WILD DIRTY SECRET

SKYE WARREN

Thank you for reading the Broken series! You can join my Facebook group for fans to discuss the series here: Skye Warren's Dark Room. And you can sign up for my newsletter to find out about new releases at skyewarren.com/newsletter.

Enjoy the story…

WILD

Once upon a time I was the girl who had everything, the clothes, the car. The rich dad who spoiled me. But the truth was, the only thing I had was my body. I used it to buy my way out.

I took a bite of the apple knowing full well what would happen.

That's how I became a call girl. That's the story of how I ended up in hell.

There's only one man who makes me wish things had been different. One man who could never be with a girl like me. Luke is a cop. Untouchable. Unbreakable. And dangerous in his own way.

When I end up on the run, he's the only one I can turn to.

And he just might be my downfall.

CHAPTER ONE

SOME DAYS ARE thick with anticipation, a portent that things will finally look up. Today was not one of those days. Instead I felt awkward, out of place among the ordinary. Unworthy.

I smoothed the paper one last time, and the dampness of my palms smudged the ink. But even the ruin of my careful work didn't distract me from the incriminating empty boxes where my work experience should go.

In a city's worth of Help Wanted, I might actually be qualified for this job. More importantly, the small indie bookstore wouldn't have a corporate HR department to balk at the gaping hole in my professional history.

They wouldn't require a background check, uncovering my arrest for solicitation.

I tugged at the sleeve of my shapeless suit, wavered on my half-inch heels. This was as close to normal as I could get. Swallowing past the lump in my throat, I approached the counter.

Without looking at me, the young woman with pink hair and pierced eyebrows automatically reached for the books I was purchasing. I hesitated, and she glanced up, her gaze flitting from the piece of paper to me.

"Oh, hi. Are you applying for the cashier position?"

You can do this. I smiled. "That's right. You haven't filled it, have you?"

"The position is definitely open. It always is, to be honest. The cashiers come and go like this is a revolving door. I've been here for over a year, though." She grinned. "Sucker for punishment. But don't let me scare you away."

"Oh no." I handed her the paper, then slid my palms over my skirt to dry them. "I'd very much like to apply." She gave the application a quick read through—nothing in her expression indicated she'd seen a problem.

"Nice to meet you, Shelly Laurent. I'm Dawn. Let me get the manager. He can interview you right now if you have the time."

She picked up the phone before I could even say *yes, please.*

"Get your butt up here," Dawn said, her eyes sparkling. "We've got a candidate, and she actually doesn't suck."

Biting her lip to hide a smile, Dawn caught a lock of hair between her fingers. No doubt about it—she had a crush on the boss.

"Okay, Jason. I'll start, but hurry up."

She hung up. "He's on his way, so I'll just ask a few

basic questions." She looked down at the application. "Get the preliminaries out of the way."

Unfortunately, the preliminaries were huge barriers, at least to my mind. After all, that's why they asked these questions. Who cared what month Johnny stopped showing up at Quickie Mart, at least for a cashier's position? No, this application wasn't about ability or even dependability. It was a test to make sure I was the right kind of person.

Which I wasn't.

One time I'd mentioned it in passing to my best friend, Allie. She had laughed, not understanding. How could I fake it all those times, but I couldn't lie for this? No, she didn't see.

That stuff was easy: *I love what you do to me. I'm coming. You're so big.*

This was different. Every attempt at normalcy felt like a tear in my gut.

I'd only be able to try so many times before coming undone.

Dawn leaned on the counter, still looking at the paper. "Have you worked in retail before?"

I had plenty of experience in customer service—but not the way she meant. I cleared my throat. "When I was in high school, I had a part-time job in the library."

"That's cool." Her brow crinkled—there it was. "Oh, I'm sorry. Am I reading these dates right? Because that would make it…"

"Three years ago."

"You didn't put down where you worked since then. Don't worry if it's not related to books or anything." She laughed. "We're not picky. The last guy quit a month ago—we're desperate."

Right. This should be easy. They were desperate; so was I.

I didn't even have to lie, exactly. I had watched Bailey while Allie had been at work. I would leave out that she hadn't paid me, that I had been the one to spot her a few hundred bucks when rent was due. I wouldn't mention how I'd earned all that money, at night when Allie and Bailey were tucked in their beds.

"Well, the thing is…I didn't have a proper job." An understatement. "I worked for my friend, taking care of her daughter. A nanny, all this time."

Dawn's gaze surreptitiously slipped down my body, her doubt couched behind generous politeness. I didn't look like the nurturing type, unless it was the kind with a fake nurse's costume. Even the drab gray cloth that clashed with my blonde hair and was one size too large couldn't hide what I was made for.

"Oh." Dawn paused, seeming to mull it over. Then she brightened. "So you can provide references, right?"

My heart sank. I hadn't wanted to ask Allie for help with this. If she knew I was looking at a minimum-wage job, she would know I was running low on money. She'd worry what I'd do when I ran out. Well, I was worried too.

"Absolutely." My voice was faint. "References."

She chatted to me about schedules. Schedules, as if I'd already gotten the job. I could walk out of here a legally employed woman. How mundane. How terrifying. I smiled at all the right places, cued more by her tone than an understanding of the inner workings of retail. I had always considered myself world-wise, world-weary, but it amazed me all the things I did not know. Things like clocking in instead of meeting for cocktails in the hotel bar, like getting a smoke break instead of a warm washcloth between clients.

A salesclerk at a bookstore. *My girlfriend works at a bookstore*, he could say. It was unremarkable. Respectable. As long as I didn't fuck it up.

The thud of steps down the stairs alerted me to an arrival. I turned. My first impression was of a middle-aged guy looking trim in a polo and slacks. Too prissy for Dawn, I thought with some disappointment, and then he looked up.

I froze as my heart skipped a beat, then two. I couldn't place him, exactly, but it was definitely a hotel room somewhere. Maybe a year ago. He was coming closer and—Fuck. Fuck.

A client. I'd had this nightmare, but it had always been me behind some counter and him a customer. Our encounter would be short and awkward, and with any luck, he wouldn't look close enough to recognize me. But this was an interview. He would see me—he would know.

"Yo, boss. This is Shelly."

My gut tightened. Dawn was practically breathless at the sight of him.

"She's cool, and you should hire her. Trust me on this."

"Shelly." He looked at me, smiling, his warm brown eyes not registering a thing. "Two minutes, and you've already earned an endorsement."

My heart threatened to beat through my chest. "Nice to meet you, sir."

He laughed. "The last time someone called me sir, it was a cop half my age, and he was writing me a speeding ticket. Call me Jason."

"Right. Jason." Nervously, I licked my lips.

His gaze lowered to my mouth; his brow furrowed.

Distantly I heard Dawn make another pitch for me, a complaint about the guys working here being lazy bums and how she really needed another girl to commiserate with. I wanted to say something, to put a stop to the train that was about to crash into me, but the air was too thin—I couldn't speak. I couldn't breathe.

Frowning slightly, he took the application and scanned it. I saw when he passed the work history section; his gaze skittered back up. His mouth opened, snapped shut. If he had already suspected, he'd definitely figured it out now. My stomach hollowed out.

He stared at the paper, clearly unseeing—frozen like me. The last time I had seen him, he'd been lounging naked on white sheets, his skin flushed and sweat-dampened as he'd handed me a nice tip from his wallet. Now both of us were trapped in this moment by our sins and by Dawn's hopeful expression.

"Um, boss?" she said. "Remember you were just saying how much we needed someone."

She laughed, but we must have been giving it away, because the sound was thin.

"I figure she's gotta be better than Damion. He wiped his nose on the books."

Jason remained silent—damnably so. *Yes*, the quiet said. *She's worse than you know, worse than the guy who put snot on books.* His lips worked, closing around empty air. The silence stretched, bottomed out. And then I started to pity him.

He had dipped his toe into the dark pool of Chicago's underworld. Paid-for sex with a pretty girl and a strap-on was par for the course in my world, but he'd probably sweated the morality—and possibly the cost—for a long time after. I was the one out of my element. I was the one who didn't belong here.

It was time to leave.

"I probably should mention that I have a busy schedule," I said.

"What?" He blinked at me with those puppy-dog brown eyes, the pleading look that once had words attached to them: *"Please, spank my ass. Harder, harder."*

I sighed. "I have a life, you know. So I don't want to work weekends, and I need to be out of here by five on the weekdays."

Understanding lit his eyes—and gratitude. "I'm

afraid weekends are required for this position. Lots of them."

I snorted. "Good luck if you expect me to show up."

Dawn's mouth hung open. Maybe I was laying it on too thick.

"Look," I said. "I thought this might work out, but…I see now that it won't. Sorry to waste your time." I snatched the application from the hands of a very relieved Jason.

On my way to the door, I heard Dawn's scandalized whisper. "What's wrong with her?"

Dark curiosity slowed my step.

"No wonder she doesn't have a job," I heard Jason say. "She's probably on drugs."

Outside I threw the crumpled application into a trash can. Hell, if sweetly rebellious Dawn thought I was a stoner, so what? Better that than the truth. Those years hadn't been empty. They'd been full of things not to discuss in polite company. Nothing to qualify me for participating in the real world. He was right not to hire me. Why did I even care?

CHAPTER TWO

BACK IN THE car, I looked at my phone and flipped to the number I never called. My thumb hovered over the Call button. If I told him I had tried to get a real job, would he laugh? No, but he'd pity me when he learned why I failed.

I put the phone down and drove home.

In the lobby of my apartment building, the doorman Evan sat behind the security desk, looking spiffy in his uniform. He always broke my heart just to look at him, perpetually deflated. He needed a sweet-faced woman to dote on him, to do dirty things to his skinny body and fill him up with pride. He brightened when he saw me.

"Hi there, Shelly."

"Hey, Ev. How's the view?" I could have been talking about the city vista through the large bay windows. But I knew he would check me out. And he did.

"It's great." He blushed. "I mean good. How are you?"

I've been bad, Mr. Thomas. You should punish me. Today, the script hovered on the tip of my tongue. "A rough day," I said.

Concern lit his face. "Can I do something to help?"

I could imagine it. I would ask for a hug and then wriggle closer, put my breath against his neck and my breasts against his chest. Then he'd be in the back office with his pants around his ankles, having an afternoon he would never forget.

I really was bad to imagine it, but my skin was still raw and his admiration was a balm. What would it feel like to be that girl even for an afternoon? "I'll be fine. I've got to run."

"Okay."

He drew the word out, stalling. Maybe he sensed how close he had come to rapture. It wasn't worth the price. I wished I could tell him. Even for free.

"But if you need anything…"

"I'll call you," I lied.

I leaned against the satin-covered wall as the elevator took me up. The glass bubbles that held the security cameras reflected my progress down the hallway. I keyed the combination into the keypad and pushed open the heavy door, pretending not to mind that this felt more like a gilded prison than a home—at least it was safe.

Once inside, I breathed out a sigh of relief and threw my keys on the kitchen bar.

A flash of black caught my eye. I turned, but a large body already held me in its bruising grip. The second asshole flanked me from the other side, though it would only have taken one to subdue me. None, really, considering who else would be in the room.

"How have you been, sweetheart?" came the voice from my nightmares.

I had mastered this. For years, I had trained for this moment, to respond coolly, act casually. But not now, not so soon after the humiliation at the bookstore. Henri's gravelly voice rubbed salt into my wounds. At one time he'd been my savior. Now he was just a pimp.

He strolled out of the shadows, his pale, strong face impassive. High cheekbones and white-blond hair spoke of a Nordic ancestry, though his accent was slight. As usual, he wore a three-piece suit, all in black except the vest and tie in matching teal.

How did he get in? How did he know where I lived? He shouldn't even have been searching for me. I had quit the life, and he had agreed at the time, but that had been a lie. The question of how was superfluous, because here he was. The question of why was too obvious to bear; I made him an awful lot of money. Now I saw. His return was inevitable, like trying to keep the ocean off the beach. Maybe for a time it would leave, but it would always come back.

Thick fingers cut into my arms, but I flipped my hair out of my face in a charade of unconcern. "I went shopping."

Henri gave me a detached perusal, inspecting his wares. "You look like a secretary."

"I'm a professional," I managed drily. And it was true, just not of the business variety. A hundred men in

Chicago's upper echelon could attest to what a pro I was. "What are you doing here?"

"Is that how you greet me?" His voice was too mild. "And here I've missed you."

My blood began to pound. He wouldn't beat me in my fancy apartment in the middle of the day. It would make too much noise, and someone would call the cops. Unless he had them on his payroll. Unless the fancy security I paid for, that had served me so well until now, also included soundproofed walls. No one would hear. No one ever cared.

He set the glass he was holding down on a side table with a quiet thud. "I blame myself. I should have known better than to let you go with him."

He never should have let me stay with Philip, he meant, even though he had gotten a placement fee and a monthly stipend the entire time I'd been Philip's mistress. Hardly anything to complain about, but he was right. Philip had given me the financial means to leave. He'd also given me the confidence. Though now it seemed more like hubris. Leave it to Philip to confuse the two.

Henri gripped my chin with his fingers and grunted. "Such a pretty face."

I slid my gaze away from his flat eyes to stare straight ahead. My pretty face, my beautiful, hated face and matching body that made me want to puke just to think of them. Let him look. Didn't he know he burned us both? Like trapping a butterfly, the only way to catch one was to kill it.

"You're wondering if I'm going to hurt you. Probably." He ran his thumb over my lips, his fingernail catching on the tender skin. "Can't dirty you up now, though. Tomorrow you have a party."

My gaze met his. I hated parties. All the girls did. Decent money, but not enough to compensate for too many men getting drunk and nasty. An escort was never more than an object to get off in, but a hooker at a party was a piñata.

But I would do it because I had no choice. I would do it because I needed more money to afford this fancy apartment with all the security that clearly did not work. And most of all, I would do it because I could do nothing else. I'd known it all along, from when I was young, too damned young, and this afternoon underscored that.

"A party," I repeated dully.

"Good girl." He leaned in and pressed a kiss to my lips. "I'll send you the details."

Then they were gone, and I crumpled to the floor. Belated, terror swept over me, drenching me and then leaving me chilled in its absence.

Stupid, thinking I could work at a bookstore as a clerk. Stupid that I'd want to. I would make more money in fifteen minutes at this party than Dawn would make all day. And she, confined to her feet. I would earn mine on my back, on my hands and knees, any which way they pleased.

Hooking had been the only thing I could do, once upon a time. Seemed it still was.

In the interim since I'd quit, I had counted down the days until I wouldn't stink of dirty money. Until I would be worthy of him. But yearning wasn't enough to buy a new life. Pity was worth nothing, and self-pity even less. I, however, was worth a whole awful lot. My daddy had taught me early and taught me often. I may have been born a whore, but I'd always been high priced.

My fancy, high-rise condo was suddenly unbearable, the pictures of Allie and Bailey tainted, the extravagant knickknacks lining the mantel muddied. This had never been a home, but now it wasn't even safe. My skin crawled, and with nothing on me but my keys and a crumpled gray suit, I left my apartment and hit the stairs.

CHAPTER THREE

Parties were dangerous, but they were nothing compared to streetwalking. I didn't look like a working girl tonight, just a poor sap whose car had broken down in the wrong part of town. Because even though I paid a ridiculous sum to live in my condo off the books, the streets were a different stratosphere.

Glossy buildings jutted from the concrete like shards of glass, untouchable from the smog-drenched alleyways. Bums gathered behind Dumpsters, burning pinches of weed in a bonfire to keep warm. Urgent sounds of cars squealing, slamming, speeding ricocheted off the concrete walls.

I saw a girl hovering against a building. Her clothes were tight and revealing, ordinary. As a whore, she looked downright virtuous, but I recognized that stillness.

Her too-young body and timid posture would attract only the worst kind of client—if she even found anyone. The sallow light of the streetlamps only lit cracks in the sidewalk tonight. If she was counting on a john to buy her dinner, her stomach would probably go empty.

Cautious, I approached her. No sudden movements. She froze when she noticed me but didn't meet my eyes. Smart girl.

I stopped a few feet away and leaned back against the wall, looking out. "Hey."

"Am I in your spot?" Her voice trembled.

Was she too scared to notice how I was dressed? Or maybe just too damned perceptive. "I don't work the street."

"Oh."

I cast her a sideways glance. She stared at the ground, clutching the dirty concrete wall behind her.

"You don't want to be out here," I said.

"No?" she said on an exhale.

"The men here—they're rough. You know what I mean?"

Her mouth tightened. She could only be all of fifteen or so, but she knew what I meant.

She licked her lips. "Wh-where should I go?"

"I know a place." She wouldn't like it, not at first, but it was where she needed to go. "I can show you."

She examined me, trying to see beneath the surface, but I could have told her it was a futile occupation. There wasn't anything there.

"Maybe we'll pick up a burger on the way," I said.

A low-pitched grumble emanated from her stomach. She clasped her arms around her waist.

"I'm not going with you."

A hint of scorn entered her voice. Where she'd gotten that lick of spirit from, I didn't know—not when she looked about to keel over from hunger and fear.

"Sweetheart, do you think I'm going to hurt you worse than a guy you find out here?"

She shook her head, more in denial at what I was suggesting. Better she hear it from me than suffer it at their hands. "They won't just fuck you, honey. They'll make it hurt. In your cunt, in your mouth. You ever take it in the ass?"

Her eyes widened. Her upper body canted forward, bent over at her arms. I might have worried she would throw up if I thought she'd had anything to eat today.

If I told her I wasn't going to do anything to her, she wouldn't believe me. Hell, I wouldn't have. "Some of them don't even care about the fuck. They just want someone to wail on. Beat you up, leave you for dead. Whatever I'm going to do to you, it's gotta be better than that, right?"

"P-p-please," she said. "I'll do it."

She looked so pitiful, so desperate for comfort as she stood there hugging herself. I wouldn't touch her, but I could take her to someone who could. They would take care of her, and I would be absolved once again.

"Come on," I said, then turned and walked back toward my place.

The pitter-patter of her feet on the pavement followed me.

I'd parked in a secure garage, and I waved at the

guard as we passed. When we reached my car, I opened the door and gestured inside. She stared at the passenger seat like it was a torture chamber.

I sighed. "What's your name?"

"Laura," came out on a whoosh.

Breathing was good. I didn't want her passing out on me. The last thing I needed was to deliver a limp body.

"All right, Laura. I see you're stressing, but there's no need to worry. I'm not going to hurt you. We're going to grab a bite to eat, you and me, okay? Maybe get some rest. No one's going to hurt you." Ah, empty promises. I'd do my best to make sure they came true, but she was still a broken girl in an indifferent world. That rarely worked out well.

I steeled myself and touched her back, her arm, to steer her into the car. She didn't resist, at least, and sat in the passenger's seat.

"You're okay, Laura. My name's Shelly, and you're going to be okay, got it?"

Without waiting for an answer, I shut the door and hurried around to the other side. I drove her to a drive-through and ordered enough to feed a football team before driving to the brick building on Wicklow Street.

I stopped the car and looked over at her. Laura stared blankly at the unmarked building, though I didn't know if she was still in her stupor or just confused about where we were. This place could never have a sign, though. It was removed from the maps. It didn't exist.

With some coaxing and a bit more nudging, she got out of the car. I fished an envelope from the glove box, thick and unmarked on the outside. There weren't many of these envelopes left. But if I was really going to work a party, they would soon be replenished.

The glass of the door was bulletproof and tinted dark against peeping eyes. I pressed the cracked button tucked into a brick. A few minutes later, Marguerite opened the door.

Her hair was such a pale, glossy blonde it was almost white, curled into a neat coif. Dressed in a slimming black suit, she looked more like a high-powered executive than the hands-on manager for a small shelter. She had run this place since its inception at, oh, the beginning of time. This place or one like it had always existed, always been needed, and always would be so long as men took what they wanted and women let them.

She ushered us both inside. "What happened?"

Any number of things could have happened to this girl. Drugs or violence or rape, that sort of thing. Likely some of them had already happened, but not tonight. "Nothing. I think I got her before she… Well, she's just been like this since she got in the car." I shrugged. "Shock, maybe."

"Wait for me," Marguerite ordered as she pressed the intercom.

I nodded and leaned against the wall, relieved to

release my charge. These little field trips were a glass of cold water in a parched expanse of desert, but there was a cost. There was always a cost, and in this case, it was the removal of my blinders—but only temporarily. The ones that said this was all my choice, it was all okay. Because if the life was something for her to escape from, then what the hell was I still doing in it? Oh God, why couldn't I get out?

But we weren't the same, Laura and I. I didn't have that lost look in my eyes. No confusion, no pain. When blue-gray eyes stared back at me from the mirror, I saw nothing there at all.

Chapter Four

WHOEVER RAN THE desk buzzed the door open, and Marguerite ushered them both inside. There was another inside-locked door between the administrative areas and the dormitories, every level another chance to stall a rampaging ex-husband or ex-pimp before they could do harm.

I wondered if Henri could make it inside the inner sanctum. Probably. My boss had oodles of money, much of which I'd made for him, and he hired military dropouts like they were going out of style. Good thing this place only housed girls from fifty-dollar pimps—small-timers lucky to find their own tiny dicks, much less track down a missing girl and break their way in here.

This place wasn't a haven for me. I had always known that, but it seemed to matter more now, when I needed one, when my own safe place had been violated.

Maybe it had been foolish to send my resources here. I could have flown to Tahiti, never to have been heard from again. Never would have seen Allie again either, or her daughter.

Never seen *him* again. No, it hadn't been an option. Still wasn't.

The girl would probably go through medical first, get checked out. Lucky for me, I wouldn't be around for that. Wouldn't find out the dirty little details, and that was the only reason I continued to do this.

Make it right. It had become a mantra, a compulsion. I was too far gone, but I could bring them to safety. The contained little community was a refuge, but not for me. The dingy walls and speckled floor tiles of the entryway were already closing in on me. I didn't suffer poverty gladly. There were only so many compensations for being a prostitute. One, really—money, and I intended to use it to the fullest. Initially, I had given Allie financial support. Now I resorted to luxury fabrics and label clothing, and when they didn't fill the void, I came here.

Marguerite came back into the foyer. "Thank you."

Her businesslike demeanor was the only reason I could handle her gratitude. "At your service, of course."

"She said she's thirteen."

Unexpectedly, my stomach lurched. She wasn't the youngest I'd seen on the streets, but suddenly she seemed like a baby. I was getting too old for this. How long had it been since I was her age? At least a decade—more. Back then, I'd lived in a fancy house with a princess bed and frilly clothes. I'd earned them.

"So," I managed to say. "Everyone's gotta start somewhere."

"Shelly."

Her voice was too soft, too kind. Too damned understanding when she didn't know a single thing.

"You look tired. Have you been sleeping okay?"

I went to sleep just fine, to my regret. The nightmares were like quicksand—the more I struggled, the faster they pulled me under. "I'm fine."

"We have therapists here. They can—"

"What can they do?" I scoffed. What could they do except make things worse?

"PTSD is not uncommon in women who—"

"Enough." I took a deep breath, looked away.

Was it true? Did I have PTSD? Maybe. Probably. What did it matter?

When I was in the tenth grade, I tried to seduce my World History teacher into a higher test score. He'd looked at me with shock, which had morphed into that damned understanding I'd learned to despise. Then came the therapists.

At the end, the teacher had been fired, courtesy of good old dad, and my home life got a hell of a lot tougher in retaliation for making trouble. I'd figured out then I was better off alone, and nothing had changed. Nothing ever changed.

"You're breaking the rules," I told Marguerite.

She made a little sound of resignation. "Okay, we won't talk about it."

"Thank you."

"I don't know why you pretend you don't care."

So much for not talking. "You should know by

now that no one cares about whores."

"Then why do you do it?" she challenged.

I flashed her my wicked smile. "Getting rid of the competition."

"Okay, Shelly." She blew out her breath. "You're right. I broke the rules."

I handed her the envelope. Marguerite accepted it with a grim face. Ah, something Ms. Faust and I had in common: taking money from someone we didn't like. I wondered if it ever got easier for her. Every month I brought a wayward girl to this place. Each time, Marguerite pried another secret from my lips. I wasn't worried. It would take far too many months, years even, to get them all, and I would never last that long.

"How's your cop?" Marguerite asked, as if we were two girlfriends shooting the shit.

My heart beat faster, but I donned a mask of polite curiosity. I had mentioned Luke once, offered his services in getting a restraining order for one of the boyfriend pimps. Marguerite had refused, housing the girl until she could move her to another city through her network of shelters. The operation was costly and dangerous but still preferable to dealing with cops. Another thing we shared.

"Haven't spoken to him in a while." Unfortunately, the truth. "Why do you ask?"

"Just wondering what he thought about you getting out."

She was fishing. No way she could know I had quit

or had tried to.

"It's not really his business," I said blandly. *Not really your business.*

She shrugged. "Seemed like you really liked him."

Except he didn't want a prostitute for a girlfriend; he'd basically said as much. More than that, he didn't deserve one. I had quit, fled, had wanted to never go back to hooking, but clearly that wasn't in the cards. My lip curled. "Come on, sweetheart. Do you really think someone like him can have a real relationship with someone like me?"

It was a joke, but I held my breath.

"No," she said finally. "But you deserve to have some fun, even if it's only for a little while."

Yeah. That was what I thought. Maybe it was for the best anyway, that I would go back to the one thing I could do so well. I never could have afforded to fund this place on what I made as a cashier or any other normal job. I swept out the door with a "Bye, honey" and a swing of my hips. Girl's got a reputation to rebuild.

I drove home on fumes and climbed directly into a scalding-hot shower. I scrubbed away the rejection from earlier, the fear and the stench of the streets. After using up half the bottle, I poured the rest of the soap out and watched as the peach-colored gel swirled down the drain. I couldn't have used it again anyway, not after using it today. Maybe it was strange, but the rituals kept me sane, and what did they hurt? Who did they hurt? I lay down on the cold, hard floor of the tub and curled into a ball on my side, letting the water rain down on me.

Distantly, I heard the phone ringing, but I couldn't have moved. Not until the water turned cold and I began to shake. I pulled myself up and turned off the shower. After throwing on a large shirt to sleep in, I grabbed the answering machine and climbed into my plush bed with six-hundred-thread-count sheets. I curled my body around the little black box and pressed Play.

"Hey, it's me." He sounded tired. "I guess you're busy."

There was a pause, which I scribbled in with well-deserved recriminations. I might not have been with a client today, but I would be tomorrow. This was my life. I could apologize for it, but I couldn't change it any more than a ship could change the tides.

"I worked a double shift today," he said on the re-cording. "One of the other guys, his wife went into labor, so I took over for him. Wasn't too bad, though. Just tiring. For her, I mean. It took her ten hours to push him out, so what the hell do I have to complain about? Nine pounds, a boy. I didn't see him yet, came straight home." There was silence. "Straight home and called you. Funny."

The answering machine broke the awkwardness with a *click.*

There were no more messages. I pressed the button

again.

"Hey, it's me. I guess you're busy. I worked a double shift today. One of the other guys, his wife went into labor…"

Chapter Five

THE PARTY TURNED out to be a corporate affair in the penthouse of a swanky modern hotel. A bunch of high-profile CEOs getting high and horny amid miles of glass surfaces—what a brilliant idea.

The guys at the front desk checked me out, but discreetly. With furtive glances instead of leers, as befitted an escort of my price range. For all they knew, I was a spoiled girlfriend, not a prostitute. But then, what was the difference?

Outside the suite, I sank my stilettos into the carpet. The dull beat shook from behind the door, already matching the throb in my head. I had the sudden urge to call him as I brushed my fingers against the little black clutch.

What could I say? *I know I promised I wouldn't do it anymore, but I'm about to go bang assholes for money. I tried to join the regular world, but they didn't want me. I'm sorry. Don't hate me. Help me.*

The door swung open, revealing a man with a shiny forehead and a bulbous belly hanging from between his open dress shirt. "I call dibs," he shouted, spittle flying in my face.

Fabulous.

"Sure, lover." I tried to squeeze by him, but he caught me in the doorway. His hands were everywhere, his foul liquor-breath suffocated me, and the doorjamb cut into my back. "No need to rush, handsome. We've got all night."

He grunted and stuck his tongue into my cleavage. His sweat-sheened head filled my vision, and I swallowed bile.

Shit, I wasn't ready to go back. I never would be.

I had to. It was a miracle Henri had let me off so easily. The least I could do was bear my punishment gracefully.

But my new boyfriend's face felt slimy. *I* felt slimy.

I'd only been out of the game for a few months. Maybe more, if I didn't count Philip, which was debatable. Still, there was no reason to freak out over a simple groping. I'd made it through much worse.

Just let him. Let him.

Let him touch and grab and pinch. Let him slobber. Let him treat me like I was a piece of meat, no thoughts, no feelings. Let him treat me like this was all I was good for. Do it for long enough, and I might start to believe it. Lord knew I already did.

Think of something else.

Not him, the man on my speed dial I never called, not while I did this. I didn't understand why it hurt him to see what I was when he met a dozen other hookers in his daily work, each worse off than me, but it did. I couldn't think of my best friend Allie or her daughter either, because to imagine them in this position was a weight too heavy to carry.

His fingers were inside me, pumping away. Thank goodness I'd lubed up, or this would really hurt.

It still hurt. God.

Philip, now he understood me. He wouldn't mourn for me or feel guilty. We did what we had to and didn't waste time on remorse. But I'd told him I was done with the life. I'd promised I'd let him know if I needed help. I needed help, needed…

"Stop," I gasped.

He froze and then gently rocked his fingers back and forth, like a child testing his boundaries.

I lowered my voice. "Wait, lover. I just need to freshen up."

He raised his head and blinked, confused. "You look pretty to me."

My stomach twisted at the compliment. He looked so earnest, his eyes slack with lust and his mouth covered in his own spit. This wasn't a guy who got off on hurting or humiliating. He just didn't know how to deal with people, wouldn't know how to please a woman if he tried. Hell, maybe he was trying.

"Thank you." I choked on the words. "I want to look good for you. Make it good for you. Give me five minutes. Please." Because if he didn't, I would freak. If he didn't get his thick fingers out of me and off my skin this very second, I was liable to do something really stupid. Like leave and to hell with Henri and his hired fists.

The guy backed up, though. His face contorted into an uncertain composition of wounded lover and dissatisfied customer, but he released me, stepped back. I attempted a smile, ignored the pounding in my ears. I wanted to tell him that I would be right back, that everything would be fabulous, but how could I when I didn't believe it myself?

I'd forgotten how to lie. In this business, I was as good as dead.

I pushed off the wall and stumbled my way down the hall. I passed the sitting area, catching flashes of rumpled suits and one lace-clad female body straddling a guy probably twice her age. What was her name? Jenny, Janey, what the fuck ever because it was all a lie. All fake.

The bathroom was empty—thank God for small favors. The sound of the door slamming cracked loud in my head, even though surely it wouldn't be heard above the music. I locked it anyway, turning the little knob. So flimsy, an illusion of safety.

I rested my palms on the counter and stared at myself in the mirror. Blonde hair that I'd straightened this afternoon, sleek and shiny. Makeup—perfect, even though lover boy had slobbered down the side of it. Waterproof stuff, cum-proof stuff—never let them see you sweat.

Even my eyes were steady. Clear. Empty.

I searched my appearance for something, any sign of weakness—none. This was what strength looked like, then. Oh, I had confidence aplenty. I strolled and drawled and acted my fucking heart out, but that was the secret. For me, it had never been an act. I hadn't been hiding what was inside me. There was nothing inside me.

So what was one more empty promise? If he really cared, he would be here right now. He would have protected me from this. What was one more trick? If the life was all I had, I might as well live it.

I touched up my makeup, just because. My hand trembled only a little, but my face came out flawless, like always. And then there was nothing left to pretend, no way left to stall.

The hallway was still empty, and I started to head back to the sitting area. I heard a sound over the pulse of the music: a muffled cry. The hair on the back of my neck stood on end; my heart began to race.

No big deal. Of course there would be those sounds at a party like this, where women were paid to perform, to endure. Probably she had faked it on purpose. But I knew she hadn't.

Still, don't get involved. That was the first rule of staying alive. Even that pitiful kid from yesterday had instinctively understood how it worked: look away, pretend you don't see, don't start trouble.

But there it was again, that sound. It curled sharp nails into my gut, signaling danger. Get away.

I was twenty-four, had stayed alive for six years by keeping to myself. Those latent self-protective instincts were still there, still honed, and yet I couldn't walk away, couldn't leave her there without knowing.

I crept down the empty hallway and paused at one closed door. At first there was nothing. I almost turned away, left, but then I heard a moan. A female moan of fake pleasure, and that was fine, just fine. Time to go.

A thud sounded from the end of the hall and then echoed in my chest. Inexorably I walked to the last door, knowing through instinct or experience exactly what was happening here. It didn't matter the men or the woman; it was always the same. Too much, too fast, too hard. *I didn't know, wasn't expecting. Too late, bitch.*

A tear slid down my cheek. It was more than just my safety at stake here. *Get away.*

I twisted the knob and pushed the door open a crack, exposing just a sliver of the scene. The face of a girl, her face contorted in fury. The grin of a man. Hands holding down arms. The low sound of laughter. A little slice of hell, and what was I supposed to do about it?

I could do nothing.

This wasn't a young girl on an empty street corner who could be cured with a fast-food burger and a lifetime of therapy. This was one of Henri's girls, off-limits for me and mother-fucking-hen Marguerite Faust. No one could help her, just like no one could help me.

I saw her body jerk with purpose. Heard the crack as her kick landed on someone's skin. The laughter grew louder, more combative.

Shit. She was going to get herself killed that way. Beaten, at the least. Didn't she know that? Didn't she care?

But Hemi didn't do hand-holding. Had he recruited this girl fresh out of high school? Given her money she desperately needed to get away, to help her friend, only to indebt herself to him forever? Dumped her at this party without any training or knowledge or a goddamned thing?

This wasn't about me. I told myself that, but it didn't help.

I pushed the door open and stepped inside. Four guys, not counting the ones out in the sitting area or my erstwhile boyfriend.

I smiled and set my hips to sway. "Hello, gentlemen. I see you've started the party without me."

Three of them shifted their attention to me, though one kept struggling with the girl. And she kept fighting, clearly too panicked or just stubborn to let me take the lead.

The one with an earring in his eyebrow grinned and patted his knee. "There's always room for one more girl."

I trailed my finger across his jaw as I passed him. "Always, honey, but not before the big show."

"The show?" another one asked, his voice breaking.

Jesus, younger and younger.

"Didn't you know about that?" I paused in my contemplative pose, often applied to men who liked to kneel, to pretend submissiveness while I spanked their behinds—at least until they turned the tables. "I wouldn't want you to be late."

I stopped by the bed, where both the girl and the guy half sitting on her were watching me with bemusement. They actually made a cute couple if I ignored the whole sordid violence routine. It was always the handsome ones.

With a wink for the good-looking asshole, I leaned over the girl and skimmed a finger up the middle of her belly and between her breasts, hoping it would cause her the least discomfort. Then I kissed her, soft, gently, for show, not pleasure. Never that.

The tension prickled at my skin as the men in the room held their breath. Without asking, the man eased up on her, more interested in seeing where this would lead than expressing his dominance.

I frowned slightly, a little slow on the uptake. "We had it all planned out. Practiced it just to show you. But I guess if you've already started, we don't have to do it." I straightened and tugged at my dress, all businesslike. "We can just get it over with, if you want."

Before my words were even out, the girl was released and practically thrown at me. They wanted to see it, they assured me. *Please*, they asked so nicely. *Yes, absolutely, whatever you wish. I'm at your command, but give us a moment, just a moment.* The men obediently trooped out to the sitting area, almost tripping over each other to nab a good seat for the nonexistent show.

The girl yanked her shirt on, still shaking. "Who the hell are you?"

My eyebrows rose. "Your fairy godmother. Who do you think?"

"I think you're just a dirty prostitute. Like the other girl out there."

Her voice caught, but the unspoken words hovered in the air. *Like me.*

I softened my tone. "Look, hon. It won't be that bad. I'll take the rough ones for myself, and—"

"Fuck you. I'm not doing that." Her words were angry, but fear radiated from her.

This night was going from bad to worse. A sigh escaped me. "What's your name, sweetheart?"

"Go to hell!"

I took in her wide eyes, her flared nostrils. She looked like a pixie—a pissed-off, belligerent, terrified pixie. Selling her body for possibly the first time was a big drop, but she couldn't get off the ride at the top of the hill.

"You've at least had sex before, right?" I asked.

"Of course I have!" she squeaked.

Ah shit. There was definite glistening happening in her ocular area. And that annoying snuffling sound. Apparently it was contagious, because now my insides had gone all quivery as well. This was exactly why I didn't do people, why I didn't do touching, at least not without the cold accompaniment of currency.

I forced down my emotions, pushed back my own revulsion and anger and fear, and patted her shoulder, proud of myself for managing it. There.

She swung around, and before I could blink, her fist connected with my face. Surprise and pain forced me back, and I fell against the wall.

Goddamn, that skinny little body packed a punch.

By the time my vision had cleared, she was gone, with only her footsteps giving away her run down the hall. I grabbed my purse from the table where I'd dropped it and ran after her the best I could in my heels and slinky dress.

The men in the sitting room hadn't noticed her passing by, but they sure saw me.

"Hey," the handsome one called. "Where do you think you're going?"

"Change of plans," I called out, but he'd already caught me by the elbow. I winced, unable to smother the reaction when the right side of my face ached, but he didn't hit me. Instead, he towed me back to the group like a recalcitrant child, and I stammered just like one. "It's…her. She has a little problem."

The silver-ringed eyebrow of the other guy lifted. "What kind of problem?"

Think, damn it. I could have come up with some sort of "show" on the fly, maybe a little girl-on-girl action with Jenny. This wouldn't have been a problem. But if I was the fairy godmother, then my Cinderella had just fled the ball. The only thing she would get up to with a torn, skimpy outfit and a bad attitude was trouble.

From the lap of a man old enough to be her father, Jenny stared at me uncomprehendingly. Her pose was relaxed, her eyes glassy. Flying high, probably.

"Drugs," I said. "The girl, um…Ella—she's having a bad reaction."

A round of curses filled the air.

"We don't have any drugs," said Prince Charming, sounding disappointed.

"Right, well. Perk of the job, I guess." I waved my hand, ergo… "But the last thing we need is her passing out in the hotel, cops asking questions. Then the reporters… They're like vultures over sex stories. But hey, I can round her up. Take care of it for you. Fair enough?"

They agreed and thanked me profusely. By the time I was unceremoniously shoved out the door, they had already cranked the music back up. Briefly I felt regret for leaving Jenny behind. But I couldn't save all of us. In fact, odds were high I couldn't save any of us.

I leaned against the wall. What the hell had I done? There hadn't been any ambiguity or wiggle room in Henri's instructions. Work the party so I didn't end up facedown in an alley. I had done this before, so how had this gone wrong so quickly?

Ella, I'd named her. Oh, fabulous. Because of course all she needed was a pet name and a muzzle for that right hook and I could bring her home with me. I allowed myself a small smile and started down the hallway.

CHAPTER SIX

IT WAS TOO much to hope that she'd caught a cab and been halfway across Chicago by now. Instead, the whispers between the front desk staff pointed me to the back offices, and then the ruckus in the back kitchens drew me like a homing beacon.

I found Ella in the back room, wrestling with a member of security. He was armed only with a walkie-talkie, it appeared, but he used it furiously, shouting into it as he gripped Ella's arm with his other hand.

"There you are," I accused.

She subsided in his grip, looking relieved. It was a sad state of affairs if I had to play knight in shining armor.

The guard looked me up and down with a faint curl to his lips, as if he couldn't make up his mind whether to permit a sneer. Young woman in a sexy dress with a fresh shiner—I could have been a rich bitch housewife with an abusive sugar daddy. Sadly, no. My sugar daddy had cast me out, both for my betrayal and for my own good.

"Ella, I've been looking all over you," I chided.

She raised her eyebrows at the made-up name.

Well, I could hardly have called her Princess without him assuming we were strippers. And the other names I called her in my head were even less flattering.

"You know Daddy doesn't like to be kept waiting," I added.

On that note, the guy released her. Anyone named Daddy who had two girls like us answering to him was either scary or crazy, probably both.

"She dropped this," he said, holding up a sleek leather wallet that she must have lifted from one of the men upstairs while grappling with them.

A little impressive, actually.

"I assumed it wasn't hers," he added, seeming less certain now.

I sighed. "Really, Ella? Wrecking the Mercedes wasn't good enough? Now you have to steal something? Where'd you pick that up—the hotel restaurant?"

Ella crossed her arms, teenage angst at its finest. "Bet Daddy didn't even notice I was gone."

She fell into the game so smoothly I almost cracked a smile and ruined the whole thing.

"So…you know her?" the guard asked, clearly a bit confused as to what he should do.

"Unfortunately, yes," I said. "We're family."

"You're not my real mom," she said hotly.

"But you're stuck with me, darling," I said with saccharine sweetness.

"Right, well," the man stammered. "I don't want to get involved with a domestic dispute."

"Oh no," I said. "It's too late for that. She stole something. Isn't that like, a felony?"

"I don't know." The guy flipped through the wallet, flashing several hundred dollars. "It looks like it's all here. No harm, no foul, I say."

Ella smirked. "Guess not every old guy falls for your fake boobs."

"They're not—" I clasped a hand to my very real boobs. "You can't just let her go. Call the police. She needs to be locked up. She's horrible!"

"I'm sorry, ma'am," he said with glossy patience.

He seemed much more comfortable now, dealing with a bitchy guest rather than the lowlifes that we were.

"It's hotel policy not to involve the authorities unless there's been property damage, and since I've recovered the wallet, I'm afraid I'm going to have to release her into your custody."

I turned to her, dismissing the man. "I'm telling Daddy. He'll cut you off."

"Bite me, mother."

I grabbed her by the arm and dragged her down a hallway. Who knew where it went, didn't matter. I chanced a look behind us. The guard was shaking his head as he spoke into his walkie-talkie. *Never mind. Silly rich people.*

"You little brat," I said, partly to complete the charade and partly because my face hurt like hell. "I can't believe you hit me. I was helping you."

She snorted. "Yeah, helping me whore myself. No, thanks."

Her words jolted me. It was one thing to accept the life for myself, but why would I ever have tried to ease her into it? Ah, right. Because we were both dead if we didn't.

"Jail won't be any better for you, sweetheart. Not if Henri's pissed, and he will be once he hears you bailed on the VIPs." A sideways glance showed her pouting profile. "Are you at least going to tell me your name now?"

"I'm Polly-fucking-Anna. Pleased to meet you."

Oh good, because more sarcasm was exactly what my life needed. "Fine, don't tell me. I'm calling you Ella."

She yanked her arm out of my hold. "Whatever you want."

"Sweetheart, if you'd said that twenty minutes ago, I wouldn't be in this mess."

"What's keeping you?" She crossed her arms. "Leave already. I don't give a shit." Her youthful hurt and depression were all too real now, like she knew better than to expect people to stick around and was pissed at herself for hoping it would be different.

"Come on. We need to get you out of here before Henri shows up."

She winced at the mention of his name. "I'm not going with you."

Her wide, slanted eyes shimmered with fierce anger

and glassy hope. What a curious mixture of courage and vulnerability. She was a flower disguised as a weed, but Henri was a bulldozer; he wouldn't care at all.

"We don't have time for this." Running out on the party like that would have been bad enough, but stealing from a client? We were both a lesson waiting to be taught. "Let's go."

"Why, so you can take me to him?"

Christ, was that what she thought? Here I was trying to save her scrawny behind. But she wouldn't know that. Like she said, I was just a dirty prostitute. Another person who'd tried to convince her to spread her legs. Hell.

"The truth is," I said, "I've been thinking of getting out myself. Well, now I'm out. Maybe you did me a favor, kid."

"I'm not a kid. And isn't he going to be angry at you too?"

"*Favor* may have been too strong a word." More like pain in the ass, but I doubted she'd appreciate that, and I didn't feel up to chasing her in my heels again. "I'm going to try to keep you safe."

"Try?" she asked.

"I can promise you this: you'll be as safe as I am." I hoped that would be enough. "Now, how the hell do we get out of here?" I didn't want to risk going back out into the lobby, where the men from the party or even Henri's men could be waiting, but the doors all had the hotel card locks on them.

Ella produced a plastic card attached to a cord. "Got it covered."

She'd picked the security guard's pocket. Lovely.

"Come on." I grabbed the master key from her and used it to get us into a stairwell. From there we'd go to the basement and then out onto the street. And then I'd make the call I had been avoiding for so long.

Chapter Seven

L UKE HANDED ME a couple of pills and a glass of water.

I swallowed the plain white tablets, clearly prescription stuff. "You poisoning me?"

"Depends. You gonna tell me who did that?"

His tone was casual, but beneath the sweatpants and T-shirt, his lean body was taut with tension. At least he'd finished cursing, which had gone on for a few minutes after seeing my bruise.

I handed back the glass, and he set it on the bedside table. I watched him pace from my perch on his bed. His face had a light layer of scruff and bloodshot green eyes, courtesy of a long day at work. And it was even longer now, thanks to me.

I turned away, unable to see the worry in his eyes. Instead I watched Ella through the crack in the doorway. She sulked in the living room, poking at the pile of papers and takeout containers on the coffee table. "I don't suppose you'll believe me when I say it was her who hit me."

"Oh, sure. She just lifted the cash from my jacket in there, so assault's not a stretch."

My mouth firmed. Luke knew exactly why I'd brought her here, but he was going to make me say it. "She's just a kid."

His look was dark, hinting at a deeper turmoil. "Only a few years younger than you."

"Look, can you keep her safe or not?"

He laughed softly. I loved his laugh, but this one was ugly and sad, like a sneer had deflated.

"What an interesting question. But perhaps you can define the parameters for me."

Something hurt in the vicinity of my chest. Probably my wound acting up at the reminder. He was mocking himself, making a joke of his inability to protect a girl under his care.

Eight months ago, I had been shot during an undercover operation led by Luke. He blamed himself, although the department considered the whole operation a success. They'd been trying to expose Luke's partner as a dirty cop, but they had managed to shake out an arms deal in the process.

Luke was a decent guy and a good cop, so of course he'd feel guilty for an injury sustained by his informant on his watch. But the truth was, he didn't have a claim on me. As much as I might have stupidly hoped, he never had.

He knelt in front of me and gently pressed an ice pack to my face. "I'm sorry. You didn't deserve that."

He had no idea. I deserved so much worse. And I was going to get it too if Henri had his way.

That was for later, tomorrow maybe. Right now I had a grungy little apartment with a nice view: mournful emerald eyes and sensual lips. A light sheen of facial hair in golden brown. I'd been scratched, scuffed a thousand times—more. I had felt degraded, humiliated, or blissful nothing those times. But then, I had never wanted those men.

"You're staring at me," he muttered, keeping his gaze on the side of my face where he pressed the ice to the bruise.

I faked a wince, just to see him flinch and soften the pressure.

I felt the corner of my mouth turn up. "You're an easy mark."

"Hmm." He slanted me a look. "Does it hurt? Tell the truth."

Of course it hurt; the side of my face looked like a cantaloupe and… Oh. The wince had been intentional, but it hadn't technically been a lie.

The side of his lips quirked up. "See? You tell me the truth, even when you fake it."

"Baby, when I fake it—"

"Don't." His smile disappeared. "Don't fake it with me, and that includes the things you say. Save the smooth lines for someone else."

My breath caught, but then he'd always been able to see through me—a weakness I couldn't afford. I had to pull it together; we were here for a reason. "She's in trouble." I paused. "She's not cut out for this line of work."

Luke finally turned away from me, disappointment and frustration filling the air like smoke. His broad shoulders were tense, his whole body strung out. "You said it was finished."

I had promised him I'd go straight. No more hooking. But I hadn't really understood, hadn't known. No one wanted a pretty girl with no actual skills or work experience. Well, that wasn't quite true. One guy had offered me a job standing outside his nightclub in a wet T-shirt. Then he had smirked while telling me about the opportunities for bonuses. "It's complicated."

"I understand," Luke said in a low voice.

But he couldn't really. He could go to the zoo every day and still not know how it felt to be caged. This was the only thing I could do. He would see that; I would show him. I drew him down onto the bed. He sat on the side of the bed, still but not passive—he vibrated like a tuning fork.

"Shh," I murmured, stroking his back.

"Shelly, goddamn it."

But his protests fell away as I pressed my breasts to his arm and my tongue to his ear. His harsh inhalation sounded broken, shattered, or maybe that was me.

I tasted salt and man, earth and spring. Slow licks alongside his lobe and upward, more suggestive than sensation, but for a man like this, anticipation would be everything. Or so I had imagined, all the times I had dreamed of it.

A small sound escaped him, somewhere between a grunt and groan. I took it as encouragement and smoothed my hands along the hard planes of his shoulders, his chest. Not anywhere near the bulge in his jeans, because this wasn't about pleasure—it was about wanting.

Anything to get closer, I let my knees slide apart around his side, the faint heat of his body a shock to my core. His hands clenched and opened on his knees, and again, the muscles rippled beneath his darkly tanned skin. Was he restraining himself from touching me or pushing me off?

"Baby, no," he groaned, letting his head fall back onto my shoulder.

No, I would never deserve to have him as more than a sex partner. And he had never fucked me, though I knew he wanted to. Every time he saw me, his eyes would darken and my stomach would bottom out, but we'd never touch. But maybe for one brief, inconvenient moment, while the door was open and the young woman beyond it needed help, we could pretend. Maybe it could be enough.

I shut my eyes tightly and pressed a kiss to his temple. Pretend, just pretend. I would give him the sex he had craved, and in return, he'd give me memories. It would be a payment just the same.

"You want this," I whispered.

He shuddered in my arms; it was like hugging a wild animal, one who could just as easily maul me as cuddle.

"Can I touch you?" he whispered. "Please."

It unraveled me, that plea. As if he understood that a little bit of my soul slipped away every time someone touched me. As if he would cherish the part I gave him.

I scrambled away from him as if burned, breathing hard. No.

No one understood, which was exactly the way I liked it. I ran a shaking hand over my face to smooth away the panic.

Sure, he knew the score better than most people. He had worked the beat as a patrol cop and then as a detective. Life as a high-priced escort wasn't glamorous; it was sweat and blood sprinkled with glitter. But he didn't know the full extent, and I prayed he never would. Henri didn't sell bodies; he gutted them.

I panted against the headboard, unable to walk away but unwilling to beg. Luke remained carved in stone where I'd left him sitting on the edge of the bed. The air pulsed with doubt and longing—with sex.

"I want it to be real between us." He spoke low and hoarse.

A quiet sound escaped me. Every caress, every pinch. Every slur ever spoken. "It's always real. That's the problem, Luke. It's always too damn real."

He hung his head, and I thought for a moment I heard him say "I know," but the moment slipped away; the sweet intimacy sailed away like clouds on the horizon—never really mine.

Without turning he asked, "Why not take her to your shelter?"

My heart stuttered in shock, distracted at least from its injuries. "Wh-what on earth are you talking about?"

"Yeah, I know about that." He turned to me, his eyes dark emerald—fathomless. "You told me about it when you were in the hospital."

For days after I was shot, I had lain in the hospital bed. He had been by my bedside every time I woke. What else had I said?

He continued. "You told me that girls don't like outsiders to interfere. What did you call me? 'An interfering bastard who doesn't know when to quit.'"

"Well, you are a bastard," I mumbled. "And I'm not an outsider. Besides, she can't go there. Even the security there won't hold up against Henri, and I can't put all the other girls at risk—"

He swore. "Henri? As in Henri Denikin, who owns two whole streets in the Fifth Ward? How the fuck did you get mixed up with him?"

I blinked with feigned innocence. "I work for him—from the beginning. Didn't I mention that?"

Of course I hadn't. Even when I'd reluctantly agreed to leak information about Philip, I had never let on that I knew Henri. I was conflicted, not suicidal.

"You know you didn't." Luke stalked away only to come right back. "He's one crazy SOB. If I had known… Damn it, you should have told me."

"So you see." Relief swept through me. He understood what kind of danger she was in. "You'll help her?"

"Child Protective Services will help her," he corrected. "I'm betting she's under eighteen, if barely. They'll give her a place to live."

I gaped. "You mean a place to die, because no broken-down group home is going to be safe from Henri."

"No place is safe from him. That's what makes him terrifying." But he didn't sound terrified; he sounded angry.

"You can protect her. Someplace better than that, somewhere safe." Something illegal.

"I can't," he said, but it sounded like *I won't*. "I can't legally keep an underage girl when she has parents somewhere worried about her. You want me to break the law for her."

For me. He had off-the-books connections, he could pull strings, but only if he wanted to. Disappointment churned like bile. He didn't, but I was desperate enough to keep trying. "What about changing her name? Witness protection?"

"Sure, if she's a witness. If she can nail an actual case against him." His look was pure disbelief. "Can she?"

Doubtful. She was brand-new here, whereas I'd worked with Henri for years. I scrolled through everything I knew about Henri, every illegal thing I'd ever seen him do. All of it incriminating, but none of it would stick. A working girl, I'd never been in his inner circle. I never knew much. And now that I'd been out of the life for months…not anything.

"I'm sorry," he said, softer now. His eyes pleading like the guy at the goddamned bookstore, the backside of betrayal. "If I helped every one of Henri's girls—"

"I'm not asking you to help all of them, just one. Just me." I swallowed. "Do it for me."

"Would you go away too—disappear?"

Change my name, fine. And there'd be no love lost for this harsh city. But never to see Allie or Bailey again? There'd be no point to any of it. No chance of seeing Luke again? Something inside me ached at the thought.

Could I give them up to save the girl?

"Please," I said, not sure what I was asking.

Light flickered through his eyes like the moonlight on water. He lived and breathed his work. His crusade against the pimps of Chicago was his mission, the rules and regulations of the Chicago Police Department his scripture. How could I ask a man to sacrifice his religion?

How could I not?

I thought of Ella and the potent fear-hope mixture in her stormy eyes. I needed this. Maybe it would be enough. Maybe, for once, I'd beat fate.

"No, I'm sorry," he said, and I knew what the answer meant. I wasn't enough.

I'd thought maybe with a fresh start, a real job… But it hadn't worked out. It was more than a little

PTSD and a shitty coincidence at a bookstore. I'd built my life by fucking the men he fought to put behind bars.

"You don't understand. There's more to it than just you or me. I can't risk…"

He ran a hand through his hair, making it stick up at odd angles. I shouldn't find him so adorable, shouldn't trust him. We were enemies, by breed if not inclination. The criminal and the cop, temporarily on a truce, because I couldn't say no when he had asked me for help. I'd hoped he'd return the favor now that I needed it—more fool me. You scratch my back, and I'll scratch yours. The rules of the street but not for Luke. He followed the law instead.

"Look," he finally said. "She'll be as safe at the precinct as anywhere. And you… Let me call this in, and we can go from there."

"Damn it, Luke."

"Trust me," he pleaded.

But I couldn't. So I plastered on a fake half smile and nodded. Any man would fall for it, and he did. Grimly, I shut him in the bedroom and found Ella rummaging through the drawers in the kitchen. Her expression blanked when she saw me. She lifted her face, like an animal sensing trouble.

"What's going on?"

Oh, Luke was about to give up our position to his coworkers, some of whom might be on Henri's payroll. "Nothing."

"Liar."

Yes, lies. What else did we have to work with? The truth had never set me free. None of us were safe. Even Luke could be in danger. If Henri found out we were here, if he sent someone… I peeked out the window and saw only an empty street.

"Shit, you're making me nervous." Ella flopped onto the couch.

"Sorry," I muttered.

I never quite knew why I did it or what I hoped to hear, but I wandered back to the bedroom where the shut door muted the low, strained sound of Luke's voice.

"Yeah, they're here. Her and another girl. She won't give her name, but the description matches."

Uncertainty unfurled in my belly, but why? Everything was fine, fine.

"Give me an hour. No, don't send anyone."

My breath came shorter, and then not at all.

"I'll bring them in myself."

I turned to face Ella, whose eyes reflected the fear I felt even though she was too far away to hear. She pointed to the TV. On lead feet, I walked over.

The local news was broadcasting a multiple homicide at an upscale hotel in the city. There were businessmen, and they were dead. Police had two suspects, and then sketches of Ella and me flashed on the screen.

"They think we killed them," Ella said incredulously. "They set us up."

It shouldn't have been possible, but I had underestimated Henri. What better way to punish us than this? And I had overestimated Luke. I felt the betrayal like acid. They must have told him we were wanted for questioning, fugitives, and he would lead them right to us. I was tempted to let him. Let them take me. When I ended up mysteriously dead in the cell, maybe then Luke would see the truth about his precious system. Either way, I would be free of it, bereft of him.

Ella looked to me, her doe eyes frightened and hopeful.

Make this right.

"Come on, then," I said grimly. "Looks like you're stuck with me."

In two minutes flat, we were out the door, down the stairs, and far away. We were gone, he'd never find us, and I was lost.

CHAPTER EIGHT

THE STREETLIGHTS BLINKED rapid-fire as we hurtled over Chicago's I-90. I longed to call my best friend, Allie, to hear her daughter babbling in the background, but any contact could put them at risk. Same went for the shelter. We could be followed or traced or any number of scary things, and all I had was a knockoff Prada clutch with my cell phone and two hundred dollars' cash.

Well, besides Ella. "Are you going to tell me your real name now?"

Her fingers clutched the leather seat. "How about bite me?"

"For someone running low on friends, you're not very nice."

"Why should I be nice?" she demanded. "Are you still trying to turn me into a hooker?"

"Still got your pockets full of other people's stuff?"

She tightened her lips, and then there was only the steady *thump*, *thump*, *thump* as the tires rubbed strips on the road. I drove in a kind of stupor, grateful for the reprieve. I didn't want to think about the implications of being set up for murder—or how stupid I'd been to trust Luke. I didn't want to contemplate what my lapse could have cost us, or what it still could if we didn't get somewhere safe.

On autopilot I took us into an opulent pocket neighborhood in Schaumburg and pulled into the winding driveway. We rolled to a stop at the gate and stared up at the house—mansion, really. The building drew lines with metal and stacked irregular planes of glass. It should have been the gawky teenager of houses but was instead a revered eccentric, splitting the lush lawn and twilight sky to suit it rather than conforming to the landscape.

"I don't want to go here." Ella's voice shook.

I looked at her curiously, surprised by the intensity of her response. She was shadows and wide eyes, the portrait of a cornered animal. Her lips were pursed. Her skin looked like it had always been light, a stark contrast to midnight eyes, but she seemed to pale further.

"Sorry to say, we're running low on options," I said. "What, you don't like rich people?"

"I don't like men."

"Men aren't for liking, Ella."

"What are they for, then? Fucking?" Her lip curled. "For money?"

"At least I provide a service when I take their money."

She scowled as she stared straight ahead: the silent treatment. I really was getting a crash course in parenting a teenager today. Maybe I'd pick up a few tips to share with Allie for down the road. Once I got out of this mess—if I got out of this.

I squinted at the shiny freestanding number pad as if I could solve its puzzle. The green talk light blinked mildly, but idling outside the gate seemed a poor place to beg Philip's pardon.

On impulse I typed in my old code. It shouldn't have worked. But it did, in a strange but convenient lapse in Philip's security. Surely he would have cut off my access the day he'd found out I betrayed him. He was meticulous in his paranoia. Had he expected me to come back? I almost would have suspected a trap if this had happened sooner. But now, months later, there was no expectancy, only relief.

I pulled into the circular drive and stopped. The engine popped, cooling down. I toyed with the hem of my dress, come loose at some point in the evening, the silky fabric unraveling.

"You seem nervous," Ella said.

I was nervous, so I kept my mouth shut.

"I mean, why wouldn't you come here first—a loaded guy like this in your address book?" She swallowed audibly. "Unless he's really bad."

Philip was bad, in his own way, but not like she thought. No matter how angry he was at me, he wouldn't hurt her. I was almost sure. "He's my friend. It's just that… Well, he might be upset with me."

"What'd you do?"

"I sold him out." I let out a breath. "Almost got him killed."

"Oh." Even sarcasm seemed to have deserted Ella under the weight of just how desperate we were. She crossed her hands over her chest in a protective gesture.

I had sold Philip out to Luke as an informant, and just earlier tonight, Luke had sold me out. Irony was the madam of life: I could resent the situation she'd forced me into, but deep down, I knew I deserved to be there.

The gate code wasn't an oversight, I realized as the front door opened to reveal an annoyed Adrian Scott. He was Philip's butler, on paper, though his true role also encompassed security guard, resident techie, and, I suspected, confessional. Adrian manned all the fancy monitoring equipment; he would have seen us through the cameras. We were only here because he'd allowed us to be. Adrian looked me up and down, his face impassive but his eyes turbulent.

"Philip's not here."

Panic crept into my lungs, drowning out his next words. Of course Philip was a busy man, but I'd been so focused on our total lack of options and how I would beg him for forgiveness that it hadn't even occurred to me that he wouldn't be here. Where would we go? We might as well head straight for Henri and throw ourselves at his Italian leather-clad feet. At least he'd be amused while he dumped our bodies.

"But you're free to wait here until he returns,"

Adrian finally said.

My heart started beating again. "Thanks," came out on an exhale.

He allowed us into the large living room and threw me a disapproving look before closing us in with one of the impenetrable fingerprint locks. Fine by me. The tight security here would keep the monsters out as much as it would lock us in.

I went to the bar and poured myself a shot of 80 proof. After throwing it back, I poured another. Ella reached for my glass, but I slapped her hand away.

"There should be sodas in the minifridge."

She gave me a wounded look but pulled out a Coke. "You seem at home here."

I collapsed onto the plush leather sofa. "And you look like you might barf on the marble. What's eating you?"

"I told you I don't like men."

"You don't like *rich* men. Did one of them catch you lifting his Rolex?"

She took a swig of soda. "I'm too good for that."

"So am I, sweetheart. So am I."

Our idle bragging lapsed into silence, and I closed my eyes and let my head fall back onto the buttery leather. Was there any chance in hell Philip would accept my apology? Where would we go if he didn't?

Best not to think too much, especially now that my mind was pleasantly fuzzy from the liquor flooding my veins. I peeked at Ella. For once she didn't appear to be getting into trouble. Instead she lounged in an oversize armchair, her head listing to the side.

Hot pink glitter shone from her drooping eyelids, and my insides twisted at the thought of her painting on makeup in preparation for this evening. I wondered what had brought her to this, but I was too afraid to ask. Last thing I needed was another reason to feel beholden to her.

It had been a long night—a long week, a long year. All I had wanted was peace, and here it was. A clock chimed softly from somewhere far away—one, two, three. Then quiet.

CHAPTER NINE

I WOKE IN terror, remaining still and silent through force of will. The smell of leather, the cool brush of air. It took me a few moments to realize that this wasn't my old house, I wasn't a child anymore, and that shadow standing over me wasn't my father.

"Good, you're up."

Philip sounded angry, but the fact that he spoke to me at all, as opposed to one of the many other things he could have done—with his hands or other, nastier implements—was a good sign. Or hell, he could have just called Henri up and had me carted away. My groggy brain registered relief even as the sharp pain of exhaustion lanced through it.

Disoriented, I forced myself to sit. "I'm sorry."

As my vision cleared, his stony expression came into focus. His face was always a study in angles—chiseled, not sculpted—but when he was angry, the hollows became more defined.

He raised an eyebrow. "For arriving uninvited in the middle of the night, or for ratting me out?"

"Um…both?" *Very smooth, Shelly.* My charm completely deserted me.

That seemed to surprise him too. He looked away, down along my body. I held myself still, figuring my sleepy splayed position was the only thing I had to my advantage right now.

He frowned. "What are you wearing?"

"Twenty bucks on the clearance rack. Sorry, babe. Not everyone keeps me in Dior." And damned if I was going to let those guys get their grubby fingers on the dresses Philip had bought me. They hung in the closet of my condo right now, well guarded and unreachable.

He grunted, not impressed. "I take it you're desperate, since you're here."

"Fishing for a compliment, Philip?" At his wry look, I allowed a soft laugh. "Yes, you're right. I wouldn't have come back otherwise. I figured you'd have me strung up by now."

"I would have, if I'd thought you wanted it too. Adrian's made up rooms for the two of you. You'll be safe for the night, at least."

I couldn't resist asking softly, "And after?"

"Don't press your luck, Shelly. One of these days, it's going to run out." He turned on his heel and strode out of the room before I'd managed a weak protest. Well, it could have gone worse. I rubbed the sleep from my eyes and turned to Ella. She slept with her head leaning against the wing of the chair, her lips parted. A blanket lay over her, tucked under her chin, that hadn't been there before.

I woke her with a gentle shake to her shoulder, dislodging the blanket and revealing the low-slung neckline of her cheap dress.

"Where are we?" she asked, blinking sleepily.

How quickly she recognized me, despite forgetting where we were. How completely she trusted. My eyes pricked, and I hid my face as I pulled her up. "Somewhere safe. Come on, let's put you to bed."

She was pliant, more like a seven-year-old than a seventeen-year-old. I towed her upstairs to one of the guest rooms with a light on and tucked her in between the satin sheets.

Adrian waited for me outside, like a stubby guard dog. "Your room's next door."

"I'm going to talk to him." I studied his stony expression, then said, "I'm not going to hurt him."

"You weren't supposed to hurt him last time."

"I'm sorry about that. I want to make it up to him. Please?"

He wavered. "No."

"Keeping me away won't make him gay," I said softly.

His laugh was a caustic sound, grating the air.

"Go, then. Who am I to stop you?"

He stepped back with his hand outstretched in a parody of the obedient servant. I had no doubt he would monitor me through the hallways, but some rooms would be blind.

Philip was in his bedroom, a place I knew well. I knocked and entered but hovered just inside the door.

He tugged at his tie. "Go away."

"Okay," I said but remained there.

He kicked off his shoes, threw his jacket on the bed. "Whatever it is, we'll deal with it the morning."

"All right," I said, padding across the room and curling into the chair beside the bed. So many nights we had sat like this, exhausted from parading around some god-awful black-tie event. It was all so familiar my throat hurt.

Once, I had been his live-in prostitute, his mistress, his well-compensated girlfriend—whatever he wanted me to be. Just a job, and a high-paying one. At least that was what the contract stipulated. Until he'd begun to develop feelings for me, unwanted, unprecedented, and I'd started to care for him too, as a friend anyway. But the wheel was already in motion. As an informant, I had been feeding Luke information about Philip's criminal activities. The truth has a way of coming out and biting you in the ass—or shooting me in the shoulder, in my case.

When he was bared down to his formfitting boxers, I went to him. He was trim, as always. I caressed his sleek muscles, but though I could admire his form, I didn't feel the same visceral pull from it that I did for Luke's. Philip was a starry night, beautiful and mysterious. Luke was like the sun, so bright he blinded me, but I couldn't stop looking up.

"You seem tired," Philip said.

My hands paused in their exploration just a beat

before continuing. The light skim of my fingertips alternated with a firm touch, perfectly measured to arouse. It worked, always.

"Is this payment?" he asked. "A businessman would insist on knowing the terms of the deal."

Funny, I didn't realize I had any leverage with which to barter. "You can always refuse."

"Can I? I'll try to keep that in mind."

He pulled me to the bed, turned me over, and ran his hands along me, checking that I was all there, his breath scalding on my neck.

"Why did you come here, Shelly? Do you want to get fucked? All hot and bothered, but he won't hold you down and give it to you like I will?"

His body was flush against mine, weighing me down, all hardness and heat. Anger and pain.

"Or did you want me to hurt you? Am I your punishment?"

"No." I shouldn't encourage this—it wasn't true—but I had to know. "For what?"

"For not being good enough for him."

He paused, crowding closer, the ridge of his cock pressed against the cleft of my ass.

"You know that, don't you?"

A sharp pain stunned me as his hand met the flat of my ass, and I released the shock in a gasp.

"You think I mind that you're all wet for that cop? This is just business, you and I. I'll help you, and you'll help me right back. I don't care if you want it." He pushed against me, the length of his cock against the flesh of my ass, and grunted.

"Does he know to touch you like this?"

His fingers found my sex, playing me with the strokes he knew so well, and all I could see beneath my closed eyes was Luke touching me—knowing me this well.

"Does he hurt you like this?" With his other hand, Philip grasped my hair and pulled. "Does he?"

"No, no." Luke didn't touch me, wouldn't hurt me. Even if we were together, he would never know my dark side. But I would hide it; for him I could. "He doesn't want me."

Philip froze, the bar of his cock still hot against my skin, the ragged heat of his breath against my shoulder. The murmur of my name sounded like good-bye. He lifted off me, and air cooled my flushed skin. I remained bent over, but he pulled me upright. He hadn't fucked me. He wasn't going to. His hands tightened on my arms when he saw my face.

"Damn," he said. "Damn. I didn't mean for it to be like that."

"I want it to be real between us."

I swiped at my cheeks. "It's okay."

Philip sat down heavily in the armchair and let his head fall back. "Tell me, then. What was so horrible that it sent you running to the likes of me at three in the morning?"

I slanted him a look as I fiddled with the jagged

hem of my dress, the cheap fabric torn somewhere during our fight or flight. For maybe the first time in so many years, I mumbled at the floor. "It's possible I'm the lead suspect in a multiple homicide."

He stared at me for a moment and then burst into a laugh. "Bet your cop shit a brick."

Sure, right before he promised to turn me in. "Do you have to find this amusing?"

"Tell me you did it, that you murdered some bastard." He was grinning. "Fuck, you didn't. Oh, that would have made my night."

"You really are perverted."

"I know." He sobered. "They would have deserved it, if you'd done it. But okay, to business. Who knows you're here—anyone?"

I shook my head. "I don't think we were followed. If we were, there would have been cops knocking on the door by now."

"Sweetheart, cops know better than to knock on my door."

A smile tugged at my lips. Was that what I sounded like? "You're an ass."

"Go."

He pulled me to standing and pushed me gently toward the door.

"Get some sleep. We'll figure it out in the morning. And if we don't, you can just live here forever."

There was a note in his voice that said he wouldn't mind that outcome too much; I shivered. As I shut the door, he was still chuckling to himself. "My little murderer," I heard him say.

I slipped through the hallways, the shadows both foreign and familiar, but I turned away from the cold guest room I'd been assigned. Metal stairs shook under my weight as I climbed up to the observatory. Philip's mansion was like a life-size dollhouse, made for play, not living. But there were a few perks, and the stargazing nook at the top of the tower ranked high among them.

I nestled among the pillows there, hoping that whatever girls Philip had brought in to replace me hadn't found this spot. The thought of another person's left-behind hair and skin and fluids on the pillows, of touching those things, was enough to mar the experience—almost. At least until I let out a breath and looked up at the sky.

At first I had thought it was stupid to build an observatory in the heart of Chicago, where only a few stars ever pierced the blanket of smog and bright city lights. But one night, after leaving Philip's bed, I had slunk up here like a dog hiding away to lick her wounds.

The small windowed room gave me space to fall apart. The endless black expanse above let me do it in privacy.

I still smarted where Philip's hands had smacked me, where his cock had branded me. Small acts, almost innocent compared to what I had done in the past, but it felt all new to me now. All dirty and so wrong, when

SKYE WARREN

it was with anyone but Luke.

And Luke. Oh, Luke. I had called Philip perverted, which was accurate enough, considering. But here I had access to a face chiseled from marble, and I wanted the one studded with stubble. Here I lay swathed in silks, wishing they were coarse blue cotton sheets instead.

Why did he have to turn on me so quickly, after what I had done for him? I supposed that showing up so late, frantic and with a black eye, it was conceivable that I had just committed murder.

Although, after the messages he'd left me, I believed he didn't mean for us to be hurt. A small comfort, when he might have gotten us killed. He trusted the system too much. He thought his precious fucking colleagues would exonerate me if I was innocent.

Maybe that was the problem. I didn't just want him to believe in me. I wanted him to think the worst and protect me anyway.

CHAPTER TEN

A QUIET DRIZZLE pattered the windows above me in a gentle morning song. I wandered back to the guest rooms. Ella's room was empty. I checked my assigned room in case she'd come to wait there. Empty as well, but there was a tray with still-warm coffee sitting beside the bed on a side table.

The closet door lay open, revealing a few of my clothes. Damn, and my favorite pair of jeans. Philip must have held them back when he sent the rest of my stuff. Figured, the sadist.

I checked my clutch, which was now minus my phone. Since the cash was intact, that meant Ella hadn't found my stash. So who had taken my phone? Maybe Philip. More likely it was Adrian, acting on his orders. It could have felt violating, to have so little left and then have it taken. But a sense of melancholy still muted my emotions, and I embraced it.

Get dressed. Wash up.

I went through the motions, almost able to pretend I was still Philip's mistress, that I'd never left this unexpected haven. That I wasn't now responsible for a hurt young woman whose life was in danger.

At least until I heard Philip bellow my name from below. After a small moment of regret for my undeserved peaceful morning, I started down the stairs.

Ella ran smack into me at the bottom, full of indignant sniffles. "Fucking bastard. I hate him!"

My melancholy was over—interrupted, at least. "What did you do?"

"I didn't do anything! I was nice. Like you told me to be!"

Nice? Her idea of nice was probably bank robbery.

I pushed past her and found Philip behind his desk, scowling at some papers he held.

He looked up. "Keep her away from me, or you won't like what happens."

"What did you do?"

His frown deepened. "Why do you assume I did something?"

I answered him by sinking into one of the armchairs by the cold fireplace and leaning my head back on the plush leather.

He sighed. "She came on to me."

"On to you," I said dumbly. She freaked out when a guy looked at her wrong. She had been nervous as hell about Philip. "You're mistaken."

His look was droll. "I realize your own opinion of my allure may be low, considering I paid for your attentions, but I assure you, I know when I'm getting hit on. Particularly when the girl in question strips in my office."

My mouth fell open. Philip was a handsome man, but this was ridiculous. "She doesn't even like men. She hates them. She hates you."

"She does now, because I told her to stop embarrassing herself. It had the intended effect."

A mixture of shock and shame flushed through me. "Even if you're right, then she's confused. It was a rough night. There was no reason to be mean. I told her she'd be safe here."

"Well, I didn't beat her," he said. "Would you have preferred I did?"

Philip's tastes were extreme, perverted, violent—and strictly consensual. That was my cue. I got up and strolled over, resting my hip against his desk. "I'm sure I can stand in, if that's what you want. You know I can keep you satisfied."

"We're not doing that."

I paused. "Not now."

"Not ever." His face was set into a mask of implacability.

"Is this about what happened with Ella? I'll talk to her. She won't bother you again."

"And neither will you."

"Philip—"

Abruptly, he slammed his fist on the desk, and I jumped.

"How many ways do I have to say it? I don't want her. I don't want your desperation or your fucking gratitude."

I stared at his fist where it pressed against the mahogany. "Then what do you want?"

Slowly, his hand unfurled, and he leaned back. "Nothing. You can stay here as long as you need. No one will fuck anyone."

"Hmm." He didn't sound sure about that. "Where's my phone?"

"We couldn't risk it being tracked," he answered smoothly. "I'd get you a temporary, but you don't need one anyway while you're here."

There was my answer. I had lived in this house once as a pampered pet. Now it seemed the leash had tightened.

"Those charges are nothing but smoke and mirrors. I've already sent out some inquiries," he said. "This will all be fixed soon enough."

I watched his gaze flicker away for just long enough to let me know he was bluffing.

CHAPTER ELEVEN

I TRACKED ELLA to the kitchen, which came as something of a surprise unless she was there to steal the silverware. Only the appliances gleamed gray, the flat-brushed metal nestled among swirled granite and knotted-wood cabinetry. The room was beautiful, warm, and complex—Adrian's domain.

Ella sipped from a steaming mug as Adrian set a plate of biscotti down in front of her. He frowned when he saw me but without the usual mixture of distrust and anger in his eyes.

"Would you like some coffee?" he asked, and it sounded like *What the fuck did Philip do?*

Seemed I wasn't the only one adopting pets.

"I'm good. Can you give us a minute?"

Adrian left us, shooting daggers at me with his gaze that I interpreted as a warning to play nice. Obviously he wasn't as familiar with Ella's right hook as I was.

Ella stared fiercely at her coffee, stirring it with a piece of biscotti.

I pulled up a chair to the hand-scraped oak table. "Wanna tell me about it?"

"About what?"

"Any of it, sweetheart. What happened with Philip. Why you were working for Henri. What your damn name is. You're killing me here."

"I thought if I could… I didn't want…" She dropped the soggy biscotti into the mug with a weak splash. "Like you said, if I had just done what I was supposed to do, you wouldn't be in this mess. I didn't want you to have to…have sex with Philip because of me."

A too-full emotion welled in my chest. I looked away. "It's not so bad."

"I wouldn't know," she said drily. "Apparently even when I want to seduce someone, I do it wrong."

"Well, you don't have to do that. Neither of us does." I tried to infuse an optimism I didn't quite feel into my voice. "We're his guests."

She looked doubtful.

"Philip and I will take care of Henri," I said with more false assurance. "So you just stay put. Let me know if you need anything. I'm sure we can order you some clothes so you're not stuck wearing my hand-me-downs. Right, Adrian?"

"Right," came the muffled answer from the hall-way.

"Um…" Ella's gaze darted to the closed kitchen door.

"Adrian's a terrible gossip," I explained.

Muttering drifted through the thick, knotted oak.

"We love him anyway," I said. "Couldn't live without him."

"Damn straight." Adrian bustled back into the kitchen, armed with a laptop. "As if I needed to eavesdrop. You can be sure, I have more advanced surveillance methods if I were even interested in what you were saying."

He flipped the laptop open on the table and pulled up the Web site for Nordstrom. Ella's wardrobe would probably be better than mine, as retribution.

I suppressed my smile. "You two have fun."

Philip was a bit of a Luddite. I used to call him a sixty-year-old man trapped in a thirty-year-old body. He retaliated by fucking me silly. But there were laptops and tablets sprinkled throughout the house if you knew where to look. I found one in one of the cozier sitting rooms. In my mind, I had dubbed it the library for its cushy chairs and dark paneling, even though there weren't any books.

I pulled up my cell phone's Web site to check my call logs.

Shortly after we left the party, I had received the first call from Henri. A series of calls from him after that, where I guessed he was trying to figure out what had happened. And then nothing, which I supposed was when he'd ordered the hit on the men in the hotel suite, and thus on me and Ella by proxy. If those men had spilled their story, Henri's elite escort business would have suffered. Normally he would have compensated them with girls, but considering Ella's complete unsuitability, maybe he was low on them too.

Henri wouldn't have been happy about our desertion, and even less so once he found out we'd taken some of their money on the way out. But what had happened after, the murder and our framing, had been both brutal and quick. The message was clear. Return to him or be hunted down. Assassination by cop. It was one of his finer ideas, really.

In the minutes after we had left his apartment, Luke had called. Then again, ten more times. Well, sure, he had just promised to produce the lead suspect in a murder investigation. Naturally he would be concerned after finding us gone.

I should delete the handful of messages from him without listening. I couldn't.

The first one was frantic, out of breath: "Damn it, Shelly, where did you go? Come back."

The second was more thoughtful, pleading: "I know you saw the news. It looks bad, but we can fix this. Whatever happened at the hotel, we can fix it. Just come back. Call me."

By the third, he had realized his error: "Did you hear me on the phone? Is that why you left? I had to keep them from sending guys out. They're going crazy at the station, trying to find you, but they haven't yet. They're keeping me out of the search after…but I know that much. I'm not going to help them. You know that, don't you? I wouldn't. You know me. Right?"

Then the last:

"I don't—you don't have to come back. I just want to know you got somewhere safe. If you can, let me know you're safe."

The message clicked off, and I closed my eyes, letting the silence and the sorrow envelop me. I couldn't trust Luke, but I still wanted to throw myself at his feet. The pendulum of my indecision was never ending where he was concerned, but Ella was my new and trusty lodestone. Her safety trumped my quasi-suicidal desire for malachite eyes and gold-spun hair.

A commotion erupted outside, and with selfish relief, I heard my best friend's voice demanding, "Where is she? I swear, if you've hurt her…"

I slipped into the hallway, only to be caught in a crushing hug. I sagged against her for a brief minute, basking in the ache of contact, until she reluctantly released me.

"There you are. Damn it!" Allie swiped at her eyes. "What happened? I'll kill him."

I laughed, surprised to find myself a little watery as well. "Kill who?"

"The guy who hurt you. God, I know you've already taken care of him, but I don't care. I'll kill him again."

First Philip believed I'd committed murder in retaliation for some imagined offense, now Allie. Did I really come across so bloodthirsty? "I didn't kill anyone, sweetie. And no one hurt me."

She glanced pointedly at my eye, her disbelief clear. "You can tell me the truth. I already know, and I don't judge you. Seriously, it's about time. The only thing I'm surprised about is that you didn't start with this one."

She nodded at Philip, and I realized we had an audience. Philip was stone-faced, as he tended to be around Allie; exuberance made him nervous. Standing behind Allie was her fiancé, Colin. Though he filled the hallway, his stillness and stoicism caused him to blend into the background. I had always liked that about him. He was the blackness behind Allie's bright star, each one vital to the other.

"Oh hey, Colin. Where's pip-squeak?" I asked about Allie's little girl. Bailey wasn't Colin's real daughter, but that didn't stop him from doting on her.

"At preschool," Allie said. "She goes two days a week now, which you'd know if you came by anymore. Nope, you're not going to distract me. Tell me what happened and how we can help. Here, let's go someplace private, where the guys aren't glaring at each other."

Colin also happened to be Philip's brother, and last I heard, the two siblings weren't speaking. They'd had a little falling-out last year when Philip had tried to kill Allie. I was surprised he'd even come, except that Allie probably insisted on seeing me, and Colin wouldn't have let her come here alone—just in case.

"Allie," Colin warned, apparently still concerned.

"The testosterone is suffocating." She patted his chest, the gesture infused with both obstinacy and affection. "We need to have girl talk. You two try not to kill each other."

Most likely Philip would be cordial, but just to make sure, I kissed him on the cheek to placate him before Allie and I shut ourselves into the library. I sank into the plush armchair, relieved to be away from the tension.

As soon as the heavy doors clicked shut, Allie whirled on me. "What the hell is going on?"

I explained what had happened, from Henri's visit to the party. I omitted the part about Luke, knowing Allie would take the fact that I had run to him as a sign that we were an item. Behind all her bluster, she was constantly watching me. She knew something was there, and she thought Luke would be a good influence on me. If I told her what I'd overheard, she would defend him. Odd that she trusted him better than me.

"I wish you would have called me," she said quietly.

"You know why I didn't." I would never let anything happen to Allie or her daughter. I had made that silent promise years ago, when a hurting Allie held a positive pregnancy test in her trembling hand. No matter what happened now, I could never regret my time with Henri, because it had given us all the security she and Bailey had needed.

She stood at the window. "One of these days, you're going to have to rely on someone."

A repeat of earlier? No, thank you. I much preferred my precarious position with Philip. Our relationship was like a stream, shimmering and shallow with no chance of drowning.

"How did you know to find me here?" I asked.

She flopped into an armchair beside mine. "I don't want to tell you."

"Do you guys have Philip under surveillance?"

She laughed. "No, but I like the way your mind works. I'll tell you, but you have to promise not to do anything stupid. Like leaving this very safe fortress to wander around the shittiest part of town. That counts as stupid, just so we're clear."

Excitement ran through me. This was a lead. "Jade called you," I guessed.

Jade was a small-time madam with a few brothels in a seedy part of Chicago. She had been in the game a long time—an eternity, it seemed—and she knew everything that went down, everyone who went down. If she was contacting me, then she had information.

Allie scowled. "She showed up with a couple of muscle guys. Colin practically shit a brick to see those bozos come around the corner of the house. Apparently she doesn't believe in phones. There is something wrong with that woman. And don't say cultural differences. She's not right in the head."

I shrugged. "What did she say?"

"She claimed to have something important to tell you, that you have to visit her. She knew you were here, but she couldn't come—"

"Without Henri finding out," I finished. And since Colin was related to Philip, he could visit without arousing suspicion, like the childhood game of Telephone.

Allie continued. "I told her absolutely not. But at the time, I was going out of my mind trying to find you, wondering if you were hurt or… You know, and she made a deal to tell me where you were as long as I delivered the message. So, message delivered, and you're not going anywhere."

"I have to. Henri is after me. He's after the girl. You know Jade always has the best information. She wouldn't have asked me to come if it wasn't good."

"I was afraid you'd say that."

Already my mind was spinning on how to get out of here undetected. Philip would forbid it, and Ella would insist on coming. So I wouldn't tell them.

Allie poked violently at a wrinkle in the leather. Uh-oh. "What are you hiding?"

She scrunched her nose. "Well, if you're going to go anyway, I might as well tell you. Jade said that her information… It's about Luke."

CHAPTER TWELVE

WITHOUT MUCH TIME, our plan was simple: Allie swiped their keys for me and then distracted both men while I got away. I knew Allie could hold her own, but I hoped Colin wasn't too annoyed at her on my behalf. At least his old truck didn't stand out so much in this neighborhood.

Jade's house sat at the end of the street, the hinge between a poor residential neighborhood and a row of ratty strip malls. I parked in the small paved lot and climbed the creaking wooden steps. The glass in the front door had been painted black for privacy, which proclaimed the type of establishment this was as much as the neon THAI MASSAGE sign.

My eyes took a moment to adjust to the dim interior. It looked the same as when I'd first been introduced here years ago, summoned by Jade and escorted by one of Henri's senior girls. Only later had I learned that an audience with Jade was a commodity in Chicago's sex industry.

The city was fractured in half, the upstanding and the underworld, each with its own customs. The bookstore had a chatty sales girl to usher a new hire in.

Jade was my guide. She ruled with a power none of us completely understood but we all respected if we were going to last in the business.

Technically she didn't control anything outside these walls, but everyone showed her deference. Even Henri had always stepped carefully where she was concerned. I wondered about them, what bound them together, which one of them was the devil and which had struck the deal. There was something deeper there, but that was the old guard, and I was the new girl.

Back then, the bright red vinyl banners with gold lettering had seemed jarring over the cracked yellowed walls, the irony almost mocking. A little cat statue waved its paw, representing prosperity, next to the sign listing $75 FOR 30 MINUTES. The good-luck pendant hung over the door leading to the "massage" rooms. Over time I had come to appreciate the blending of noble tradition with harsh reality, the evidence of hope within a brothel.

I wasn't the new girl anymore.

After ringing the small desk bell, I scooted one of the metal folding chairs away from the wall and gingerly sat down to wait. I had only seen a cockroach on the wall once, but it made me eternally grateful for the expensive hotel rooms where I usually worked.

Two men came in, squinting and laughing and stumbling. Boys, really. They sobered at the sight of me, a woman in the waiting area of a whorehouse. The one with his hair in two-inch spikes whispered to the other furiously; the other argued back.

I couldn't make out their words, but as if channeling some animal instinct, well sharpened, I sensed their lust, their anticipation at having it soon slaked, and their terror at this taboo venture. First timers. I disliked being a man's first paid sex experience, vicariously living their thrill and shame over less money than they'd have dropped on a nice date. Plus, invariably, first timers tipped like shit.

They leaned against the opposite corners, seemingly deciding to stay, shooting me dirty, desirous looks. Possibly they wondered if I was for hire, but of course I never would be here. It wasn't even the prices, which were low but not offensive. There was a caste system to these things, and Jade's house was as low as you could get and still warrant a bed.

It wasn't usually an Asian fetish that drew men here. Like a prime-time sitcom, any escort agency offered an assortment of white girls, with a token black and Asian to round out the group. Men usually came here for the convenience—women available without an appointment, location secured.

Jade stepped out, wearing her usual uniform of a floral-patterned pajama suit cinched at the waist and cheap leather and cardboard sandals. Her hair was sleek black in a crop that would be hip on someone thirty years younger. There was an era of timelessness to her; she was ancient with smooth, pale skin, not a wrinkle or age spot to give her away. Still, no one would mistake her intensity; even the boys straightened under her hawk-like gaze.

"What you want?" she asked them.

"Uh…" They hemmed and shuffled, clearly reluctant to reveal any lascivious intentions to a woman who could have been their friend's mom, but too polite—and horny—to leave now.

"You want massage? Why you come here if you don't want massage?"

"We do, we do."

The quieter one stepped forward, not willing to lose his shot at a happy ending over his dumbfounded friend.

"We just were wondering… I mean, when you say massage… Because we heard…"

Jade glared at them, her irritation almost palpable. This place was full-service, but everyone knew not to talk about options or anything sexual outside the room. It was part of the way they protected themselves from narcs, but it was obvious these two boneheads weren't undercover; they were just stupid.

"Massage only," she said flatly. "Very relaxing. You like. No refunds."

Flustered, they dug around in their pockets to come up with the right amount, thirty-minute sessions for each of them. Watching their reluctance as they handed over the cash, I wondered if they had even kept any back to pay for extras. And yeah, they'd be shitty tippers.

After Jade led them to the back, she motioned me upstairs into her office, which was arranged more like a regular sitting room. Out of courtesy, I accepted her offer of a drink and received a very small glass of flat soda. Here, alone, her accent dwindled to a lilt, her tone still sharp but less abrasive.

"So, you in trouble. It was going to happen. Just matter of time with that one."

"With…" Henri?

"You know Jenny? Pretty girl. Stoner."

The girl at the party, the one we'd left behind in the hotel room. The reporter had made no mention of a dead hooker, which was certainly newsworthy if only for the salacious appeal. She had probably bailed shortly after we did, I assured myself. "Is she okay?" I asked.

Jade snorted. "How should I know? Maybe, maybe not. Henri knows it was you, and she makes him money, so why would he hurt her?"

"Great," I said faintly.

"She start maybe three years before you."

"Jenny? I guess. She was pretty far in when I started, but she isn't the type to pull rank."

She seemed not to hear me. "Her mother was a nurse, gone during the day. Jenny started getting high, so her mom kicked her out. Tough love, they say. Jenny quit school and moved in with her boyfriend. A common story."

"Mmm-hmm." It was a common story. The kind that made Jade's business possible. So I wasn't sure why

Jade was telling me this, but conversations with her were often circuitous. Once she had talked for fifteen minutes about her kidney stones before segueing into telling me about Marguerite and the women's shelter she ran, concluding they were both a pain in her side. At least this seemed more relevant.

Jade flipped through a *Vogue* magazine and pulled out a yellowed newspaper clipping. She slid it across the glass coffee table toward me. It appeared to be a small inner-page article titled "Dead End in Drug-Related Shooting." The piece explained that a twenty-three-year-old male had been found shot dead in his apartment. Due to his previous history of dealing charges and the circumstances of the break-in, police assumed the hit was drug related. Rumors indicated that the victim had poached the territory of a well-known dealer in the city, Henri Denikin, but there was insufficient evidence to link him to the shooting. A chill ran through me.

The last paragraph remarked that the only possible witness, the victim's seventeen-year-old live-in girl-friend, had been missing since the shooting. Her name was Jennifer Ponds. There was a grainy black-and-white photograph of a girl who looked about nine years old, dressed up for her school picture. A younger, happier version of the Jenny I knew, one who couldn't imagine the indignities that would be visited on her body.

Beneath the photo was a number for the missing-persons hotline. With a jerky motion, I threw the clipping back on the coffee table, but it caught on the air and floated to my feet. My fingers had black smudges left from the ink.

"What is this?" I asked. "What does this have to do with me?"

Jade shrugged. "Maybe nothing."

Unaccountably, I felt angry. "This is from the original paper, not a printout. So you knew about this at the time. Did you call this number? Did Jenny even have a chance?"

"Call them?" she asked scornfully. "What for, call them?"

I shook my head, throat tight. Her words replayed in my head: *"What for, call them?"* That wasn't how this worked; I knew that. Every one of these girls had a story. Every one of us had a story, and it didn't matter. I had a story. Don't think about it. What for?

"Hey," Jade chastised. "Did the rich bastard fuck you so hard your brains are broken, huh? You want to save your skin, or the girl you have, then pay attention."

I looked down, feeling properly chastised. Of course Jade was helping me. My gut told me this was important, and I would never have found it without her.

Focus on Jenny. On Ella. This wasn't about me.

I picked up the clipping again and stared at her

bright smile. Was this the most recent picture her mother had owned of her daughter?

"Yesterday Henri had those men shot in retaliation. The same thing he did before, with her dealer boy-friend."

Jade shook her head. "You are determined not to see truth."

"It could be a pattern," I said more gently. "Maybe those guys at the party had done something to Henri. Cheated him."

She gave me a look not unlike the one she'd used on the customers earlier. Idiot.

Okay, then. "So if it's not that… That's how he acquired Jenny. It wasn't random. Maybe it was even a little bit of revenge, to whore out the girlfriend of a man who screwed him over."

She looked approving, if that was what the retreat of her scowl meant.

I continued, "And if that's how he acquired Ella too, then it explains why she was so clueless about it. It also explains why he doesn't want to give her up."

"Face," Jade said curtly.

Everything was face with her. Face meant a man's reputation, his respect, his ruthlessness. If Ella repre-sented some sort of revenge to Henri, he wouldn't let her slip away so easily. Killing the men and framing her for the murder might have been the most convenient way of finding her in the large city.

"So what do we do?" I asked.

"If you hand over the girl, Henri will owe you." At my shocked look, she raised her eyebrow. "Maybe owe you enough to let you go."

My freedom or the girl. Oh, she was good. Maybe she had been sent by Henri after all.

"No," I said, my voice just a little too loud to be confident.

She didn't look overly perturbed by my refusal. "I assume you won't send the girl away to live on the run and turn tricks for her money. Otherwise you would have already let her go. The last option is look to the source. If you restore face in some other way, maybe Henri will be happy. He will make cops look somewhere else. You both free."

I was skeptical. "Did Henri tell you that?"

"He tells me nothing. I hear things. You know this." Her surprise looked genuine. "So don't listen to me. What do I know?"

"No, no. I'm sorry. I've been messed up from this whole thing. How can I find out what happened? Please tell me."

"I should make you ask girl for that." Then she seemed to reconsider. "I tell you what I know. I always like you. Henri is scared of the girl, because she is only one who can put him away."

"No." The word slipped out of my mouth, the thought of Henri afraid so preposterous. Though he was hands-on, he still had his men do the dirty work. If the heat for one of his employees became too much, that person disappeared. And on the rare occasion that failed, he had his hands in CPD's pockets and the best lawyers dirty money could buy.

Something gleamed in Jade's eye. "Not only what she sees. She has proof of this."

Her accent slipped—not completely absent but not nearly as thick. I had a sudden vision of her playing a part. The most garish representations of her culture propped up like a prostitute's slutty clothes. This plastic-covered sofa her version of a hotel room bed. Maybe she sold herself as much as any girl down the hall. Maybe she spent every day faking it too.

"You want Henri brought down," I said, knowing it to be true.

She slipped back into her role. "I been waiting long time. This will be return favor enough."

I paused, mulling it over. "What does this have to do with Luke?"

Her smooth face split into a smile, showing white, even teeth. "I wonder when you bring him up. Luke should come with you. Alone, you will probably get raped and killed. With him is the only way. He is only one cares enough."

"I'm not sure he wants to help me."

"Tell him you are looking how Henri acquire girl. He will come."

Jade's awareness of the underground certainly proved useful, but it was disconcerting to think she might have better understanding of those close to me than I did. She seemed to know Ella's mind, Luke's motivations, when I could barely manage not to piss them both off.

Well, it seemed I needed to have a very stern, pointed talk with Ella. If this was true, she had been hiding something that had damn near got us killed, something that might be salvation for us both.

"You want pay respects?" she asked softly.

Along the side wall, a small, fragile-looking table held a meditating Buddha—surprisingly, this was the thin, serious-looking version and not a jolly fat one. A thin reed of incense sent smoke into the air. I knelt in front of the table and deposited my two-hundred-dollar tithe into a small tin box in the back.

After a moment of quiet, I heard the swish of Jade's clothing as she came closer.

"Your Luke," she said. "He searches for someone. Another girl in the life."

My breath caught. All this time, Luke had been religiously following the rules. All this time, he had been going after Henri to find some other girl, some other prostitute. Not me. It shouldn't have mattered. Shouldn't have been a surprise—since when had I been anyone's end goal? Since when had I been more than a way to pass the time? A stepping stone to the girl he really wanted. Yes, that was me.

I stood. "I will do you this favor." I hardened my voice, infusing it with whatever influence, whatever face I held in my own right. "But don't go to Allie's house. Don't ever bother her again."

Chapter Thirteen

"**I** swear I don't know anything," Ella insisted, falling back onto the bed.

She hadn't strayed from that line the entire time, probably because my interrogation technique amounted to some variation of *Come on! Please?*

I sighed. This was getting us nowhere. If Jade had lied, if she'd been wrong... But I didn't think so. It made too much sense and hurt too damn much to be wrong.

"It would be easier to believe you," I said, "if you told me anything useful. Who you are, what your name is. How did you end up in that hotel room?"

"This is stupid. I didn't see any crime."

But I could feel her relenting. My breath quickened. "Just tell me." I played my trump card, since I had already figured out she had a weakness for sacrifice. "This is my ass in trouble too, remember?"

She flung her arm over her eyes—defeat. "Okay. So I'm with some friends, going to this party downtown. You have to be twenty-one to get in, but my friend hooked up with this guy who makes fake IDs. He was the one who told us about it, actually."

I sat down cross-legged on the bed beside her. "Go on."

"So we get there, and you know, it's crazy loud. Everyone's drinking a lot, smoking weed, and other stuff. I'm just standing around, and these guys kind of cornered me. At first I liked it. I guess I was flattered, but then I started to get scared. I didn't know how to make them leave me alone. People were only a few feet away, but no one looked over, while those men were just…herding me along."

Closing my eyes, I could almost see her uncertain smile, feel her nervous energy, smell the pungent smoke. I had been there myself, the teenager with too much curiosity and money for her own good. I'd been hit on, fended off the drunk and slightly violent, only to scamper away breathless. I had always been lucky on my wild excursions, like some sort of cosmic payment to balance out the unluckiness I found at home. But I already knew the ending to Ella's story, and whatever had gone down, she hadn't been blessed with the same unnatural immunity. She was too young, too inexperienced, like a tight bud just bloomed, unknowing of the world around her but more fragile than ever before.

"We ended up in this room." She moved restlessly as she spoke. "It was kind of like what happened in the hotel room, except everything was dirtier and… Well, I guess that was the main difference."

"There aren't many differences in fucking men, but that's an important one. That and tipping, so you can see why I prefer them rich."

"I don't want any sort of guy, rich or poor. Can't I just stay here? It seems safe. I could…I don't know, be the maid or something."

Boy, what a visual. "I don't think Philip needs that kind of temptation."

"He doesn't even like me," she scoffed. Then, aggrieved, "I know, I know, they don't have to like me to have sex with me."

That brought a brief smile to my face. She was learning. "So how'd you end up with Henri?"

"They took me out the back, where there's a bunch of men standing around a limo. The guys are pushing me forward, like here, we did it. This scary dude from the limo—I guess that's Henri—he says, 'Take her.' The men pull me inside, but not before I saw them shoot the guys from the club. I was so freaked out, just like half crying and half screaming. Henri is cool as snow, asking me all these questions. What am I doing in a place like this. How have I been. First I thought he was going to take me home. Then when I realized he wasn't going to help me, I thought he was going to… You know."

Yeah, I knew, but it wasn't like Henri to gangbang underage chicks in a nightclub. Even acquiring a girl that way seemed too lowbrow for him. Most escorts in Chicago would have killed to work with Henri for how much money he would make them. And status, because there was nothing a hooker longed for more than respect. Face, Jade would say.

I examined Ella, her soft brown hair and smooth, creamy skin. Her nose tipped up, her eyes slanted up, doe-like. She was an attractive girl, no doubt, but there would have been plenty of them at that club, more sexed up than her. And the fact that he hadn't fucked her before sending her on a job meant he didn't have a sexual interest in her.

For the most part, Henri didn't take seconds on his girls. He fucked them first or not at all.

Neither did he bother with rape. Henri liked his women willing; it made the girl's inevitable fall more perverse. I shuddered—a residual reaction, a creak in the shadows of my memory. Only twice had I ever let Henri fuck me. Once upon a time, it was the price of entry to work with him and to gain access to the best clients.

Later, I'd been desperate to help my friend Allie fight for her daughter. I'd gotten the cash, but the experience had been painful and humiliating. That night I had made a promise to myself. That had been the last day I worked for him—until the night I met Ella.

Life was about finding the positive, picking the wildflower from a field of brittle grass. At least she didn't know that pain, and if I could keep her safe, she never would.

Resolved, I turned back to her story. "Are you sure the guys were bringing you out to him? Maybe they were looking for somewhere private, and you guys saw him doing some deal."

"No, I remember one of the guys saying how the rich guy needs to pay up."

Shadows flitted across her face, pain and horror and grief for a man she didn't even know, a man who'd hurt her. This was more than innocence, her instinctive caring for her enemy—it was goodness. No wonder we fought all the time. We were oil and water, destined never to mix.

"He was the one I saw on the ground as the door closed."

I thought back to what Jade had said. "And Henri wasn't doing any shady business when you got there? Drugs, women, something?"

"No. He was just standing outside, waiting."

"Did he give you anything?"

She pursed her lips in frustration. "Like what? No, nothing. See, this is pointless."

"The point is saving your ungrateful behind," I said mildly.

From her position where she reclined on the bed, she suddenly turned onto her belly and rested her forehead on my jeans-clad knee. Her words were muffled when she spoke.

"I don't know what he wanted with me. I didn't do anything to him. I don't know. I don't know."

She was bowed down to me, her words like a prayer. I felt uncomfortable in my own skin, a fake object of worship, a fraud. My skin itched, too tight, all wrong. She probably needed comfort, but I couldn't give her that. I'd known all along I wasn't cut out for this. I'd said all along that this wasn't my thing. I would protect her, not baby her.

I slipped out from her grasp and out of the room, leaving her arms outstretched to nothing, ignoring the darkened stains of her tears on the bed. I really didn't care at all.

Chapter Fourteen

I FOUND A workaround to the phone situation in the form of Adrian's cell phone and a well-placed Chanel catalog for distraction. Locking myself in my room, I dialed Luke's number. I wasn't ready to deal with his desperate search for some other girl, but this situation needed him. Ella needed him.

"He is only one cares enough," Jade had said.

I called his apartment first, disconnected. Then his cell phone; it rang and rang. If he cared so much, then where was he? Not just now, but every time I had ever been hurt, ever been humiliated, why hadn't he been there to protect me? It was irrational to think he could have saved me before we'd even met, but my love for him was irrational. It was obsession and affection, all blackened with the taint of resentment that I wasn't pure enough. It was lust and it was familial, but then those two things had always been twist-dyed for me.

I kept thinking if I only had a name for what I felt for him, the solution would reveal itself to me. But there were no words for it, only sensations. Only the hollow sound of my voice calling out in a well where no one could hear me. There was only this churning, choking feeling in my gut, the remembered bite of a whip I had sworn never to feel again. Now I felt it always—phantom pain.

How much would I pay to keep my friends safe? It began as a mantra, a way to help someone who needed it at the time, a way to prove I wasn't the shallow rich girl everyone thought I was. How much of myself could I give away and still be me? I feared we had already passed the mark, the sacrifice like a cancer that ate away at me inside, always hungry, never full.

A knock at the door startled me. I flung it open, expecting to see Ella: penitent, indignant, forgiving. Instead Philip glowered there.

"Where the fuck did you go?"

"Don't start with me." The look I gave him was pure venom, my whole body a poison. "I'm not in the mood."

He brushed past me. "You and your moods. Everyone living at your whim. You're like the goddamned queen sometimes, Shelly."

"I'm a queen?" It was so ludicrous, a laugh puffed out of me. Resigned, I locked us inside, lest Ella get the idea to check on me after all. Can't let the kids see Mommy and Daddy fighting. Or fucking, if that was what we were going to do here. I recognized the gleam in Philip's eyes along with the bulge in his trousers. So he'd finally decided to collect, which felt like a relief. Why shouldn't we fuck? No reason. Let it wash over me.

"I work my ass off to keep you safe here," he was saying, "and come to find out, you run off at the first opportunity. No one knows where you are, except Allie."

"Your sister-in-law," I said, just to annoy him.

"My soon-to-be sister-in-law, who apparently doesn't give a damn about your safety either, because she helped you. I mean, fucking hell. I told Colin—"

"Ooh, you told Colin how to handle Allie, didn't you? I would have loved see his face when you did that." I grinned, though it felt more feral than amused. I wasn't sure why I was needling him this way, except that the only thing that sounded more appealing than sex right now was angry sex.

"Why are you taking this so lightly?"

I stepped close to him, bathed myself in his heat. "Because it doesn't really matter what happens to me. It's sweet that you worry, baby."

He pushed back, uncharacteristically hesitant. "Jesus Christ, Shelly. What's gotten into you?"

The glitter of silver in his onyx eyes gave lie to his refusal; he pulsed with lust, he breathed it out, filling the air between us with heat and spice. His desire might not have been for me, but caring had never been a requisite, so I purred anyway, rubbed my body against his in response, because ohh, he felt so very solid and aroused...so present. Yes, this was a little bit of payback to a man who'd used me and then turned me loose. And so what? That man didn't want me anyway.

Another girl.

"I'm trying to make it up to you," I told him.

"And then worst of all," he continued as if I hadn't spoken, as if his erection weren't pressing into my belly now, "you leave that girl here. She's got claws, that one, and here you're a cat in heat."

"So kick us out." I stepped back, waving my hand as if I didn't care—and I didn't. I was halfway to suicidal on a good day, and this wasn't one.

He smiled, and I shivered. "I came up here to make a deal with you, Shelly. You know how this works."

"I said I'd give you what you wanted."

"You don't have that anymore, sweet girl."

I stiffened, not aroused nor pliant any longer. He wanted Ella. He wanted her fight, her youth. Or maybe, as I had learned, there was no rhyme or reason to who we wanted. "You can't have her."

"Why not? She's old enough."

"I saved her from that life."

"Saved her? You've got half of Chicago trying to arrest her and the other half trying to kill her. If this is how you save someone, I'd hate to see you angry."

I narrowed my eyes. "Then help me. I know you can."

"My money. My favors. Mine. I've worked damned hard so that no one can tell me what to do, so that everyone owes me something, and I'm not about to give one goddamned inch because you ask me to. Once upon a time, maybe, but not now. Not after you sold me out."

So it had come to this, finally.

"I'm sorry for that." My voice dropped to a whisper. "Please, don't make her pay for my mistakes."

His voice slid into a seductive murmur. "I'm not going to hurt her. Is that what you're worried about? I understand she's new. I'd be gentle. You know I can be."

The temptation nudged at me, as soft and potent as any caress. I could walk away from this, just like I had done every time at the shelter. It wouldn't be so bad. The shelter was a sort of prison too, and this one was much prettier. I could even pretend I had saved her still, since Philip was a far kinder master than Henri would have been.

"I won't let anyone touch her," I said. "She's going to get her old life back, and when she does, she'll be…" Pure. I wanted her to have the life I hadn't. I wanted her to be worthy of the men I wasn't. "She'll be safe."

"I would keep her safe."

He would keep her, but would he let her go? And if he touched her, even once, she wouldn't be the same anymore. Always remembering that her first time was with a man not of her choosing, even if he'd been kind enough to make her come. Forever wondering whether she would have to pay with sex one more time. Offering her body, again and again, because she knew at least that much worked.

"No."

His face darkened. "You're not in a position to negotiate, Shelly."

"You won't touch her." That much I was sure of. There was a twisted honor among thieves, or in this case, sexual deviants. According to the rules of the street, by saving her and bringing her here, she was mine. Mine to sell, if I chose, and mine to keep. He wouldn't touch her without my agreement.

"You're here under my protection," he reminded me.

But he could kick us out. He had no obligation to me or to her. Street etiquette was to not get involved, and by our very presence here, he was involved.

"Just give me a few days," I said, my voice raw, naked. "Let her stay here, and I'll fix this."

He looked doubtful. "And if you can't?"

She was mine to use as a backup plan. I swallowed. "Then we'll see."

"Then you'll give her to me, wrapped up in lace," he said amiably.

"Yes." I choked on the word.

"I think we should ink the deal. Something to tide me over."

I would, I swore silently. I would fix this and free her, the way no one had done for me, not even Luke. Yes, I could ink that deal, with blood, with sex. "I saw the way you talked about her. The way you got hard thinking of her. You're hard right now with it, aren't you?" Another roll of my hips; his sharp intake of breath. "What is it you like about her? Her age?"

"It's... No... She's not too young."

Stammering was deliciously out of character for Philip. I worked at the buttons of his shirt. "Not too young. And she'll learn." Inside, I ran my hands through the light fur there, touched my mouth to his heated skin. "Wouldn't that be fun, directing her? Guiding her?"

He groaned, almost there.

"Show me what you'd do." I flicked my tongue at the base of his throat. "Teach me a lesson."

His restraint fell away; he caved in completely, pulling off the rest of his clothes while I took off mine. I fell to my knees, eyes wide and innocent. "I want to please you. Will you show me how?"

It was so wrong. Not only to play the ingénue, but to do it in the guise of Ella. But Philip had always gotten off on the strange, the deviant, and I had been right about his desire for her. The fact that he thought she was too innocent, out-of-bounds, just made the lust sharper. I would play the part in her place, and in doing so, keep her safe.

He slipped his hand behind my head and guided his cock to my mouth. There he paused, giving me time to feel it on my lips, the patient instructor to a curious pupil.

"That's right," he murmured. "Let it inside."

I opened wider, only a fraction. It seemed too big; suddenly it was too big, and I had never done this before. I felt poignant fear, both of this foreign male member and of the possibility of failure as I donned my role.

He bolstered me with praise while feeding the air of pretense. "It's going to feel so good, your mouth around me, sucking me. I love your lips, so pink and full. It's all I can think about when I see them, spreading them wide around my cock."

I wondered briefly if he was really thinking of my lips or hers, but it didn't matter. This wasn't about me and him; it was about our unfulfilled fantasies played out with another, and the wrongness of it was just right.

He slid inside, and I worked the head of his cock in clumsy swipes of my tongue. The more I flustered and bungled it, the more excited he got, hard and urgent, seeping cum into my mouth. His words were sweeter than he had ever used with me, almost painful to hear: *yes, you've got it, just like that, you're so brave.*

For my part, I played the role like I had been paid to do it. That was how I liked it; I didn't have to care, and that couldn't be real fear. It was just a job, just another part to play.

Despite my play at inexperience, or because of it, he was close. So close his pretty words cracked into grunts and groans.

A knock came at the door. "Shelly, are you in there?"

Oh, Ella. Uncertain, stricken, I looked at Philip

and saw that it was too late. He was panting, flushed, already there, the sound of her voice triggering his release into my throat. His orgasm was quiet, the raw sounds of his breathing easily muffled by the rattling of the doorknob.

I swallowed.

After a moment, Ella said, "Okay, I know you're in there. Are you mad at me because of what I said?"

On my knees, with my mouth still tasting of salt and sex, I couldn't remember why I would ever be mad at her. I could barely remember a thing she said either, except *"I don't know."*

"I didn't do anything to him."

"I don't know. I don't know."

It was a puzzle. If I found all the pieces, then Ella got her life back. And I got...what? Redemption, though the idea seemed laughable as I knelt on the floor, naked and well used.

Philip nudged me, handed me my clothes, and I realized he'd already quietly dressed. I tried to read his expression, but he could hide his thoughts, even from me if he tried.

But Ella's expression was clear as day when Philip opened the door and strode past her: hurt. And then at me: betrayal. With a soft hiccup, she turned and walked away. That's right, I thought, because this was all I had to offer.

Take of me, but all that was left was flesh.

CHAPTER FIFTEEN

Eight months earlier

I WOKE WITH a start, blinking eyelids that felt sore and cracked. They felt broken too, jagged red seeping through and orange blurred so that I wasn't sure they were open at all. But then a dark face hovered over me. I couldn't make out the features, but his eyes were hazy pools of green rimmed with red, and I knew it was him. Luke.

He hadn't left me or had me killed or any other of the rather unlikely things I had feared. No, he was too good to act on his justified anger. He was too good for me, but at least he knew it. He'd been careful to couch his lust for me in furtive glances. We both knew he wanted my body, and we both knew he wouldn't fuck me.

If I had been smarter, I would have taken what I could get. A rich, handsome man had been willing to pay me for my company, for sex, and that should have been enough for someone like me. So what if he was a little bit criminal? So what if it was nothing more than bodily transactions? Philip was a decent guy. He deserved my loyalty. He certainly paid for it.

But then Luke had contacted me, with his soulful eyes and his stiff-as-a-flagpole ideals, and the longing had hit me so hard I couldn't breathe. I held myself back from all-out begging, but I found a way to stay near him: I'd agreed to become his informant. And so I traded in the security of my benefactor for the hopeless wish on a star.

It had all come out, and I'd gotten shot, so this was what I got for it. The white-walled brightness of a sterile room and the *beep-beep-beep* of some machinery that was no doubt attached to me through plastic and metal. And Luke's face, frowning and worrying and caring about me, and suddenly this whole mess seemed like the best idea I'd ever had.

"Don't go," I said, but it came out as a groan.

He seemed to understand anyway. "I'm here," he said. "I'm right here. You're going to be okay."

How could I be? And though I'd never seen it coming, it was somehow a cliché. Shot through the heart. I had been sure that was a metaphor, but Bon Jovi had known. They'd called it. It's all part of this game that we call love. But maybe it wasn't really love, this thing I felt for Luke. Just a pale shadow, because I hadn't been shot through my heart, just near it. Just a loud sound in my ears and a sudden pressure in my chest.

I had no idea how close the bullet had come to the organ now pumping liquid thick as mud. Certainly my whole midsection felt tight and too large. It was like the time with that man who must have weighed over two fifty and not in the good-shape kind of way, which hadn't been so bad until I had started to panic. But the face above me wasn't his. It was Luke, and he was talking to me.

"Expect a full recovery," he finished in his cop voice. That was the fake voice, the one he used when he needed to hide the truth. It was the booming mirage, and he was the man behind the curtain.

I shook my head slightly, and for a half second, the whole world shook too before righting itself. I didn't want a full recovery. I wanted this body broken and bleeding. I wanted it unable to perform. That was what I deserved. It was what I longed for, maybe more than I longed for Luke.

"How long?" I pushed through my cracked lips.

His brows drew together, and I sympathized, because even I didn't fully understand the question. How long until I made this miraculous recovery? How long would he stay?

But he answered something different entirely. "Five days. You've been here for a week. You woke up a few times, but nothing coherent until now."

It took me a few minutes to process that. In fact, it was possible I'd blacked out sometime during my study of what he'd said. For five days, I had been laid up in this hospital bed, and he had been by my side often enough to see me wake, incoherently, and coincidentally been here when I woke up just now.

"This whole time?" I asked, incredulous. He had

been here this whole time?

He looked me in the eye, and it was like the curtain lifted, not because I had nosed my way back and exposed him, but because he was revealing himself, the man behind the curtain. All that earnestness was made more potent by the slight tilt of his lips. "Where else would I go?"

And then, like a dam breaking, he unleashed it all. "I'm so sorry, Shelly. It was my fault, not yours, not yours at all. I should never have gotten you involved in this. I should have protected you, not put you in danger. I should have convinced you to get out, and this never would have happened."

Maybe the bullet had gone higher than I'd thought. It felt like there was swelling in the vicinity of my throat, making it hard to swallow. And some sort of malfunction too, in my eyes, causing them to water and spill down my cheeks. But he was there to fix it, drawing the tears away with his lips. Kiss it where it hurts.

"But you're done with them now, aren't you?"

His voice sounded thick, like maybe he was afflicted too. Like maybe it was contagious, this horrible, hopeful feeling.

"You won't go back to Philip now, or anyone else. You can start a new life. Anywhere you want, doing anything you want."

"I can't—I don't know—"

"You can, Shelly," he said fiercely. "I know you can

do this. I believe in you."

He couldn't know how much I wanted to quit. For so long I had dreamed of leaving, like drifting away on a cloud—nothing practical, no concrete plans that would disintegrate into dust the minute sunlight touched them. But how could I... And then I looked into his eyes, and I thought, how could I not? He was the goal here; he was the prize. All I had to do was the impossible. Walk through fire, and I would win a chance with him. Be a normal girl with a normal job, and I would be worthy of it.

"I will," I said. "I'll quit, I swear it. I'll find a new job and a new apartment, where they can't find me. I'll never...do that..." Suddenly I couldn't say it. I had performed the act a hundred different ways with a hundred different men, but I couldn't say the words.

"You don't have to say. I know. I trust you."

Chapter Sixteen

Present day

THE WORST PART of the whole thing was that he had. He'd trusted me, and I'd fucking lied. I hadn't meant it as a lie, but I should have known it was impossible for someone with my past to live a normal life. But there I went, wishing on another star, and this time there wasn't even Luke's worried face above me, just a pissed-off, anxious teenager at nine o'clock in the morning. After opening up to her, I hadn't had any energy left—nor any desire to hear her pity. So I'd hit the sack. It looked like my reprieve was over.

Ella wanted to talk about the past. She wanted a plan for the future. But I only ever lived in the present. It kept me from hyperventilating and was cheaper than therapy.

"So what, are we just going to wait around until they find us?" she asked.

Still frustrated from my dream, from my failures, I rolled over. "Give me a few minutes."

"You've been sleeping all morning. It's afternoon now. Did you know that?"

Sighing, I tried to rub the old hurt and bitterness

from my eyes. Now wasn't the time to mess with me, but she didn't know that or she didn't care. Wasn't she supposed to be pissed at me for blowing Philip? Or maybe she was glad about it now, because she didn't sound angry. I couldn't keep up.

I glared at her as the pounding in my head grew louder. "I should have left you there at that fucking hotel."

"I did *tell* you to leave me alone, if you recall. You're the one who didn't listen."

"And I'm not listening now either. Notice a pattern?"

"I'm just trying to help."

I rolled my eyes. "Go fuck Philip if you want to make yourself useful."

She looked stricken right before she ran from the room.

I flopped back on the bed, beating my head against the wall. Shit. I shouldn't have said that. It had just hurt so much to see Luke's brilliant eyes in my dream, then Ella's with the same hopeful shine. I was failing them both.

At least I was awake now. Self-loathing would do that to a person.

Though it wasn't all bad. I needed to make a visit, and illicit anticipation rushed through me at the thought. I had broken my promise to Luke, but I would still take whatever pleasure I could get from him, wring every second of his company.

I thought about going to the club alone. Being Henri's girl had always afforded me a certain amount of protection. But now, this time, my identity would be a secret. A lone girl in a place like that... Well, look at what happened to Ella. Instead, my disguise would be commonplace, and strung-out, drugged-up girls being dragged around by a grungy boyfriend, dealer, and occasional pimp were a dime a dozen in Chicago's underground scene.

Luke should come with you.

Jade's words kept repeating in my head, a slippery invitation to my darkest desires, excuses to cling to when I slid down, down. Besides, I reasoned, this way I could see Luke and not break down at the thought that he'd never wanted me. What had he been thinking when I'd pushed myself on him? Before, I would have said repressed desire. Now I thought maybe disgust. The whore who couldn't even be in the same room with a man without humping him. And my actions with Philip last night proved it.

I didn't waste much time on regret. Why poke the base of a house of cards? And yet my situation with Ella irked me. I hadn't really done anything wrong. Why was she even mad? That I'd slept with a man on her behalf? Or that I'd slept with the man who'd rejected her? Goddamn teenagers. I couldn't get her hurt expression from when she'd found us out of my mind.

Downstairs, I found Ella sulking into a coffee mug that smelled like chocolate.

"So, did you have a good night?" I asked.

She said nothing, glaring at her drink like she could bring it to boil through sheer force of will.

"I did," I said, sitting across from her. "I always sleep great. It's a gift and a curse."

"Why would that be a curse?" she asked before catching herself.

"Isn't that the proverbial moral compass? That way I could know when I'd done something bad. Though I'd probably get permanent insomnia."

She snorted.

"Hey, I know. You can just tell me why exactly you're upset, and we won't have to rely on my faulty internal equipment."

She frowned at me.

"Lay it on me. I'll even let you smack me around if it'll make you feel better. I normally charge extra for that."

She choked a laugh. "I can't believe some of the things you say."

"Believe it, baby. Here's a lesson about lying: tell the truth. You don't have to tell the whole truth, just the parts that work for you. Me, I hardly ever lie."

"That statement could be a lie."

"What is this, a paradox? I'm trying to be a mentor here."

"And for reasons that are beyond me at the moment, I'm trying to learn from you. It doesn't make sense, because I don't want be a...a..."

"Hooker. Say it, or I'm going to start calling it the-profession-that-must-not-be-named, and the last thing I need is another mouthful."

"An escort," she finished. "I don't want to be one, but I still want to be like you. Is that crazy?"

It was sweet. Humbling. And a really bad idea. "If that's crazy, then so am I. I want the same thing, honey."

"So why were you there, at the penthouse? Why not just quit?"

Ah, what a question. If prostitution was the oldest profession, then how to quit was the oldest dilemma. "It's hard to explain." I thought for a moment. "Did you know a spider has venom to paralyze its prey? Most people just think about the web, but it's the venom that incapacitates them. Then it liquefies them, all before the spider takes a sip."

"That's disgusting. Also, please stop being creepy."

"My point is, the guns and the beatings, even the money, that's the web. It's easy to see, so people think that's why prostitutes stay in the life. But really they're stuck because of the venom, the sick poison of shame and fear that we'll never fit in with regular people again—it paralyzes us. We stay there, frozen, even knowing that we're going to get eaten."

"Oh, Shelly," came Allie's voice from the door. "You are like normal people."

Something caught in my chest before I breathed it out. "This is why you don't lie," I told Ella. "Too easy to spot."

Allie dropped a box of doughnuts on the table, and Ella grabbed one.

"Now what is this I hear about a trip to a club?" Allie asked as she grabbed her own doughnut.

"Who told you that?"

"A little birdie." When I stared at her, she conceded. "Okay, Adrian may have told me about your clothes. And the fake IDs."

"Traitor," I said, snatching the doughnut from Allie's hand.

She rolled her eyes and grabbed another. "Someone has to talk you out of it. It's a dumb idea."

"It's the only idea," I said. "Which makes it a good one."

"I assume you're bringing Philip along for protection," Allie said, probing.

I examined my nails, feigning nonchalance even though I'd never get it past her. "Actually, I'm bringing Luke. Or I will, as soon as I ask him and he says yes."

Allie's eyes never left mine. "Ella, can you excuse us a moment?"

"Uh-oh. It must be time for my spanking."

She grabbed an extra doughnut before heading out. "Okay. If I hear any screaming, I'm going to assume they're cries of ecstasy."

"What are you teaching that girl?" Allie asked when Ella had cleared the room.

"I think she's been watching too much HBO."

"And what's this about Luke?"

"Yeah, you know, the detective who can gather clues and make arrests and stuff. I figure he'll be useful to have around, since we want to get our names cleared. Legally. Philip would probably start World War III before our drinks came."

"Whatever, it's always about Luke with you. Seriously, can you guys just go fuck it out? The world would be grateful."

"Tried that. He didn't want me."

She made a sound of disbelief. "The way he looks at you, the way he talks about you. He's into you. Bigtime."

"Yeah, and he still doesn't fuck me. Makes you wonder what's holding him back, doesn't it?"

"Honestly? Not really, no. He's a nice guy and all, but I'm much more concerned about you. Why don't you just forget about him? There are other cops, other men."

She didn't sound convinced, though, as if she knew her words were falling on deaf ears, and oh, they were. Other cops? To pay off so I could work uninterrupted. Other men? Other paychecks. There was no one but Luke for me. There wasn't even him. Just me and my wanting of him.

"Don't you think I'd let him go if I could?" I dropped my voice. "I can't. I think...I think I might love him."

"Bullshit," she said with a roll of her eyes.

"Excuse me?"

"What do you care about, exactly? His penchant for singing show tunes in the shower? Or maybe it's the way he cuddles with you after sex. No, wait, you guys don't have sex. And you don't know anything at all about him."

Righteous anger flooded me, a relief really, because what the hell? "And I suppose you knew every secret of Colin's life before you fell in love with him."

"I didn't pretend to love him when he barely gave me the time of day."

I suppressed my gasp of pain with ruthless efficiency. I could control my breath, my body, the goddamned spasms in my cunt to fake an orgasm. That was why every man wanted me, everyone except for Luke. *"I want it to be real,"* he'd said. Except I'd faked it for so long I didn't know how to stop. If I wasn't pretending, wasn't modeling every word, every turn of my head to elicit the proper reaction, what would I do? If I stripped away the sultry sexpot and the ruthless working girl and even the doting godmother, what would be left?

"Then tell me." I swallowed hard, willing to beg. "Tell me what I have to do to make him want me."

Her laugh was harsh, metal on metal. "You're like some sort of man whisperer. You know what they're thinking, what they want. You know how to be around them so that they all fall at your feet. With Luke, you're dumb as a rock. And maybe that's the best argument

I've ever heard for you two getting together."

"I'll make him want me," I said grimly. "And you'll eat your words."

Allie stared straight ahead, her expression closed, her body rigid. It was clear she didn't understand me. We used to see men the same way. They used us, and we used them right back. But she was in love now, happy now, and I guess she didn't have the black heart to keep up the charade.

Tiredly, she said, "I'm not going to argue with you."

"Well, there's a first time for everything." I hated the nasty turn in my voice; I reveled in it. "You think you've got me figured out? Because you landed yourself a man, the only one in the city who was willing to put up with your bullshit?"

Shock widened her eyes, parted her lips.

"I bet you repay him nicely too. Do you give him shit if he stays out late? Nag him to put the toilet seat down? That's what wives do, but you'll make it up to him at night. Make him forget about all the trouble you cause, because hell, I told you what to do with your mouth."

Once upon a time, she would have called me a bitch. She would have put me in my place.

She turned to me, her frown slight, more thoughtful than hurt. "You went too far."

The quiet words stung more than epithets. "So leave."

"I will," she said, and I held my breath. "But I'll come back. You'll keep pushing me, and I'll keep coming back, because I owe you my life. You saved me a hundred times over, and nothing you could ever say or do to me will be enough to repay that."

She turned back at the door. "You know, if it was a pride thing, I wouldn't mind at all. The one man who could resist you, so you have to bring him to his knees. That would be fine. But I don't think that's it. You seek him because you know it's impossible. You're setting yourself up for failure, just so it won't be your fault when you're alone. So you can be alone and blame every asshole john and every uptight cop instead of yourself."

Chapter Seventeen

INHERITANCES ARE FUNNY things. They aren't earned, except by being born; we get them whether we deserve them or not. But I had learned long ago that everything came at a price.

On the first day my father came to my room, he didn't touch me.

He sat on my bed and told me that my mother had abandoned us both. She was weak, and he was strong. He hoped I would be strong too.

He left a small velvet bag of rocks on the bed. Mostly diamonds but other types of gems too, rubies and emeralds all beautifully cut and glittering by my bedside lamp. He explained that he had melted down my mother's jewelry after she left. It was rightfully mine, considering I would take her place.

Only years later, when I left the house with them in my possession, did I realize that she would have taken her jewelry with her. Which meant her leaving had been an unplanned escape or that she hadn't left at all—at least not willingly. Part of me preferred this rendition, since it meant my mother hadn't abandoned me to a monster. But these were all stories, part of the

Laurent family legacy.

I hadn't sold the jewels, even when Allie and I had desperately needed the money. I had preferred to sell my skin than part with them, for reasons I couldn't quite understand. I set out in the world with both my dignity and my inheritance intact, and now I only had the latter.

My dependence on those stones was fading, though. I could feel the weight of them lifting, their manacles unlatched. Their worth to me was measured not in blood but money—what I could buy with them. A new life for Ella, maybe. And if I bestowed the money upon her, like our own makeshift inheritance, what price would she pay?

The large sitting room and wet bar were usually empty unless Philip was entertaining. I slipped along the wall, trailing my finger over a lesser-known Matisse. In his private rooms, Philip's taste was spare and masculine. However, he spent a small fortune decorating the public rooms with artwork and bric-a-brac. The only style was expensive, and that was the point. I had once teased him about being so obvious. He replied that he had to be—people often didn't see what was in front of their eyes.

I had taken this lesson to heart.

Nestled in a bookshelf was an abstract sculpture of a rainbow with metal rays jutting from an unpolished block of concrete. Without the muted colors on each thin pipe, this would just be a piece of construction refuse. Maybe it had been once, though Philip had paid five figures in an auction at Christie's in New York to acquire it. I loved the way the artist had taken something ugly and made it valuable and unique—but without hiding its true nature. I also loved the way it stored my gemstones, which filled a dip in the concrete. I assumed that no one would look twice at the treasure at the end of the rainbow. Hiding in plain sight. Isn't that what I did every day, every trick? Even if the maid had dared to steal from Philip, the rainbow statuette hardly seemed like the most valuable trinket in the room. It looked like Swarovski had thrown up on a brick.

I had brought the stones with me when I lived with Philip. My departure had been abrupt, and I'd never gotten to retrieve them. That turned out to be a good thing. If this had been at my apartment, it would have been stuck there along with the rest of my belongings.

I scooped them out, a handful of glittering color, my own tainted rainbow that I had been following for years, a hopeless quest for treasure at the end. An emerald sparkled against my palm, the same green that had gazed at me with heat and passion and distrust, endless facets of light and dark, of blind hope and a long tumble to fathomless depths. It mesmerized me against my will, held me in its thrall so that I'd never be able to let it go.

"Find what you're looking for?"

I whirled at the sound of Philip's voice. His hands

were slung into the pockets of his dress slacks, his shirtsleeves rolled up. I searched his face for signs of accusation but found only a sort of sheepish tension. His dark eyes were hooded.

Slipping the stones into my pocket, I perused the textbooks on the shelf. "Not yet. Got any recommendations?"

He strolled closer, his distracted gaze flicking over the titles. "I didn't think you were interested in architecture."

I lowered my voice. "I'm interested in what you want me to be."

Mild amusement lit his face. "Very pretty. Actually, your erstwhile profession is what I came to talk to you about."

I glanced around the large room, with its wall-to-wall marble flooring and columned door frames. "Here? I think this may be the one room we never christened."

"Talk wasn't a euphemism. Come, sit."

Oh, fine. We had an entire relationship built on empty sex, but now he wanted to talk. I perched on the cool leather recliner while he took the one opposite me.

He stared out the distant window, unseeing, then turned to me. "Last night, I was…hasty. I was stressed out and fell back into our routine, but I didn't mean to have sex with you, and not that way."

"I'm shocked. Are you apologizing to me?"

"No. I'm saying I should have taken the time to negotiate. Clear terms make sure everyone is on the same page."

"Ah."

"I'd like you to reconsider the situation with Ella."

I made a noncommittal sound.

"It wouldn't be as…sleazy as it may have seemed before."

"*Sleazy* is not a word I associate with you. Perverted, deranged—"

"All right, your point is made."

"I'm not selling her to you."

"And I wasn't planning on paying you. I find that sex by the hour holds less interest for me now that a certain woman is out of the game."

"How flattering," I said flatly.

He shrugged. "Money is a means to an end. You know that. You were perfectly happy with our arrangement at one time."

"That's true."

"Fine, so I'm feeling a little guilty."

I shook my head in affectionate exasperation. "This isn't the first time I've had to make a guy feel better about what I do, but I never expected to do it for you."

"I had everything perfectly justified in my head." He scowled. "Until she came here."

"She has a way of disrupting the status quo," I agreed.

"With you, it was different. You had been doing this already. You knew what you were getting into. It was a job for you, and you did it well."

I inclined my head. "Thank you."

"But she's…"

He looked lost in thought, bewildered.

"I don't know what she is. She seems so young, and yet she's clearly old enough. She's innocent, but she swears like a sailor. She wants to have sex, but she doesn't… She hasn't…"

"A virgin. I think that's the word you're looking for."

"Christ. Is she really?"

"Pretty sure."

"How unsavory." He looked fascinated.

"Hmm. You remember that you promised to keep your hands off. Do I need to fit her with a chastity belt around you?"

His arousal thrummed through the air. "Only if you want me to physically pry it from her body and fuck her raw."

Of course, if her purity turned him on, it made sense that chastity would too. Apparently he'd found a new fetish, although whether his trigger was purity or just Ella, I wasn't sure. "Never mind. We'll just have to rely on your honor."

"We really are in danger." He grew serious. "I want to keep her, but if I did… If she were really with me, she wouldn't be able to go back."

"She doesn't belong here. She's not like you and me."

"So get her the hell out of my house," he snapped,

but his anger deflated quickly.

I spoke quietly. "I don't see why you're in knots over her anyway. You were like meat on a slab to those women when we went out. And yet you never fucked any of them."

"I had you," he said.

My heart melted a little at the simplicity of that statement. As if he had no reason to look elsewhere when he had me. As if we had been a real couple.

"You could have slept with other women when we were together. It's not like I would have quit."

"I wouldn't have. I thought of you as my girl-friend."

His honesty was touching and guilt inducing. Sure, it had been the girlfriend experience all the way. He hadn't just taken me out on dates. I had lived here. The envelope that appeared on my bedside table could have been an allowance in a certain kind of relationship. And I had cared about him. I still did.

But if it was possible to cheat on him emotionally, I had done so. All along, I had wanted another man. From the look on Philip's face, self-deprecating and a little weary, he knew it too.

CHAPTER EIGHTEEN

EANS AND A Bears cap flattened me into just another Chicago citizen. Anyway, no one would expect me to sniff around at the station while on the CPD's most-wanted list. Even I was a little surprised that I dared. It was almost like I wanted to get caught.

But I had reasons for coming here, and they weren't only about seeing a certain cop. I couldn't stop thinking about what Jade had said. It niggled at me, the way Jenny was connected to Henri through her boyfriend. The way she had been targeted for her relationship to him.

Henri kept a few girls in his inner circle, and she was one of them. So was I. What if I had been targeted the same way?

I had dismissed the idea at first. I hadn't had a druggie boyfriend who could have screwed Henri over. I had just been a dumb blonde in need of large quantities of cash. Open and shut. No mystery. But the thought had come back, worrying and worrying at me until I had to come here just to prove it wrong.

The old colonial building bustled with distracted cops and jaded public attorneys. A rumpled suit held the door open for me, and I walked in, hiding in plain sight, immersing myself in the spill of sweaty worker bees. Some people might think a prostitute would get nervous here, but what was a police station except a brick box of men with something to prove? Criminals, law enforcement officers. Customers, all of them.

I didn't quite have the audacity, or the suicidal fortitude, to walk straight into the detective's bull pen. Instead I exited the flow near the back offices. A shudder ran through me as I passed the double doors to the morgue; I preferred my marks alive, thank you very much. Ah, there it was: the evidence room. Possibly the safest place in this joint and definitely the friendliest.

A small bulletproof window had an opening at the bottom, like one of those banks from the eighties that screamed "we don't trust you" to their customers. At least they were honest.

I rapped on the window. A few minutes later, Chase appeared. His face went slack with disbelief when he saw me. I imagined he would have gone pale too, if his skin weren't practically obsidian.

"What the hell are you doing here?" he muttered, his white teeth flashing. Not a smile; a grimace.

"And here I thought you liked me."

"I do like you. That's why I don't want you raped and dumped in the river."

His words sobered me, but I refused to let it show. Never let them see you sweat. I raised an eyebrow. "Are you going to let me in or not?"

A buzz sounded from the door beside me, signaling it was unlocked. With a quick glance at the distended mass of distracted people, I slipped inside. Chase grabbed my hand and yanked me to the back room. The dimly lit space had only room for two. Once there, he pulled me into a bear hug. It should have been all bones and angles, with his thin form, but instead warmth enveloped me, outside and in. Cardboard particles and dust tickled my nose and brought tears to my eyes.

"Damn, girl," he said, releasing me. "I'm sorry I freaked out on you, but give a guy some warning. I almost had a heart attack when I saw you."

"Next time, I'll put an announcement in the paper, let you know I'm coming."

"There isn't going to be a next time. You shouldn't be here, not in the station, not in Chicago. Just start over. Start a new life somewhere else."

"And let them win?" I teased, although the joke was really on me. I had long ago given up any delusions of triumph, licking the boots and sucking the cocks of Chicago's elite.

"If you want to beat them, stay alive."

"So earnest, so loyal," I cooed. "I love that about you, Chase."

He sent me a cross look. "Stop it."

"Stop what?"

"Acting fake."

That's what I got for being honest. I did love

Chase, in a little-brother kind of way. I had always appreciated that he'd never made a move on me. Sure, he was gay, but I found that most men weren't too discriminating about the warm, wet place they put their dicks.

We'd met in my early days in the life. He'd worked for some dealer. Now he was on the city's payroll. Not much of a step up, in my humble opinion, but at least it gave him the respectability and confidence he'd always wanted.

"Fine," I murmured. "If you want the truth, I came here to see Luke."

"Now how did I know that?"

I ticked off the reasons. "Because I'm his informant. Because he's working my case."

"Not anymore. You stopped being his informant a long time ago, and he just got kicked off your case, off all his cases. He's on administrative leave."

"The hell he is." Luke must be going crazy. Administrative leave was an insult, like getting fucked in the ass, too fast and too hard, and I knew exactly how that felt.

"Yeah, well, the captain was a little pissed when he found out you had been to his apartment."

Guilt turned my gut. "I didn't know where else to go." As soon as the words were out, I realized how pathetic that sounded. "I didn't know who to trust at the time."

He shrugged, unconcerned, except I saw the way

his mouth was set. Frustrated. Protective?

"You don't need to involve him in this, and you know it."

If Jade was right, Luke was already involved in this, maybe more than me. He'd been on the scene longer, fighting Henri when I was just an unholy gleam in my father's eye. "I need to talk to him."

He wanted to refuse; I could tell. But he wouldn't. I hadn't given away his previous life to Luke or anyone else, so he owed me. I wouldn't have told anyway, but he didn't need to know that.

"I'll bring him here, but don't…" He looked away. "Don't do that other thing you do."

I grew still. The only sounds were the muffled and nebulous rush of people through the wall, as if I held my ear to a shell. Empty, hollow, how I felt inside. "Fuck him?" I offered quietly. "Is that what I shouldn't do? Don't worry that we'd make a mess in here. I'm a professional."

"Hurt him," he said, his mouth taut, body tense. "Don't hurt him."

Without looking at me, he turned and disappeared out the back room door. I heard the front room door clang shut. I stared at the rows of dusty boxes. Hurt Luke? A laugh escaped me. As if I could. I leaned against the stack of boxes and let the irony wash over me. Hurt Luke, when I ached for him. Hurt him while he searched for some other girl.

She probably had a case file in here. All the more

recent reports were digitized, but the police department still kept the hand-scrawled, dead-tree documents around, right in this room. What would hers say? Missing persons, maybe. Solicitation, drug-related arrests were all par for the course if she was in the life. Without a name, I'd never find her. If Luke had a file, it would be in some internal affairs lockdown, not here. I didn't even know Ella's real name.

I only had a few minutes. My file was a pathetically thin bundle, considering my current fugitive status. There were the solicitation charges Henri had set up for me to keep me in line. There were a few blacked-out pages from the incident where I'd gotten shot. And a note: *Full immunity.* The benefits of being an informant.

In the back, there was a brief report from when the police had interviewed me over a fellow escort who'd disappeared. It didn't include the outcome of that investigation, but I knew she'd never been found, because I still got an anonymous postcard every Christmas with a palm tree on it.

I replaced my file and skipped a few files down to dear old Dad's. Stephan Laurent. It wasn't a big surprise that he had a file. It meant nothing. I flipped it open.

Suspected for embezzlement. I tsked softly. *Couldn't afford the current year's Mercedes? Or did Juanita finally nail you for knocking up her daughter?*

Where had he embezzled from? It didn't say, and I

couldn't remember who he worked for or even what he did. My only memories were of roaming eyes and cruel words. How he'd made his money had been the last thing on my child's mind, and when I was older, I had more important things to worry about than angry conference calls in veiled business-speak behind closed doors, but now the question took my breath away. So much money. No morals to speak of. It could have been anything.

A whole slew of blacked-out pages followed. Unease fluttered in my gut. It meant nothing.

On the last page: *Full immunity.*

What had he done that needed immunity? Who had he fucked over to get it?

I heard a scratch at the door. I slipped the file into its place and shoved the box back where it belonged, my stomach churning. Would he see the marks in the dust where I'd pulled it out? Was it even Luke who'd come? I trusted Chase well enough, but only a fool let down her guard in the belly of the beast. I clasped my hands together, the picture of innocence; meanwhile the words were emblazoned across my vision.

Above me, a lone lightbulb flickered in a rusted cage.

Then it went out, plunging me into darkness.

Chapter Nineteen

THE DOOR OPENED, and yellow light sluiced around a familiar silhouette before the latch clicked shut. My breath caught in my chest, a heavy bundle of anticipation—and fear.

Luke?

I wouldn't speak his name out loud, in case it wasn't him.

Faint squeaking of rubber on concrete put him squarely in front of me. As my eyes adjusted, the slim light from underneath the door lent him a faint glow. I could even smell his soap through the haze of dust between us. But none of those things confirmed his identity as much as the simmering tension that pulsed through my veins when he was near.

It *was* him. "How's the sexiest detective?" I murmured into the darkness.

"Were you sure it was me, or is that just how you greet everyone here?"

"Jealous?"

"Pissed, Shelly. I'm pissed. Why are you here?"

Neither pissed nor jealous accurately described what he felt. Something closer to despair. I knew it, the way I knew what every man wanted, their dirty desires marking me, degrading me whether they touched me or not. Allie had called me the man whisperer, but she thought I didn't understand Luke. I did. Maybe not completely, but enough to know he was like the rest of them. He wanted my body, my mind; he wanted to consume me whole more than any other man.

But he didn't. It fascinated me, or it had until I'd found out the reason—some old loyalty and Luke too steadfast to ever stray. Mystery solved.

"I had to see you," I purred. "I couldn't be apart from you one minute longer."

"Save the BS for someone who's paying you."

I blinked. "Yeah, okay." Deep breath. *It's not personal, just business.* "I need you to come with me to a club Saturday night. That's where Ella got taken."

A beat passed. "I'll go. Alone."

"Where would the fun be in that? Besides, you'll have to excuse me if I don't quite trust you after that stint at your apartment."

"I was caught off guard when I heard you had a warrant out. I had to improvise."

"With my head on a platter? Nice play."

"I've done everything to keep you safe. I can't help you if you don't trust me. Goddamn it, Shelly, you walked into the middle of a fucking snake nest. Sometimes I think you want to get yourself shot, for someone to do what you can't do yourself."

Shock numbed me, but slowly feeling crept back in.

Of course, he wasn't just a pretty face. Allie knew me better than anyone, but even she wouldn't have called that one. This was a new side of him, more aggressive. I wasn't sure I liked it. "What's gotten into you? If I'm so annoying, you should hope I'm caught."

A pause. "I didn't mean to say that. I've taken a lot of shit around here since you came to my place."

"I'm sorry. I shouldn't have—"

"Yes, you damn well should have. Should have come to me, should have trusted me. Do you really think I care what those fuckhead bureaucrats think? I went insane thinking you were caught, hurt, dead. Thinking the next Jane Doe in the morgue was going to be you. Checking in case it was. You want to know what's gotten into me? You, goddamn it, you. Too goddamned selfish to let me know you're okay, so fucking cavalier, walking right into headquarters. Jesus."

Pride was a funny thing for a prostitute. We really shouldn't have had any left, and yet haughtiness was practically the hallmark of a sex worker. The last time I was with Henri, he made me do every degrading thing in his repertoire, waiting for me to balk. It would have been his crowning moment. I'd come to him for help, and if I said no to anything, even once, the deal would have been off. Victorious, I'd made it through, physically broken, mentally numb, and when I held the money in my hand, this was how I'd felt. The same way I felt now, standing in front of Luke in the dark, his

I'll make him want me. Both of us so determined. He would fuck me, and I would come, and then where would we be? Right here. No future, just sex. Broad fingers opened me for his tongue, pumped inside. I pushed back, halfway there.

I discovered that he swore during sex. I clenched every time, and God help me, he noticed, using it to bring me closer. "So fucking wet," he muttered. "This can't be fake. You didn't lube yourself up before coming to see me, did you?"

That gave me pause, but then his finger reached a spot inside me, and I cried out.

"Shh." He stood up, though his fingers stayed inside me, pressing right there, pushing and pulsing and oh Jesus, right there. His hand covered my mouth, muffling my cries and catching a pool of tears on my cheeks.

"Let go, let go," he muttered against my ear, and I didn't understand. I had come. What more did he want? He explained with his hands, massaging my clit through the aftershocks until suddenly lights burst behind my eyes, and I came again weakly against his palm.

It wasn't the first time a man had made me come. Some clients knew their way around a woman's body, demanding a real orgasm.

Limp, I waited for him to push me to my knees, to bend me over the table in the corner, anything. He didn't move except for the bellow of his chest, in-out, in-out, and the occasional twitch of his cock at my hip.

"How do you want me?" I asked, my voice husky.

"I don't."

"Nice words." I slid against his hard length. "But your body calls you a liar."

"I want you to come with me."

"What, you think I can't come from anal?" I taunted. "Want me to put on a teddy bear costume? I assure you, if it turns you on, I can do it. If you can think of it, I've probably already done it. Or is that what bothers you? Do you want someone pure, a little innocent for the pristine cop?"

"Jesus. For a girl who's seen everything, you can be really blind sometimes."

"So let me see." I found the thick bulge in the dark. One stroke, and he sucked in a breath. Two, and he jerked against me, his body hot, burning. I had him to hold, to touch, to finally see what it would be like, if he could be different from a hundred other men. Already I felt more than flesh, heard more than low animal sounds from him. Already I wanted this, and that made it new.

A knock came at the door; then Chase hissed, "Time's up."

Luke froze, his body taut with arousal and indecision.

"Let me finish you," I whispered.

He pulled my hand away, groaning. "We can't. You can't be caught. I couldn't protect you here."

I let my head fall back against the wall, clearing my head, finding my footing. "No? Well, we can make our last stand here. The star-crossed lovers have to die together, you know. That's how the story goes."

"Is that what we are?" he murmured.

"The hooker and the cop," I said. "We're from opposing families. Fated to tragedy."

His green eyes flashed in the dark, like a cat. "We'll call that plan B."

"Then what's plan A?"

"Let me take you somewhere safe."

At his very first words, *let me*, my body tautened, leaned forward as if to follow him. *Yes, anything, take me.* Like the Pied Piper, he could lead me into the sea. Already I was enthralled, tethered to him by an invisible string of yearning. I waded through the shark-infested waters of headquarters, going deeper and deeper just to hear his voice.

I couldn't breathe, the dust or the tension filling my lungs. "I can't."

"You still don't trust me." It wasn't a question.

My head tilted back, letting me draw in air from the surface. "Don't take it personally. I don't trust men."

"I'm not *men*," he said, his voice low. "I'm Luke, the man who's been fucking torn over you since I first met you. The man who's almost throwing away his whole career for you. Doesn't that count for anything?"

It meant everything to me, but gratitude was a long

way from trust. I was thankful for him, undeserving of him, but I couldn't make myself go with him. I couldn't make myself weak.

"Not enough," I whispered.

I couldn't forget the word *almost*. He was *almost* throwing his career away for me, and that was a hell of a lot different than actually doing it. Maybe that was too much to ask of a man—almost definitely it was—but it was the only thing that could let us be together.

A cop and a prostitute had no future.

"You know I can't," I whispered. "What would happen when the dust settles, would I be some hooker you keep stashed away? Would you come and visit me, bring me presents?"

He made a rough sound of denial. "Fuck, Shelly."

I laughed without humor. "There's nothing for us."

There was nothing for me. I knew it was true, but I waited for him to tell me I was wrong—that we did have a chance. He was a goddamned optimist. If anyone could believe in us, he could. I waited, and hoped, and held my breath.

"I'm not asking for forever, Shelly," he said low.

No, he was asking for the same thing every man had ever wanted. At the end of the day, in the dark and on the run, he wanted what every other man did. My body and my desire. My trust just for a short and wild ride.

DIRTY

CHAPTER ONE

L UKE FLASHED A small enigmatic smile. "I ought to drag you out of here myself."

I tensed.

"But since you don't trust me, you'd probably make a scene. Then we'd both be screwed." His lips flattened. "Which is why you felt safe enough to show up here. You pretend you don't trust me, but you come here, wriggle under my thumb, knowing I could trap you so easily."

Apparently done waiting, Chase opened the door, blinding us both. I leaned against the wall, unembarrassed by my breathless state, and felt Luke's hands straighten my shirt. He buttoned my jeans. I had been undressed by many men, but it was a novel experience to be dressed by one. Everything with him felt that way. I looked up. A wash of orange light fell over Luke's face, revealing his small, knowing smile.

"What?" I asked.

"Now," Chase murmured. "She needs to go now."

"What is that, some kind of psychobabble? I trust you, but I don't want to trust you?"

"You said it, not me." A glint entered his eyes. "I'd

tell you to make up your mind, but I'm starting to think it doesn't matter. One of these days, I'm going to take you. And then I'm going to keep you."

In a blur of black-suited coat and sandy-brown hair, he disappeared from the room as quickly as he'd come. I stared after him, a little shell-shocked. I had expected him to push me for sex. *Do the right thing, Shelly. Trust me, Shelly. Be a good girl so I can fuck you without feeling like an abuser, Shelly.*

But what did he mean by keeping me? Like some sort of concubine. Crazy.

I straightened my jeans and smoothed my hair. Hadn't I worn a cap? I glanced around but didn't find it. Dim light pooled through the open door, revealing a dusty concrete floor and rows of brown boxes. Well, this worked too. I would take a different exit from the one in front, in case anyone tried to track me through security footage later. They wouldn't, but paranoia was the constant churn that kept me above water.

In the main inventory room, Chase glared at me. I wondered if there had been any real urgency or if he'd just wanted me to stop sucking face with his favorite detective. It didn't matter. I'd accomplished what I came here to do.

"I know what you did in there," he said.

"Oh really, was it the pornographic sounds we made or the fact that I'm half-dressed that gave it away?"

"I told you," he accused. "I told you not to touch

him."

"No, you told me not to hurt him. And he doesn't swing that way, so it really wasn't likely."

"Don't act naive, like you don't know what effect you have on men."

"Of course I know what effect I have," I said lightly. "It's big and hard and hurts every time."

He shut up then, pursing his lips lest I forget he was pissed. Once I had straightened my clothes, I gave him a kiss on the cheek. Never leave a man angry; it only gave them more time to stew.

His expression eased. "Shelly, I don't like you two together."

"Get in line. After me. Then him."

"You say that. Excuse me if I don't believe you while you're all flushed from making out with him like teenagers."

"Teenagers?" I glanced at the back room. "Is that who you bring back there?"

He snorted. "Such charm. I don't know why I like you."

"Ah, but you do like me. That's part of what makes me mysterious. Men like mysteries," I said sagely.

He waved me toward the exit. "Yeah, I'm sure it has nothing to do with the fact that you're beautiful and way too smart to be doing the job you do."

"Stop. I'll blush."

"Get lost, squirt. And don't get into any trouble on your way out."

"Actually I was thinking I might start a fire. Maybe you should pull the alarm, just in case."

He groaned. "You're killing me."

"We'll call it even, then. No more visits, cross my heart."

He shook his head. "Fine. I'll do it. But you better be serious about that. If I see you back here, I'll turn you in myself."

In the hallway, I followed the flow until I found an empty broom closet. One benefit to these old historical buildings was that security was never quite up to modern standards. They could install all the fancy systems and safeguards, but the floor plan was designed with comfortable nooks instead of open spaces.

I pulled out the little plastic badge that allowed Luke to come and go into secure areas of the building—and to log into the network. It was a dirty trick, using sex against him like that, so of course I'd had to. I hoped he wouldn't be too mad.

Right on cue, a loud clanging fell from the ceiling, shaking the walls. The footsteps sounded like thunder down the hallway as everyone slipped outside. When it quieted, I returned to the storeroom. It was empty, since of course Chase had evacuated with everyone. Such a good boy.

I got on his computer and found the files I needed.

Stephan Laurent had been wanted in connection with multiple homicides. All young girls, all prostitutes. Full immunity. Murder probably wasn't beyond him, but what was the point? Young girls weren't any good to him dead. Besides, if he was guilty, that didn't explain the immunity. He needed to turn on someone. And ah, here. Known associations: Henri Denikin. The answer had been sitting in the corner, just waiting for me to turn and see it. My descent into prostitution hadn't been random at all. I put my hand to my mouth to keep the bile in. My eyes fell shut, and I took a few deep breaths of musty air to clear my head. I needed to focus. I needed to get the hell out of here.

I tossed the little badge on the floor in the storeroom where Luke could find it and maybe even think it was an accident, that he'd dropped it. It had slipped from its clip while we'd kissed, and the fire alarm had been a coincidence. Sure, he'd believe that, just like I believed my father's criminal connections meant nothing.

Jade had known. I remembered the look in her eyes.

In elementary school, my class had gone on a field trip to the zoo. Not the Brookfield Zoo, but a wild animal sanctuary out by Lake Michigan. We'd huddled outside the chain-link fence while the tour guide gave us a speech about rehabilitation. Inside, the tiger prowled the far corner, watching us warily. The woman told us he was more afraid of us than we were of him, and I believed her, but I didn't see why that should make me feel better. The air vibrated with thinly leashed violence. The tiger's eyes were filled with malevolence, and through them, I hated myself for being a part of his captivity.

We left uneventfully, but the next week there was an "accident" with one of the trainers, and the tiger was put down. Murder, my ten-year-old mind had thought. They had caged the animal and then killed it when it didn't obey. No one else seemed fazed by the news. Our venerable teacher trilled a laugh and thanked God we hadn't been there that day.

Bitch.

The next day, Allie left the tiger refrigerator magnet she'd bought from the gift shop on my desk. It was a white tiger, not orange, and the plastic represented the commercial value of his life, like a cheapened version of a rhinoceros horn, but I still fell in love with Allie that day. I twined between her legs like a stray cat, and she let me stay because she knew I had nowhere else to go. I would still be there, bringing her dead rodents, the only gifts I knew how to make, except for Colin. He was like me, operating on an animal frequency, and he had claimed her.

For that, I should hate him. I didn't.

Loving her meant wanting her to be happy; that was what made it love.

Luke was a different story. I wanted him near me, over me, inside me—his happiness secondary. And so I would continue to seek him out, endangering his career, his life, manipulating him into helping me for my own benefit. The little plastic badge that I'd stolen and used and discarded was no better than the plastic tiger replica on my fridge, a symbol to covet, a trophy of misuse.

Underneath her usual brusqueness, Jade had looked like the tiger that day, hunted, haunted. Ready to lash out, and God, I knew—I knew exactly how she felt. Reading my father's files had brought it all back to the fore, all the quiet rage and seething shame, every gentle touch and cruel, wrathful word. Each paid-for fuck had pressed it all down, pushed back old hurts in favor of new ones. But seeing Luke seemed to soften me, weaken me, and now I felt each memory like a sharp new cut.

Somehow I ended up in front of the shelter. The squat brick building looked the same, but I felt a world apart from the last time I had visited Marguerite. I didn't have an envelope for her today, but I did have a girl who needed help, one who was fearful and helpless.

This time, it was me.

CHAPTER TWO

I FELT HOLLOW inside, from the base of my neck to the pit of my stomach. Empty and cold, the dubious relief of frostbite. Instead of pain, syrupy languor spread through my veins.

My reflection waited in the black-mirrored door of the shelter, and I watched it with a casual detachment. How pretty. A marble statue to be desecrated and then washed clean in the next rainfall. But there was no water this time, only parched lips and broken eyes.

The door opened. Relief flooded Marguerite's face before she dammed it behind studied professionalism. Her minimal makeup was flawless as usual, her curves safely hidden beneath a severe black suit and skirt. She smoothed that skirt now, her hands twitching as if she wanted to reach out to me—or slap me. It could always go either way with her, and right now, I would have been grateful for both. Anything to make me feel again.

"I saw you on the news," she said. "I assume you're here to stay."

Would she let me, if I asked? But I wouldn't, for the very same reason I hadn't brought Ella here in the first place. Henri was on the hunt, and this place was a

161

too-easy target.

I shook my head. "I just stopped by… I came here because…" Because I thought she could give me advice. Something without pity, because I knew she didn't have any.

Her lips tightened. Her hesitation drummed in my ears. She had helped a thousand girls. Why not me? Was I beyond repair, a lost cause? Then put me out of my misery.

Finally she gestured me inside. "Come with me."

Our shoes clopped on the rubber floor, the sound bouncing off the egg-speckled walls. The fluorescent lights burned into my eyes, but despite that, some of my shock thawed. My tension eased. Strange, considering I'd just entered the human equivalent of the pound. The unwanted, the abused all crammed into cages, waiting for the world to want them again. But the air was bright and clean, and that was more than most of us would have asked for. The two girls who passed us in the hallway glanced at me curiously from beneath lowered lashes. No fear.

The sound of laughter and clinking metal on ceramic floated out from the cafeteria as we passed, comforting, familiar. It was like high school without the confusing and soul-deadening home life. Still, I didn't doubt this place had its demons. They must have been banished to the shadows—neat trick, that.

I realized I'd lagged behind, and I hurried to catch up. "What do you do when someone doesn't follow the rules?"

She didn't look back. "It depends on the rule."

"A big rule. Let's say one of them punches the other in the face."

"We don't allow violence here."

"She's a rebel," I said about my fictional rule breaker.

"We have a sliding scale of punishments, depending on the severity of the offense. There are a series of warnings. Then certain privileges will be removed. And finally, there are punishments."

I grinned slightly, feeling back on solid ground. "Don't tell me you paddle their behinds. That's very naughty, Ms. Faust."

Marguerite flashed me a repressive look. "If a girl is truly a danger to the others, we separate them. They eat their meals in their rooms and are given study work until they've shown they can interact with the other girls."

We grew quiet, passing girls filing out of a classroom, giggling and bumping into each other.

"So basically, solitary confinement," I said when they were out of earshot.

She sighed. "This is why I didn't want to tell you. I knew you'd frame it that way."

"The truthful way?"

"The worst possible way. We do what we have to do to make this work. There are only so many ways to keep teenagers in line short of beating them, which no, we don't do. Do you think some legalized group home does it better?"

"Hardly."

"These kids don't have the luxury of a two-parent support system and the family dog. We are their family."

"What if someone wants to leave Casa Faust?"

"When they turn eighteen, we help each girl with placement and relocation."

"And if they want to leave before then?"

She paused with her hand on a metal doorway. "Then we keep them safe. And that means here. Don't flip out. You had to know we couldn't let them run back to guys who would hurt them and force them to say where they'd been staying."

"It's always about you, Marguerite."

She sobered. "No man is going to hurt me or any one of the girls here. And one day, that will include you. You know that, right?"

Well, that was both comforting and creepy. "But not today."

"Not today," she agreed, opening the door and waving me inside. I followed her up a dimly lit metal staircase. We exited into a hallway exactly like the one downstairs, except this one was quiet. Empty. Eerie.

"You aren't going to lock me up, right?" I asked. "Because I asked about leaving?"

I was joking, but this floor unnerved me. While downstairs had felt happy, up here the air vibrated with expectation and something else I didn't recognize. Over the years, I had learned to trust my gut feeling more than what I could see. Right now, it didn't feel like danger, just anticipation of it. Like fear.

She unlocked a door. "I'm giving you what you came for."

"And what's that?" My breath held while she considered me.

"What do you most want?"

To be safe. "To be free."

"You want to feel like you're in control again. I understand. This isn't a group therapy session where I tell you everything will be okay. That wouldn't work for you anyway. This is better."

Curious now, I stepped inside. She shut the door behind me, and my eyes adjusted. I blinked. Equipment and wires nestled among—yes, those were guns. Two men worked laptops at the foldout tables. The guy in the far corner looked up blearily, then turned back to his screen.

I couldn't take my eyes off the sleek metal. "I thought you said there wasn't any violence here."

"There isn't, because we have these. All our security works to keep us safe."

"There's irony here, but I can't put my finger on it."

She hefted a gun with a chilling nonchalance. "Are you telling me you've never held a gun?"

"Yeah, that's what I'm telling you. I have gotten

shot before, and I'm not really looking to repeat the experience."

"Good, because I'm not planning on shooting you. You need to know how to defend yourself."

"I use my feminine wiles for that."

"And yet you're in hiding." She raised her eyebrow. "How's that working out?"

Ouch.

"As long as you're running, you're prey. Take a stand; see how it feels. You may still get hurt, but isn't that happening anyway? This way you're in control. This way you have a chance."

I let my expression convey my doubt.

She shrugged. "So don't. You came here for my advice, and this is it. You want to win a fight without getting your hands dirty. Go ahead and try."

When she put it that way, it sounded silly. Cowardly too. "Okay," I said. "What exactly would this entail? Do I need to buy chaps? My ass looks great in leather, but it's a little restrictive, don't you think?"

"It's not a costume, Shelly. It's a gun."

And yeah, she was holding one out. As if I was supposed to take it.

I stared at it like it might magically float in the air, turn, and shoot me. I could see it in my mind's eye. Absently, my hand went to my shoulder, where the old wound seemed to pulse.

"It won't hurt you," she said. "They will, though, if you don't defend yourself."

My breath stuttered out of me. I gingerly took it from her. It was lighter than I expected. So sleek and shiny.

"Point it down," she said sharply. "Finger off the trigger."

I almost dropped it. "Is it loaded?"

"No." She softened a fraction. "That's not the point. You need to be careful. As careful as they are, or they'll win. They'll beat you."

Her words rang in my ear like a premonition. "I don't know what I'm doing with this."

"Practice. Prepare yourself. You'll only have time for one shot. Make it count."

I frowned. "You make it sound like I'm going to assassinate someone."

"Aren't you?" she asked. "About damn time, really. You're going to find the son of a bitch who's hunting you, and you're going to kill him. That's the only chance you have of being free. It's the only chance you have of being with that cop you're mooning over."

Kill Henri? No. "You're insane."

"Tell me I'm wrong. Tell me you can take him down another way."

Mess him up, sure, most likely with money. That was my ill-formed plan. After all, Al Capone was brought down by tax evasion. Maybe Henri had an assload of unpaid parking tickets, and Luke could waltz in and arrest him.

But probably not.

"Not me," I said. "Someone else—"

She laughed. "Who, the cops? If they were willing to, he would already be dead." She grew serious. "You want to help people, but you don't want to touch them, talk to them. You want to be the martyr, so be one."

I blinked, taken aback by her observation and its accuracy. It made me feel a little dirty to hear my motivations spoken so plainly, but it also cleared my mind. This was what I wanted, to help those girls, to help myself. In that way, Luke and I weren't so different, although we came at the problem from different sides.

Still, I couldn't kill Henri. Could I? The idea made me terrified…and giddy. But I wasn't sure I could even shoot this thing. I still dreamed occasionally, flashing back to that split second when I realized I was going to die. The metal barrel glinted in the moonlight as it swung toward me. I heard the report like an explosion in my ears and found myself already on my back, already bleeding, blissfully gone.

I hadn't died, though. I'd gotten almost completely better. My shoulder still didn't stretch all the way up or back, but what was I, an Olympic gymnast? And when the weather changed, I felt a chill run through the puckered skin all the way to the bone. My imagination, probably.

"I don't think I can."

"Don't be selfish. This isn't just about you, Shelly."

A shiver ran through me, an echo of accusations I had run from all my life, even though I knew they were true. I was selfish to my core, working everyone around me like a master puppeteer. Never stop moving, never stop manipulating, or they'd crumple to the ground like lifeless dolls and prove I'd been alone all along.

"He's after you," she continued. "He's after that girl I'm sure you've stashed away someplace safe while you play the hero. He has whole apartment buildings of girls he's using right now, hurting right now. But as long as you can walk away, it's okay to leave those girls behind. As long as you get yours."

I swallowed, unable to say a word in my defense. Compared to her, to all she had done for these girls, I'd done nothing at all. So I would go to the club and fix this, for Ella, for Marguerite—for myself, so that I could feel something other than hate.

"I need something else from you," I said quietly. "A couple fake IDs."

She raised her eyebrows. "What makes you think I can get them for you?"

I shrugged. "You deal in false identities, and you do a better job of it than WitSec. Pretty sure that includes a little laminate."

"Going hunting?"

"We'll call it scouting."

She considered me. "Give me the information."

I told her mine first. She typed away on a laptop, taking it down. Then I said, "And one for my cop, as you call him. He'll be coming with me."

She smiled. "Very good. What's his name?"

"Luke. Luke Cameron."

Her smile slipped, just a fraction.

I frowned. "Do you know him?"

"No," she said, turning back to the keyboard. "He's a stranger."

CHAPTER THREE

I TOOK THE gun with me. It sat on my passenger seat, seemingly innocuous. Just plastic and metal melded together, like the seat buckle it rested on. Except it was lethal, if I used it right. Marguerite had given me a quick crash course. Would I remember? One shot, one chance.

As I drove through the city, my eyes fixated on every Dumpster or trash can, on every litter-strewn ditch I saw. I could get rid of it and call the whole thing off. And be alone again, afraid again. Was it really power or just the illusion? The pain in my shoulder felt real enough. I wasn't sure if I could kill in cold blood, even knowing it was for the greater good, but I was sold on using it to protect myself. I would go to the club and carry it with me. If I was going to win this fight, I'd need to get my hands dirty.

Henri was out there searching for me. Philip was waiting for me to fail so he could take what he wanted. And now my father was out there too, with actions unknown and repercussions that could run deep.

Suddenly Luke's hesitance didn't seem bad at all. It sounded downright heavenly. The gun might be another wedge between us. He wouldn't want me to use it. Hell, I didn't want to use it either. But I would. With Ella's neck on the line, I would. With my honor against the wall. I wasn't selfish, despite what my father thought. Maybe this was the final test. The last gift, and then what? I'd do what money hadn't done for Allie. What innocence hadn't for Ella. I'd save us all, and then I'd finally prove my father wrong.

Inside Philip's house, I skated around the kitchen and living rooms, hoping to avoid any contact with anyone. Instead I went up to the observatory, where I dozed into a mindless coma. It didn't matter whether my eyes were open or closed. They were still blanketed with black and dotted with stars. I could still taste the sour night air through the double-paned glass. Such were the dreams of a hothouse flower, imagining she knew freedom in a cage, reaching for the earth at the bottom of her pot.

"Shelly?" came a whispered question. Then again, closer.

If I didn't say anything, Ella might go away. And spend the next quarter of a century searching the whole damn house. I sighed. There really was no rest for the wicked.

"What do you need?" I called, knowing my voice would reflect off the glass around us.

"Where are you?"

"Climb the stairs in the far corner."

A few minutes later, she crawled into the loft sectional. "Hey, this is nice. Peaceful. Kind of private."

"Yeah," I said drily. Private.

She nestled among the pillows beside me. "Oh, did you want me to leave?"

I didn't, really. I liked her chattering presence, her unflagging spirit, her undeserved devotion to me. She filled the void that Allie had once occupied, sharing herself in a way I never could.

"You can stay."

"The house is just so big. And empty. Where do you suppose Philip went? Do you think he's coming back?"

"Probably. Don't go looking for him, okay?"

"Okay. I get it." She fell silent, but the air still buzzed with her energy.

Maybe I had gone about this all wrong. I had asked question after question, receiving very little back. If I offered answers first, she would... What, trust me? I rolled my eyes in the dark. Love me? The lost little girl who needs everyone to love her.

Pathetic.

"I've been thinking," I said, "about what we talked about, about why I didn't leave. Or why I didn't leave successfully."

"Yeah, the poison." Her voice grew cautious, as if she expected me to pounce.

Not yet, though. First I needed to spin my web, using the strongest net I knew. No words held more power than the truth. I would speak a few honest words tonight, in the hush of twilight, in the presence of innocence, and my only purpose was to draw out something useful in return. This wasn't for me. There weren't enough prostitutes in Amsterdam to offer me absolution.

"It's not about where we end up. It's about where we came from. Prostitution was always in my future. I just figured I'd be fucking one old guy for money instead of several and that we'd be married."

Her voice lilted, uncertain. "Why not make your own money?"

"This is my own money. You mean, why not put on a pinched suit and sit in a cubicle for ten hours a day? We have very few choices in life, but one thing we can do is pick our poison. I'll take a couple of sweaty men over a marketing department full of them any day. Except…"

"Except?"

"I thought about changing, once. That was when I met you. I was completely out. Until I wasn't. I'm still not sure how it happened. At the time, I thought it meant Henri was too powerful to deny. But now I wonder if it doesn't go further back than him. Like maybe someone above him is pulling the strings."

"You mean God?"

I laughed. "I meant my father, but I'm sure he wouldn't mind your assessment of the situation."

"What does your father have to do with it?"

"I don't know. Nothing, probably. But if he does, if

I'm right…then all this shit really was preordained." I laughed again. "Like God. Like fate. Just another fool on Fortune's Wheel."

Her throat worked audibly. "You're scaring me."

"Sorry," I said, contrite. "I'm not the best company right now. You should probably go."

Her hand fumbled for mine, burning where it touched. "It's okay. You can tell me."

Strangely, I believed her. Or maybe I just needed it to be true.

CHAPTER FOUR

I N HISTORY CLASS, we learned that each new civilization plows over the existing one. Archaeologists cut
through rock and measure the years based on the layers
within. Pottery shards of one culture sit only yards
above, feet above the broken pieces that came before it.
That was what our neighborhood in south Chicago did.

Some big-shot community development folks
bought up a rectangle right in the middle of the
projects, razed it down, and built a handful of million-
dollar homes. The poor, run-down houses surrounding
the gated neighborhood were the murky waters of a
moat, something to be crossed between the castle at
home and the freeway.

Except for the kids. We were all zoned to the same
school district, and since dear old Dad didn't see fit to
send me to private school, I got to mingle with the
commoners. The rich and the privileged usually
dominate, but not there. There the strong and the
fearless would—and did—cut an uppity white kid and
take his iPod.

Luckily I've always had a pretty face and a nice
rack. Or maybe not so luckily, since men tended to

notice, and the kind of men who notice such things on a thirteen-year-old aren't very good. Like my father. He touched me and had sex with me, and what are you going to do? Even then, I knew better than to bite the hand that feeds me. Even then, I knew what I was.

I wasn't bitter about what my father did. It was the way of the world.

I also learned that Cleopatra's daughter was only fifteen years old when she was forced to marry an older man, and I imagined myself an exotic princess fulfilling her birthright. Some Egyptian royalty married their relatives, even. The analogy fit, because my mother had been beautiful and selfish, leaving her daughter to face the world alone. Not that I was bitter about it, but life went on, for me at least.

The important part of this story began when I left home. That day I approached his office.

I knocked.

The long wait indicated how annoyed he'd be at the interruption. "Come in."

I slipped inside and stood before his desk. "Hello, sir."

He didn't look up, rifling through papers on his desk. His hair was rumpled, shirtsleeves rolled up. "Speak," he said.

My stomach sank. I had hoped for a good day, when he took me on his lap, took what he wanted, and then asked what he could do to make me happy. "Can I come back when you're free?"

"I won't be." He slammed the papers with his fist, finally looking me in the eye. "This is what I do, Shelly. I work so that you can live here, wear the clothes you wear, so that Juanita can clean up after you. Now what is so important that you had to disturb me?"

Deep breath. "My friend. Allie. You may remember her. She came over a few times when… Anyway, she's in trouble."

An eyebrow rose. "Trouble?"

I flushed. "She's pregnant."

"I see."

If he thought she was a bad influence, he wouldn't help. "It wasn't her fault, I swear. She said no. He wasn't even her boyfriend. He just—"

"Quiet."

I stilled, stomach churning.

He got up from his desk and strolled over to the window. "Do you know what I see when I look out there?" He glanced back at me. "At the rattraps that litter our lawn, where your friend no doubt lives?"

I licked my lips. "She doesn't have a choice."

"No," he said. "I doubt she does. Which is what makes her an animal, only acting on instinct and fear. Those rotting apartment buildings are the cages we keep them in, like unwanted pets we're too soft to kill. So what does that make me?"

Failure tightened my throat. "Sir…"

"Come and see, Shelly."

My leaden feet carried me to the window. I stared

at the jagged landscape of concrete and flesh, of rust and blood, while he brushed my hair aside and kissed my neck.

"What does that make you?" he whispered.

Cold air slipped under my skirt. His fingers bruised my hips. A sharp burn before I blocked out everything physical, pushed away anything warm and feeling and human. I was an animal, only acting on instinct and fear. I heard his footsteps as he returned to his desk and the rasp of pen on paper.

"Come here."

He handed me a wad of cash. Five thousand dollars, I counted out later.

"Thank you, sir," I whispered.

"After this, I don't want you to see her again. A girl like that could be a bad influence on you."

I took a cab to the county hospital, where the uninsured were allowed, where two other pregnant women shared her room, and sat at Allie's side, the folded wad of money in my purse burning a hole in my gut.

Her brown hair splayed across the pillow, her face was damp with sweat. Pain wrenched her sweet features, but she smiled weakly at me. "I wondered where you'd got off to."

"Had to stop at the bank," I said lightly.

My best friend for years, she knew what that meant. Not the specifics, of course. There were some things better left unshared. But she knew that my father was a bastard.

Her forehead creased in worry. "Are you okay?"

"Don't worry about me. I'm not the one in labor. How are you? What are they saying?"

"Any minute now." She grimaced. "That's what they said nine hours ago."

"There's nothing they can do? I'll talk to the nurse."

She caught my hand. "No. I just want you to sit with me. Can you?"

So I did, crawling into the bed beside her. The cold steel of the railing bit into my side, but I needed the contact as much as she did, maybe more. I needed the hard, contracting bump on her belly, the mysterious, elusive hope born of a nightmare, to make me forget.

The woman on the next bed began to cough, ragged and thick. I held Allie's hand, pretending this was normal and okay and a perfectly safe environment for her child to be born into. A child, when we could barely take care of ourselves. What would she do? Her dad had sent her two hundred dollars when she'd called him. That was all the money she had. And now my five thousand.

If I told her. She would take that money, spread it thin, and make it last. Then what would she need me for?

She clenched and keened as a contraction hit, and I rocked with her through it, wincing as she squeezed my hand. It wasn't enough to distract me from the ache lower down my body.

"Have you thought about where you're going to live?" I asked.

Her brow furrowed. "I don't know, but I can't stay at the shelter forever."

"Yeah, I guess… I mean, you'll probably get a full time job or something, right?"

"I already talked to Rick. He's going to up my hours at the bakery."

"Oh. Who's going to watch the baby? I mean, a decent day care will be expensive."

Her lower lip trembled. "I know. But I'll make it work. I have to, right?"

Forgive me, Allie. "And what about when she gets sick? They don't let sick kids go to day care. You'll have to stay home and take her to the doctor. Rick isn't exactly the lenient type. Plus paying for the doctor… Is your paycheck there really going to cover all that?"

A tear fell down her cheek. "I don't know. What can I do?"

"I'm just worried about you. I want to help." Five thousand dollars wouldn't last forever, but it would be a good start. Something to comfort her. But what about me? I couldn't go back. Something had snapped. *What does that make you?* A pretty bird in a gilded cage, its wings clipped for its own health and safety. "I'll stay with you. I can help with the baby and with money. You'll see. We'll do it together."

She blinked wetly. "What about your dad?"

I despised my dad. "I'm an adult now. It's time I

left the nest."

She knew better. "Will he let you go?"

"He doesn't have a choice. Shh, now. Don't worry." I pressed my lips to her forehead. "You don't have to be alone anymore."

And I didn't have to be alone either.

I placed an ad online and met up with a few average johns before Henri called me up. He was exceedingly polite over the phone and brutal in person. A few weeks later, I was earning four times as much on his payroll.

For two years, I played babysitter by day and prostitute by night. A few times I had tried to leave the life, but something always dragged me back. Usually money. Occasionally the rough hands of Henri's men. Every time, a small part of me sighed in relief. At least I knew how to do this. This way, I was wanted.

My complacency had been a fool's gold. I had worked the upper echelon of Chicago's sex trade and never run into my father. He ran in the same circles as these men, the rich and the cruel, but it was a big city. There were plenty to go around. Or had he been avoiding me? He said I'd always be his little slut.

It spun a silvered web in the shadows of my mind. Henri had targeted Jenny as revenge over her boyfriend's shady business. He ripped each dime right out of her skin and gained face in the process.

What does this have to do with me?

Maybe nothing.

But it was everything. How had Henri known to

contact me? I had always assumed that call had been random. It wasn't. I knew that now, certain to my bones. For some reason, Henri had contacted me, worked me over, and offered me a job. Payback for some business deal gone wrong with my father? Maybe. Either way, I had never despised him more.

I had been fooling myself that this was about protecting Ella. That was a fringe benefit to what I really wanted: to nail Henri. If I could take down my father in the process, all the better. Both seemed impossible, like trying to touch the twinkling lights above me. But I had never had so many people fighting for the same purpose before. I had never had so little to lose.

Allie and her daughter were away from me now, under Colin's protection. My obsession with Luke was threadbare, exposed as physical chemistry and a perverse desire to see myself fail. And then there was Ella, whose lower lip trembled in response to my rambled life's tale.

Chapter Five

I FROWNED AT her. "Don't cry over me. There are sadder stories every day."

"But I'm not holding their hands," she said thickly, tears pooling in damp spots on the silk pillow.

I pulled my hand free and wiped the dampness from my palms. She needed to get herself under control. She needed to calm down. No, I did.

"Tell me about yourself, Ella. I told you about me, things I've never told anyone. Now it's your turn."

"Is that all this was about? Make me feel guilty so I'll trust you?"

"Yes."

She soured. "Sometimes I think you're the most selfless person I've ever met. Other times, I think you're a manipulative bitch."

"Why can't I be both?" I asked mildly.

"Fuck you. I'm not telling you anything."

"Such language. Come on. Telling you about my dad fucking me has got be worth something. What's your name? Your real name."

"Fine. You care so much? Claire. It's Claire."

I suppressed a smile. It was too sweet for her and

just right. "Claire?"

"I know. It's like an old lady's name."

"Kind of old-fashioned."

"Whatever, it's stupid. But you know what? It doesn't matter. Claire was a problem child. Ella is the prostitute that couldn't. I fail at everything. It doesn't matter what my namc is. I'm nobody."

I swallowed. I should have seen her hurt. No, I had seen it and ignored it. "You're somebody, Claire."

"Don't call me that. I don't want to be her anymore. I'm nothing but a pain in your backside. You don't like me."

"Sure I do."

"You didn't know my name until two seconds ago. You don't even know me."

"You like Philip because he makes you feel safe. You figure even if he beats you, he's strong enough and possessive enough to make sure no one else does. You like nice things, which is why you steal them. It's simple really, but the psychologist your parents pay for tries to turn it into something about your self-esteem, like maybe if you win a cheerleading trophy, you won't care anymore. But the truth is, you like power and money and having these things when other girls don't. You want to be a good girl and have everyone love you for it, except you know you'll never succeed, so you push them away before they can reject you. You're scared and you're sad, but most of all you're lonely, and you'd rather risk death than be alone."

Her eyes were wide and luminous, as deep as the sky above us.

"That's you," she whispered.

Shit.

"Just tell me why you're helping me," she said in a rush. "If this is some sort of new-age training program for escorts or hazing the new girl or something like that."

I stared at her wide, owlish eyes, incredulous at her thought process. Although maybe it was a relief—for a second there, I'd thought she was uncannily intuitive. "That's ridiculous. This isn't a game. I'm trying to help you."

"I know. I mean, I think so. You have this way of talking and looking at me like you really see me, and I want to believe what you say. But then I think you must do that for everyone, right? Everyone thinks you really like them. They want to believe it's true. That's why you're so good at…"

"Whoring?"

"Sex."

"Same thing. If you want to believe something that comes out of my mouth, believe this: you're safe here."

"Then what was that before? You and Philip. I know you were doing it. Fucking." She forced the word out. "If you have to have sex with him to keep us safe…to keep me safe, I don't want that."

"It was consensual."

She looked doubtful. "You're telling me you have

paid sex and recreational sex?"

Hmm, when she put it that way, it sounded excessive. In fact, I didn't understand it myself, how I ended up having sex for money, how I just couldn't stop. I was trapped in the fun house, the mirrors showing ever more incarnations of me fucking for money, distorted depictions of my depravity. I couldn't escape. Philip was a sleek tiger, lethal within his cage, and Henri the ringmaster. The only player I didn't understand was Luke. He wanted to protect me, and he wanted to punish us all, and I wasn't sure which one would win out. He looked at me with grave sympathy, an experience I both hated and craved, and yet at other times, though he tried to hide it, I felt his bone-deep revulsion.

"Prostitution isn't black or white. If our goal was just to get off, we could curl up with our hands and be done with it. Sex is about wanting something from the other person, whether it's affection or intimacy, security or money. I'll admit I owed Philip something, but I wasn't coerced. If I had said no and meant it, he would have listened."

She frowned. "When do you say no and not mean it?"

"We'll save that lesson for another day, grasshopper."

CHAPTER SIX

I SUSPECTED PHILIP hadn't left at all. He could have been at a meeting or at another one of his houses, but given his fascination with Ella, I figured he would stay close. Which meant he was probably in the basement. True to paranoid form, it was a fully decked-out storm shelter, probably designed to withstand a nuclear explosion. Probably filled with the latest gadgetry and every comfort. Though in my mind, the basement was darker and definitely damper, like canal-woven caves in *The Phantom of the Opera*, and there he dwelled, hiding his face, listening to the sounds from above and feeding off the gaiety.

With a closed-circuit audio feed, most likely.

So we would give him that. It gave me the opportunity to patch things up between Allie and me. I went downstairs to call her from the kitchen.

"Hello?" Her tone was guarded. Clearly she had checked caller ID.

"Hey, sweets. How's my best girl?"

"Don't let Ella hear you say that," she said, though I could tell she'd loosened already.

"I was talking about Bailey," I said, referring to Allie's daughter.

"She's fine. She learned the Hulk smash. The cat is not happy."

"You let her watch *The Hulk*?"

"Nah, I think she learned it from a boy in school."

I tsked. "Goddamn boys in school. They're a nuisance."

"Tell me about it. I think Colin's going to have an aneurysm when she hits middle school. And the situation with Ella isn't helping any."

"Her name's Claire," I said absently.

"Oh yeah? So she's talking to you."

"A little bit. But I need my best girl on hand for tonight. Emotional support."

"You need emotional support?" Begrudging curiosity laced her words. "This I've got to see."

"Don't sound so eager to see me fall, you blood-thirsty bitch."

"I don't want to see you fall, but if you tripped every once in a while, I might believe you were human like the rest of us. As long as I'm around, I'll catch you."

Pretty sentiment, but she wouldn't be around on Saturday.

"Come over tonight," I demanded. "Girls' night in. Poor thing has been cooped up here for days with only Adrian for a friend."

"Poor thing," Allie said and meant it. She had never been partial to his formal charms.

I waited in the kitchen for her to arrive, poking at

the contents of the fridge. Plenty of fruit, seedless grapes and chocolate-covered strawberries. Various spritzers and organic colas. Some homemade chicken salad in a Tupperware container. A far cry from fuzzy tacos.

"Need anything?"

I jumped and turned to see Adrian standing behind me. "You surprised me."

"Sorry," he said, contrite. "I forget sometimes."

"Forget what?"

His smile was wry. "That this isn't my room."

I looked around the kitchen. It was more his room than anyone else's. "It's yours," I said. "I just feel comfortable enough with you to invade your space."

"Invade away. Are you hungry? I can make you something. I was about to get dinner started."

"Let me make something for you," I said on impulse.

"You can cook?" He sounded doubtful.

"I have lived alone for many years now. Surely you didn't think I subsist solely on the fruits of my illicit labor."

His face screwed up in disapproval. "I figured you subsisted on prepared foods from the grocery store with a frequent helping of takeout."

Bingo. And men had called me mysterious. Ha! I was an open book. "Look, just let me give it a shot. There's plenty of food in here. And you've cooked for me so many times. I want to return the favor."

"That was different," he hedged. "I'm paid to do that."

"I'm paid to do things too, but sometimes we like to have things done for free." He got a speculative and slightly lustful look on his face. "Don't think too hard about that. I just want to do something nice for you. Is that so strange?"

"Frankly, yes," he muttered, although he left when I shooed him away.

Damn. I wished Allie would get here already. I really couldn't cook at all. I couldn't even figure out why I wanted to do this, except for a burning desire to please—the same desire that always simmered beneath the surface, now burning white-hot, fanned by my lingering unease from the gun I'd gotten yesterday and my trepidation about tomorrow night. I would get to see Luke again. Then after it was all done, I would return here. I would come back, but something compelled me to fix things with Allie, with Claire, with everyone before I left, tying a knot in the loose, winding threads before they ran out.

Claire found me in the kitchen, and together we prepared a big grilled steak to share and asparagus, something fitting for a last meal. Claire, Adrian, and I ate together, a mishmash family, human trinkets collected by a reclusive owner. Allie arrived with dessert, as she most often did, and we all four feasted.

Although Adrian was just as comfortable with a girl's night as me, maybe more, he excused himself, perhaps sensing the particular gravity of the night's festivities. I wished the mood were lighter, my apprehension further from the surface.

At least Claire and Allie seemed mostly unaffected. They chatted as if they didn't notice my quietness, as if they had known each other forever. I loved that about them. They were both so vibrant, fighting and laughing their way through life. I paled in comparison, a single note in contrast to their harmonies, a single trick to perform again and again.

As they bent their heads together, their laughing faces lit by the glow of a laptop, I noticed how much they looked like each other. Both petite, both brunettes. Claire's face was thinner, her nose a little longer, but the resemblance was remarkable. It wasn't an altogether uncommon look, but uneasily, I wondered if I would still have saved Claire if she hadn't looked so much like Allie.

When Claire looked up at me slyly, I had to ask. "What are you two up to?"

Allie grinned. "Claire wanted to see him in uniform."

Claire smacked Allie's arm. "Hey, that was you."

I came around the laptop. On the screen, the CPD's Web site was pulled open to Luke's profile. He stared unseeing at the camera, his green eyes more of a misty hazel in the camera's lighting. He seemed younger than I remembered, but possibly the picture was old. His youth didn't detract from his severity. And in his full uniform regalia, he looked very upstanding. The very opposite of what a prostitute could aspire to have for herself.

Both Allie and Claire waited expectantly. Claire seemed a little nervous, as though I might get mad at them. Allie looked mischievous, probably expecting the same thing but knowing she could handle me.

"Well?" I raised my eyebrow. "What are we rating him?"

"Eight out of ten," Allie said. "Would let him bang my best friend."

"Next," I said.

Luke blinked off the screen, taking his solemn sexiness with him. The next guy had olive skin and a Hispanic heritage. More than that, he had a gleam in his eye that was sadly not wicked at all.

"Four out of ten," Claire said. "Would steal his wallet but not his rosary."

"You can tell religious fervor from his face?" Allie asked doubtfully.

I concurred. "Virgin Mary tattoo on his back."

The next listing was a butch female cop and then another man, older but with a decidedly roguish smile.

"This one's a good tipper," I remarked.

"Follow the formula," Claire said.

I examined the picture, mentally comparing him to hundreds of other men. "My guess is…good hygiene. Corny dirty talk."

"I'd hit that," Allie said. "He has a silver-fox thing

going on."

"Oh no," I teased. "Are you panting after a cop? I should tell Colin what you've been up to."

"No, don't." Her voice filled with playful fear. "I wouldn't be able to walk for a week."

Claire looked up sharply.

"It's a figure of speech," I said to soothe her.

Allie's face softened. "I didn't mean it that way."

"So you've never really been sore?" Claire demanded. "It never really hurts?"

"Not the way you're thinking. Not with someone who cares about you."

Allie's eyes clouded over, and I wondered whether she really believed that. If so, she had healed more than I realized. More than I had. Years ago, our friend had hurt her—raped her. We had both been shell-shocked. He had cared about her. Not enough, though. Not in the right way. No, I still didn't understand. Who could comprehend evil? Who understood what made friends and fathers do what they did? Claire's quiet questions disrupted my thoughts.

"How do you know guys won't go too far? How can you trust them?"

Two pairs of wide eyes blinked at me. I laughed softly. "You're asking me? I wouldn't know. That's why I collect payment before, not after."

Allie kicked me under the table.

"Ow." I turned to Claire. "I take more abuse from this one."

Allie sobered. "Yeah. That's probably true."

"It was a joke."

"I know." She went to stand at the window, looking out over the rolling hills of Philip's backyard.

I followed. "Hey, don't be like that."

"I'm not being like anything, except maybe guilty as hell."

She had always blamed herself for my prostitution, as if she were responsible for planting the tree just because she had eaten its fruit. She wasn't. The roots of my shame ran too deep for that. "Nothing that happened to me was your fault. We've been over this."

"No, you said it wasn't my fault. I disagreed."

"We'll agree to disagree. Are we going to argue or have girls' night?"

"Is that not what we do on girls' nights? I need a handbook or something."

"I was thinking girlier. Like, way girlier."

Allie stared at me blankly. "If you mean what I think you mean, you should know by now, I really don't swing that way. Plus, I don't think Colin would approve."

I rolled my eyes, then pulled out the two cheap boxes of dye I'd had Adrian pick up at the drugstore. "I want to color my hair."

"No," Ella exclaimed. "I love your hair. It's so pretty."

Allie's eyes narrowed a bit. Finally she nodded. "Okay. A new look, a new life."

It did have a nice ring to it. The truth was, my hair was too distinctive. Too blonde, too bright. I'd stand right out in the club. Dull, slightly damaged brown ought to do the trick. And hey, if I was really lucky, we'd find a way out of this mess.

I smiled. "A new life."

The chemicals burned my eyes, but the laughter and camaraderie were well worth it. I soaked it up, storing it away for some future time drearier than this. As Allie was leaving, for maybe the first time I leaned in for a hug. I felt her little jolt of surprise before she returned it. It felt like good-bye.

CHAPTER SEVEN

A CAB DROPPED me off a few blocks from the club. Even from here, the bass could be heard like rolling thunder, vibrating the gravel on the sidewalk. Though this had ceased to be a good part of town a decade ago, most of the shops were still operating. A pharmacy, cash loans—but right now they were dark, closed for the night, encased in metal gates.

Only the pawnshop was open at this hour, because partygoers might pick up some ecstasy on the way. I slipped inside, withholding my wince as a loud doorbell rang out. The sickly sweet smell of pot assailed me. Clearly someone here was a fan of Mardi Gras; brightly colored plastic beads decorated the cluttered shelves like garlands.

Raine poked his head out. "Can I help you?"

I looked down, suddenly nervous. I had seen the man many times. How had I thought I could disguise myself like this? He would see right through me—and worse, expose my presence here if questions were asked later. But I'd met him in smoke-filled rooms, standing behind powerful men. I had been an accessory just like the watches in the glass cases.

"I'm looking to pawn something."

"Yeah, yeah, that's what the sign on the door says. Don't think just 'cause it's late that a pretty little thing like you is gonna get the jump on me. You got something to sell, show me the goods."

I pulled out the velvet bag that contained the last of my inheritance. The small stones rolled onto the glass countertop, reflecting the dim light with disproportionate brilliance. Only the gemstones were here; the diamonds had been left for Ella with a small note of farewell. They had been earned with my skin and blood. Hopefully she would find a better use for them.

"Whoa, girl." He rushed over to rally them onto a ratty velvet tray. "Be careful with those. This shit doesn't grow on trees."

He seemed genuinely offended by my callous treatment. It made me glad someone would finally appreciate them. A sort of wistfulness filled his eyes as he nudged them over, like a small boy who's caught a caterpillar in his palm.

"These are beautiful. But I don't know if I have the cash on hand for something like this."

"Make me an offer."

He did, and it was surprisingly good. He really wanted them. "Done."

Squinting at me, he said, "Look, how hot are we talking here? I don't need no fucking search warrants, if you know what I mean."

"They aren't stolen." Well, not really. I hadn't exactly had permission from my father to take them, but it had been years, and he'd never tried to get them back from me. They definitely weren't hot in the way Raine meant, stolen from a robbery or something.

"You would say that. For all I know, you have cops on your tail, about to bust me as an accomplice."

He was practically panting over them. No way he'd let me walk. I started to gather them back up. "Okay, I'll take them somewhere else tomorrow. I just really needed the money tonight, that's all, and—"

"Okay, wait. Give them to me. This one's off-the-books, though. No fucking pawn slip for this, you hear? When you walk out that door, I never want to see your pretty face again."

My breath caught as I ducked my head. I didn't want him examining my looks at all. "Just hurry up, okay? I have a party to go to."

He snorted. "I have a party in the back room. Come see."

I shook my head. "I'm meeting someone."

"I'll bet you are." He squinted. "Do I know you from somewhere? You look familiar."

I shrugged as my heart beat wildly. "I come and go. Chicago's a big city."

"Yeah. A big windy fucking city." He finally turned away and counted out a slim pack of bills. "You remember what I said, now. I don't want to see you back here. If anyone comes around asking, you were never here."

"Perfect."

I tucked the money into my jacket pocket, wishing I could stash it somewhere safe. But at least I had the money now. If I needed to run, I could. Strange thoughts. I wouldn't run. I had nowhere to go. And yet the premonition nagged at me. I was free, unencumbered. I had a gun, I had money—this was power. I didn't feel powerful, though. I felt melancholy, already missing a life I had tried so hard to escape.

A block away from the store, a slight scuff of a shoe on pavement caught my attention. I slowed and heard the quiet *clop-clop* of footsteps following. Ducking into an alley, I waited for the person to pass me. Nothing came. No club visitors sauntered by, no more sounds at all. I was getting paranoid. I stepped out to head toward the club again. A hand reached out and sealed over my mouth before I could utter a squeak. Then I was pulled back into the alley. Farther, farther into the inky black, until all I could see were the stars above me.

"Be still." Luke's whisper was harsh in my ear.

"Jesus," I gasped when he took his hand off my mouth, my heart pounding. I blinked up at the stars, stiff against him, filled with relief I couldn't examine right now. "Did you do that just to scare the shit out of me?"

His hands softened; his hold turned from a cage to an embrace. "Probably for the same reason you waltzed into headquarters and lifted my ID."

"Okay," I grumbled. "You had your revenge. Let

me go."

I pushed against him, halfheartedly, turning to face him, and became aware of the hardness of his body, the tautness everywhere, and the firm length of him against my stomach. I didn't want to breathe his bitter-soap scent or hear the catch in his voice whenever he spoke near me—but God, I needed it. Like stepping out of my heels, peeling off the tight garments after an evening of work; like collapsing on the couch, finally safe; like standing beneath the hot beat of the shower, finally clean—meeting Luke was like coming home.

He cupped the back of my neck, and I let my head fall back. With slow, aching deliberation, waiting for me to deny him, forcing me to choose, he lowered his head. I strained for him. Not just my breath—my whole body panted for him.

The touch of his lips on my neck was so light I barely felt them. Like the flicker of moonlight on water, the moment my nerves centered on his kiss, he was gone, skimming over the surface, alighting on a new slip of my skin. And myself, the dark, fathomless depths—liquid, effervescent, effortlessly languorous. Pleasure rippled over me, while something long hidden stirred beneath the surface.

"What are you doing?" My voice trembled.

He didn't pause in his exploration. "If this little game of yours is going to work, we have to look like lovers."

A game, then. "I'm great at faking it," I said blandly.

His laugh was soft—seductive. Did he know how he sounded? Did he do that on purpose? "I'm sure you are. Though I'll know. Don't doubt that."

I attempted to snort my derision at his statement, but it came out breathy. "Spare me the promise of your magic dick."

"I didn't say I'd make you come. I said I'd know if you didn't. I'm sure you can moan very nicely, but the truth is in the eyes. I bet you close them when you're pretending."

"By that point, the guy is usually too far gone to notice," I admitted.

"I wouldn't go so easily."

No, he wouldn't. Even though his thumb stroked the column of my neck and his mouth grazed the curve of my ear, this wasn't surrender. If I were to pull up my skirts right here, right now, he wouldn't take me.

"Then don't tease," I said crossly. "There's a word for people who do that."

His laugh turned husky. "I'm not the one holding back. But that will change. Very soon."

Before I could process that unnerving declaration, he stiffened and stepped back, letting the stale stink of the street flood between us. In his raised hand, I recognized the ominous shape of a gun. My heart beat an erratic tattoo of fear and disbelief and relief. This would be the end.

His voice turned cold as he said, "What is this?"

Mine. The gun was mine, not his. He wasn't going to use it on me. Of course not. I wasn't going to be shot again—what were the odds? I blinked away the sense of inevitability that had claimed me for a few surreal moments.

"A girl's got to protect herself. Surely you didn't expect me to meet you unarmed, now that I'm without that lovely security of headquarters."

Even in the dark, I could see his scowl. Or maybe just feel it wafting in the air, slipping along the invisible cord that connected us.

"Ah, so we are back to that. I wonder what I would have to do to make you trust me."

"Don't sell me out to your boss. That's a start."

"Because of what I did, what you did, I'm walking around with his boot shoved up my ass. Try again."

Stop using me. Want me. Fight for me. "I want you to go inside that club and pretend to be my pimp. Help me get proof that the girl was kidnapped. Even if she played a part in their deaths, which she didn't, it would have been within her rights. Self-defense."

"And you? If you're serious about clearing her legally, that's going to mean taking this to my boss. It means working with the DA. It means testifying."

Every cell in my body revolted at that idea. "That's what she deserves. She should have her life back, a clear name. She deserves a regular life."

"It means going public with your identity, with what you did. Everyone in Chicago will know." His tone was grim.

"Afraid of what people would think of me?" I asked, feigning disinterest, though the idea of him ashamed of me made my insides tighten.

"I'm afraid of what your father will do if it comes out," he said quietly. "I'm fucking terrified of what you'll do if he lashes out at you."

It shouldn't have surprised me that he knew. He had seen every crack and flaw in me, so why not this? Even stranger that Luke should worry about such an eventuality. Surely it would happen one day. So strong was my certainty that it had never occurred to me to fear it. Luke would be reunited with his long-lost prostitute, and I would be returned to the waiting hands of my father, both of us where we belonged. No reason to worry over it, no reason to fret.

"I'll be fine," I said gently, feeling unaccountably protective. Did he stay up nights worrying about each of his informants, about each prostitute he tried to help? Did it break his heart to think of his lost love in my place? Even the thought of her couldn't dampen my warmth toward him. A man in love was a beautiful thing, even if he wasn't in love with me.

"If we go in there, then it's real. I'm really your pimp. You do whatever I say."

I smiled. "Playing out a fantasy? I like that."

"I'm not kidding. Going in there half-cocked is asking for trouble." He put up his hand. "Don't say anything."

"Wasn't going to. Too easy."

"I'm just worried that you—" He turned away, the troubled sound of his voice ringing through the chilly night air.

"That I can't cut it? Oh, come on." And here I'd been worried about him being able to handle himself in disguise. "I've done worse than this. I've lived this."

"No, you haven't. Not like this, in the slums. Half the time, you look like you belong in a country club. You couch everything you say with sexual innuendo, putting everyone else at a disadvantage. You turn prostitution into a little rich girl's game so you don't have to face the reality. I'm not blaming you for any of it. But that's not what we're going to do in there."

"Right, because you're a goddamned expert on life in the slums."

"Never mind. If we're going to do this, let's go." He sounded grim but resolved. "We go in, we get out. We keep a low profile. What's my name tonight? I assume you had a fake ID made."

I huffed. "You ruin my surprises."

"You're reckless and intermittently suicidal, but you've got a practical streak that really works for me."

A laugh escaped me. He saw me clearly enough. It made me wonder what else he saw in me. "If you wanted me to work for you, all you had to do was ask."

I pulled out the fakes Marguerite had made me and went over our stories. He was a small-time street dealer who liked to pimp out his girlfriend when money was tight. I would be too coked out to care. He would be slimy, I would be skanky, and with any luck, one of us would get the scoop on what had happened the night Ella was here. Ever the Boy Scout, Luke wanted to talk exit plans.

"I'm serious," he said. "If things start to go south, you get out. We can meet up later."

And leave him to the wolves? Not likely. He was strong and capable, but this was my turf. "Are you going to split if I'm in trouble?"

"Of course not. That's different."

I rolled my eyes in the dark. "How chivalrous."

"If you ask me, you could do with a little more chivalry from the men in your life. A lot more."

"And you are volunteering."

"Actually, I insist. Now come into the light. I need to rough you up a little."

"What a gentleman," I said, following him onto the street.

"You look gorgeous," he said. "Like you stepped off the pages of a magazine. That's not going to work for us."

Under the flickering streetlamp, I finally got a good look at him. Gone were the rumpled suits and casually messy hair. In their place was a stereotype of a different sort. He wore a loose blue shirt hanging open to reveal a sweaty undershirt and cargo pants, with a mottled gray wool cap covering his hair, dirty blond scruff on his jaw.

I wanted him because he was good and I was bad. Because he was worthy and I was not. And yet seeing him like this, like the lowest of men, made me hotter for him. Every excuse I made for wanting him fell away. I wanted him in every incarnation, in any form I could get him.

He pulled out a small round tin. "Your turn."

I didn't ask what the black substance was. He smeared it across my cheeks and along my arms. At least it didn't smell bad.

When he started to work it into the ends of my hair, I protested. "Is this really necessary? I already changed the color."

His eyebrow rose. "Did I recognize you immediately?"

"Fair point."

He circled behind me, gently combing the grease through my hair. His hands settled on my shoulders. The heat of his body seared into me from behind, more acute now that I couldn't see him. My hair swept away from my neck, replaced by the kiss of his breath.

"It wasn't really fair," he murmured. "I would recognize you no matter how you looked. I would find you anywhere. I haven't learned every secret of your body, but I know what's inside. I know you."

My eyes fell shut, releasing a tear on both cheeks. They would make tracks in the dirt, I thought inanely. And then realized that would be more authentic. He removed his hands, a loss that felt like a blow.

"When you believe that, then you'll be ready."

I couldn't put voice to the question. Ready for what? For I already knew the answer. I had been waiting for it, carefully cultivating the seed. Telling myself a thousand times it wouldn't grow, until, like magic, a tendril of green peeked through the cold, packed earth. Us, he meant. When I believed he knew me and not the persona, not the prostitute, then I would be ready for us.

CHAPTER EIGHT

A THICK LINE of eager partygoers blocked the entrance. In front of us, a pair of girls shivered in their halter tops and short skirts. Those thigh-high striped stockings were to show how hip they were, not for warmth. They clung to each other like vines; even from the back they were clearly too nervous for the giggling and flirting that marked the other women in line. One of the girls whispered to the other, briefly pulling out an ID and then slipping it back into her shiny black purse. There was no way for me to see if it was fake—but it was. That much was loud and clear from their body language. This must be how Ella had looked, all vibrating anticipation. I wanted them gone, out of this line, off the street, far away from the life Ella would be leading right now if I hadn't found her. But anything we did would draw attention to us.

I sneaked a look at Luke. He wore his gangbanger appearance well, so I almost didn't know him. Underneath the soot and ratty white-gray fabric, it was still Luke. Wasn't it? Like studying an optical illusion, I could look at him once and see Luke. I blinked, and the noble cop receded, replaced by the sooty criminal. The same image, different perspective, and my mind didn't know what to make of it. His blank expression gave no clue as to whether he had noticed the girls in front of us, but I knew he had.

"Don't," I said.

His green eyes flicked to me. "Don't what?"

I raised my eyebrow. He already knew. *Don't pull your cop routine to get these girls out of line. Don't mess up our plan to assuage your goddamned integrity.*

"They won't let them in," he said quietly. "Then they'll look at ours more closely."

"You don't know that. Ella got in."

A line appeared between his eyes, the only sign he was disturbed. "Look what happened to her. We can't let them go in."

"We'll be inside too," I pointed out. "We can help if there's any trouble."

"Us being there increases the odds for trouble," he said drily. "Besides, it would blow our cover to help."

"It would blow our cover to stop them from going in."

We shuffled forward with the line, quiet for a moment as people resettled.

The girl with the striped stockings checked her phone. "My dad's calling."

"Don't answer it," the other whispered. "Text him. Tell him you're at my house."

I approved of Striped Stockings. The anxiety in her voice made it clear she didn't want to be here. Her friend Blondie was the troublemaker.

"What if he calls there?" she persisted.

I mentally cheered. *That's right. Think of the conse-quences.*

"Say you're going to sleep now."

From the side, I saw her bite her lip.

"It is pretty late. I'm usually asleep by now."

It was barely ten o'clock. Luke didn't have to look at me to make his point. *See?*

Okay, I did see. He couldn't stand by and let them inside, knowing they might be targeted. And maybe that was beyond my capability too—damn Ella for messing with my sangfroid—but hell, I didn't know how to make them leave. I sure as hell couldn't make Ella do anything. We were nearing the entrance. The bouncers stood impassive, disinterested in the crowd, but any attempts to dissuade the girls would surely attract attention.

The group at the front slipped inside, and we all inched forward, a giant lumbering caterpillar with a multitude of feet.

I held my breath, hoping he would stay silent. Hoping he wouldn't.

Luke cleared his throat.

A nervous sound of objection or surprise escaped me—Oh!

The bouncer in front looked over at me, bored at first, but his expression rapidly turning to one of interest. Sexual interest, hopefully, because if I had been identified before I even made it through the doors, I really had lost my touch. Like some sort of cartoon sketch, the bouncer pointed at me—directly at me, and I half expected a trapdoor to open in the concrete, sending me to a pit of crocodiles.

Instead the bouncer said, "Go ahead."

"Me?" I managed to say.

"You in or out?"

"In." I gestured to Luke. "He's with me."

The bouncer gave him a thorough once-over, which Luke returned coolly. The bouncer nodded a grudging approval. We started to slip past the girls, but the blonde one blocked our way.

"Hey, why do they get to go? We're next in line."

I stopped myself from rolling my eyes. Naive much, Blondie?

The bouncer's face was like granite. "Wait here for your turn."

"This is our turn," she complained. "No fair."

No fair? Oh Lord. Then I realized this would be an opportunity to get them booted from the club—maybe my only opportunity.

I drew myself up to full haughtiness. "Let me give you a little life advice. When someone insults you, it's best not to draw attention to that."

Two lipsticked mouths fell open, but the blonde recovered first. "Who the hell do you think you are?"

"Are you confused, sweetheart? I'm the girl getting bumped to the front of the line. You are the loser standing outside."

Her face turned mottled red. She looked ready to blow.

"Is there a problem?" the bouncer asked.

She stammered. "I… She… Did you hear what she said?"

"Maybe we should just go," Striped Stockings pleaded.

Blondie's face twisted into a cross between a sneer and a pout. She was pretty and slender and probably used to getting her way—I should know.

Luke had viewed the whole exchange with the mild amusement typical of a lowlife watching a girl fight, though I didn't know if that was genuine or part of his act. He stepped forward. "There's no need to get upset," he said in an oily voice I hadn't even known he was capable of. "Nice-looking girls like you two deserve to party. I'll bring you guys in, get us a table." He leered rather convincingly. "I'm sure you can think of some way to repay me."

With a flurry of rushed excuses, Striped Stockings dragged her friend away, out of the line and out of sight.

Turning back to the bouncer, Luke shrugged. "Their loss."

Chapter Nine

INSIDE THE DOOR, we handed over the IDs to another bouncer who examined them under a bright light. A cold line of sweat ran down my back as I waited. There was no way they would catch them as fakes, and really, they would have known within two seconds. It was almost as if the extended wait, with the guy glancing from me to the card, was designed to elicit a reaction, the telltale heart of underage clubbing.

Finally, he handed back the cards and stamped our hands with Xs. I plunged into the sweaty mass, eager to blend in. Luke was right behind me, his slick fingers entwined with mine. Everywhere I looked, people laughed and frowned, flirted and fucked with their eyes, their words, their hips against hips. Too many people, too little space. We reached an empty back wall, and I melted against it, sucking in the air at the edges of the room.

Luke's body closed in on me from behind, and we could have been fucking like this, except for the kindness in his touch.

He murmured into my ear. "What's wrong? If you're pretending some sort of overdose, it's very convincing."

I shook my head. Even the wall shook with the effort of holding this many bodies, but then I realized it was me moaning. Underwater, unable to hear the sound of my own voice except for its vibrations in my throat. Unable to hear anything at all except the rush in my ears. I let the currents pull me, the too-tight grip on my arm like a hook yanking me out of the water. We stumbled together into a bathroom. I staggered back, supporting myself on the ceramic sink. Luke grabbed a dirty mop and slung it through the metal handle, keeping everyone out.

He turned on me. "What the hell happened out there?"

"Sorry," I muttered. "Freaked out a little."

"Yeah, I got that. Want to tell me why?"

"I don't know. So many people."

"There were plenty of people at headquarters, and you didn't lose your shit. So tell me why."

"I don't know. Those girls, the way you looked at them."

He seemed genuinely puzzled. "How did I look at them?"

"You know," I choked out.

"Like I wanted to smack them for being little idiots. Is that what you mean?"

"No, no. Like you wanted them."

Understanding dawned in his green eyes, and with it, bright shame within me.

"I didn't want them," he said gently.

The kind of soothing tone you use with a child. It's only lightning. It can't hurt you. But I had seen the lightning and the lustful light in his eyes. I had felt its burn and knew well how it hurt.

"I know you didn't." Did I? Oh shit, I was losing it. "Breathe."

The low command penetrated my haze, drew me back to the surface. I breathed. When his face came into focus, it was concerned. That part would have been fine. The part that really sickened me was the kindness. *Poor Shelly. She can't help what she does. This was all predetermined years ago*. No way to change my course.

"I'm fine," I said. "Got a little derailed, but I'm fine."

He looked doubtful. Extremely doubtful, and I worried if I didn't convince him soon, he would abandon our entire mission.

"Look, I'm okay. See? I'm standing all by myself, breathing without you having to tell me. Very mature-like."

"Mmm-hmm."

"And I realize I'm jumpy, so as a gesture of good faith, I'll let you hold on to my gun for me," I said magnanimously.

"I've already got it," he said, reaching back to where he'd stashed it in his belt. He swore as he came up empty.

I handed it to him. "Sorry. But not really, because you had no right to take it from me in the first place."

"I had every right. Do I even want to check the registration on this?"

"Only if you want your worst suspicions confirmed."

"No, thanks."

"This way is better. I'm giving you permission to hang on to it. Because I trust you." My emphasis on the last few words could not go unnoticed.

A slow smile spread across his face. "I see."

The door rattled, then shook violently as someone banged on it. Shouting came from the other side, too muffled to understand through the steel door and the roar of the club.

"Gee," I said. "Do you think he wants to come in here?"

"Occupied," Luke called over his shoulder.

I started toward the door. "I think we're done here."

"Oh no." He stopped me. "We need to snort a few lines. Then I'll probably make you pay me back. On your knees. All that takes a while, so he's just going to have to wait."

The picture he painted was so accurate it chilled me. "It creeps me out how well you fall into this role."

He raised an eyebrow. "Would you rather I open every conversation with the Miranda rights?"

The banging on the door grew louder, stronger. I

wondered if the rusty metal pole of the mop could bend. More likely the door handle would break off first.

Luke prowled over to the door and rattled the mop in the door handle. "Hold your fucking horses." He turned to me. "We should give them a show."

"Oh my God, you're so long," I said in a loud voice. "And thin. And with all those bristles on the end."

"You're complimenting the mop here?" He strolled back.

I smirked. "He's the only hard rod in the room, I believe."

He reached me, standing close, then ducked his head to my neck. With his hands on my hips, he pushed me onto the ledge of the sink.

"He can't please you like I can, baby."

"I don't know about that." My legs parted as he closed the space between us. I stared at the fuzzy exposed pipes above us, wondering exactly how far this little show would go. "I like a man who cleans up nice."

His fingers walked up my thigh. "It's all show. He's limp where it counts."

"And you?" I matched his wandering fingers with my own, traveling down his lean belly. "How are you?"

"Thorough," he whispered, and my legs fell open a little more.

He found the damp string of my thong and slipped past it. The touch of his fingers on my slick skin was electric, sending waterlogged sparks through my body. The thought alone was almost enough to bring me to orgasm. He was touching me. Luke had his hand on my cunt, and what's more—I liked it. I was wet for him, not freaking out for him. As his fingers slipped deeper, I began to rock against him. This was real, the most real sex I'd ever had, in a dirty bathroom, with the door rattling angrily, while we both pretended to be different people.

He stilled.

"What's wrong?" I asked, breathless.

"Be louder," he whispered.

His words poured cold water over my body. The tender skin around his fingers ached; the dampness chilled. All this was a show.

I moaned loudly. "Is this right?" I muttered. "Am I doing it right?"

His hands began to work their magic again, and to my frustration, I slipped under their spell. My moans grew louder, fake and gaudy, but beneath the wild cries resonated true pleasure. Underneath the facade of a prostitute was a woman in heat. My long moans and heated encouragements gave way to breathy pants.

"Why are you doing this?" Why taint the act with something real? Why show me what I couldn't have?

Without answering, he ducked down, matching his mouth to his fingers. I let out a shout of surprise—one that would surely satisfy a curious audience. I held myself suspended on shaking arms, a picture of wanton depravity, spread open on the bathroom sink. He licked my clit while his fingers fucked me, winding me tighter, dragging me higher, until the air was too thin to breathe and the drop too high to look down. My hips rocked into his mouth and waiting fingers, wanting more, seeking his generous tongue and the sweet friction.

"Let go," he muttered against me, and the vibrations, right there, almost pushed me over. Almost, but not quite. I didn't like to come with a man. It had happened before, and each time, I had felt dirty.

"Stop thinking."

"I can't." My lips formed the words silently.

"You can do this," he insisted.

A desperate laugh escaped me. "The magic cock again?"

"My cock isn't a part of this."

He paused with his fingers inside me and looked at me, his green eyes pure and bright and pained.

"This is just about you. Giving you pleasure. Making you come."

I had to ask. "Why?"

Not breaking his stare, he pushed his fingers deeper inside me, searching, searching for a certain spot. I knew where—a little left—but I wouldn't help him. I didn't want this, did I?

"Don't you think you deserve it?" he asked. "Pleasure. Orgasms."

"You know I don't," I moaned, bucking against

him.

"No," he said, a little sadly, his fingers still rubbing and stroking and searching. "You don't think so. But you'll let me do this. You'll let me lock you in a bathroom and force you, because then it wouldn't matter if you deserved it or not. You'd just be doing your job."

"Ahhh," I cried out as he found the right spot.

"There?" he asked, the tease.

"No, no," I begged, because I didn't deserve it, didn't want it, except for the burning desire to have him and keep him and feel this way forever.

"Just take it," he murmured. "You're not responsible for this."

He closed his mouth over my clit once more, sucking and lashing it as his fingers pushed me over. My entire body jerked once in a futile protest before giving in to the flood of pleasure. Wave after wave crashed over me, until my vision blurred to a distorted hue and my mouth filled with water, and then he was kissing me, soothing me, rocking me gently back to shore. I shuddered against his still hand as the last vestiges of my orgasm left me.

Like the insistent cawing of seagulls, the rattling on the door was too distant to disturb my stupor.

"Oh, Luke," I sighed, resting my forehead against the softness of his neck.

Tension tightened his body broken only by the tremors that ran through him.

"Let me touch you," I said, knowing he wouldn't. In that way, he was like me.

"I didn't mean for this to happen," he said gruffly.

"Sex in a dirty bathroom is usually a spur-of-the-moment activity. Or so I assume. I have never done it before."

"Really?" His voice was wry. "An accomplished sexual maestro like yourself?"

"Yes, well, usually I have standards about these things."

"Except with me." The amusement was gone.

"You're my new standard," I said softly. "Anything else doesn't compare."

He pulled back, his features strained. "God, Shelly. The things you do to me, the things you say. I can't even lust after you properly. I want to devour you, swallow you whole. I want to secret you away where no one can ever take you from me, not even you."

My breath caught at the jagged edge of longing that grated his voice. If ever I had imagined us together, there were silk petals on satin sheets and scented candles in the window. Sweet words and courtly manners were a safe fantasy. But this feral desire did more than woo me—it thrilled me. A dark and primal part of me awoke from deep slumber and stretched, its sleek black body rippling with its urge to claim, to mark, to devour him right back until we were inseparable. I wanted to drown in the sea of possession, to tie myself to his weight and throw myself into the water, so that even if I lost my nerve, we would still be together. "You won't be satisfied until I'm ruined, will you?"

His eyes swirled green and black, molten malachite, as he murmured, "Turnabout is fair play."

As we left the small bathroom, sauntering past the angry line of people, I wondered if it was true. Would I be willing to ruin his career to make him want me? And if he did abandon his principles for me, would I even want him still?

CHAPTER TEN

W E HANDED OVER a few hundreds to get into the back areas with large booths and thick tables, probably made for dancing on. Low platforms skirted the length of the room, studded with poles to the ceiling, but no strippers graced them. Testosterone filled the room like dust in the desert, emanating from the lounging men. A few women perched on laps. They were eye candy as much as the gold chains and flashy watches the men wore.

I recognized about a third of the people, but Luke had been right. I had glimpsed these people as they interacted with Henri, but these weren't my clients. This wasn't my scene. I kept my eyes downcast. It would help prevent anyone from recognizing me, plus that was proper submissive behavior. Luke slung his arm around my neck, a mark of ownership. I could feel the eyes on us, their heat and judgment. New meat would always be a novelty, whether it was a feisty virgin escort or a new couple in the scene.

A man waved us over. He wore a similar grunge uniform to Luke, though a stripped-down version— and he seemed far more intimidating. Tattoos blanketed his scalp, visible through his cropped hair. A flat look in his eyes said he was no stranger to death. He introduced himself as Todd and spoke to Luke, but he kept his eyes on me.

"Haven't seen you around."

"We're new in town," Luke said coolly. "Just checking things out."

"Maybe we don't need anyone poaching on our turf."

Todd wasn't a particularly menacing name, but this guy gave it a new edge. I imagined a young mother in a hospital, naming her infant Todd, counting his fingers and toes, raising him with high hopes, and then her disappointment and fear as he turned into one of the scariest motherfuckers I'd ever seen. More likely, she'd been a crack whore and this was all he'd ever been destined for. It didn't make him any less terrifying. Anyone else would have been quaking in their boots. Luke's body was as solid as a tree, his arm like a noose around my neck. He was just protecting me, just playing a part, but I got the strangest sense he was holding me back.

"That's one way of looking at it," Luke said. "I'm not looking to take anyone's piece of the pie. I figure, let's just make a bigger pie."

My eyes must have bugged out of my head. Insulting a guy one minute in—shit. So much for blending in. What the hell was the exit strategy again?

Todd laughed. "I like the way you think. Sit down,

and tell me more about it."

The man at the end of the booth had full sleeves of colorful tattoos and three visible gold teeth. He glared at us but scooted over to make room. I went first, ending up pushed tight between Gold Teeth and Luke. Luke and Todd conversed in vague, barely understandable language about the types of drugs they sold, about how much volume Luke had supposedly dealt. I wasn't sure what this was supposed to get us. Was he working on a drug bust? Although we'd first have to get in with them to get any information. Meanwhile, Gold Teeth's fingers inched up my thigh.

Luke stretched beside me. "What I'm curious about is who the big players are."

Todd snorted. He seemed to like Luke's chutzpah. "Are you saying I'm not big enough for you?"

"You run a nice pack," Luke said with a nod to the heavily armed and heavy-lidded group around us. "But like I said, I like to expand the pie. That means more than chemical merchandise." In a swift move, he pulled me onto his lap, far enough away that the wandering hand slipped from my leg.

Todd eyed me. "She's a nice piece, but there's only so many times a ride can run in a night. Unless you're hiding a harem in your boots, you don't have any business thinking big."

Luke's hand skated up my arm, sending goose bumps along my skin.

"I don't have any girls with me, no, but I know

how to get them."

Todd's arms had been spread out along the back of the bench. With slow intensity, he leaned forward. The chain bracelets clunked against the table. "And just how do you do that? You got a clone machine stashed away? 'Cause I'd sure as hell take one of those to order."

He nodded toward me on the last, and a shudder ran through me. I could have sworn he saw it, and a ghost of a smile graced his face.

"I used to run a program," Luke said. "We'd target a certain kind of girl. There are certain criteria you can use to figure out the good ones. Then you train them."

An uneasy look crossed Todd's face before he bolstered himself. "If you were so successful, then why'd you move here?"

"Things got too hot," Luke said easily. "Only so many girls can go missing before people start poking around. That's bad for everyone. Cops are not discriminating, if you know what I mean. It can be a mess. But this place would be fresh."

The other woman at the table seemed to snap out of her coked stupor. "There was that girl who went missing. She was on the news."

Luke snorted. "In a city this size? That probably happens every hour."

"No, it was right here in this club," she insisted. "We saw them—"

"Shut up, Lee," Todd snapped. "Go clean yourself up."

She sulked off to the corner, toward the same single-stall bathroom Luke and I had used earlier.

Luke pushed me off him and smacked my bottom. "Good idea. You need to use the little girl's room too."

Wow, he had this whole degrading-women routine down pat. Inside the bathroom, I found the woman with her face pushed under the faucet. She blew her nose repeatedly, splattering water onto the peeling mirror and cracked tiles. I tried to ignore the fact that my ass had been where her hands now rested. This place seemed a whole lot seedier without Luke.

"Are you okay?" I asked her.

"Can't get it out," she muttered, wiping her face on the sleeve of her shirt. Her brown-black hair was pulled back into cornrows, her lips a deep-stained red. She wore a black sleeveless T-shirt, revealing arms that were thin but well-defined with muscle.

"Yeah." I tried to sound sympathetic. "I know how that goes. Listen, about that girl who was taken—"

"Fuck, what are you doing here?" she cried.

I gestured lamely at the door. "My boyfriend told me to come here."

She rolled her eyes, her most lucid expression yet. "Not here, in the bathroom. Here with a guy like that. In Chicago. You don't belong in this life."

Oh, the irony—she didn't believe I was a prostitute. "Listen, I've been doing this for a long time."

"Then you need to get out," she demanded. "Some crazy shit is going on. It's not just the girl that was here.

There was some kind of fucking massacre, and two of the rich-bitch escorts were killed."

Rich bitch? Ouch. "Yeah," I agreed. "Crazy shit. But I'm really curious about that girl."

She continued as if I hadn't spoken. "It's like a fucking sinking ship around here. You need to get out while you can. I mean, I can understand why you stay. I've seen your boyfriend. It's the eyes, right? Fucking green eyes."

Yeah. Fucking green eyes. "Pretty much, but here's the thing. He's bent on running this little scheme here in the club, so unless I can convince him otherwise…"

"Nah, that'll bring trouble to all of us. He said it himself."

"I just want to show that it really happened. I mean, were you there?"

"I was there that night. I thought I saw her earlier, because some of the boys were roughing her up, and I thought it was sad. I mean, kind of funny but also sad. And then I found out later she was dead. You can check the news. They said she was at large, but that really means they didn't know shit. If they haven't found her after all this time, and if Henri didn't find her either, then she's got to be dead, right?"

My heart started to pound at the mention. "Henri? Who's that?"

Her eyes glazed over. She stared at the brown leak stains on the wall as if hypnotized.

"Hey," I said. "Don't do this. Henri, remember?

The girl."

She snapped out of it again. I wasn't sure if she was high like I thought or whether she had some sort of condition. I wondered idly if she needed medical attention. It wouldn't matter either way.

"Henri's a scary guy," she said. "Some advice, woman to woman? Stay away from him."

It was good advice. Unfortunately I couldn't take it. "My boyfriend really wants to talk to him. From there…" She shrugged. "He's cool once he gets an audience."

She frowned. "You should ditch him."

Even when we were in disguise, no one wanted us to be together. "I'm just trying to help him out." I took a deep breath. "The truth is, he's been really focused on breaking into Chicago's business. It's like his life goal, and if I could help him do that, I'd be in, you know?"

She nodded, her expression sad. "Yeah, I know."

"So you'll help me?"

She shook her head but not in refusal. "I think you're going to regret this."

I thought so too. "Tell me anyway."

She told me what she remembered about that night, naming the guys who had cornered Claire and likely brought her outside to Henri. I recognized the names but hadn't met them before. She said she hadn't heard any commotion the rest of the night, only that she saw Claire's picture on the news the next day. They had considered shutting down the club but decided that would look more suspicious. Plus, it would be a major interruption to their service business.

"Did anyone talk to Henri about what happened?"

She wouldn't meet my eyes. "Why should we? It doesn't have nothing to do with him."

"But you said the hit was put out by him."

"Correction. It doesn't have nothing to do with us. Look, sister, no one gets in Henri's business. Not my boss, and sure as hell not your boyfriend." She looked me up and down. "You don't want to get on his radar, if you get my drift. You're pretty, and you want to stay that way."

Actually, Henri was very careful to preserve prettiness. There were many ways to hurt someone without leaving permanent damage. The worst hurt came on the inside anyway.

"Tell me where to find him. I'll just tell my boyfriend, and he'll be so happy with me. Please."

She deliberated for a few quiet moments. "He's been taking plenty of heat lately, so he's gone to ground. No one knows where he is. But I happened to overhear someone saying he had a new location. The Barracks."

"The what?"

"That's what they call it, the Barracks. It's some sort of big silo west of here. I think it used to be an airport. Anyway, I've never been there. That's all I know."

"That helps. Really. Thank you."

"It's supposed to be haunted." She considered. "You don't think that stuff is real, ghosts and shit?"

"Probably not. But I figure, even if it were real, there's a lot scarier things in this world than white floaty beings."

"Amen to that."

Chapter Eleven

WE RETURNED TO the men, who seemed to have moved on from talk of criminal activity to sports. Some languages were universal as a way of bonding, which meant Luke had said the right things when I'd been gone. Our eyes met as I returned to his side, but I couldn't get a read on him. His sleazy persona felt like a physical barrier between us. He blended in so well here, almost seamlessly, and an uneasy curiosity rose within me. He seemed more comfortable here than me. I had given him a hard time for knocking my knowledge of this underworld, and yet he'd been casual and cool while I'd had a nervous breakdown in the bathroom. What if he had real experience with this, beyond the occasional undercover sting with the CPD? What if he had been a part of this world once?

As soon as I thought it, I knew it was true. It made too much sense. It explained why I had never been able to see though his stalwart cop facade. It exposed the root cause of his noble quest. He was trying to atone for whatever he had done in his past. Had he slept with prostitutes like me? Apparently, if he had a girl he was looking for. Had he even pimped them out, for real instead of pretend? Guilt was a powerful motivator. Maybe our little game of the boyfriend as pimp was more fatalistic than I'd thought. Except that picture didn't work for Luke, despite the lock-and-click way he fit in here. His sort of unerring integrity wasn't born of a single mistake. I couldn't imagine him being so far gone as to really cause harm to someone he loved.

Far more likely he had been unable to save the girl he loved, instilling in himself a deep and abiding need to save every other one—including me. In the span of seconds, I sketched the fairy tale in my head. He had been lonely and, in a moment of whiskey-induced weakness, called an escort service. The girl had been so beautiful she took his breath away with a knowing touch but an innocent look of hope in her eyes. He was smitten at first sight and swore to rescue her from the life. Except something had gone wrong. Her pimp wouldn't let her go. These things happened—I should know. And then he lost her…though he never gave up wanting her. He would never give up. I could see it all so clearly, as if it had happened, as if I had been there. I wondered if she thought of Luke still. If she appreciated him and longed for him in return. She must, I thought.

Luke's body tensed beside me in the booth, snapping my attention back to the present.

"Maybe some other time," he said.

Todd frowned. "I'll pay you, of course. I'm not looking for a handout."

I realized they were talking about me. Specifically, Todd wanted something from me. Sex, of course. Revulsion rolled through me. He looked decent enough if a little scary. But I thought I was done with that. I wanted to be done with it so badly that I wasn't sure I could do it. Would Luke ask me to?

"I don't share her," he said flatly. "Or sell her."

This seemed to intrigue Todd. "That seems like a hard line to take, especially in this business."

"I don't shit where I eat. She's mine." He nodded toward the mass of dancers beyond the moldy velvet curtain. "I'll have plenty of girls available to you once I establish myself here."

Todd seemed provoked by Luke's refusal. "Maybe that makes it the perfect test. After all, you're the new guy here. You got something to prove. How do I know I can trust you? So maybe I'll have a taste of what you like so much. She must be good if you're keeping her to yourself."

Luke snorted. "Bullshit. This is a test, all right, but if I broke line now, you wouldn't respect me or trust me, and I wouldn't blame you."

"I like that you're a straight talker," Todd mused. "I don't like that you're telling me no. Over some chick, of all things. What, afraid to make her do something she doesn't want to? If you hurt her feelings, will she run home to Daddy?"

"She's not going anywhere," he said. "Not home to Daddy, not with you."

Todd leaned forward. *Clink*—his chain bracelets on the rough tabletop.

"What if I give you the information you wanted?"

The information about Ella? Luke's hands tightened on my hips. "No."

"I don't just mean hooking you up with Henri," Todd said. "As I said, I'll do that anyway. It's good business sense. I like the bigger-pie analogy. That's sweet. But I meant information about the other thing." He smiled at me. "The other girl."

My heart did a little flip. The other girl. Was that what Luke had been asking about? Was that why he'd sent me to the bathroom, so I wouldn't know?

Luke's hand felt like warm iron around my thigh, his grip tightening with every word from Todd's lips. He crowded me, his body blatantly interested in the offer, despite his denials. The smug look on Todd's face said he knew exactly what effect his words were having.

"You said you didn't know anything," Luke said with a hint of question.

"I lied. There wasn't any incentive for me to tell you. Now there is."

"You're bluffing."

"What was her name? Ah, that's right. Daisy. Very pretty, like the flower." Todd lifted one bare tattooed shoulder. "I may have fucked her."

A shudder ran through Luke's body, visible to anyone at the table. But even if they hadn't seen it, they could feel it. His rage rolled off him in almost-palpable waves. I had felt his intensity before, his lust, but never this. Never unadulterated hatred, and sure as hell never a love so strong as to generate such a thing. How he must have loved her. How he loved her still. But he wouldn't do it, would he? He wouldn't give me to them, even if it meant finding his long-lost love.

His voice was hoarse. "How do I know you're telling the truth?"

Todd considered that, looking off to the right. Everything, from the stillness of his hands to the steady, unflared slope of his nostrils, indicated he was remembering something, not making it up.

The din of the club seemed to quiet, as if someone had turned the volume down. I heard my blood pumping in my ears, fast against the backdrop of Luke's harsh breathing. I realized that his rigid discipline hadn't been him all along but a container for years upon years of unfulfilled fury. Through force of will, he had carefully tunneled his energy into the places he could effect change. His almost inhuman efforts to help me and the other girls were merely steam from the release valve. All the while pressure had built, waiting for someone to set it free.

"She was a natural blonde," Todd finally said. Then he glanced at me. "Not as hot as this one, though."

It happened so quickly. Luke pushed me out of the booth and lunged across the table. Half of the people spilled out from the seats while the others stared, slack-jawed. That was when I knew we weren't getting out of this alive. This was an insult of the highest order to the woman who meant the most to him. Luke couldn't find her, but he wouldn't let her go unavenged.

He had his hands around Todd's neck, while the larger man grappled futilely, unable to shake him. He landed blows on Luke's side, on his head, but nothing would shake him. Would Luke kill in his rage? I saw no other way out. Unless Todd killed him first. I fumbled for my gun before remembering I had given it to Luke for safekeeping. Where had he put it? He had reached back and tucked it behind him.

I yelled out a warning, but it was lost to the melee, evaporated like sound underwater. Helpless, I watched in horror as Todd's wild blows found the gun, as he whipped it out and pointed it at Luke's cheek. The two men froze, one on top of the other, panting. Slowly, Luke levered himself up and stepped back. I breathed a sigh of relief. I had been half expecting him to continue fighting, blind to his rage. At least he had this much self-preservation. Though it was unclear whether it would be enough, whether we would get out of this after all, considering the look of vengeance on Todd's face.

He let out a stream of incoherent curses, promising all manner of retribution upon Luke, his mother, any pets he might or might not have. But when Todd turned to me and our eyes met, I knew exactly how he meant to exact revenge.

Still holding the gun, he spread his arms wide. "I

know what will make me feel better after this. We'll have a party. And your girl will be our main attraction."

"Try it," Luke snarled. "And count how many breaths you have left."

Despite his clear disadvantage, his words seemed to give Todd pause and me too. There was something unbreakable about him then, as if a bullet couldn't stop him. It was only his will, his decision to stand there instead of beating Todd to a bloody pulp, that kept him safe. Todd seemed to think this over while wiping a dribbling line of blood from his brow. He looked around, as if aware that everyone in the room was watching us—far too many witnesses to keep quiet, far too much bother to rape and murder us for what amounted to a barroom brawl.

"Get your bitch and get out," he said. "I never want to see you back here."

I seemed to have been rooted to the spot, but Luke grabbed my arm and pulled me from the club. Cold night air slashed at my sweated skin and seeped into my bones. The streetlamps blurred before my eyes, as if I watched them through a car window on the freeway instead of stumbling down the street away from the club. My limbs felt like lead. I remembered this feeling from once before. My brain was filled with white dewy mist. Ah, shock. That was it. Knowing its name didn't lift the fog.

If anything, I sank deeper. Nothing could touch me here. No one could.

Chapter Twelve

AT LEAST LUKE seemed to have all his faculties, buckling me into the car. His hands were smooth as they tucked my hair behind my ear. He pressed a kiss to my forehead. "Close your eyes. We'll be home soon."

Only when I felt the car move did I realize I had followed his instructions. I kept them closed, luxuriating in the cottony comfort. We were safe; that much I knew. And really, wasn't that all I'd ever wanted for us? Safe and together.

Whether minutes or hours passed, I didn't know, but I felt the car slow to a halt. I opened my eyes, and first things I saw were trees. I squinted. Where were we, a park? Luke circled the car and let me out. Then I saw the cottage. In the twilight, dark crisscross beams could be seen shadow-framing the cottage, and a dark leafy carpet blanketed the side. I hadn't been sure what he'd meant by *home*, but it sure as hell wasn't this. "What is this place?"

"A safe house."

I grew alarmed. "The CPD?"

"No," he said shortly. "It's mine."

"She's mine," he had said to Todd. All part of the game that had almost blown up in our faces.

It was too dark to see inside properly, even with the small table-side lamp Luke switched on. I registered vague, ranch-style furniture crowding the small living space. It all looked very ordinary, as if a sleepy-headed child might wander out for a glass of water. But maybe that was what made it a safe house. Not just its location as a hideout, but its ability to bring ease to the people who stayed here.

Luke prepared a cup of tea for me and coffee for himself. I warmed my hands on the bowled mug and took a sip.

At length, I asked the question that had sat on the tip of my tongue all this time. "Do you regret it?"

He leaned back in the wood-and-wicker armchair he'd chosen and closed his eyes. A lock of golden-brown hair fell across his forehead, softening the hard, chiseled lines of his face.

"I should. I can't. He deserved every fucking bruise."

I dipped my pinkie finger into the scalding tea, then brought the wobbly drop to my lips. "Still. He might have had information. You might have found her."

"He didn't know anything. Not anything current, anyway."

I shrugged. "I would have done it. In case you were wondering."

"Done what?"

"I would have fucked him if you'd asked me to. So he would tell what he knew. So that you could find her."

His eyes snapped open, glowing green in the dim light, like a cheetah ready to hunt. "I didn't ask you to do that."

"I know she's important to you."

"Did you know about her? You don't seem surprised."

"I had an idea." More like Jade spelling it out for me. There had been other clues, but a girl would go to great mental lengths for love—even the doomed kind.

He reached forward and set his coffee mug on the side table, then rested his elbows on his knees, his head down. "Daisy is my sister. Was my sister. Three years younger. Though she probably isn't alive anymore, I've never been able to make myself accept that."

"Your sister?" Of course it shouldn't bring me any happiness, knowing that his sister had been a prostitute, that she was likely dead, and yet pure inappropriate relief flooded me. This was exactly the sort of selfish response that made me unsuitable for him. "Why didn't you tell me?"

"What for? You were my informant, at great risk to yourself. Then before you had even fully recovered from the gunshot, you were on the run. I owed you my help, not the other way around."

He glanced up, his gaze hooded—and tired. He

needed sleep. And possibly medical attention.

I stood and found an ice pack in the freezer and placed it against his temple. He winced, then pushed it more firmly against the swelling there, taking it from me. I sat again, trying to order my thoughts. He had been searching for his sister all this time. Contrary to my impassioned imaginings, the discovery didn't diminish his integrity—it strengthened it. Any prostitute who denied ever having a white-knight fantasy was lying. And here he was, loyal to her cause. Considering she was his sister, he wouldn't even expect sex in gratitude. The savior scenario didn't get better than that.

"I could have helped you," I said. "That's why you were so invested in us girls, right? You were looking for her. I could have helped."

"I didn't want you to," he said, so fiercely I blinked. Then, "That wasn't why I was so invested, okay? Yes, I've been looking for her, but that didn't have anything to do with us."

Sadly, I thought it had everything to do with us. He never would have met me if he hadn't been so bent on finding his sister. He wouldn't have gone after the pimps…Henri, especially.

"Was she with Henri?" I asked, incredulous.

After a pause, he admitted, "I think so."

So we were back to this. It was a small comfort that he didn't feel romantic love for this girl, but she was his goal all the same. I was merely a means to an end.

Something to use and discard. And he was just another man to use me. How unoriginal of him.

Well, far be it for me to let him down. "Tell me about her. Something other than the fact that she's a natural blonde. Maybe I've met her."

He scowled. "Stop it. Stop using that voice with me."

"My helpful voice?"

"The one you use with johns. The one that sounds sweet and subservient, unless they know you. Then it says you despise them."

I did despise him. I despised him for seeing me, for knowing me, exactly as he had so arrogantly claimed to in the alley.

"Fine," I said brusquely. "This is me. My regular voice. My pissed-off voice, actually. Better?"

A smile tilted his split lips. "Better."

"So tell me. Tell me about your sister."

He sobered. "Blonde hair. Hazel eyes. They change by the light. Blue in the sun, brown in the dark. Five feet six, a hundred twenty pounds, although those measurements may be wildly different, even assuming…"

Assuming she was alive. "There's no chance, then?"

His eyes grew distant. "It was so many years ago. Long enough to come to terms with it, long enough to give up the ghost. As a cop, I can figure out the facts, same as if it were a case. She's likely dead. If she's alive, she's probably not in Chicago anymore."

"What makes you say that?"

"Because I've looked. Everywhere." He ran his hands through his hair, then hissed out a breath as he found a sore spot. "I can't let her go. I can't shake the feeling that she's here, right outside my grasp. But I have to accept that she's gone. All I'm doing now is investigating her death. If she were here, and if she were alive, I would have found her by now."

"There's one other option you left out."

Green eyes locked on mine. "What's that?"

It occurred to me, because it hit upon my own hidden desire. If she was alive, if she was in Chicago… "She may not want to be found."

CHAPTER THIRTEEN

Luke reclined on the chair, stress wrinkling the skin between his brows. I knew he was thinking about his sister. I wished I could help, though if I knew for sure she had overdosed or met some other grisly fate, I wasn't sure I could tell him. It didn't matter because his description of her matched half the prostitutes I'd ever met. Even Jenny, from the blowout at the corporate party, fit the physical description.

Except she was too young, and so was I. With the beginnings of leathery skin and crinkles at his eyes when he smiled, Luke was in his midthirties. At thirty, his sister would be ancient in the realm of prostitution. If I had met a woman that old working for Henri, I would have remembered.

But I hadn't. "I'm sorry."

"I know it's too late to help her. I just wish I knew what happened to her. Then maybe I could…"

"Avenge her?"

His lids were hooded. "Maybe I could move on."

A shiver ran through me, a sense of camaraderie. That was what I wanted too—for myself. Both of us were trapped by the ghosts of our pasts, him by his sister and me by my father.

"What then?" I asked. "Would you still work for the CPD?"

He shrugged. "Being a cop is all I know, but the only reason I became one was to find Daisy. I couldn't get them to help me, to care about her. So I figured if I was on the inside, I could look for her myself. I didn't understand then how many girls go missing, how little time there is. You can't do this job and get choked up about every little injustice. I turned into the cops I hated. Putting in my hours and, at the end of the day, barely making a difference."

"Don't sell yourself short. You did a lot for me. You were the one who convinced me to quit."

He laughed sharply. "Some good that did you."

"Hey, things aren't so bad." As I spoke the words, I realized they were true. This cottage felt like it was a million miles from civilization—and from danger. In the whole world, there was only the two of us. The darkness and distance wove a cocoon around us, keeping the scary predators and unkind world out of sight and out of mind.

"How long can we stay here?" I asked.

He shrugged. "From my talk with Todd, it's clear Henri has gone to ground. I have a few people who can help me with tracking him down, but I can coordinate that from here. It's a secure location, completely untraceable. We can stay here until we find him."

I thought of Henri's new hideout, the Barracks. But

if I told Luke, we would have to leave. If I told him, the cocoon would dissolve. Henri would still be there a week from now, but I would never have this chance again. Of course, it was selfish. This wasn't just about me or Claire. Luke wanted to take Henri down for reasons of his own. He might finally get closure on his sister. He certainly wouldn't thank me for withholding information that could help. But I couldn't make myself say the words. I couldn't destroy the one thing I had longed for.

I looked away, as if the lie of omission were written in my eyes.

"Are you okay?" he asked. "You didn't get hurt in the fight, did you?"

I swallowed my guilt. "No, I'm fine. Just a little tired."

He stood. "Sure, let me show you the bedroom."

He led me to a small room, which had a large bed and an oak side table and dresser. Across the bed, a ruffled bedspread with large white flowers was both ostentatious and humble at the same time. Matching drapes covered the windows.

"It came with the place," he said from behind me. "In case you were thinking of mocking me."

"It suits you."

"I have always felt that about magnolias."

"I meant the ruffles."

"Thanks. At least the bed is comfortable. The bathroom is down the hall, so I'll let you use that before you turn in. I keep spare toothbrushes and everything else in the cabinet."

Exhausted, I only planned to wash up in the sink, but the prospect of a bath was too alluring. The tub was bare, no shower curtain and no drain stopper. I indulged in a hot shower instead, spilling water over the side and feeling guilty for using this much hot water. I cleaned the greasy residue from my hair, reveling in the bitter-soap scent I recognized from Luke. It was harsh stuff, the kind that took my skin off as it cleaned, but I appreciated its strength. The residue of my sins went too deep for regular soap.

A small pile of neatly folded clothes waited for me outside the door. A man's white undershirt and a pair of boxers. Well, that answered the boxers-or-briefs question. I rolled the waist until it promised to stay on me, while the shirt draped over me. Luke didn't look like a large man from far away, mostly due to his leanness. But up close he was tall and filled out with muscle. His was a deceptive power, which made me adore him even more.

I found him in the bedroom, turning down the thick blankets. He stepped back when I came inside. Would we have sex here tonight? Almost as if I had voiced the question, he answered.

"I'm sleeping on the couch."

"Oh." I slipped past him and climbed into bed. It was a relief, the lack of expectation. So why did my stomach feel so hollow?

I thought for a moment he might tuck me in, maybe even sit on the bed, and I realized with alarm that I might fall apart if he did. Already, with him just standing beside the bed, my heart rate had increased. Heavy blankets, in the dark, couldn't breathe.

He turned and left without a word.

My eyes slid shut. Maybe this hadn't been such a good idea. My clothes and makeup and sultry sarcasm were all part of my armor, but here they were stripped away. Just me, as lonely and scared as I had been at sixteen, desperate to get out of my father's house.

From the bathroom, I heard the shower turn on. I imagined him under the spray, rivulets of sweat and dirt running over roughened skin. I pictured the pleasure on his face as hot water soothed the tension in his muscles.

I stared at the little dots on the ceiling, wondering how I could have been so tired before but so awake now. How just knowing he was naked had drained all the sleep from my body.

I heard a groan from the bathroom. Or had I? It was hard to tell over the rush of the shower. What if he had been really hurt? He might need my help.

Chapter Fourteen

PUSHING THE COVERS back, I slipped from the bed. The carpet was thin and brown, as if I walked on a soft dirt path. The bathroom door was open a crack. I pushed it a little farther.

The overhead light blinded me for a minute until my eyes adjusted. Luke stood in the shower, facing away from the spigot, letting the water beat his back. One of his hands was on the wall, supporting his weight. The other was on his cock, thick and long and clearly right in the middle of something. Something dirty, something private—I couldn't look away.

His eyes were shut, his entire face tight in concentration. What did he think of? Who?

He moaned again, and it was so clearly a sound of pleasure. How could I have missed it? Maybe I had known all along. Maybe I had come here to see this, to press my nose against the window and dream of the future.

He fisted his cock, slow and easy, and I found myself storing that information away for a future when I would use it—this was how he liked to be touched.

His whole body glistened, his chest and arms

adorned with glimmering droplets while swaths of steaming water ran down his back and legs. I wondered if the water slipped between them, caressing his tender sac as a warm tongue might do.

As I would have, if he had come to me. And yet I couldn't be bitter, not to watch this. Like watching a tornado, so self-contained in its strength, so natural in its glory, and I wanted it to sweep me away. I wanted him to let me in. I wanted so badly to know what he was thinking.

"Shelly," came out on a breath.

At least I thought he said my name. It wafted to me on the thick, moist air. I couldn't be sure if it was my wishful thinking, until he said it again. He mumbled it this time, and I imagined it was more than a fleeting thought, that he was looking at me, speaking to me. My gaze snapped back to his face, but his eyes were still shut. If he saw me at all, it was in his mind. A specter with my body but none of my issues, one who didn't freeze up when a man stood by the bed. It was that Shelly he spoke to, that one he wanted.

He stroked himself faster, and my body responded with heat of its own, dampening and softening as if he were already inside me, preparing my body so that his size and his speed wouldn't damage me. The human body was an amazing thing that way. The mind, not so much. As he came on the tile wall, my body twinged, but all I could think was—not for me.

He wanted me enough to speak my name, but he'd

chosen the fantasy of me instead. Smart man. Self-disgust curdled any lingering arousal.

Returning to the plush comfort of the bed, I listened as the shower squeaked off, as he brushed his teeth and dressed. The bathroom door opened all the way, draping yellow light over me before he flicked it off. I waited for his footsteps to move away, to settle into the couch in the next room. Instead his dark silhouette remained in the doorway, leaning against the frame, arms crossed.

Had he detected me outside the bathroom? Maybe he would demand an apology. At length I realized he wasn't waiting for anything. He was merely watching me sleep—a voyeurism of his own.

I spoke into the darkness. "Hi, Luke."

"Shelly." He returned the greeting without hesitation, apparently unsurprised to find me awake.

"Can't sleep?"

"It's the adrenaline rush. After a situation like that, it's not uncommon for me to stay up half the night."

"Oh. What do you usually do on those nights?" I had meant watching TV or reading a book but mentally kicked myself, because I had just invited him to tell me about his sex life.

He sounded amused. "That's a little different. I'd usually finish out my shift, fill out paperwork. If we made an arrest, there'd be processing and questioning. I don't usually go straight home."

I tried to match his light tone. "This was your first

time doing something illegal, then? How does it feel to be a criminal like me?"

His voice lowered. "It wasn't my first time doing something criminal."

"Really?" I sat up a little. "Did you once run a red light? Never say so."

"Nah. Not without the flashers on."

"Did you abuse your badge?" I teased. "I can see it now. You pull her over. *Oh, Officer, I had no idea I was going so fast.* Next thing you know, your belt is around your ankles, and she's out of a speeding ticket."

"What a flattering portrayal of me," he said drily.

"Well, I'm out of ideas. I really can't imagine you breaking the law at all, with the exception of...you know, punching and choking the guy earlier. That was probably illegal."

"Probably."

"That was different, though. He was totally baiting you. You had a good reason."

"All criminals have a good reason."

I considered that. "I don't. I did it to get money. That's hardly a noble cause."

"You had your reasons. I know you helped Allie."

"I should be excused, then." I nodded as if I agreed. "Besides, I didn't hurt anybody, so that should count for something. What do they call that?"

"A victimless crime."

"That's it. Mine was a victimless crime. Except if you talk to the lady who runs the shelter, she'd say I was the victim. Which would make me the victim of my own crime. Isn't that funny?"

"Fucking hilarious," he said darkly, turning to leave.

"Wait. I don't know why I say that stuff."

He had stopped, facing away. "It's how you cope, and you don't have to apologize for it. It's just… It's a touchy subject for me."

Of course it was, because of his sister. And here I was making a joke about it. "I'm sorry. Please stay."

"You should get some rest."

"I don't want to be alone."

CHAPTER FIFTEEN

A FTER A LONG beat, Luke slid into bed. He didn't just lie next to me. He wrapped me up in his arms, tucked my body inside his. He was wearing jeans and nothing else, no shirt to shield me from his skin, his maleness. It was more than I was expecting, more than I was prepared for. We were so close, enveloped in each other, and I wasn't cut out for genuine intimacy. It was suffocating. The backs of my eyelids pricked. I struggled to get away.

He held me tighter. "Shh. I won't hurt you."

My laugh was watery. "I think I could stand that better."

"Yeah," he said softly. "You probably could. But you can let me hold you."

I lay in his arms, tense. I wanted to relax, to enjoy this like a normal person, but I couldn't shake the old, now stale panic. I knew he wouldn't hurt me. It wasn't for fear of him, but fear of the past. When I lay in his arms without the rote mechanics of a job, the fear took over.

He spoke in a tone so certain it soothed me. "One day you'll be free of this. You won't have to look over your shoulder all the time or be scared anymore. You'll have a place of your own. But bigger. And nicer. No ruffles for you. You'll have a whole life. All this will fade away into the past."

But I didn't want to forget him. I didn't want to forget the rough timbre of his voice as he tried to imagine me, happy and whole.

"Keep going," I begged.

He paused. "I know you think guys only want you for your body. What else could you think, considering what you've been through? But it doesn't have to be that way. You'll find a guy who sees what's inside you, who loves you for that more than anything else."

Past the serious insights, a glint of humor touched my lips. "Are you telling me about my life with another guy while your dick is hard against my hip?"

"Ignore that." I heard the smile in his voice. "Every guy has a part of him that's a greedy bastard. Right now that's the only part of us you see."

"I can't see it right now, but from what I can feel, it's very impressive."

He snorted. "Don't act like you prefer them larger."

"Don't act like you didn't appreciate the compliment anyway."

His laugh confirmed my words. "You don't need to pretend with me. That's all I'm saying."

"Ah, we're back to the fake orgasms. Do they offend you so much?"

"They aren't necessary. If I wanted to fuck you

without making you come, I would do it."

The harsh language reverberated within me, but it was the truth. He could have had me by now, for free or by the hour. He hadn't. I wanted to know the reason even as I was terrified to find out. Whatever my fatal flaw was would haunt me forever after. "Why haven't you?"

Tension rolled through him. His voice flattened. "I have a different view of the situation than you."

"The situation?"

"Prostitution. I don't care if I'm paying you or if you say you consent. You don't want this."

"How do you know that?"

"I'm not so vain as to believe I'm the one man you actually want to have sex with."

"What if I told you I had watched your body with lust? That I wanted to feel you inside me?"

"You're under my protection right now." His voice was strained. "It's in your best interest to stay in my good graces, to develop a bond with me."

"So now I don't even know what I want? My desires are invalid? Oh please, spare me from another man who tells me what to feel."

"I'm trying to protect you. From me." His erection loomed thick and hard against my side, belying his words. "God, there's a million reasons why this is a bad idea. You're too young. You've been hurt too badly and used too much. How can you consent to me and mean it? It would be rape if I touched you."

I pulled back and turned to face him, incredulous. "You're saying I'm not even capable of consenting. I'm so far beyond broken that I can't even do what another woman can. Do you know how much that insults me? When you take away my choice, it diminishes me. I don't want to be less than anyone else. I want to be whole."

"Christ," he said. "I know. I'm sorry. I know."

His apologies were like a prayer, heartfelt but falling on deaf ears. I pushed away, scrambling to the edge of the bed.

"Get away from me. Don't touch me. Or am I not allowed to say that either? I don't even know what I want. Is that right?"

It was right, though, whether he said it or not. I was so torn up inside, wanting him near me but fearing and loathing myself. Tears slipped down my cheeks.

"I will leave," he said quietly. "If you want me to go. Is that what you want?"

"No," I sobbed. "Don't go. Don't leave me. Even if I tell you to, that's not what I really want. I just can't say it all the time. I can't say what I want anymore. I'm so afraid."

He pulled me down into his arms. It hurt again, in that old familiar pain, but I didn't fight it this time. I let him hold me and rock me and soothe me, until the tears dried up and my hurt faded into tiredness. I drifted in the cradle of his arms, in and out of sleep. Slumber wasn't a destination but a journey, allowing my body to rest and my mind to recover.

When I woke with a soft start, he soothed me. "Shh. I'm here."

"Luke?" Sleep weighted my voice.

"That's right. Go back to sleep."

"Have you been awake all this time?"

"I told you. I usually stay awake after a rush like that. I'm fine, though. You should rest."

"I want to stay up with you. To keep you company." I struggled awake. My mind felt like it was underwater. I stretched a little and felt him tense beside me.

"Hold still," he said tautly.

As awareness seeped into me, I recognized the sexual tension that he held at bay. It was more than passing arousal. Gentle tremors betrayed his restraint.

"Let me help you," I whispered. "I want to." At his hesitation, I said, "Don't turn me away."

He groaned. "God help me, I don't think I can."

When he rolled over me, it wasn't with a savage lust. He touched me with infinite care, his hands on the most innocuous parts of me—the bare skin of my waist, the curve of my shoulder. If it weren't for the hard brand of his cock against my leg or the gentle thrusts he seemed unable to control, I wouldn't have known his urgency. But he held it in check, preferring to explore my skin with the gradual caresses of a reverent lover.

Heat flared through me, urging me onward, faster,

oh God, more—I needed so much more. More pressure, more of Luke.

"Do you want…?" I caught myself.

"Want what?" he panted.

"Nothing."

But he wouldn't let me forget. Finally I muttered, "To kiss. It's okay if you don't."

A shudder ran through him at my words. "You're going to kill me, I swear it," he said and then kissed me.

Chapter Sixteen

W ARM. HIS LIPS, his hands, the tenderness he showed me. All of it filled me with warmth, from heart-full comfort to simmering sexual awareness. The brush of his bristled jaw sent sparks along my skin. His tongue pressed to mine, and I gasped into his mouth, breathing in his air, his scent, the care he imbued in every touch.

He slid his hand beneath my shirt, slowly, slowly, giving me plenty of time to stop him, while I counted the seconds until he finally touched me there. The feel of his hand cupping my breast sent a shock through me. A whimper reached my ears—it was me. I felt drugged, by him, by giving myself over with no business and no force. This was what I had demanded from him, the right to choose this, and now that I had it, the heady taste of him threatened to overwhelm me. I had wanted the power, but this felt like surrender.

In a brief show of impatience, he tugged my shirt over my head, tossing it away. I was unraveling here, coming apart at the seams, and who knew what would be revealed underneath. It didn't matter, not when he put his mouth to my breast, closed his lips over my nipple, and flicked it with the soft wetness of his tongue.

He kissed my breasts with reverence, and a few seconds of false worship had my hips lifting up to him. Restless, I moved my legs, allowing him to fall between me, his hardness nudging against the fabric of the boxers I wore. He pulled back, though not enough to tear our clothes off and complete the act. No, he settled himself above me, content to touch and lick and tease. He was teasing me, I realized through my haze. Pulling back when I reached for him, stoking the fires so that I wanted more and more, helpless in his thrall until he decided to grant me release. I knew this trick. I had performed it so often from the other side.

"Don't," I murmured.

He paused, panting, then rested his forehead beneath my breasts. "Do you need me to stop?"

"Stop playing. Give me what I want. What you want."

I expected him to deny it, to say that was what he had been doing all along. Instead he shook his head. "I can't let go. It would be too much."

He added as an afterthought, "For you," and I wondered whether it meant the opposite. Whether it would be too much for him.

Stroking his hair, I felt a rush of longing. "I don't want the watered-down version of you. I don't want some experience you think I should have—the careful boyfriend, the gentle lover. I want you."

He placed openmouthed kisses on my skin. "You deserve all of that."

I groaned in lust and apprehension as he reached the crease below my belly. "I don't know."

"Say no if you don't want it. I'll stop." Though it didn't feel like he would when he pulled off my shorts and spread my thighs, his hands like iron bands holding me open. It didn't feel like he was capable of stopping or hearing me at all, when he licked and sucked at my cunt as if he were starving, dying, and could think of no better way to go. I bucked into his mouth, my body confused, caught between sensitivity and arousal, between overexposure and never having enough.

Rough groans escaped me, animalistic sounds of pain and pleasure, nothing like the sexy moans I could make on command. I grabbed at the sheets, searching for something to anchor me. There was no seduction from either one of us, only desire. There was no teasing, only taking. I took pleasure from his mouth, and he took all my reserve, all my fear and loneliness, leaving only wild abandon and a sense of pure acceptance.

His fingers pushed inside me, rocking, working their way between tender flesh, but it wasn't enough. I wanted to tell him, but I couldn't speak, couldn't breathe, couldn't think of anything but the sharp ache he drew forth. Then his mouth was over my clit, and his hands rough and insistent, and I tumbled off the cliff, crying out in wordless relief. I could feel my inner muscles clench around his fingers, pulling at them in an attempt to bring him deeper. Even as my body floated in blissful stupor, I wanted him inside me.

He rested his cheek against my hip for a moment before sliding off beside me. Rolling to my side, I examined him. My orgasm softened my vision, as if I were seeing him in a dream. His eyes were closed, the angles of his face more distinct from the darkness and his arousal.

I peeled the clothes from his body with a foreign sense of wonder. I had done this so many times but never with him. He stayed passive for my perusal, taut with arousal but too conscious to rush me, too kind to force me. His body was corded with bands of muscle, a sinewy sculpture dusted with light brown hair. As I tugged his briefs down his hips, his erection hung heavy over his lean stomach, thick and dark.

I reached over and stroked a finger from tip to base.

"Don't," he gasped.

I smiled lazily, echoing his words. "Do you need me to stop?"

"God, no. Just go slow. I'm so fucking close."

I fisted his cock, relishing the burn of his hot, silky skin against my palm. He sucked in a breath. I stroked him with the same rhythm he had used on himself. He bucked and moaned, delirious in a matter of seconds.

His hand enclosed mine for two strokes and then fell back onto the bed. His head fell back too as he ceded control to me. I could see the struggle in the lines of his neck, in his teeth, in his lip, in the grunts that matched each downward stroke of my hand. But he must have thought it was important to give me this power, and so I resolved to use it well.

Leaning over, I flicked my tongue over the tip of his cock, tasting saltiness and sex as he pushed up into my fist. I let him linger there, the head of his cock glistening and begging for more. I gave another quick lap at the slit to match another downward thrust. Again and again, I exacted sweet revenge for some nameless slight. For bringing me to this point where I wanted his arousal more than his release. Where I wanted to hold him at the brink for eternity, if only to see his eyes saturated with lust and desire and need.

I varied my licks—at the tip, riding the vein along the side, at the base where his cock met his groin. A tease, all of it, trying to see how far I could push him, how much he would take. It seemed limitless, his agony, as he staved off his climax. This wasn't the pleasurable pastime in the shower but a fight, a struggle—an exercise in torture and devotion.

"Shit, shit, shit," he chanted under his breath.

I loved that he swore during sex. He would occasionally swear around me but was for the most part very respectful. Fuck respectful. I wanted his coarseness, his crudity, every dirty thought he ever had.

"Do it," I whispered.

"I don't—" He gave up midsentence—gave up pretending not to know, not to want, not to dream of owning me the way I dreamed of being owned. With his hand behind my head, he guided me to the tip, not to lick or suck him, but to take all of him, to swallow him down. I moaned with my mouth full of his flesh and felt his balls tighten under my caress.

Even in this, I wouldn't give in too easily. I went slowly, laving my tongue along the underside but without the proper rhythm to bring him to orgasm. It was far too early to submit completely. He understood what no other man ever had—for me, pleasure was freely given, easily bought. It was the withholding that measured my trust, and the permission for him to bring me in line.

He nudged my head down, and when I acquiesced, he did it again, over and over, until he let out a choked sound and released warm, salty cum onto my tongue. I caressed him softly with my tongue as he shuddered through his climax, his hands tangled in my hair, grasping and reaching as if he couldn't get close enough.

I felt languorous from making him come, more gratified by his pleasure than my own. I climbed up his body and rested my chin on the ridges of his abs.

"Well, did you survive it after all?" My voice came out husky.

After a moment, he said, "No. Not ever, Jesus."

Which wasn't really a complete or coherent sentence but felt just about perfect. We dozed in bed. By which I meant, he fell asleep almost immediately, a stuttered snore emanating from him. Typical man. But I didn't have to wake him so he could tip me or anything, so I felt pretty good about it.

Instead I could lie there and overthink everything. Was that part of the typical, noncommercial sex experience?

What did we just do? I asked myself, even though the faint saltiness on my tongue was answer enough. Would everything change, or nothing? What did he feel for me, and was it exactly the same as what I felt for him? How stressful. On the whole, I might have preferred a couple crisp C-notes.

Well, almost. Except for the amazingly wonderful part that made me feel bursty inside.

It was an urban legend that prostitutes don't kiss on the mouth. I preferred to think of it as the greatest PR campaign ever run. Since everyone thought we never did it, we didn't have to, all without insulting the client or lowering our price.

But kissing is far from the most heinous of sexual acts, and money will buy every single one of them. Every client I kissed thought they were the one exception… Now, *that* was the way to receive a great tip. Undercommit and overdeliver, the recipe for success in every industry.

I had kissed countless men, endless clients, but never had I lost myself in it. Kissing had always been a messy clash of mouth and teeth and tongue, and never had I gloried in it.

"I want it to be real between us," Luke had said, but this wasn't real, just the opposite. Real was flesh and blood, and this was so much more. When Luke kissed me, I ceased being the sum of my past, and he was no longer the next man in line. I was no longer a body to be used, and he wasn't a grunting weight to use me. In that moment, I was a woman, and he was a man. We were lovers with no time to bind us, no secrets to thwart us, no enemies to hurt us—but none of that was real at all.

Chapter Seventeen

THE NEXT MORNING, I woke up with only the ruffles for company. I heard intermittent clicking from outside the bedroom and a low voice I recognized as Luke's. I padded out and found him seated at the kitchen table with a laptop and a spread of maps and papers.

"No." He spoke into his cell. "That will take too long. I'm talking hours, not days. He's weak now. The longer we wait, the more time he has to build back up." There was a pause. "Okay, let me know what you find. This is it. If we're ever going to bring him down, it's right now."

After setting down the phone, he stood and greeted me with a kiss on the cheek. He wore loose-slung jeans and a soft gray T-shirt that gave his green eyes a smoky look. His jaw was silky smooth and smelled of after-shave. It was so domestic, so casual, that I felt my throat tightening.

I turned away. "Is there any coffee?"

"You don't drink coffee."

Then I remembered that he had made me tea last night. "How do you know that?"

"I didn't realize it was a state secret," he said lightly, reaching over to the stove and pouring me a mug of steaming water. He handed it to me along with a box of assorted teas. "Sorry I don't have anything better."

"I'm not a tea snob. Just wondering how you know I don't drink coffee."

He rolled his eyes. "I pay attention, okay? All those meetings we had when you were my informant. You drank soda or tea or water, but never coffee."

"Are you always so observant?" I asked.

"Are you always this suspicious?"

"Yes."

"Yeah, well, I'm a detective. Being observant is part of the job description. Besides, I was into you. By that, I mean hopelessly obsessed and crazy into you. You tend to notice someone's beverage choices in that state."

I stared, mouth agape, as he made his casual pronunciation of being into me. What did that even mean? Besides amazing. He had already turned back to his laptop and was squinting at the bright glare.

"Excuse me," I said. "I'm not usually so slow on the uptake, but it's early, and in my defense, we almost died last night. Did you say you were into me?"

He looked up, seeming slightly amused by my confusion. "Sure. I'm pretty sure everyone knew that. Except possibly you."

"There's a reason for that. I just can't think of it right now. Oh, wait. I know. It's because you refused to touch me or really even look at me the entire time I was your informant, which is almost the entire time you've known me."

"That was to keep from jumping you."

"Which would have been bad, because…"

"Aforementioned reasons."

He sounded almost cheerful. Dear God, was he a morning person?

"The age difference. The guilt. The impropriety, considering my position of authority. The impossibility of a long-term relationship while you were an escort and I was a cop."

I had written off his objections last night, but in the sunny light of morning, they did seem like awfully big hurdles. "And now?"

"It's a little late for regrets." He raised his eyebrow. "Do you regret what we did?"

Did I? It terrified me, but I wasn't sure that counted. It thrilled me, but I wasn't sure I was ready to admit that. "As sexual escapades go, it was rather tame."

"That doesn't answer the question."

"You're not the first cop I've slept with, if that's what you're asking."

"It wasn't."

I threw up my hands. "Then I don't know what you want from me."

He was definitely amused. "It's the morning after. I declared my feelings for you. Now is generally the time you do the same for me. Unless you don't have feelings for me."

There was a protocol for this?

"Is that it, Shelly?"

He stood up and approached me, blocking me against the counter. His green eyes leveled with mine, measuring me, assessing.

"Is that all? Was I nothing more than a quick, meaningless fuck?"

Oh God, he was going to make me say it. And if I didn't—what then? There were rules, apparently. Maybe he wouldn't touch me again. "I have feelings," I admitted sourly.

I waited for him to throw it back in my face, to smirk or boast. Instead he dropped a quick kiss on my lips and said, "Good." Then he returned to his work, adding, "There's bread for toast or fruit in the fridge if you're hungry."

Leaning on the counter for support, I caught my breath. Could it really be that simple, one declaration, then another? Could there really be hope for us, just two ordinary people caring for each other?

"I need to send an e-mail off. Can I use your computer?"

He hesitated for a moment before standing. He gestured to his laptop. "Go for it. It's not traceable."

I pulled up a browser and typed off a quick e-mail to Allie, asking her to check on Ella—and Philip. *Trust but verify* seemed like a good policy with them, the self-destructive good girl and the honorable bastard.

I believed that Philip would honor the terms of our deal, and Adrian could play nanny with the best of them. Ella was the unknown quantity. A girl with a crush was a dangerous thing.

But leaving her there had been more than convenience; it was a life insurance policy. If I succeeded with Luke, she'd go back to her old life, untouched and intact. If I failed, if I died, then the safest place for her was with Philip. Even if she had to pay rent with her body, at least she'd be alive.

After hitting Send, I turned my attention to the maps spread under and around the laptop.

"What are you working on?" I asked.

"Tracing Henri's payment from the brothels in Roseland."

"Ah." Not so ordinary after all. I sat down heavily at the table.

"He wouldn't have skipped town, not with his entire business running out of Chicago. He'd stay near the money, which means he's around here somewhere." Lines of tension appeared in his forehead. "We need to find him soon. He's already running. It's time to go in for the kill."

Guiltily, I thought of the Barracks. For all I knew, it might not be a good lead. It could even be a trap. Maybe I was protecting him by not telling him. But that was a bunch of bullshit. He'd want to know. As it was, he would be pissed at me for keeping it from him.

I was distracted from my guilt when he pulled out a

gun and set it on the table. It was slightly smaller than the one Marguerite had given me but shaped the same.

"Why'd you bring a gun to the club?" he asked, his voice deceptively mild.

I shrugged. "A girl's gotta stay safe."

He made a noncommittal sound. "Speaking of safety, do you know how to use the safety?"

I gave a nervous laugh. "Duh."

Marguerite had showed me a little metal ridge before I left. I couldn't have reproduced her smooth actions, though. I had been too scared to touch the thing. From the look on Luke's face, he knew that too, and he didn't seem very happy about it.

"I'm going to teach you how to use this."

"Really?" I was sure he'd tell me never to touch one again, not encourage the behavior.

He shook his head. "I don't like you with this, but if you're determined to have a gun, I know you can just get another one. I'd rather you know what you're doing with it than shoot your leg off."

Chapter Eighteen

W<small>E SPENT THE</small> next hour with him showing me how to load and unload the subcompact and covering the many safety rules. When I had passed each of his instructions and questions multiple times, he took me outside, armed with rubber earmuffs and eyewear. Red concentric circles had been painted on a couple of trees. With me standing behind him, he took aim and shot. The report was loud even through the earmuffs, and a small tuft of tree bark flew out from the center of the red circle and fell to the ground.

He handed the gun to me and stepped back. I looked at the gun, then back at him, but he only waited. Right.

I tried to remember what he'd told me. Widen my legs for a firm stance. Left thumb on the side, not wrapped around the back. Aim using the sights. Finger off the trigger until I was ready to shoot, and then pull, slowly, steadily, until—I blinked. A new hole had been created in one of the outer circles. Not even close to the center, but…I had hit a tree. That was a hell of an improvement over barely being able to look at the target. I laughed, giddy.

He was smiling too, but he nodded again toward the tree. I turned and shot off the rest of the clip. A few of them even landed inside the smallest circle.

When I was done, I set the empty gun down and jumped at him. It felt…freeing. Violent too, but maybe a little violence was what I needed in my life, perpetrated by me this time. It was exactly like Marguerite had said. I felt empowered, like I was doing something more than running, like I was finally fighting back. I knew that a single shooting session wasn't enough to combat all of Henri's men, but the real value was the power that coursed through me. I could fight back.

His grin faded slightly. "How's your shoulder? Did the kick bother it at all?"

He was referring to my gunshot wound.

"It's never felt better," I said honestly. That small radius had always made me feel like a victim. Maybe it didn't have to be that way.

"Listen," I said. "Do you remember when I went in the bathroom with that girl?"

"Yeah, I wanted to talk to you about that." He got a faraway look. "I'm sorry I waited until you were gone to ask about Daisy. That wasn't fair to you."

Deep breath. "She told me something about Henri while we were talking."

He continued as if I hadn't spoken. "We were partners in there, and you should have had all the information."

"There's a warehouse or airport hangar or—"

"I just didn't want you to think less of me," he said.

Distracted, I asked, "Why would that make me think less of you?"

"The way I grew up." He focused on me. "There was a reason I fit in so well at the club. I know you noticed."

I had. "I figured it was your cop prowess."

He laughed shortly. "Not exactly. I grew up dirt-poor, in the scariest fucking neighborhood around. It's gone now. They razed it down, built some fancy houses on top. It was for the best. That place needed to go."

My hand found his.

"We lived in the basement of this house, renting, but my mom was a nurse, so she was gone for full days at a time. The guy who owned the house was a real jerk. It was worse when I got a job after school. Daisy would lock herself in her room until one of us got home." He looked down at our linked fingers. "I don't know why I'm telling you this."

I squeezed gently. "Because you can. Remember? You don't have to pretend around me."

A faint smile brushed his lips. "That was supposed to go the other way. So that you could relax."

"I'm relaxed. And I don't think less of you."

"It got worse." He grew grim. "My mom died when I was fifteen. Some lunatic came into the ER, waving a gun around. Shot her and three other people because his wife had died there. How does that make sense? What kind of logic is that?"

"I'm so sorry." My heart ached for the grief on his face.

He shook his head as if to clear it. "Anyway, the guy who owned the house ransacked our rooms. He took the money, any documents, everything important. When the police came, they said Daisy and I should stay there, that he had allowed us to live there and continue going to school until they determined a permanent solution. I guess he was supposed to be our temporary guardian, but we knew it would be bad. Maybe if I had said something. If I had spoken out against him then, they might have removed us from the home."

The way he spoke, it was clear he'd been down this line of questioning before, that the path was deeply rutted with guilt and what-ifs. I knew how dangerous that path could be. "You did what you thought was right at the time. You were a kid."

"That night when he came for Daisy, I fought him. I punched him, and he went down, hitting his head on a table. There was blood everywhere. I thought I'd killed him." He met my eyes, a little dark, a little rueful. "I was sure I had. Only years later I looked him up and found out he'd lived another six months before his liver gave out."

"It was self-defense," I said, stating the obvious, knowing it wouldn't have mattered to a scared kid protecting his little sister.

He stood up and paced, as if unable to stay still.

"We didn't wait to see if they'd believe us or where they'd put us next. We ran. For a while it wasn't too bad. I was motivated. I worked all day and all night instead of going to school. I made enough to buy food, and that was about it. I'd bring her library books to read, but she had all day to sit around in the abandoned house we were staying in. She was bored and restless, like any twelve-year-old girl would be day after day."

"It wasn't your fault," I said, heart heavy. After all, I already knew the ending to this story.

"Yeah," he said quietly, but I knew he didn't believe it. "She just wanted to make friends. But the only other street kids around stole shit and did drugs. She got caught up in it. We argued all the time, but I wasn't there. I was out working for us so much of the time, and then when I was home, I was exhausted." Regret stained his words. "I didn't have enough patience with her, nor did I try to see her side of things. I just yelled at her to stop seeing them."

"A fifteen-year-old boy is not ready to parent a teenage girl. He's not supposed to be ready to do that. That's what parents are for." Although it seemed like we'd both got the shaft in the parental department.

"Then one day, she disappeared. She had gone missing a couple of nights and come back in the morning. The first few times, I had looked everywhere and given her a bunch of shit when she came back. This time I was going to be tough. I was going to tell her she had to shape up, or I wouldn't help her anymore. No more giving money to her so-called friends for drugs. When she came back, I was going to cut her off. Only she never came back."

I hugged him, and he wrapped his arms around me and rested his chin on the top of my head.

"I looked for her, of course. Beat the shit out of a few of her friends; they told me she'd started hooking. Didn't get very far on my own. I got my GED and enrolled into the academy."

"You've never stopped looking," I said softly.

"I can't," he admitted. "Even when I tell myself I'm done, that I've moved on, I find myself pulling up Jane Doe records. I hadn't even planned on asking about her last night. Or maybe I knew I would. I don't know anymore. But the guy told me he'd been with Henri from the early days, and the timing was right. Next thing I know, I'm questioning him and risking the whole damn operation, risking your safety, on a lost cause."

Frustration rolled off him in waves. Like a lion caught in a trap, he would pull and gnaw until he'd torn his paw off just to be free—maim himself to escape his demons.

"Of course," I said. "Of course you should have."

"I risked my cover. I put you in danger." He vibrated with guilt.

It would tear him apart—guilt for his sister, for me. "I'm glad you asked about her. At least now you know for sure she was with Henri, right?"

"Yeah. I had suspected as much, but now I know for sure." He pressed his lips to my temple. "You're sweet."

I laughed softly. "All I did was listen."

"Always undervaluing yourself."

"I assure you, my price is very high," I said in a mocking voice. "Don't assume that because I gave it to you for free that I'm cheap."

"Hey."

He turned me in his arms so that I faced him. When I wouldn't look at him, he raised my chin. Solemn green eyes met mine.

"You honored me."

My eyes burned; my throat tightened. I was seconds away from embarrassing myself. I kissed him, using my sexuality as a shield like I'd always done. He responded at once, taking the lead with his hand on the back of my neck, holding me open. His grip on me was implacable, inescapable, but his lips were infinitely gentle. He ran his tongue along my lips, soothing, calming, and it felt like gratitude. I hoped he did feel lighter, having shared his burden. I hoped he would slake any remaining tension with my body. All of it food for my ramshackle soul. To be wanted, needed— even adored. Men praised me, they used me, and so I found sustenance.

He deepened the kiss, grew rougher, more demanding.

"Come into the bedroom," he said, both question and demand.

It didn't matter. Anything, always. "Yes."

CHAPTER NINETEEN

WE TUMBLED TOGETHER, bare skin against abrasive ruffles, naked bodies to streaming sunlight. Playfully, I pulled away. He pounced, trapping me beneath his. I lay my cheek against the bed in surrender.

"Stay," he said. His weight lifted, but I felt the light pressure of his hand on the small of my back.

I remained bent over the bed, with my feet touching the floor and my face turned into the sheets. Cool air brushed my backside, and I knew he was watching me. I had very few qualms about my body. My waist was slim, and the five pounds I'd gained in the past year went straight to my hips. My skin was waxed and shaved with careful precision, and I had a small blue vein running down my left thigh. I couldn't shake the nervousness about what he thought. I already knew I turned him on; shouldn't that be enough? But this was Luke.

Nervously, I shifted on the bed.

He hissed a breath. His hand on me moved lower, over the curve of my ass, down the sensitive stretch on my thigh. Between my thighs, I felt his hot breath.

Probing, possessive fingers spread me open, exposed me to his tongue.

I moaned at the touch and ground myself against the bed. My thighs quivered as he spread them farther, reaching deeper.

His exploration was so careful, so slow. Far too slow. Not a manipulation but a lesson, as if he was learning what I liked and where I liked it. It should have felt clinical, but instead my arousal reached a fever pitch. Being desired by a man who knew me inside as well as out, being helpless to a man who would never hurt me. It was foreign—and addictive. I wanted to lie open to his emerald gaze, to his careful fingers, to his sweetly curling tongue until eternity. I wanted to shake and cry out and come against his mouth forever. And then I couldn't want anymore, couldn't think at all— just feel. Oh God, the things I felt. There was anguish and ecstasy; there was anger and a sublime sense of connection.

The tear of foil pierced my haze, but I didn't move, not until he turned me over. I spread my legs, eager and hopeful. He entered me in a smooth, painless thrust. A gasp escaped me at the shock of being filled, at the pure joy of being filled by him. His answering groan sent shivers down my arms.

We moved together in an ancient dance, a universal rhythm—one I had done a hundred times, more, and each one had been a sham. A parody of this act and this intimacy. I hooked my legs around him, pulling him closer, forcing him deeper. His lips found mine with no hesitation this time. He was joined to me at every point—my mouth, my sex, the hard planes of his chest against my breasts, and still it wasn't enough. I scrabbled at his back, desperate and clawing, like some sort of wild sex animal, and he responded in kind, shoving his hand into my hair, holding down my hip, and growling a low sound of approval into my mouth. I spasmed and clenched around his cock, coming countless times, my orgasms bleeding together to form one long litany of sensual rapture.

There was violence in his movements, pain in my response, but there had never been a more pure expression of his love. There was no better gift from a man of meticulous restraint than letting go. No greater way for me to thank him than to give myself, unhindered by payments, free of the cool ice shell that always encased me. I was more naked than I had been a hundred other times, a hundred other beds. I was exposed, raw—and vulnerable. He could break me this way, if he chose to.

Impossibly, his thrusts grew more powerful, more frantic, as if he wanted to reach the farthest place inside me, and God, he had. He squeezed his eyes shut, and I knew he would come soon. I reached up and mouthed the skin at the base of his neck. A flick of my tongue, and he shouted his climax, the cords of his neck vibrating against my lips. At his orgasm, he pushed into me once, twice, then again, stroking himself with my body. I whispered words of encouragement and praise, wishing he might never stop.

He slumped down on me, heavy and supple. The most vulnerable time for a man, I'd always thought. I found myself protective of him in this moment, that he would expose himself this way—not the baring of skin, which I was too familiar with, but the lowering of his guard. He didn't have to be wary of me. No, I would guard him. At all times, and especially when he was made slack and unseeing with bliss, I would watch over him and keep him safe.

Placing kisses over the tops of my breasts, he leisurely pushed inside me and then out, as if he wasn't quite ready to end it.

He froze when he saw the scar.

I lay still, allowing him to look his fill, to pass judgment. The reddish skin puckered just under my collarbone. Almost perfectly circular, a clean shot with no additional scarring from when they had pulled the bullet back out. It might fade in a few years, the doctors said. It might not.

"Does it hurt you?" he asked hoarsely.

"Not really. Not on the surface anyway. Sometimes deeper, if I move the wrong way."

I expected him to pull out, to pull away after seeing the scar. It was ugly, but worse than that were the ugly memories. I knew he blamed himself. Everyone blamed themselves for my mistakes, first Allie, then him. But he didn't move away; he stayed inside me. His eyes were on that scar, filled with a kind of mourning.

He touched the space beside it, the pale, unmarred skin. "So strong."

I turned my face away. He kissed my cheek, capturing a tear on his lips.

"What would it take for you to believe that?" he asked.

"What would it take for you to stop searching for your sister?" The words were meant to push him away so that he would stop pushing me. But they came out with no bitterness, no rancor, only an earnestness that revealed too much.

"I don't know," he admitted. "But I'm here now. That's something, right?"

"That's something," I whispered.

He replaced his condom and entered me again. I was tender, sore from our previous rough session, but he moved slowly, soothing me until I felt a soft glow of pleasure. There was no bruising grip or frenzied thrusts this time, only the smooth glide of his cock inside me, the steady rise of his broad shoulders over me. Only the press of his temple to mine, as if we were connected by more than our bodies—we were. He came with a soft expulsion of, "Oh, shit."

We fell side by side, limbs entangled and hearts beating rapidly.

This was what he'd always wanted, if his declaration in the kitchen was to be believed. We had always been heading to this—to ruin, for a prostitute and a cop had no future. Neither of us had a future, caught as we were in the past. Still, I couldn't help feeling that something else drove his fascination with me. So bent on saving me, as if a guilt much older than the past year propelled him. There were too many similarities to ignore. His sister was a prostitute with Henri; so was I. His sister was blonde; so was I—well, usually. Now my hair was dyed brown, and to his credit, that didn't seem to slow him down. But maybe the strongest sign was that his sister had paved her own road to destruction…just like me. A decade younger. The do over.

"It wasn't your fault. I brought this on myself. This gunshot. My entire life." More softly, "I'm not your sister."

"I…I think I know that," he said drily. "Considering what we just did? Yeah, I'm pretty sure."

"I don't mean literally."

"I know what you meant." He spoke in a low, almost teasing tone. "You aren't trying to diminish me, are you? By taking away my choice?"

I laughed, recognizing my words from last night. Then, I had been self-righteous and defensive, aggressive and fearful, but now… "God, no."

He continued. "Because I seem to remember you telling me that no matter what had happened in the past, you could choose your present. No matter how broken you were, it didn't take away your right to consent. It seems only fair I should get the same treatment."

"You are very pleased with yourself right about

now, aren't you?"

"Very. But that probably has more to do with the two amazing orgasms I just had."

The trill of a cell phone sounded from the kitchen. An echoing alarm rang in my chest. It was happening, dissolving in my hands, and nothing I could do would stop it.

"I've got to check that." He ducked into the bathroom and emerged, slinging on his clothes. "There might be news on Henri."

"What if there is?" I sat up, pulling the sheet to cover me.

"Then we've got to get over there. I do, anyway. You can stay here."

I frowned. "You're not going without me."

He made an impatient motion as the phone abruptly cut off, probably going to voice mail. "We can figure that out later."

"That means you can tell me no later. I'm going."

"Look, for all I know, it's a wrong number," he said, though that seemed more unlikely as the phone rang a second time. He gave me a curious look. "What's wrong, Shelly?"

Everything. "I'm just trying to figure out if that was our last time, that's all. If we go back to Chicago and confront Henri, then what? Will I go back to being your informant? Or not even that? Will you call me and leave voice mails about how your day went? Just tell me where we'll stand."

A frustrated sound left his throat. "I don't know, but if we don't find Henri soon, we're all fucked. That has to be our first priority."

Priorities, responsibilities. There was Claire and the shelter. So many girls who needed help, when our failure was all but guaranteed.

"Why can't we just stay here?" I heard the pleading in my voice and hated it. I knew it was unreasonable, but we were flying here. Almost delirious with weight-lessness, I would rather burn up in the sun than fall in the grit of the earth. "You said that it's safe. Undetectable. Why do we need to go back?"

"And never leave?" The doubt in his voice conveyed just how ridiculous that idea was.

"I don't need anyone but you."

His face softened. "I understand it's scary. But this is the best way for everyone. What about Ella?" He paused. "And I thought you understood. This is my best chance to find out what happened to my sister."

Tightness formed in my chest, one I recognized well. The disgrace of selfishness, the feeling of inevitability. Like staring out the window, looking over the houses of my friends, feeling cold hands lift my skirt. I couldn't stop any of this. Once upon a time, I had tried to escape my fate. To my eternal shame, I had been willing to use my friends as an excuse. I had pretended to help Allie so that I could be free. Here I was, years later, doing the same thing, desperate to stay with Luke at his expense.

I swallowed. "I know where Henri is."

"Right. We'll find him and—What?"

"Or at least a clue. The girl in the bathroom said he was in a building called the Barracks. It might be an old airport just outside Chicago."

He blinked. "You're just now telling me this?"

"I'm sorry."

"Christ, Shelly. I don't need an apology." The anger in his voice made me wince. "Tell me why."

I'm a coward. I angled my head, looking up beneath my lashes. "I wanted to spend a little more time with you."

He made a slashing motion, green eyes flashing. "I told you not to play the hooker with me."

"Don't play the hooker? This isn't a game, Luke. It's who I am. Don't you get that? I can't stop being one any more than I can cut away my skin."

His harsh breaths filled the space between us.

I liked to think he understood all the things I couldn't say. I liked to think he felt it too, the melodious tumble of locks fitting together that happened whenever we came close. From our professions to our backgrounds, everything conspired to keep us apart. But from the moment we'd met, all I could think about was being together.

The shrill tone of his phone broke the spell. He turned and left the room.

Naked on the bed. How many times had I found myself this way?

I was tired of it, so weary of being used and discarded. It was my own fault for flying so close to the sun. Maybe this was what Allie had been trying to protect me from. I lay in bed alone, listening to him make plans without me, the low sound of his voice was a cold and somber lullaby.

SECRET

CHAPTER ONE

LUKE GOT EVERYTHING together quickly, just like I knew he would.

That was him—a boy scout until the end.

He and his buddies had a vague idea of the location, and they were tracking down schematics and anything else they could find. I was back in my clothes from the club, high heels and all, and we were ready to go.

After only a few minutes on the road, it began to thunder.

Slashing rain battered the car window. I had passed out on the ride out here, with no inkling how far we really were from the city. The storm slowed us even more, turning a two-hour drive into three. The steady back-and-forth of the windshield wipers was a metronome to the tension within.

"I'm sorry," I said. Again.

I seemed to be saying that a lot lately.

He stared straight ahead. "It's fine."

"It's not fine. If it were fine, you would look at me. Talk to me. Something."

"I am talking to you. I'm not looking at you because I'm driving."

"Bullshit. You haven't looked at me since you found out I didn't tell you. It was a mistake, okay? I'm not allowed to make mistakes?"

"You're allowed to make mistakes," he said evenly.

I faced away, watching a drop trail from the top of the window. It darted from one drop to another, joining and then separating, never staying long in one place. It was at the whim of the wind, of this car—of everything. No will of its own.

"I'm sorry." My voice broke on the end.

He muttered a curse and pulled off the road. I peeked out the window, seeing only driving rain and grass and a line of trees in the distance.

"If you're going to dump me, can you at least find a rest stop or something? I don't want to get my hair all wet."

"Jesus, Shelly. Some of the things that come out of your mouth."

"Is that a request?" I eyed the space beneath the steering wheel. "Because I don't normally do drive-bys, but I might make an exception for you."

"I just want to strangle you. Or make love to you until you stop baiting the world."

I smirked. "Kinky, with a touch of philosophy. I like it."

"I can't stand the idea of letting you go, okay? That's why I'm not talking about it. It's why I'm not talking to you. I'm not mad."

"Then don't let me go. Take me with you."

"That's not what I meant. I meant after. I can't bring you with us."

"I have to go."

"You would just get in the way. We'd be watching out for you instead of focusing on the job."

"I know Henri better than you or anyone else you have working for you. What if things get tough and you can't find him or can't get close? I can. He'll see me. He'll talk to me." It was a low blow. "If it comes to getting information about your sister, no one has a better shot than me."

He stared straight ahead. "I don't know if I can do that. Put you in danger."

After what happened last time, he meant. "I won't get shot again."

"You can't know that."

There was real worry in his voice, and it shook me. So of course I had to lighten the mood.

"I promise I won't get shot. Cross my heart and hope to die."

"Surprisingly, that isn't giving me confidence."

I sobered. "I need to go. For me, to get closure. There are some questions of my own I need to ask."

He considered that, watching the rain batter the windshield. "Okay," he finally said. "But you need to understand there's no guarantee you'll get to ask them. I might just shoot him on first sight."

"As long as I get to watch."

"Bloodthirsty woman." He sounded approving.

Chapter Two

WE DROVE STRAIGHT to a hotel, where purple beaded lighting and black leather couches adorned the lounge. Bypassing the check-in, we took the elevators up.

I tapped the art deco paneling. "Why the fancy place?"

"Not my choice. Major doesn't like anything affordable."

"Major?" I wasn't sure how I felt about bringing another person in on this, even though it seemed a little late for shyness. Mostly I didn't want to share Luke in the time we had left.

"A guy I know. A few guys willing to help. They're friends; don't be nervous. What am I saying? They're the ones who need to be nervous. Don't bite."

"Don't worry. That costs extra."

His frown was very intimidating. I wondered if he used that on perps. I considered asking, but that would probably just aggravate him further.

"Okay, okay." I put my hands up. "I can behave. You know, GFE. The Girlfriend Experience."

He grimaced. "If you actually were my girlfriend,

then we wouldn't have to pretend."

Girlfriend? That sounded so high school. Which was easier to focus on than the flutter of happiness in my belly. "I'm sorry, did you ask me to be your girlfriend? Because I feel sure I would have remembered that."

"What are the chances of you not mocking me for this?"

"Are you going to ask me to prom too? I don't think I have a dress, but maybe we can go shopping together. That's probably best. What color is your tux?"

"And this is why I didn't ask."

"Pass me a note in homeroom, and we'll see."

He snorted, but I detected humor dancing in his eyes.

We rode the rest of the way to the hotel in silence.

Inside, the elevator doors opened to a narrow hallway with light-beige vinyl walls. An older couple left their room and began walking toward us. The woman stared at my boobs, her face puckered in disgust.

I rolled my eyes. Typical closet lesbian.

"Behave," Luke murmured.

I scooted over to make room for them to pass, but the woman's hips bumped into me. I stumbled and would have fallen straight on her cleavage if Luke hadn't caught me. He firmly pulled me forward, his hand on my elbow.

Rather than resist him, I draped myself over him in dramatic relief. "I can't wait to get to our room."

He shot me a quelling look.

I lowered my voice. "I've been thinking about this the whole drive." Glancing back, I saw the woman shoot me one last murderous glare before rounding the corner. I shrugged at Luke's raised brow. "What? She practically felt me up."

He just shook his head.

We reached the room, and I was disappointed that there seemed to be no special knock or secret code for entry. He just knocked and said, "It's me," and we were let inside. A flutter of nerves upset my stomach, which surprised me. Since when did I get nervous about meeting new people? Most guys were nervous to meet me, not the other way around. But these were Luke's friends.

And wow. I had expected other cops, ones who cared more about doing what was right than following the rules, like Luke. But these guys were faux military and street thugs.

Luke introduced me to Jeff, who sported green-brown fatigues, a buzz cut, and a gold hoop through his ear. He smiled shyly.

"Nice to meet you," I said. "I like your earring."

Jeff blushed a deep rose. "Nice to meet you too, ma'am."

"Oh, and a southern accent. I bet the ladies line up to hear you speak."

"Naw." He practically scuffed his thick black boots on the glass-tile floor.

Luke drew me over to meet the next man, muttering under his breath, "No flirting."

The next guy was a local gang member, judging by both the tats down his neck and the red bandanna hanging from his pocket.

"You can call me Rico," he said. "Because that's my name."

I met his fist bump with a smile. "It's a pleasure."

"And that's Major." Luke nodded toward a guy in the corner.

Major was dressed all in black, his square-set face impassive. He gave a brief wave, more like a salute.

I wondered if Luke had given them some kind of warning about me. None of them let their gazes linger below my neck. At least Rico would know who I was—what I was. Probably all of them did, considering they were helping Luke with the situation, but there was no judgment in their gazes. Judgment usually came from the ladies, but there was none of the speculation, none of the wink-wink-nudge-nudge guys tended to do when they knew, as if they turned into adolescent virgins at the thought of paying for it. There were exceptions to this rule, but rarely zero out of three like this.

The four men gathered around the glass coffee table. Even Major gave up his post in the corner, although he still drew a chair from the kitchenette, turning it backward and straddling it, distancing himself.

They had confirmed the location and were discussing the best way to get there while avoiding detection. I stood aside, not pointedly excluded but clearly unhelpful to any tactical discussions. The unique cultural norms of Henri and the prostitution community at large—color me an anthropological expert. Breaking through a state-of-the-art security system, not so much.

From my perch against the window, I considered the assembly. Were they from Luke's past as a homeless kid? Or his present as a cop, maybe other informants? The two sides of Luke had seemed disparate when he first told me the story, as if he had been reborn as a different person. Slowly I had come to merge them in my mind, to see glimmers of his boyhood in the man. He was fiercely determined, unafraid—like a gutter dog. He was unflinchingly loyal, in a way inherent to street life. On the streets, you either ran pack or died. Luke was a survivor all the way.

I only hoped that carried through to the mission, as the boys were fond of calling it.

There was a basket of snacks and candy on top of the counter, a sort of high-trust minibar. Luke hadn't eaten since we were at the cottage. He needed to keep up his strength if we were going over tonight. I prepared a tray of sodas and arranged snacks and carried it to the coffee table, as if this were fucking game night and I was the little lady.

Luke and Major had their heads bent together over a laptop, murmuring quietly, but Jeff immediately reached for a cola with a quiet thanks.

"Is there anything noncaffeinated?" Rico asked.

Jeff flipped the top of his can. "Seriously?"

"Unlike some people, I don't need artificial additives to stay awake. Not when that adrenaline rush hits."

"I think there's grapefruit juice," I offered.

Rico made a face.

"I'll look for something else." I returned to the minifridge. "Sorry, but if it doesn't have caffeine, it's got alcohol. I'm guessing that counts as an artificial additive."

Rico trailed me to the counter, poking at the remaining items in the basket. "Ooh, think these are any good? Gourmet Dipping Pretzels."

Straightening, I shook my head. "They go stale fast, but hotels only replace them if someone eats them. Here, stick with a classic." I handed him a Snickers bar. "High turnover rates and low cost-to-fullness ratio."

"Will do."

He reached for a glass on the counter and turned on the faucet. He must have caught something in my expression, because he paused.

"What?"

"Nothing."

He looked from his half-full cup of tap water to me. "Now you have to tell me."

I scrunched my nose. "Don't cheap out with the water. You don't want to know about those cups."

He immediately set it on the counter but peered

into it. "It looks clean."

"I have it on good authority that the rinse-and-wipe is often employed. And you do not want to know what liquids end up in there sometimes."

"What are you, some sort of hotel connoisseur?" he joked. His face fell as he realized what he'd just said. "I didn't mean—"

"No, it's okay," I said with a small smile. "That's a new euphemism. I like it."

He seemed relieved. "I mean, it's not as if I'm in a position to judge."

"You wouldn't be the first." I handed him a bottle of water from the fridge. "Paying a hooker doesn't have quite the same stigma as being one."

"What did Luke tell you about me exactly?"

I laughed, popping the top of my cola. "Not much. Just that you were helping him out with this. He didn't tell me about your hooker-buying habits, if that's what you're asking. I'm just stereotyping." The gang symbols, the old track marks on his arms, not that I had to spell it out. "Why, you telling me you've never been with one?"

He was thoughtful for a minute. "No. I'm afraid I fit the profile in that particular regard." Then, "You aren't afraid to speak your mind."

My lips curved. "Is that an insult or a compliment?"

"I prefer honesty to lies. Though may not always like what you say." Glancing back toward the men, his expression turned speculative. "So how long have you and Luke been…you know."

I blinked. "Working together?"

"Doing the nasty."

"Oh. Umm…"

It was his turn to laugh. "All right, straight talker. I guess that answers my question."

When he smiled, I realized how handsome he was. More than that, almost pretty. He had thick black lashes and a sensual mouth most girls would kill for. It was all covered up in the gang wear and a layer of grunge, making his skin oily and darkened. I frowned. Or was it just that black gunk Luke had used as a disguise? And if so, why would Rico dress up as a gang member? Maybe it was some sort of undercover operation, although I couldn't imagine how it would work. Surely the gang members themselves wouldn't be fooled by a disguise—they would know who was in and who was out. Still, he suddenly seemed too proper underneath all that mess, his teeth too white and his speech too cultured.

"Are you a cop?" I asked.

He stared at me for a second before laughing so loud the other guys looked over. He whooped for a minute before catching his breath. "She thinks I'm a cop."

Jeff turned to me, gesturing at Rico. "This clown?"

I shrugged sheepishly. "It was just a thought."

"Come on, guys," Luke said. "Back to work."

As the men settled in again, Luke sent me a half smile over the tops of their heads. Heat warmed my cheeks, though I couldn't have said whether it was embarrassment over guessing wrong about Rico—we hookers had a certain professional detection, usually—or simply being a part of a group after so long. The only place I'd ever belonged was with Henri's other girls, but I'd never felt comfortable with them. I did here, and that had everything to do with Luke.

I listened on the sidelines as they discussed what would go down tonight. It was a simple plan, though it did involve a fair amount of walking. Or running, more likely. My high heels would be impossible. I checked my pocket. Yup, still had the few hundred in cash I'd slipped there last night before leaving for the club. We had passed a boutique in the lobby. They had mostly artsy clothes, but almost anything would be better than these heels.

Luke caught me with my hand on the knob. "Where are you going?"

I pointed to my shoes. "These aren't exactly active-wear." I reconsidered. "Well, I suppose that depends on the activity. But it sounds like there's going to be some full-fledged jogging, and these heels aren't going to cut it. I'm going to check the gift shop to see if they have something better."

"Wait, she's coming with us?" Rico askcd, incredulous.

I felt myself pout. I thought I'd made friends with

that one.

"No way," Jeff said.

Jerk. The gold earring should have been my first clue.

Major frowned at Luke, waiting for his response. The room grew quiet, the men watchful. I waited along with them, unsure of my place. Luke had told me I could go, but his reluctant promise given when we were alone faded in front of the complicated planning and camaraderie of these men.

"She's coming," Luke said.

I breathed a sigh of relief. Despite their earlier objections, both Rico and Jeff shrugged and turned back to their planning. Only Major's eyes narrowed a bit, as if he might veto the decision. I wondered if he had that power. I tried to look innocuous. Shit, I had no idea how to seem innocuous.

Luke slanted me a look. "Are you scared of him?"

"Who?" I asked innocently.

"Major."

"No, why, are you looking to do a three-way? Because I'm game for it, but you have to be in the middle. I'm allergic to all that brooding."

He shook his head, muttering to himself, "Why do I even ask?" Then to Major, "Take her downstairs."

"Wait a minute," I said. "Why is he taking me?"

"Because you're being hunted in this city, and he will make sure you don't get shot in the head."

"Okay, fair point. But why can't you take me?"

"Because it would be distracting, and I'd probably end up having sex with you in a changing room."

I bit my lip. "I'm still waiting for the downside."

"Go."

Major brushed past us, muttering, "Come on. Let's get this over with."

CHAPTER THREE

"OH, THIS'LL BE fun," I said, stepping into the boutique.

We had quickly determined that unless I wanted an I Heart Chicago T-shirt or strappy sandals with bulbous gems, the hotel gift shop wasn't going to cut it. Which meant we'd hit the street, just an anonymous guy and girl out for a stroll. No one would know that he despised me. No one would know it actually hurt to be rejected by one of Luke's friends—just another way we didn't fit.

I tried on a purple cowboy hat and posed. "How do I look?"

Major's expression was flat. "Like a gay stripper."

"So…not that far off."

A woman brushed up against me as she left the store, and I recognized her from the hallway with Luke. She sent me a scathing look before leaving the store in a huff.

"What's her problem?" Major muttered.

"She saw me with Luke earlier. She probably thinks I'm a hooker or something." I snickered. She'd lose her shit if I told her it was true.

"Well, she was totally checking you out."

"Thank you," I said, feeling vindicated.

We walked out onto the sidewalk—or rather, he strode while I hobbled on my heels, feet aching, struggling to keep up in the crowd. As bodyguards went, he left something to be desired.

A block later found us in a runner's shop. From the window we could see tennis shoes and workout clothes—perfect. We started to go inside but were blocked by runners exiting en masse. They took off like a swarm down the sidewalk in some sort of group-run activity.

"Wow," I said, watching them go.

Major snorted. "Someone will probably twist their ankles on the sidewalk."

"You remind me of someone. Eeyore, that's who."

He held the door open for me. "He speaks the truth."

"He's a downer," I said, brushing past.

He joined me by the shoe wall. "If we were doing character profiles, you'd be Winnie-the-Pooh."

"You say that like it's an insult. You do realize he's the star of the show?"

The shoe salesman waved to us. "Be just a minute."

"We'll be waiting," I said.

The salesman blushed because, yeah, my voice had been low and suggestive. Professional hazard.

Major spoke out the side of his mouth. "Winnie-the-Pooh is annoying. The other animals just let him get away with stuff because he's cute. And kinda dumb."

"Oh, very subtle. How do you even know about him? You have kids or something?"

He snorted. "No kids. Everyone knows Winnie-the-Pooh. He's been around since the Great Depression."

"You would know," I muttered, right before the salesman ran over to us. He literally ran. It seemed a little overenthusiastic, even for a running store.

"Welcome to Ralph's Running Mart," he said breezily. "What kind of racing gear are you in the market for today?"

Major glowered.

I cleared my throat. "I think just ordinary tennis shoes for me."

"Oh, we don't sell tennis shoes, ma'am. Our shoes are specifically designed with runners in mind."

"Get her some shoes," Major growled.

The poor guy seemed to be shrinking in on himself, though perhaps that was because Major seemed to be expanding, filling the space around us as if his annoyance were a balloon and the salesman kept blowing and blowing.

I smiled brightly. "Don't mind him. I'm looking for something simple. In fact, what's your simplest shoe?"

"Well," the salesman said. "Before we can get to the shoe-selection process, we need to get your stats."

"I'm a size seven," I said.

"Actually, this will be far more accurate."

The salesman led us a few feet away to a machine in the corner. The large metal base had feet stickers where my feet should go, handles along the sides to hold on to, and a large monitor that took a variety of inputs about lifestyle, dietary choices, and workout habit. It looked like some sort of arcade dance game that had gotten drunk on wheatgrass. He patted the side.

"Take off your socks and shoes and hop on. Don't be shy."

"Yeah, I'm not doing that."

The salesman blinked as if no one had ever refused it before, which I found hard to believe.

Major smiled. "Ready for me to handle it?"

"Yes, please."

Within fifteen minutes, we were headed back to the hotel. I had already changed into my new clothes: size-seven cross-training sneakers, black yoga pants and matching top, and a black hoodie. I still had my money in the bottom of my shoe. Major had insisted on paying for the clothes, which I fought until he told me the money was Luke's. So I let him do it but didn't think too hard about what that meant. Luke wasn't the type to think I owed him anything for the money. It was me who would feel beholden.

"You realize we're matching," I told Major.

He looked pained. "We're not matching. I happen to be wearing black, as are you."

"Yeah, but we're walking together. Everyone thinks we're a couple."

"Well, we're not," he snapped. "You're with Luke. You should act like it."

That shut me up. We walked the rest of the way in silence.

In the elevator, he sighed. "I guess I went beyond Eeyore and straight to asshole."

Pretty much. His words had bothered me more than I wanted to admit. The problem wasn't whether I was with Luke or not. I had no idea what it meant to be a couple. I didn't know how to act any differently if we were. The surface problems like Henri's and Luke's jobs were conveniently keeping us apart, but the truth was, even without them, we wouldn't work. I wasn't built for a relationship. I only knew how to be the other woman.

The elevator hovered to a stop. I shrugged, staring straight ahead and willing the doors to open.

"I'm sorry," he said. "I just don't want to see Luke hurt."

"So then keep him away from me."

His eyebrows rose a little. "Is that really what you want?"

"That's what you want. You and Rico and probably Jeff too. I'm not really a stuffed bear with cotton for brains. I know you guys don't want me with him."

"We're just worried about him. He deserves to have this go right. A real shot at happiness."

"Well, I can't be his reward, okay? That's too much pressure, and I'll fuck it up anyway. I'm just a messed-up girl with nowhere else to go. So don't put that on me, like I can save him or something."

The elevator door opened, and Luke stood there.

"I was just coming down to check on you guys," he said, his face blank. I couldn't get a read on how much he'd heard, if anything.

Major stalked past him. "Operation buy shit for your girlfriend is a success."

Luke turned back to me. "See, he got the girlfriend memo."

"Is he always so cheery?" I asked sourly.

"Actually, yes," Luke said, sounding thoughtful. "That last was downright playful. For him, anyway. I think you amused him."

"Oh, well, as long as the men are entertained, I suppose I have done my job."

He speared me with a dark look before turning to my clothes, his clinical gaze raking over my body. "These look nice. Comfortable."

"You're wondering how my ass looks in these yoga pants, aren't you?"

"And praying there's a God."

"I don't know about God, but I'm feeling merci-ful." I sashayed down the hall in front of him, letting him drink his fill.

Chapter Four

B ACK IN THE suite, the men all split up into separate bedrooms. We had a few hours before it was time to leave. We were supposed to be resting, but Luke was far too tense. He kept looking over the old schematics of the Barracks, even though our entry and exit routes were well laid out.

"Come here." I patted the bed. "I'll rub your shoulders."

He hesitated before throwing down the papers and lying on the bed. I climbed onto his back, and he groaned.

I laughed. "I haven't even started yet."

His words were muffled in the sheets. "But I have."

With gentle strokes, I rubbed some of the knots out of his shoulders and back. I knew his mind was on what we were going to do in a few hours, but I felt some of the worry leave his mind as the tension drained from his body. But like an electrical current, the worry seemed to flow from him to me. Our opening moves were pretty well decided, but what happened at the end? It seemed vague, which I had first assumed was because we couldn't predict Henri's reactions. Still, a question lingered.

"So assuming we get in quietly and you do arrest him. How are you going to explain that to your boss?"

It was quiet.

"Luke?"

"I'm not planning to arrest him, Shelly."

Which meant… "I thought you were joking about shooting him on first sight."

"I was. I'm going to talk to him first." He struggled to sit up.

I moved off him. "You're going to talk to him. And then shoot him. That's…that's…"

"Murder," he supplied.

"Not legal. I was going to say that's not legal."

"I told you I've done worse than you thought."

Despite his glib words, he spoke with a solemn intensity. This affected him deeply, his long-standing adherence to the rules not so easily discarded.

"If I arrest him, he'll just walk. You know that. And even if by some miracle he ended up in jail, he would be able to organize things from there. At a minimum, that would mean putting a hit out on you, on Ella."

"On you too."

"I've spent twelve years of my life fighting for the law to take him down. It hasn't. It won't. This is the only way."

The words were eerily familiar. This was the only way. Everyone wanted Henri dead, but no one had the guts enough to do it. Not Jade, not Marguerite. Not even me, only Luke. But I wondered how much it would cost him. I wondered where his breaking point was, and whether this was beyond it.

On impulse I pressed a kiss to the back of his hand. Feeling silly, I glanced up. His eyes glowed surprise and approval in the dim late-afternoon light. This close, I could see the gold-and-black striations through the deep green. I had a sudden premonition than this would be the last sight I'd ever see.

I shivered.

"Are you cold? Come lie down. We have a couple hours." Despite his casual words, none of the intensity had faded. He observed me with an almost cruel glint in his eyes.

But I knew him better. He felt the same pull of fate, the same inevitability. It had always been coming to this.

I kissed him, infusing the touch with all the love I couldn't say. I couldn't be a proper girlfriend for him, but God, I could do this. I undressed him slowly, carefully, my dreams unfolding with each touch, my hopes flayed open with each caress. His body fit him perfectly—strong and lean. He had faced down immeasurable challenges but known hunger. I kissed and nipped and sucked every part of him I found beautiful, learning the ones that brought him the most pleasure. Then I settled between his legs and filled my throat with him, drank my fill of him, and soothed him softly until he fell into a loose-slung sleep. Only then did I feel comfortable in the nook of his arm, basking in the warmth of his satisfaction.

I woke up ten minutes before the alarm was set to go off. Stumbling out of bed, I rinsed my face and went outside to the sitting area of the suite. The only one there was Jeff. He stood at the window, staring out with a brooding expression. I wondered if he was nervous about what we were going to do.

He turned when I came out. "Hey."

"Hey back. Couldn't sleep?"

His expression was sheepish. "Maybe Rico was right about the caffeine."

I laughed, heading to the minibar. "Oh man, you guys drank all the water."

"Well, you scared us with that stuff about dirty glasses." He lifted the bottle he held, cap gone but mostly full. "Here, I'm good. You can have the last one."

"Thanks, Jeff." I took a drink. "You're a gentleman."

He blushed pink. Endearing, despite the fake tough-guy act. Men with earrings always acted like they were great lovers, although they knew they really weren't. But hey, who was I to judge? We were all overcompensating for something.

He joined me at the table. "What about you—nervous?"

"I guess it hasn't sunk in yet. Feels kind of surreal. I mean, if things go well, I might be free of him by this time tomorrow. And if things don't go right…" I shuddered. "Probably best not to think about that."

"I know Luke's going to do everything he can to keep you safe."

I took a swig. "What if it's him I'm worried about?"

"Don't. He tends to land on his feet."

"You've known him a long time, then?"

"Forever," he said. "Since we were kids."

If they'd known each other since they were kids, then that meant he'd seen Luke's hard life. It meant Jeff probably had a story of his own. In fact, if they'd both been on the street together… "You weren't a…"

"A rent boy?" He snorted. "Not likely. I don't have the face for it, even if I… Well, no. I did other stuff to get by. Mostly beating up anyone who got in our way. We all had our parts to play."

I considered that. "So what can you tell me about Luke? Besides the feet-landing thing." Jeff looked away, far into the distance, though I couldn't tell whether it was the past or the future.

"He's a good guy. I mean, a really good guy. If you ever feel like you need to doubt him, you don't have to."

"Hmm. This sounds like the beginnings of another intentions speech."

"A what?" he asked blankly.

"Both Rico and Major gave me one. *What are your intentions where Luke is concerned? Don't hurt him, or you answer to us.* That sort of thing."

Jeff chuckled. "Luke's a big boy. If he's with you, I'm sure it's because he wants to be." He shrugged. "I gave up trying to control the future a long time ago."

"I hear that. Sometimes you just gotta ride it out."

He granted me a half smile, making him look boyish. "Pun intended?"

"Always." I tilted the water bottle to offer the last inch. When he shook his head, I inclined my head in thanks. "To riding it out," I said in a toast before downing the rest.

Luke came out of the bedroom and yawned. "Are you corrupting Jeff too?"

"Hardly." I went over and curved against his side. "I've been on my best behavior."

"See now, I wasn't even worried until you said that."

I started to laugh, but it became a little watery. I turned my face into his shirt, and he hugged me back.

Chapter Five

THE CRUNCH OF gravel sounded loud in my ears. The men had earpieces, but they weren't made for smaller ears, nor was I familiar with using them.

Besides, as Luke was fond of telling me, my job was to stay near him. Stay near Luke. Boy, had he drilled that into my head. Stay near Luke, and if something went wrong, stay near Major. I suppose the other guys came next in the "stay near" directive. But if things got that bad, I was probably fucked anyway. That part Luke hadn't said, but it had been in the grim set of his mouth, the veiled look in his eyes when he'd asked me one more time to stay back.

He couldn't have made me. I was tired of running. Like Marguerite had said, I ended up hurt either way. At least this time, I had a shot. *Make it count.*

Luke and Major were stuck with me, while the other two men circled around. There were several parts of the plan referred to as redundancy, and I chose not to overanalyze situations where we might need that. I would be fine, and more importantly, Luke would be fine. One day this would all just be a funny story that we never, ever told anyone.

As we approached the compound, we didn't see any signs of life, which somehow scared me worse. I leaned away from the trees, as if Henri's men were waiting there, ready to jump out and shoot us. I had seen evil in my life, but usually it was in plain sight—most often right on top of me, pushed inside me, with its hand fisted in my hair. It was the quirk of cruel lips when my teacher met my father at parents' night and told him how well behaved I had been. I wasn't used to this subterfuge, to shadows that moved and sounds without a source, and I found I did not like them.

Which was confirmed when we heard the squawk of a handheld radio nearby, and I almost squeaked in response. Luke pushed me back into a corner, then Major covered us both, like shields made of flesh and bone. The other two men were entering at a different entry point on the perimeter.

The guys slowly came closer, and I could see the red light of a cigarette. I watched the light bob in his hand, bouncing with his step.

We were not actually hidden from sight, tucked against a cutout of the building. If it were broad daylight out, we would be completely visible. But our dark clothes melded with the shadows, and so we would be missed. Probably. Except I was the only one who could see the guys and the red pinprick of light.

Luke held his body against mine, his arms holding me in, his breath light against my ear. Major was holding him in, facing me, with his breath brushing faintly against my other ear from over Luke's shoulder, so it looked like we were getting that threesome after all.

The two guards were maybe five feet away from us. If the guys noticed us, if they shot at us, Major and Luke could be dead before either of them realized they were exposed. Would they even hear anything? A slight scuff in the gravel as one of them raised his gun to aim. A high-pitched whine as the bullet zoomed near. Or maybe they'd just go down. One minute giving full-body hugs, the next—lights out.

I had known we were risking our lives here. That was what euphemisms like *fighting chance* and *get your hands dirty* really meant, after all—kill or be killed. So aside from the abject terror, I was feeling very suave and sexy about the whole thing. I had actually been shot before. Had Luke or Major been shot before? I didn't know. Which meant I might have been the badass of the group, even if I didn't get to have an earpiece. I did, however, have my gun in a holster at my side. That had been Major's last stand. I could come, he agreed, but I had to be armed.

I liked him better after that.

I watched the guys come closer, drawing crazy red circles in the dark, like some sort of screen saver reenactment. My heart pounded; my throat was dry. My breathing sounded like a racehorse, and I thought they must have heard it. They must have seen the whites of my eyes, because Lord knew I was staring, frozen, unable to blink or look away. The two men in front of me were crouched over me, shielding my body with theirs, but I felt protective of them.

"Shhh." A breath of a sound. Luke's hands ran down my arms, softly, lightly.

I didn't need his comfort. I needed him to stay alive. I should tell him to stop, but I was petrified, about to break down bawling, so I just stood there and shivered as Luke pressed a kiss to my temple.

"Almost," he said, so quietly I almost couldn't hear him. Just the sound, like a hiss but soothing. Almost what? Almost over, I guessed, but it wasn't. This was only the beginning. We weren't even inside yet.

"Hey," the smoker said, waving his cig. "When the fuck do we have to get back?"

"A few minutes."

"I'm so tired of that shit. At least out here, I can breathe."

More waving of the red light. I was like a cat with a laser pointer, watching with bated breath.

The other guy coughed pointedly. "Maybe you can, but I can't breathe for shit with all this smoke in the air. Jesus Christ, put that thing out."

"Fuck you. Maybe if you had a drag, you'd stop being so uptight."

"Excuse me if I don't want to get my ass chewed out today."

"Yeah, yeah, or maybe you're looking to get a piece of ass. The amount of fucking time you spend with that girl. You probably spend half your paycheck."

"Do I complain about where you stick your dick?"

One red circle, another. "I'm just saying this for your own good."

"Yeah, well, for your own good, put that fucking light out. If someone sees us, we'll get docked for being unsafe. And you'll be paying me back for it."

A snort. "So you can spend it on, what's her name, Candace?"

The red light lifted. The guy took a long drag, then blew out just as slow, taking a final hit.

He flicked the cigarette. It flew in a long red arc. It only took a second for my fevered, oxygen-deprived brain to figure out where it would land. On us. Almost anyway, but it was enough—I tensed. Luke felt it, and through him, Major did too. They turned, ready to strike, to defend us against an attack that wasn't coming. And in doing so, their defense would expose us. With one hand, I grabbed Major's wrist, the one pressing against the wall by my head. *Trust me.* With the barest breath, I said, "Wait," and I knew Luke heard me because his body stilled.

The little red cigarette landed at our feet, creating a small glare on Luke's shoe. Luckily, the men were already heading the other direction. When their footsteps had faded and fifty-two beats had passed, Major blew out a breath. "Jesus," he muttered. "That was too fucking close. Next time we run into someone, we don't sit around like ducks. We disarm them."

"We're too wired," Luke countermanded. "We almost blew our positions because of a fucking cigarette."

"I would have got them."

For the first time, I approved of the arrogance in Major's voice. I needed some of that surety.

"We stick to the plan," Luke said, and that appeared to be that.

The word *airport* was really overselling the Barracks. It was actually a set of five hangars, each with a small circuit of offices in the back. The hangars were organized into a pentagon, facing a circular pavement that led out to a singular runway.

The design of the place was simplistic, which would work in our favor. The downside was that we didn't know which hangar Henri would be in. If we went busting into the wrong ones, we would set off alarms, and Henri would have time to bolt. So it was important that we find the right hangar before going in.

Which is why they'd brought gadgets. Specifically, heat-sensing goggles.

The building next to us was completely empty. One down, four to go.

We crept around the side, where Major checked out the next one. "Four below, two upstairs doing the horizontal tango."

"Having fun there?" Luke asked.

"Nothing like infrared voyeurism to make my night brighter."

"Let's go in," Luke said.

"We don't know he's in there."

"Six people total? Those are good odds. And we're here. Let's go."

"Five," I whispered.

"What?"

"Five that could be Henri. Those are the odds. I'm assuming Major saw an old-fashioned boy-girl party upstairs, which means one of them is female."

"Shit, that could be him," Major said. "Having a good time while his hired helpers do all the work."

"How was he taking her?" I asked.

"What?"

"The position," I muttered impatiently. "What position was she in?"

"Uh…missionary."

"Not Henri," I said decisively. Neither man questioned my conclusion.

"He could still be on the first floor," Luke said.

"Here. Let me see." I reached for the goggles. "Come on."

With clear reluctance, Major handed them over. I peered inside. It took me a couple of minutes to line up my eyesight correctly and then to make sense of the blue-red blobs on the screen. I checked the two upstairs first. Yup, still going at it. And nope, no way would Henri resort to something as intimate or leveling as missionary. Besides, he was an ass man.

I lowered the goggles to the second floor. First I only saw a single mass, like some sort of a shapeless amoeba. Then one separated and shrank a little—sitting down, I guessed. Another moved away—and sat. I pictured guys gathered around a break-room table, talking shit and grabbing a beer.

Henri wasn't here. Even if their specific activities were slightly different, no man was singled out from the crowd, held away as Henri preferred to be. This was the disorganized chaos of jacks and marbles. Henri ruled the space around him with the rigidity of a chessboard.

"Not here," I said.

"How do you know?" Major asked impatiently.

I really didn't want to have to explain the marbles-and-chessboard thing to him. He'd just give me that frowny look and tell me I was stupid again.

"He just isn't."

Major looked ready to argue, but Luke cut him off with a glance. "Next."

Two down, three to go.

Chapter Six

THE MIDDLE HANGAR was the trickiest, because people were milling around. My heart began to race. Most likely this was it, if only because of the activity outside. I counted four men carrying machine guns. There didn't seem to be any urgency to their movements—which meant our entry wasn't detected—but energy crackled in the air. As if they were waiting.

This time Luke and I hung back while Major checked out the building with the goggles. "Too many to get an accurate count," he said when he got back. "But I'm estimating twenty total."

Twenty of them, three of us. And I probably shouldn't even have counted myself, compared to these guys. Two and a half. Could the situation get any worse?

"There's another problem," Luke said. "Rico isn't responding."

"Shit," Major said.

"Yeah, shit. You heard him when he got inside the fence, right? Then nothing. We've made it past two buildings now, and he hasn't reported in about a single one."

"What do we do?" I asked.

"We follow the plan," Luke said grimly. "We've found the right hangar. Now we go in."

"Redundancy." I felt light-headed.

"Keep breathing," he told me. Then to Major, "You stay with her. I'll go in."

"That wasn't the plan."

"Well, in the plan we had two teams, one to keep watch outside, one to go in. Since there's only two of us, that means one person per team."

"Bullshit," Major said. "She can wait outside by herself. If anyone comes close, shoot them in the fucking face. We'll hear the shot and come get you."

"No," I said. "I want to confront Henri. You said I would be able to."

"It's not a good idea," Major said, his voice oddly gentle, as if I might break.

Maybe I was shaking a little. "That's why I'm here. I know I'm slowing you guys down, but it will all be for nothing if I don't at least try. If he dies before he calls off the hit on me and Ella, we're screwed. You know that."

Luke looked away, the moonlight drawing long shadows over his eyes. "Okay. We all go in."

We waited until the side of the building was clear and then crept to the back. The night air felt suddenly as thick as fog, as rich as butter. The light beaming down on us from the stars seemed blinding, even though I couldn't quite make out anything.

I felt invincible.

"That's the adrenaline talking," Luke muttered, and I realized I had spoken aloud. "Don't let it go to your head."

Right, adrenaline. Except it already was in my head, in my body, rushing through my veins like a sweet hit of coke. I had done drugs a few times. There were men who wanted to get high and wanted the girl to ride it with them. The crash at the end had never been enough to make me want to repeat the experience without a paycheck to help me bounce back.

This racy, jittery feeling was just like shooting up. I wondered if adrenaline had a crash at the end too. But who cared when it felt this good? It felt surreal, and that kept me safe.

We crept through the quiet hallways. Where was everyone?

Major motioned with his hand. Up the stairs.

We started to climb when Luke paused. He put a hand to his ear. "Shit," he muttered.

"I love it when you say that during sex."

Major gave me a strange look.

"Not you," I assured him.

He rolled his eyes. "You *are* flying high."

"Almost," I whispered.

Luke pressed a hand to his ear, listening. "They need backup," he whispered. "Major, you go."

Major firmed his lips, as if he wanted to protest. But he didn't have a choice. With a salute and a faint look of regret in his eyes, he was gone.

"Come on." Luke waved me to follow him.

We crept down the hallway, hearing men and women moan and groan and cry out in questionable pleasure.

He looked back at me.

I shook my head. Henri didn't moan. He shouted. And anyway, I didn't really expect to find him in these upper rooms. He rarely took his prostitutes to bed. This wasn't a party to him, unlike Major had thought. This was business. This whole setup was too dirty, too common for him. Despite that, I couldn't shake the eerie feeling, as if he would be here, exactly where he would never be. It didn't make sense, but I wanted the feeling to go away. I wanted to see Rico and Major and Jeff again.

"Downstairs," I mouthed.

Luke nodded his agreement, and we slid along the wall the way we'd come.

From the stairwell came the raucous sound of male laughter and female giggling. I looked back and saw nothing but rows of doors. Trapped. Their footsteps climbed the staircase, banging along the sides, as they tumbled about in wild sexual abandon. At least he did. Her laughs were obviously fake, way too high-pitched and evenly spaced. They reached the top landing. I held my breath. Then it was pushed out of me in a whoosh as Luke slammed me inside the closest room.

He was on me, pulling off my clothes. My hand

SKYE WARREN

was caught, but it didn't matter—he yanked it free, the whole shirt whipping over my head along with my bra, tumbling my hair from its ponytail. I gasped into his mouth, trying to catch up, but I couldn't. He was moving too fast, climbing onto the bed, dragging my body beneath his as if I were prey and he a tiger gone in for the kill. His mouth glued itself to mine, taking away any sound as he settled between my legs, the hard ridge of his erection a blatant message that his lips hadn't had time to speak. He rocked against me, and it hurt. I wasn't ready, wasn't aroused, but already my body prepared itself to receive him, well practiced in this, growing wet and swollen, supple flesh to be speared repeatedly. His hands were all over me, my waist, my arms, my sides—but not my breasts.

The door slammed open, and two very drunk, possibly high people stumbled into the room. Luke finally released me, looking up. I panted audibly.

"*Ocupado*," Luke said in a guttural tone.

"Sorry, man," the guy said. They both backed out of the room, closing the door behind them.

We collapsed on the bed for long minutes after they left.

"Okay," I said, still panting. "I see what you did there."

He let out a breath. "He's not in this building, is he?"

"Don't think so." I felt a little woozy. The ceiling made lazy swirls above us, like a big upside-down bowl of batter. Allie was a baker. She loved to bake all sorts of things. I wasn't as good as her, but under her direction, I could whip up a batch of cookies. That's what this looked like, chocolate caramel cookies with streaks of beige and dots of black. Or was that the exposed pipes in the ceiling? It was hard to say. And all these thoughts about food were making me want to throw up.

"Damn." Luke's voice sounded far away. "I just assumed because there were so many. We've got to try the next one."

"Okay. Have fun."

There was a long pause. "What?"

Right. We were going now. I was sitting up…pretty sure. I stood and took a step forward and ended up slumping over in a graceless heap.

Luke caught me and hauled me back onto the bed. "Jesus, Shelly."

"That's not my name." My words were slurred.

"It wasn't just the adrenaline, was it? Oh fuck. What did you do? What did you take?"

"Don't know."

He was still talking to me, but all the sounds were like mush in my ears.

I opened my mouth to speak; I didn't know if anything came out. Until I threw up, and then stuff came out all over the floor—that came out of my mouth.

Luke was there, behind me, supporting me, talking to me, saying urgent words that washed over me. I wanted to go to sleep. Didn't he see that? I was tired. But then, bless him, he did understand. He tucked me into his arms and told me to close my eyes, don't make a sound. Hah! As if I could. Nope, I would be right here. He carried me for what felt like hours, days, or maybe just seconds, and tucked me into the backseat of the SUV we had parked a mile outside the compound. But what about the other guys?

"Just wait here," he said, and yes, I could do that. I closed my eyes and slept.

CHAPTER SEVEN

THE FIRST THING that registered was the shaking. I was going to vomit, rattling about like a loose bit of change. My eyelids felt heavy. I would have given up, just drifted off on the turbulent waves and crashed onto the waiting rocks, but for his voice. Not Luke.

Henri. Now I was really going to throw up.

My mouth felt like cotton as I tried to speak, to warn someone. Even though I knew it was too late. Even though I knew I was alone in the dragon's lair. Luke wouldn't be here. Not any of the men. They would have died first. Or they had let me go. Sometimes you had to give up a pawn to win the game.

I blinked, and everything came into a dreary focus, like looking out a rain-drenched window. Those weren't raindrops; they were tears. Not the healing kind, not cleansing—they fell on barren land.

Henri stared straight ahead, though I had no doubt he'd registered my waking. He was all black-suited cloth and shadows except for the glint of a ruby-colored vest. He was a smart man, but not the smartest. Strong, but not the strongest. Instead, he had an animal instinct about things of a dark and violent nature. It gave him an unnatural advantage, sustaining his position in the face of richer competitors. It must have been that, because he had been at the top since I had entered the scene.

"Where have you been, sweetheart?" he asked.

I shuddered, an involuntary response, inescapable remembrance.

There was a book in Philip's stargazing room. It said that every planet, every moon was constantly leaving orbit—and constantly pulled back by the gravitational force. I couldn't seem to escape Henri's pull; I couldn't seem to stop trying.

"With you." My tongue felt thick. "Where else would I be?"

He laughed. "That's a good answer, but it doesn't quite distract me. I thought we had an agreement."

"Luke didn't leave me. You lied."

"Of course," he said simply. "What else would I do?"

My eyes drooped shut, and my head lolled against the leather seats as the SUV started to move. He spoke to me distantly, his thick voice washing over me in waves of nausea. I tried to focus, but whatever drug was affecting me was still in my system, clouding everything, even my thoughts.

Henri was talking, telling me about an angry man and a woman caught, but all I could see in my mind was my mother's face speaking to me. She was telling me a bedtime story, I realized. Or a cautionary tale.

Had she really done that? I couldn't remember, but the picture seemed so clear, more refined now that I was drugged than it had ever been in my waking hours.

There was a king, and a queen so beautiful that none could equal her. On her deathbed, she made the king promise that he should only marry one as beautiful as she, one who had the same golden hair.

He grieved for her upon her passing but eventually scoured the land for a new wife who fulfilled his promise. Although many beautiful women were found, none could compare. The king's daughter, on the other hand, had grown into a woman. She was beautiful like her mother, with the same golden hair.

So the king decided to marry her, despite the protests of his counselors. Determined to escape her fate, the princess ran away from the castle with only her gold and dresses. She traveled far, and when night came, she hid in the hollow of a tree.

The next morning, a different king was hunting on his lands. The king's men found the girl and brought her back to the castle, setting the orphan to help in the kitchen. There she toiled each night and day, miserable and lonely, her beauty obscured by the dirt of her work.

One evening, she washed herself and joined the festivities in her old fine dress. The king was much taken with her, but at the end of the night, she disappeared back into the kitchens. She cooked the king's soup during the day and danced with him at night.

One night he slipped a ring on her finger, but again

she disappeared. The next day he demanded to meet the new cook who made the wonderful soup, and then he saw the ring on her finger. He washed the soot from her cheeks, and she was beautiful again, so he married her.

"You're mine again," Henri said. "We can put this whole thing behind us."

"Why are you telling me this?" I mumbled, though I spoke to a ghost.

"So you'll understand," he said. "This is for your own good. You are nothing without men and our desire to use you. You have nothing without me. Do you understand?"

In the story, the king had valued the princess without knowing her beauty. At the end of the story, the two parts of her were merged. At the end of the story, she finally made her escape.

"I know what you are thinking," he said. "You think your detective will save you."

There were those damn instincts again, right on the money.

"He and I have a lot in common," Henri continued. "We both appreciate a beautiful thing. We both understand the darker impulses, sometimes to curb them, other times to unleash them."

Luke wasn't like that. He had a dark past, but only out of necessity. He was a protector, not an aggressor...wasn't he? The lines had blurred for me, lumping all men together in one bloodthirsty heap.

"Oh yes. He knows…greed, lust, revenge. The last one especially."

"You're wrong." Luke didn't want material things. He didn't want revenge either. All he wanted was to protect women like me, to find his sister. Good intentions, honest ones.

"What does he want, then?" Henri mocked. "If he's so concerned about your safety, then why are you in the car with me?"

A mistake. He had been overpowered, outnumbered. Any number of excuses could explain it, without him having been hurt or having betrayed me. *Please let one of them be true.*

"Ah, yes. You see it now. I gave him the one thing he couldn't resist. The answer to all his searching. I gave him the truth about his sister. No, more than that. I gave him proof. As you and I talk, your Detective Cameron is on his way to Chicago with a tape of his sister. And me. It was rather brutal. Of course the statute of limitations has run out for rape. But he hopes to make a case for murder, considering she is presumed dead and I am shown hurting her. He isn't going to win. But you can understand the temptation."

"I've spent twelve years of my life fighting for the law to take him down."

Yes, Luke would do anything to nail Henri. It wasn't just that he wouldn't have to kill him. It was a question of principle. This was the system he had lived and breathed for the past decade. If it failed him, then all his work was for nothing. But to leave me here?

"It was a simple trade," said Henri. "You for the tape. If it is any consolation, he struggled with the decision. It pained him to leave you here; I could see that."

Tears streamed down my cheeks, but at least I didn't have to see Henri and the gloating on his face.

He stroked my hair back. "Shh, calm yourself. I won't kill you. Nothing will happen to you here that hasn't happened before."

Chapter Eight

THE BEST THING about being a hooker is the job security. In a good year, men had plenty of spending money. To a wealthy man, a prostitute might be a smart financial move—certainly cheaper than a high-maintenance girlfriend who rarely puts out. But even in a down economy, the stress and scattered families kept prostitutes in demand. Men would use any excuse to fulfill their biological urges.

In other words, they were always, always down to fuck.

The worst thing about being a hooker was also the job security...as in, the locks on my door and the guards I could see from my window. In the years I had worked for Henri, I had always lived in my own place and kept it sacrosanct, never bringing clients home, always traveling to out-call appointments in swanky hotels.

Then I had quit. When that didn't work, I went rogue, taking Ella with me. And finally, I'd tcamed up with men who broke into his little fortress and generally wreaked havoc. Unsurprisingly, he didn't trust me anymore—thus the need for security.

They had brought me here after the night at the Barracks, to a crumbling apartment building in south Chicago. The men who escorted me were firm but not brutal. Never mess up the goods—unless on orders. So I was Henri's girl again. He wouldn't let me go this time.

Hell, he never really had.

One week of sitting in this room, waiting for Henri to bestow his sentence on me. Would I live or die? Though my odds looked significantly worse after last night. They had sent a client in.

I had threatened to bite off his dick if he touched me.

He had requested another girl for his hour.

I'd felt triumphant for all of five minutes. Then I heard the banging against the wall and deflated. There was a certain amount of suffering in the world. I could take it upon myself or leave it for others to endure. Standing up for myself was supposed to make me stronger, but this felt cowardly.

Still, I was surprised I hadn't gotten any shit about it. In the old days, Henri would have beaten down my door within the hour, made an example of me. Now nothing? Even if he was on his way, the delay was a sign of problems, a symptom of his strange decline.

Certainly, the location of this apartment building left much to be desired, supporting the idea that his business was in trouble, that he was in a downward slide. That would have been comforting if I weren't currently tethered to him. If he drowned in the criminal mire, so would I.

The neighborhood wasn't completely abandoned, though the armed men who loitered outside the building tended to scare off most pedestrians. Every now and then, cars passed by on the street, probably keeping their doors locked and eyes straight ahead as they passed through the seedier part of town.

I imagined myself Rapunzel, sending down my long, flowing, now brown locks. Of course, for that escape plan to work, I needed a prince and—

Don't think about that.

Besides, there were burglar bars on my window and a garbage dump beneath it. Hardly the stuff of fairy tales.

A sound at the door drew my attention. Jade poked her head in, perhaps checking to see if I was going to brain her with a chair. When I had first seen her here, working for Henri, I was surprised. And then I wasn't. The sex industry was an incestuous lot. I didn't know the extent of the history between Henri and Jade, but I knew that favors were strewn like pickup sticks. And no one said no to Henri.

I didn't move from my seat at the window as she came in and set the tray down. She opened a package of saltines and put them in the canned tomato soup, stirring them around with the spoon. It was sort of sweet, aside from the whole kidnapping-and-forced-prostitution thing. She hadn't been the one to do them, but she was helping. Or maybe she was just as much a pawn in this as I was, unwilling, unthinking. Sometimes it was easier to pretend not to care. They couldn't subjugate a carved piece of marble.

"You eat," she said.

I looked out the window. A familiar rhythmic sound started up against the wall behind me. *Thump, thump, thump*—the sound of a bed frame hitting the wall, the impact of flesh hitting flesh. Henri's business may be in trouble, but there were still clients who came here to visit with the girls. I watched the men enter the building, heads down. I heard them through the walls. Even in the shitty part of town, hooking was good business. Maybe especially here.

"Now," Jade demanded.

I was a little worried about her. She looked tired, desperate—coming apart at the seams. No matter their collusion, she hated Henri. Working for him must be wearing on her.

"Come eat," she said, pleading now. "You look sick."

Hmm, maybe that would keep the clients away, if my threats and my vehemence weren't enough.

Thump, thump, thump.

Staring out the window, I spoke softly. "Why, Jade?"

Agitation rolled off her in waves. "You understand this. Business."

"You were the one who sent me after him."

"And you failed," she cried. "You were supposed to save us."

A throaty groan came from the other side of the wall, then fell silent.

"No." My whole life I had been saving people. I didn't expect gratitude—they were my sins as much as my accomplishments. But I was done with that. "I can't save anyone."

"You change mind."

Jade frowned at me one last time, the wrinkles in her face crowding out her eyes.

"Henri come today. Don't give him more reasons to punish you."

She turned and left.

So he was finally coming to deal with the problem child. I continued to stare outside as a car rolled by. A flash of green eyes caught my eye in the window. I started in my seat before realizing they were the eyes of a kid, his nose pressed to the glass.

A black Escalade pulled into the parking lot across the street. Two men in suits emerged from the front seats, then one, slightly shorter, from the back, his gold-scrolled vest glinting off the sun. Henri.

I remained in my seat by the window, though I could no longer pretend to be unaffected. My heart raced; my teeth clenched. It was facing down an army, naked and bound. Not a question of pain but how much. No doubt of failure but how far.

As usual, two men preceded him. They pulled me

up from the chair, flanking me on either side. Their fingers were like iron bands cutting into my arms.

Without looking at me, Henri strolled to the window. He looked out at the pitiful display and snorted.

"This would never have happened if you had stayed put, you realize."

If he blamed me for his turn in fortune, he was delusional…and giving me far more credit than I deserved. Still, it wouldn't save me. Nothing could, in the face of his wrath.

He pulled a gun out. With a handkerchief, he wiped the barrel of the weapon. He was a showman, and so was I.

"Why are you doing this?" My voice shook.

He looked over at me, his mouth a flat line. "You can do better than that, Shelly."

"Please," I whispered, not knowing whether the plea was real or fake, finally realizing it didn't matter at all. When I said the words, they became real. When I lived the lie, it became me.

He pointed the gun at my chest.

This was it. I swallowed hard. There was no escape, no one to distract him. Nothing at all to barter with. He knew I'd never work for him again. My body was useless to him, my mind hardened against him. My life, forfeit.

The metal was cold. His eyes were cold. What a mess it would make.

"Why her?" I whispered.

"Why you?" he said. "Eat or get eaten. That is the choice we all face. Look at Jade. She was one of you before. The prey. Now she is like me. Predator."

But Jade didn't look like a predator. She looked hunted. There was another way out. Marguerite had done it. She was neither predator nor prey but her own person, one of pride and mercy, and she didn't conform to Henri's animal kingdom. She operated outside of it, tearing down its structures with her very presence.

"You're wrong," I said, a little stronger. Because I could be like her, even here, facing death. Circumstances would batter me, but they wouldn't break me.

As if to prove me right, he told the men, "Let her go."

I was sure I hadn't heard him right, until they did. Both men released me, and I wobbled on my feet.

Henri held the gun out in the flat of his palm. "Take it."

My gaze slid to the guys beside me. They looked as confused as I felt, but they knew better than to question him. Unlike me.

"Why?" I challenged. "So you'll have an excuse to kill me? So you can say it was in self-defense?"

"I don't need an excuse to kill you," he said gently, as if explaining it to a child. "I'm giving you the chance to become the predator. Take it," he repeated.

Gingerly, I picked up the gun. Though I was hardly well practiced, my hands fell into the proper arrangement. Right fist around the base. Left hand pointed down. Only put your finger on the trigger when you're ready to shoot.

I aimed it at Henri's heart, finger on the trigger. The men beside me tensed. If I killed Henri, they would kill me. For some insane reason, he had put his life in my hands, but he had second-strike capabilities here. If he went down, so did I, and in that way, our fortunes were still tied together.

My hands were shaking. Marguerite wanted me to do this. So did Jade. Why did it fall to me? I wasn't strong enough. They had made a mistake putting their trust in me.

My finger tightened on the trigger. I pulled. A loud bang. The recoil.

Henri smiled. "Good girl."

Relief claimed me. A blank. It had been a blank, and Henri wasn't dead. It was perverse to wish him well, but he had already turned me into a prostitute. It was a relief that he hadn't also turned me into a murderer.

It didn't hurt that I also got to live.

Henri took the gun from my limp fingers. He turned it back to my forehead and shot—one, two, three. All blanks, though the sound was real and terrifying. Each shot sent a puff of hot air from the barrel to the center of my forehead.

I slid to the ground, a boneless, breathless puddle.

"Now that we both understand each other, we can talk." He sat down across from me, resting one ankle over his knee. There was an uncomfortable silence before he finally spoke. "Jade tells me you refuse to work. She says you haven't been eating."

I closed my eyes, struggling to gather myself. So this would be a face-off with words instead of bullets. At least this was a game I could play. "I'm not hungry."

"You're too skinny," he observed.

"That's my exit strategy. I'm going to stab you with my hip bone when you rape me."

"I like this. It shows you still have spirit."

"Since when are you concerned with my spirit?"

"Always, Shelly. I do not sell lifeless bodies. The clients do not come here to rape an unwilling woman. Well, most of them do not. That is not your value to me. They pay for you because of how you look and how you act. For who you are."

I couldn't help it. I laughed. "They don't know who I am. Neither do you."

"Not completely. That is part of the mystery. But there is something there; that much we can tell. It drives us to learn more. The men who pay five hundred dollars to sleep with you do not want a wet cunt to slide into, Shelly. They want a chance to understand what is inside you. They fail, and so they come back again and again."

"Hmm." He didn't look high, but I wasn't ruling it out.

"I am telling you this because right now you are not worth anything to me. You are dead like this."

"So, this was all an explanation for why you're going to kill me?" As if I could follow the twisty sex logic and agree with him: *yes, yes, I'm better off dead.*

He made a frustrated sound. "I do not want you dead. I do not want to break your spirit either."

I was doubtful.

"I have never tried to do that. I have never raped you either, have I?"

"You haven't," I agreed cautiously. That didn't mean he couldn't start. Certainly, holding me captive was not promising.

"I want to make a deal with you. You work for me. You don't die. In return, I will call off the cops on the girl."

I blinked. Claire.

"Well?" he asked, eyebrow raised.

"I guess…I want to say yes. I just want to know why. Why did you do it?"

"You know why. Those men threatened to tell everyone what had happened. My girls attacked them, stole from them. And maybe worst of all, left without delivering the goods. I would have been ruined. I didn't like the way they spoke to me. I sent some men over to take care of it. I blamed it on you, and the cops could run you to ground, where I'd be waiting."

"It was pretty diabolical," I admitted.

"Thank you. It would have worked, except word had already gotten out. Fucking social media. Combined with the news and the fact that my top girl had gone missing, clients started going elsewhere. Once that happened, I had cash-flow problems."

I felt a little like some sort of criminal therapist, listening to his sob story. *How does that make you feel?* I should ask. Instead I prompted, "So, the girl."

"There are two things I want. One, for you to work for me again. And two, for that bitch of a girl dead. But I will settle for the first one."

"Why did you take her at all?" I asked.

His eyes looked into the distance—into the past. "Everyone makes mistakes. Old ones that haunt you." He came back to himself. "I am not going to explain myself to a hooker. Take the deal or no."

So much for all that shit about my elusive spirit. "I'll take it."

"Good. Your first client will arrive tonight." He stood, shaking out the crease in his slacks. "That means you must eat." He turned back at the door. "And Shelly, if you do not obey me…I will track her down myself." An enigmatic smile lit his face.

Something unsavory roiled in my gut, and I hadn't even eaten the soup yet. After he left, I forced myself to eat. Two days of not eating and an entire bowl of soup left my stomach distended and sore, but I finished it as a show of obedience. It was a good deal, and one I hadn't been expecting. I had assumed I wouldn't be able to help Claire from here, at his mercy, with no leverage at all. Now I had a chance to save her, and all I had to do was the same job I had done for years.

I wasn't sure if I could. I had resigned myself to death, to rape. But consensual paid sex?

Unbearable.

There was a mirror each prostitute must wear. A man thought he was using me? No, I was using him. His physical impulses, his money. He was the one being manipulated. A woman looked down on me? No, I looked down on her. She spread her legs for free. She was the cheap one. The mirror was a shield, and mine was gone, shattered by a few brief hours of true happiness, of real sex, of realizing that the only person I was tricking was myself.

But I had to do it, for Claire. For myself, because this was the goal I had set, to protect her as no one had done for me.

I watched from the window as Henri and a few other men walked to the black Escalade across the street and took off. The door opened, and I turned, expecting Jade. Instead it was Jenny, from the hotel suite party that day. I sucked in a breath of surprise and relief. "You're alive."

She glanced down the hallway and then crept inside. Her step was unsteady, pupils dilated. I wondered if she'd been the one I'd heard through the wall, getting banged. I wondered if she had even felt it, as high as she probably was, though it was for the best if she couldn't.

"I can't stay long," she mumbled. "I have an appointment."

I held her hand. It was shaking. "What is it?"

"I heard what Henri told you. Don't believe him."

A sick feeling turned my stomach. Of course it would be foolhardy to trust someone like Henri, but in this position, I didn't really have a choice. "Why not?" I managed.

"That's the same deal he made with me." She shuddered. "My…my boyfriend stole money from him, too much to pay back. Henri promised he would forget his debts if I agreed to work for him."

I could guess where this story led. "And?"

"And he shot him, right in front of me. I've been hooking for him ever since."

CHAPTER NINE

I KEPT THE tomato soup down, but barely. When dinner came, I almost threw up from the smell of grilled chicken alone. Jade relented and took it away. I showered and shaved and put on makeup that came standard with each room. The same garish colors for every girl, the same skimpy clothes. I dressed with a lacy black bra and matching thigh-high stockings, a black silk sheath and high heels. Rituals I had done countless times, but they didn't steady my mind this time.

They didn't numb me.

A silver Jaguar parked in the lot across the street, conspicuous in its luxury. Men had streamed in and out all day long for other women. But I suspected this one was for me. If Henri was going to make a deal like that, he must have lined up some heavy hitters. I would be his road back to the top, the star of the show, motherfucking Winnie-the-Pooh.

A man dressed in all black crossed the street with long strides. I waited, imagining him stepping inside the darkened door, paying Jade at the front desk, being escorted up the stairs. I imagined his wife waiting for him at home, wondering why their sex life sucked. Or maybe she was relieved.

Footsteps approached down the hallway.

"This one," I heard Jade say through the door, and then it opened.

A man. Of course it was a man, but it took me a second to recognize him out of context, as he was wearing a sleek business suit. I barely stopped myself from saying his name.

Major.

Jade must have caught the recognition in my eyes. "You know him?"

I forced myself to shrug. "An old friend."

At least it felt like a million years ago. I felt older too, or maybe just wiser.

She knew I meant client, but her eyes narrowed. This was my first client since my kidnapping, after all. If I screamed rape, they'd have a hell of a time keeping it quiet. At some point, they couldn't kill every client who talked shit about them. It was bad for business.

We kept to our roles, though. Major with raw lust in his eyes. Me bored and mildly fearful. We must have been convincing, because Jade nodded and shut the door.

I opened my mouth to speak, but he gave a short shake of his head, then glanced at the door. Jade was listening.

Rising, I went to take his jacket. Before I reached him, he shrugged it off and handed it to me. I took it from him, feeling the weight and shape of a gun wrapped inside.

I raised my eyebrows. *What's this?*

He raised his back in unspoken challenge.

Okay, then. As I laid his jacket on the side table, I slipped the gun underneath the seat cushion.

"How much time do we have?" I asked in my usual voice. It was a customer question to ask at the beginning.

"Thirty minutes."

Oh, how the mighty had fallen. Once, my time had been sold by the evening. Hourly rates were available, of course. But half hour? I was a little offended. I guess a soul was worth something after all.

Major's expression was hard; his eyes glinted. Jade would have interpreted that as lust, or good old-fashioned cruelty. I knew it as tension. He was nervous, which meant I was nervous too. He glanced at the bed, then turned away and sat down in the chair Henri had used. I sat across from him.

"What…" I tried to think of something innocuous, something I would ask as an escort when all I really wanted to do was pin him to the ground and ask him if he'd heard anything in the news. "What would you like to do tonight?"

"See, I have this problem."

"You do?"

"I don't want to come too soon."

"Oh." I made a face that I hoped was sympathetic,

even though it amused me that he was using premature ejaculation as a code. He and I were cut from the same cloth.

"Right." Humor danced in his eyes. "You understand how it would be, with those urges to finish quickly. But sometimes I think it's better to go slow. Don't you agree?"

"However you want to do it," I forced out.

"How accommodating," he said, his expression sardonic. "I don't like the girl to come too quickly either. In fact, not at all while I'm here, you understand? If you need to go, you do it after I leave."

"Okay." I drew out the word, not quite sure what he meant.

"Right after I leave."

"Oh."

He stood and wandered over to the window, looking outside. He tapped lightly on the windowpane, seemingly casual. "I think it'll be a shattering climax."

It took me a second to register. He wanted me to jump out the window. Right after he left.

Oh hell, no. I shook my head frantically. "You know, I don't think I'm a shattering climax kind of girl."

He smiled wolfishly. "Tonight you will be. You'll go just the way I came."

I followed his line of sight to the Jaguar in the parking lot. I understood the plan, such as it were. I should jump out the window and head for his car. But God, this was a horrible idea. The only thing more horrible than doing it was not doing it.

"Now come to the bed, sweets. I paid a lot for my time, and I intend to walk away satisfied."

After thirty minutes of moaning for me and two hundred and forty push-ups for Major, we were ready. Jade came and knocked at the door to bring him back down. He was sweaty and panting, clothes askew. I was armed with a few more directions he'd been able to squeeze out during exhales.

I waited at the window until I heard shots fired downstairs. The men standing outside ran in, and that's when I tried the window. It wasn't locked from the outside, so after a few pushes, I managed to get it open. The bigger problem was the bars on the window. That was where the gun came in.

"Aim for the brick," he'd said, panting through his workout.

I leaned over the window, looking at the large screws that held the bars to the wall. If I blasted the bricks they were in, the whole thing would come off. Hopefully.

I took aim, squinting into the sight. Lining it up. Slowly, slowly, I pulled the trigger. Oh shit, what am I doing? I thought right before the sound of gunfire exploded in my ears.

The shell ricocheted back into my face; the gun pinged directly off metal. I ducked back into the room for a second, but the shouting from downstairs spurred me on. I peeked over the ledge and saw that the metal had bent right out of the wall.

Hah! So much for hitting the brick.

I congratulated myself on my badassery before moving to the next one. Which I missed, entirely. But there wasn't time, so I shot again and again. As the third one came off, the whole grate tilted on its axis, hanging from the last screw.

I didn't need to remove that one to get out, so I slung one leg over the window and prayed. I didn't bother with shoes, and at least the black sheath was easy to move in.

I looked down at the garbage dump. Footsteps sounded outside the door, and I jerked, almost falling headfirst out the window. The door slammed open, and I thought my heart would burst. That didn't happen, but I did pee myself—just a little.

It was Jenny, white as a sheet. "What's happening?"

"We've got to get out of here," I said.

"Okay. You jump, and I'll follow."

"Right," I said, not moving.

"Shelly," she said urgently.

I glanced down and then away. "I might have a small fear of heights."

She rolled her eyes and then pushed me.

"Wait," I cried, but it was too late. My leg scraped along the jagged edge of the bars as I fell. I landed sprawled on the lid of the Dumpster. The impact jittered up my whole body, and my teeth chattered with the agony of it. A red gash ran from the outside of my knee to the ankle.

"Move," Jenny demanded.

With shaky legs, I slid to the side and turned my face, ready to send encouragement. But by the time I called her name, she was already falling, landing in a far more graceful heap. No painful leg gashes for her.

"Well, yeah," I said. "Because you saw me go first."

She hopped onto the street beside me. "We have a plan after this?"

Damn, how had she recovered so quickly? And she looked more alert than I had ever seen. I glared at her as I stumbled onto the ground, wincing as the weight of my step shot pain up my shin.

"Come on." I took her hand, and we ran across the street. Or really, she ran. I hobbled. We crouched behind the Jaguar and peeked over the hood. No one appeared to have seen us. In fact, we couldn't see anyone at all. Everyone was inside and quiet, which meant they were either dead…or Major was.

CHAPTER TEN

I SLIPPED INTO the driver's seat, and Jenny took the passenger's. No keys. I felt around in the pockets of the car. Jenny flipped the visor down, and the keys fell on my head.

"Ouch," I said, rubbing the spot.

"Let's go," she muttered, watching the door of the complex.

"I have to wait for someone." She gave me a look, and I recoiled from the vitriol of it.

"A man?"

"The man who helped us escape," I retorted.

Her cool gaze slid to the keys in my hand, then back to me. I got the impression she was measuring me, deciding whether to take them by force. My fingers tightened on the keys as I waited.

The tension released from her in a breath as she had apparently decided to keep me around. "You better hope he comes out soon," she said, her gaze glued to the door. "If they find us, we are so fucked."

I let out a breath. "I cannot believe you were faking it all this time."

She snorted. "As if you don't."

"I don't mean orgasms. I mean pretending to be high and stupid," I said. "All the freaking time."

"We all have our masks to bear."

"You could have been straight with me. What did you think, I would go tell Henri?"

Her look was assessing. "You might have. I couldn't trust you. I still don't, but you're the one with the ticket out of here."

I touched the gash on my leg, then winced. "They really did a number on you, didn't they?"

She laughed softly. "You're one to talk."

I felt Jenny tense beside me. I looked back to see a man walking out of the building. Major.

"He's with us," I said.

Major walked across the street, focused but unhurried. When he reached the car, I climbed between the seats into the back while he got in and drove.

"You got blood on the seats," he said.

"Yes, I'm fine. Thank you for your concern," I said sarcastically, collapsing against the back. "How did you know where to find me?"

"Let's just say I have friends in low places."

"Well, you do know Shelly," Jenny said.

"That's it," I said. "I was *going* to actually help you, but since you're being rude, I'm going to sic Marguerite on you."

She scoffed. "Another pimp? Please."

"Much worse. She runs a shelter."

"A shelter?" Jenny cut in. "I don't want to go to a

shelter. Hell, no. Do I look like a poor battered woman to you?"

Major looked over at her, from her dirty, tangled hair down to her bruised arms. "This is a trick question, right?"

She crossed her arms. "I'm not going."

He looked back at me. *She's your friend. You talk to her.*

"Well, that's where we're going, so unless you're planning on doing the tuck-and-roll out of a moving vehicle, so are you. Besides, you haven't lived among regular people in years. No way are you surviving on your own."

"That's your motivational speech?" he asked me, incredulous.

I waved my hand. "I don't do positive thinking. That's what my shelter is for."

In the rearview mirror, I saw Major raise his eyebrow. "Your shelter?"

I felt heat creep up my neck. "No, not mine. I mean, I just—"

"What, like, you volunteer there or something?" Jenny asked.

"No. Definitely not."

"Spill," Major said.

I sighed, resigned to explaining my random, very nonpossessive connection to this place. Really, what did I care about them? Nope, barely at all.

"I was at the clinic to get my birth control pills and

monthly testing done. And this lady comes up to me in the waiting room, saying how I was such a beautiful soul and I didn't have to do this and she could help me live a better life."

Jenny made a disgusted sound.

"Right? So I get the hell away from her, but then I met Marguerite, who is not sweet. Honestly, she's kind of a bitch, but that's why I tolerate her. She guilted me into giving money for the girls to start new lives. Then when they got too big for the house they were using, I bought them a new building. Whatever."

"You bought them a building," Jenny repeated.

I shrugged. "By that time, I was with Philip. He's pretty generous."

"But a building?" She seemed stunned. "I have two thousand dollars stuffed inside my bra right now, which is all the money I have."

I winced. Paper cuts had never been my thing. "And that's why we're taking you to the shelter."

She spoke quietly. "I've been in hiding for the past five years, hiding inside my own body. No way am I going back to that life."

I gentled my voice. "The thing about the shelter is, they aren't hiding from life. They're living it. It took me a while to figure that out too."

She swallowed, looking scared. "Okay. I'll go."

"Good. I'll get you settled in too. It won't be so bad."

"Wait a second," she said. "After convincing me to

go to this place, you're not staying?"

"My orders are very specific," Major said. "Get you out and keep you safe until Luke can meet up with us."

"Sorry, I've got some things to take care of. Clearing my name and all that."

"I thought you knew," he said.

That sounded ominous. "Thought I knew what?"

"The police department. They've moved on. Technically, you're still wanted for questioning in connection with the crimes, but they've removed the arrest warrant on you and that other girl. You're free."

"Wow." So Henri came through for me after all.

He continued. "The cops can't justify spending their time looking for someone when everyone knows you guys aren't a threat anyway."

A small sound came from Jenny. She looked outside.

"What is it?" I asked.

"So, don't lose your shit."

"Shit." I should have known it wouldn't be that easy. "What did you do?"

"Nothing. Well, not exactly. I overheard Henri talking. Apparently he's going to talk to someone right now. Negotiating for your release."

I turned to Major. "Where exactly did you say Luke was?"

His silence was damning.

"Fuck."

"There's no way he'll actually do it," Jenny said.

"You heard him."

Yes, I had heard Henri's plans for me. More than that, I remembered Jenny's story from earlier. Henri would do anything to get even. It was the reason he was so successful. Desperate to claw his way back to the top, he wouldn't abandon his brutality now.

"Major, you know where he is."

"Goddamn it."

"Take me there. Right now." I paused. "Please."

"Luke's not going to like that," he muttered.

We drove straight to the Barracks. I spent most of the trip hyperventilating in the backseat while Major gave Jenny a kind of guided tour through Chicago. She had been incredibly sheltered under Henri's thumb and displayed a childlike excitement at every new landmark. I could tell Major was charmed. Well, Henri hadn't been an idiot. We might have been pawns, but the girls in his elite were good at what we did—making men want us.

When we got to the Barracks, Major pulled behind a copse of trees. The headlights were off, and we rolled gently over the rocky landscape.

"You guys can go," I said. "I'll go in alone."

"Hell, no," Jenny said. "If there's going to be ass-kicking, I want to be a part of it."

"No. There will be no ass-kicking for you."

She pouted. "As if you're a ninja or something."

"If you must know, I've had lessons in shooting a gun. Plus, I've been shot. It's a special club."

"A gun lesson." She sounded giddy. She turned to Major. "You mean you can teach me how to use one?"

"Your enthusiasm is disturbing but irrelevant," I told her. "We can't do a lesson now."

"I'm going," she whispered. "You can't stop me."

"Very mature."

"Look at it this way," Major murmured. "I'm going, so she's probably safer with us than alone."

We got out of the car. Every car door closing made me wince, and I waited for men to come running out. When nothing happened, I let out a breath. We crept along the line of the trees until we reached the fence. It was still cut away where we'd entered before. An odd lapse in security, but I supposed Henri had already evacuated this place for the most part. If he was just coming here for a meeting, he wouldn't need to establish a perimeter.

Slipping inside, we made it to the first hangar before Major put up his hand. He lifted his gun, signaling for us to stay back while the shadows enveloped him. I heard a low voice and then a brief scuffle. I blinked, my eyes wide, but I couldn't make him out. Pushing Jenny behind me, I was about to get us the hell out of there when Major reappeared with his arm around another man. I saw the red bandanna first, then noticed the rest of him.

"Rico," I said with relief, then realized Major was basically choking him. "What the hell?"

Rico threw Major off him and echoed my shock,

but with more profanity.

"Was it you?" Major asked. "Don't fuck with me right now; just tell me I can trust you."

Rico grew still. "You saved my ass, literally, when I was nine years old. I told you then that I had your back, and that hasn't changed."

Major stared at him, measuring, and finally blew out a breath.

"Now," Rico said. "What in the actual fuck was that?"

"Someone betrayed us," Major said.

Both men turned to look at me.

"Yes, okay," I said. "Be a stereotype and blame the hooker."

Rico frowned. "It doesn't make sense that it would be her or Luke, not with their asses on the line. And if it wasn't you or me, then…"

"It was Jeff," I said. "He must have put something in my water."

Rico shook his head in frustration. "He said you'd been shot, but we couldn't find your…" The word *body* hung in the air. "Luke was frantic. He almost got killed because he refused to leave without finding you first. We had to drag him out of there."

He'd thought I was dead? "Where is he?"

"I heard some of the guys talking," Rico said. "The meeting is happening in the middle hangar. We have to get over there before he does something crazy."

We turned to go around the back. That was when I

saw it. A faint red light glowing from the ground, the remains of a cigarette. Which meant the guards were nearby. I opened my mouth to warn them, but before a sound emerged, a shot rang out. Rico fell to the ground. Major jumped over Jenny to cover her. Heavy hands closed around my neck.

Gleaming white teeth shone in the dark, the Cheshire cat holding a machine gun. "You're back."

Chapter Eleven

T HE DARK OF a windowless room enveloped me, followed by a humid stench strong enough to gag me. Mold and copper—it smelled like pain. Henri's shoes clipped the concrete softly from behind me, incongruously civilized compared to the almost dungeon-like atmosphere…but it was a lie. This place suited him more than the well-guarded penthouse where he conducted business. It was how he saw the world, darkness and death inescapable.

An elbow rammed into my back, and I fell to the floor, landing in a thin film of grimy water. From the floor, I heard the *drip-drip* from somewhere else in the room. Slowly my senses sharpened, revealing a counterpoint—low, harsh breathing. Labored breathing.

My voice wavered. "Luke?"

"Don't worry." Henri's voice came from beside my ear as he bent to speak to me. "I punished him for taking you without payment. I know you were very concerned about that."

"Luke." I shuddered, feeling bone-deep revulsion for the breath on my ear, mourning whatever unseen pain had been inflicted. This was my fault, not his. My pain, and my body craved it with a kind of gnawing hunger—anything but have him suffer. I couldn't stand it.

I had to.

Summoning my strength, I stood. In the center of the room, I could make out a shadow. A chair. A man, slumped over.

He didn't register my approach. He was not conscious. At least, his eyes looked closed, but they might have been too puffy to see. He might have heard me call his name in horror and pain, but for the blackened blood dripping into his ears. He must have felt me when his head jerked away from my hand—though it might have been an unconscious move, like the leaves that fold at the touch of a finger.

"Oh God," I whispered. "What did they do to you?"

Hurt him, beat him, tortured him. My mind didn't want to accept it. *Find another answer, one that wouldn't leave Luke bleeding.*

Blood leaked from the corner of his eye, dried into a crusted tear. His face, his head was a mass of blue and black and purple, swollen and misshapen and beautiful because I could still hear the rasping breath from his bloodied lips. I could still see the beat of a green vein at an undisturbed patch of skin at the hollow of his neck. I touched my fingertip to that spot. He was warm and smooth there, where life and hope still beat.

I heard the steady *clop-clop* of Henri's shoes as he

came near. I shut my eyes, willing myself to remain still, remain focused, but how could I focus in the face of my worst fears? Luke hurt and Henri with nothing to lose—I didn't know which one was more terrifying. Where did I go when both dreams and waking held nightmares?

He touched a hand to the back of my neck, the soft pressure almost reassuring. "If you had only listened," he said with what sounded like regret. "I had such hopes for you. After I'm gone, the two of you could have ruled."

The force of my denial shook my body. I knew he could feel it, so I didn't bother to hide the disgust in my voice. "Never. He never would have done what you do."

After a pause, he laughed. "I didn't mean Luke." Before I could ask who he meant, he continued in a low taunt. "Though his hands are not as clean as you think."

"Lies," I spat.

"Come now. We may not always agree, but have you ever known me to lie outright?"

"Yes."

"All right." He chuckled. "But in this case, I wouldn't. The truth is far too glorious on its own. Didn't you ever wonder why Luke cared so much about the plight of the working girl?"

I had wondered, but it was only because Luke was so good—someone like Henri couldn't possibly understand motives so pure. Someone like me.

"Didn't ever wonder how he knew so much about the life? I know you did. It was part of what drew you to him."

I hated that he knew that. I had sacrificed almost everything for the shields I wore. Only a handful of people could see through them. Luke was one of them, Henri another. They were opposite sides of the coin…weren't they?

"I don't believe anything you say," I whispered, though it sounded like a weak defense even to my ears. I was so starved for anything about Luke, for something true and deep. His shields were as fortified as my own, but one thing could always pierce them. Our pasts, our history. The turning point at which we first realized we needed a shield at all, when the world had attacked.

"He was like you. A prostitute. Only worse, I think. You have to spread your legs. It is the way of a woman, for all of time, yes? A man can bear much more physical pain than a woman, but far less humiliation. To suck another man's dick for twenty dollars in an alley. To bend over. He ceases to be a man."

No, it couldn't be. He would have told me. He might have kept it from me, but I would have been able to tell. It explained so much. I could always feel that shame leaking from their heavily powdered pores, wafting on each nervous breath.

Though an unwelcomed power, I could always detect when another had undergone the same denial, the same internal negotiations: *it doesn't mean anything, they can't touch you on the inside, they can't even see you.* It was a repellant. I had enough sick deals in my own head without shouldering someone else's. But Luke… No.

He was too straitlaced. He fought prostitution because it went against his lofty morals, and that was the way I damn well liked it. We were opposites that way, light and dark, the sky and the earth, touching along the horizon but never to mix. Attached for eternity but always separate. If we were the same after all… No no no.

"I don't believe you," I said with conviction now. I wouldn't, couldn't.

"I hope you didn't suck his dick," he said. "No telling where it's been."

I whirled, catching him on the cheek with my nails. The odds were stacked so high against us, too high, but I wouldn't make it easy. Let him try to touch Luke again with me nearby. I swung, slamming my fist in the side of his neck. He wouldn't even have been the one to kill us. One of his men, as he delegated everything except for this.

He pinned me, and I panted against the wall.

"Bitch," he spat into my face. "I should kill you for that."

"So do it," I panted. "Why don't you fucking do it already?"

I realized my question had been sincere. Why was I

still alive? Why was Luke? I couldn't have much gratitude for it, considering the pain he must be in, considering the way this would have to end, a tragedy after all.

An icy fire raged in Henri's eyes, matched by the frosted blue of his vest. It wasn't any desire to whore me out that kept him from putting a bullet in my brain. He must know by now I wouldn't cooperate, and even without that, I had disrespected him enough that retribution would be death. The only reason I should still be alive was if he wanted to hurt me…except he had hurt me so very little. Yes, the emotional hurt of Luke lanced me worse than a whip, but that seemed too nuanced even for a consummate asshole like Henri.

Still leaning against the wall, I murmured, "What is it? What hold do I have over you that I don't even know I have?"

"Don't try my patience. There isn't much left."

"Then kill me. Why waste time?"

He turned back. "You're not the one in control here."

"Then who?" I whispered.

After a pause he said, "I am," but neither of us believed that anymore. "You'll find what you're looking for soon enough, but I don't think you'll enjoy it very much." He stalked from the room. His men followed, locking us in behind them.

I considered briefly falling at Luke's feet, just falling

apart. That approach had its appeal, but I had an advantage here. For once, I wasn't the remains of what my father had done to me. Not even the punishment I had inflicted on myself with my choice of profession for the years after. I'd had a friend who'd helped me, and so I knew what kindness looked like. In the clumsy way of a child copying his elders, I tugged at the knots at his wrists until they gave. I pulled him down to the floor, where I cradled his head in the nook of my arm, not shying away from his body, not using any hollow quip to buffer the bond between us. He radiated heat and pain, and so I took it into myself, not a sacrifice this time but a comfort. A tear fell from my cheek onto his. I touched it, washing the dirt and blood away from his skin.

Was it true, what Henri had said? It was an idle question, something to ponder. *Do you think it will rain tomorrow? Doesn't matter, worry about it then.*

He stirred, groaning. It was an animal sound, an agony sound.

"Shh," I soothed, but the tears came faster, and the sounds did not stop. "I'll sing to you," I offered, "but you'll probably wish I hadn't."

I sang him songs that I'd sung to my goddaughter in a different lifetime. *You are my sunshine, my only sunshine.* Morbid for a children's song, I had always thought. And of course I'd been perversely attracted to it. Now it seemed appropriate in the almost-underground area we found ourselves in, with no light and little air.

Please don't take my sunshine away.

Chapter Twelve

When he settled, I left him and explored the room, feeling around the hinges of the door, just in case, and along the walls. On the far wall, I ran my hip into a table. Some sort of workstation, judging by its height and breadth. I caught a few splinters in my palm and a few loose rocks at the bottom of the crumbling concrete wall, the occasional screw.

"Aha." My fingers clasped on cool metal, and I released a puff of satisfied breath. Some sort of tool, maybe a wrench. Hardly a fair fight against too many men armed with guns I barely knew how to hold. Still better than waiting to die.

"Shelly?" Luke's voice was hoarse, a little disoriented.

"Here." I swallowed my guilt and worry and returned to his side. "I'm here."

"Why?" A pained pause. "How?"

"I came to save you," I said with a small laugh. "It hasn't gone so great so far, but don't worry. I like to save some of my tricks for the big finish."

He groaned, whether in pain or annoyance at my joke, I wasn't sure—probably both.

"Have to…have to get out." His eyes were merely green slits, but slowly they came into focus. Awareness would only bring pain now.

I stroked the hair at his temple. "Don't worry about that. Just rest. I've got it covered. I took a self-defense class…kind of. Of course I don't have a gun, so it's not very useful, but the point is, I'm not going to let them hurt you again."

He struggled to sit up. No matter how I soothed and reprimanded him, he insisted on propping himself up against the wall, away from me. He touched his nose gingerly, then sucked in a breath.

"Broken," he muttered through swollen lips. "Hope you're not too attached to the face. Probably won't heal right by the time we get outta here."

"I appreciate the optimism, but since you're planning on living through this, maybe you shouldn't be sitting up or talking right now."

He ignored that, using his interrogation voice. "When did he leave? How long until he comes back?"

"Don't know and don't know. Must have left my glow-in-the-dark watch in my other dress."

"I'm assuming you don't have a phone either."

"Surprisingly, they didn't give me one. Guess they figured I would call someone."

The low sound he made was more frustrated than amused. "Where's Major?"

I sobered. "Lost him along the way."

"So no one knows you're here?"

"I'm sure your precious cops are on their way to help. It's a good thing they don't have red tape or bureaucracy or anything that would slow them down when they come rescue us."

His stern look was overshadowed by the mosaic of blue-green bruises across his skin. "Laying it on a little thick with the sarcasm today?"

"Well, I've been on the run for my life for weeks now. Abandoned by you. Kidnapped. Forced to become a hooker. Again. It's either irreverent sarcasm or a nervous breakdown."

"Keep on with it, then," he said gruffly.

So I did. "You'll be pleased to know I found a wrench, so if we need any furniture assembled, we're covered. Speaking of which, there are a few tables over in that corner. That's all. A table, a chair. It's all very minimalist, very contemporary. The dirt is a nice touch, kind of like tree-hugger modish."

He stood with a low moan that raised the hairs on my arms. Before he'd had time to recover or become steady on his feet, he followed the walls, feeling for himself. After a minute and some rustling I heard, "Take off your stockings."

"Just like that? No dinner date first? No down payment?"

"I'm going to fill them with rocks."

"Oh, I see. We're making homegrown weaponry, like prison inmates. It was only a matter of time, being locked up like this. It's like some kind of social experiment. Pretty soon we'll turn on each other."

He filled them with the loose nails and crumbled concrete. "I didn't abandon you, by the way. Not exactly. I thought you were dead."

"What?"

"First it just seemed like you were passed out, some kind of sedative."

"And then you left."

"I thought you'd died. I was back in fifteen minutes to get you, but you were gone. No trace, and Jeff told me…" He paused, his grief saturating the air around us. "I thought you were dead," he repeated, and I heard the uncertainty, as if he still worried it might be true. As if I were just some beating-inspired hallucination.

"I'm here."

"I know." A hollow laugh came from his chest. "I heard what Henri told you. I knew you must be real then. I couldn't have made that up even in my nightmares."

Was that a denial or confession? "Henri's a bastard," I said quietly. "I don't care what he said."

"Don't you? I sure as hell do. The whole time we've been talking, that's all I can think of. Why haven't you asked?"

Tears sprang to my eyes, warm and plump. "If you wanted me to know something, you'd tell me." No matter how I tried to placate him, it only seemed to make him more agitated. More accusatory.

"Ah, so you do believe him."

"Tell me what you want me to say," I whispered. "Just tell me what you want me to do, and I'll do it."

"Right," he said with a cruel twist, "because you're whoever I want you to be, you'll do whatever I say. God forbid you ask me a goddamn question. God forbid you care."

"Why?" I asked thickly. "Would it matter if I did? Would you actually want to be with me then, or would you keep pushing me away?"

"Oh, that's rich, coming from you. You keep everyone at a distance. Do you know how hard I had to work to get close to you? It's a struggle to get any information from you, even the goddamn time of day."

"What is there to know? You want me to spell it out for you? Home life wasn't so great. Daddy didn't like me too much, except when he did, if you know what I mean. But I showed him. I got out of there, and here's some good news. The only skill I had was worth a hell of a lot of money per hour. All I had to sell was my fucking soul, so I guess everything is just peachy. But you already knew that, didn't you? I'm a walking cliché. So tell me what secrets I've been keeping."

"Shelly." His voice cracked, and I hoped it was over. I prayed that he'd gotten whatever anger he had out of his system, that he realized I wouldn't judge him. I would, a little, but only as much as I judged myself, as anyone. How could you do that, just let them touch and use and hurt you like that? I had to; he had to. A million other jobs in the world, and somehow it had seemed like the only one.

"We don't have to talk about it," I whispered. I put my hand on his, and he jerked away.

"Don't touch me." It was a snarl, an animal sound carved into words.

I pulled back, frightened. Not of Luke but of the hurt inside him.

"I don't…I don't think of you any differently." It was a lie, and we both knew it.

Dirt scuffed into the air as he pushed off the wall. "Of course. I'm still the noble one, the guy with the best intentions. That's why you let me close, isn't it?" His voice lowered. "That's why you fell in love with me, isn't that right? Because I was just the opposite of you, so much better than you."

His words rang with truth. I shook my head. "It was you. Only you."

"Stop telling me what you think I want to hear. Just for once, say something that's you. Not a trick, just the honest-to-God truth."

I whirled on him. "Fine. You want to know the truth? I hate it. I hate that I had to hear it from him instead of you. I hate that you had to go through that. I hate that the worst part of me, the worst things I ever felt or thought or had happen to me…they happened to you. I hate that because I love you. Don't you get that, you big idiot? It kills me that you went through that. I wouldn't wish that on my worst enemy, but you? It's heartbreaking. You're breaking my heart."

He stilled. "What did you say?"

"I said you're a big idiot."

He grabbed my arms and backed me up against the wall. My toes pointed to the ground, barely touching. I felt like a doll. Like a child, though it didn't feel as bad as it should—just bad enough.

"Don't push me right now," he muttered. "I can't… It's not… I'm not myself."

No, this was finally him, unfettered and cracked open. Ironic that it had taken a brutal beating and imprisonment to release him. He was dark and angry, this man. Tortured and terrified that he wouldn't be able to control that darkness, that anger. But he didn't have to, not with me. That was the gift I could give him. That was how I'd be worthy.

I pushed at him, but he didn't release me. I didn't expect him too; we were too far in. He was too far gone. This was going to happen rough and hard and with pain so sweet we'd neither of us forget it, with a pleasure so cruel it would teach us both a lesson; it would leave marks so deep that I wouldn't regret it when it was over.

"Just let it out," I whispered.

"No," he said. "It's too much. I know how that feels. I know what it means and everything about it. You've been hurt so much. Abused and afraid and angry—so much. How could I hurt you more? How could I cause you any more pain?"

"Don't you see? I want it all. Your pleasure, your

pain. Anything you can give me, I crave it."

The last words shattered in my mouth, pressed there by the force of his body and his rage. He unleashed it on me. His anger, carefully boxed and hidden, sprang open. The fear, so neatly caged, splintered all around us. He lashed at me with hands that forced my wrists against the wall, his mouth that pried mine open and stole my breath, the painful ridge against my stomach as he pushed and threatened and warned me away, but with nowhere to go and no desire to leave him, I yielded. It hadn't been a lie; the pain he delivered was sweeter than the gentlest caress of a hundred-dollar bill. It was honest, and it was him.

I hadn't lied about that either: I loved him. I had dressed it up with excuses, with reasons that made it okay to break the cardinal rule. He was unattainable, like Allie had said. He was unlike me in every way, but when those drapes were pulled away, they revealed a blinding white-hot wound. There wasn't any reason to compel it, any logic to explain it, and that's how I knew it was love.

Copper touched my tongue—my blood, his. An anguished sound disturbed the air around us—my pain, his pleasure. But no one would play the martyr tonight. Neither of us would pretend we didn't want this, not anymore.

CHAPTER THIRTEEN

HE SHOVED ME to the floor, and I tumbled there, a flurry of dust and limbs, of bruises on my knees and a self-satisfied grunt in my throat. With fingers digging into my arm, he turned me over. I sank gratefully onto the concrete, my legs spread, body eager.

Harsh hands pushed the cloth of my panties aside. Two fingers shoved inside, dry until he added his spit to ease their way.

"Oh God," I cried. He was more than I'd thought he could be—worse and so much better.

"Take it," he muttered. "Just once, just now. Just like this."

Did he think I would refuse him? It was bliss, this pain. Did he think it was too much? It would never be. I wanted him to beat me, to transfer each blow from his body to mine so that my scars matched his, inside and out.

"Let me see it," I begged. The real him, the real me. "Let me feel it."

He knew exactly what I meant, and he was far enough gone to give it to me. His palm landed on my cheek, a slap too light to be cruel, the force of it turning my face to the floor. I groaned at the sting, at the relief. "More," I whispered.

"No. That's enough." But the words weren't meant to protect me or to soothe me. They were a denial. He wanted me to beg.

"Luke, Luke." I was helpless for anything more coherent.

"Shelly," he answered me, mournful. "I never wanted this for you."

"Me neither," I whispered, not knowing whether we were talking about me or him, but it didn't matter anyway. We couldn't change the past, only live in the present. We couldn't heal the hurts; only fill the hollows of memory with the jolt of my hips as he yanked me closer, with the softening of my body as I let him. His force and my acceptance, they were a bargain between us, a language we both understood.

The rasp of his zipper met my ears, and then he was pushing, pulsing, already inside me before I realized we didn't have a condom. I clenched around a warm length, rippled against velvety skin, no barriers between us, but that didn't matter now, couldn't matter here in the aftermath of torture, at the fringes of death. I wanted to be taken over, to be ripped and torn to shreds by him, and I was. I couldn't help it, couldn't do anything but writhe and moan and coat his cock with the fluid I had denied him before.

Tilting my hips, I let him in deeper. It hurt that

way. It pressed and pushed and stabbed that way, but it was the perfect counterpoint to the pleasure I felt spreading like a fever over my body. I was going to come; it had already started, like the first gentle curve on the horizon. It grew closer to the shore, gathering strength until it was a wave crashing over me and I gasped for breath at the surface. He never stopped, never slowed his thrusts.

I fought for air, for acknowledgment, pounding on his chest with my fists. He grunted in pain but didn't relent. He trapped my arms, holding his weight on the soft inner flesh. It was agony, and my body wrenched in response, but none of it could compare to the pain he must have felt. With those bruises, those injuries, even holding himself up would be torture; even moving inside me, against me would be pain. We rocked in it, reveled in it like hedonists who had just discovered that pain spilled over became pleasure.

My hips rode the air, reaching up for his. He slammed me back down on each thrust, an ache reverberating through my limbs.

I couldn't find an end or a beginning. "Help me."

"Stop?"

"More, more."

He released my arms and reared back. He wrapped both his hands around my neck, not squeezing or pressing. Just holding me there by my most vulnerable place. It felt like worship.

With the slightest constriction, I felt the flesh of his

palm as I breathed, as I swallowed. Like a dam torn apart, tears ran down my cheeks. Heartbroken. My heart was breaking for him.

He didn't want my pity. I gave him something else, everything else. I sobbed out a release, his every entry brought a new surge of heat, relaxing as the last of the pleasure lapped at my heels. When I had finished, he covered me with his body, filling me until it was too much before letting me breathe once again. Each thrust was marked by a small expulsion of air. *Ah, ah, ah*. And it drew out, melting together into a masculine sound, the horizon between power and helplessness.

He collapsed on top of me, a slippery weight of sweat and sex and probably blood from one of us, maybe both. It was the cleanest I had ever felt, not marred by shame or misuse. The oils of his body were like a baptism, washing away my sins and leaving me reborn. He panted there, shudders gripping his body as he caught his breath. His stillness worried me. *Don't let him regret this. Don't let him withdraw.*

"Hell," he said, rolling off me.

I followed, tucking my body against his, heedful of the jagged cut that ran wetly along his side and the matching one on my leg.

In the aftermath, cold settled over us by degrees. With it came dread, that he would forget or go back to the old way.

"Are you okay?" he asked gruffly.

"I'm fine, I promise."

He turned his face away, and I clutched his arm as if it were a life raft. Where did this clinginess come from? I didn't know, but it gripped me, and in turn, I couldn't let him go. I didn't mind his roughness earlier, didn't mind the bruises. I couldn't stand for him to push me away. If he left me now, there wouldn't be any time to make it right between us. It wasn't fair to him, putting all that pressure on one experience. Was it real? Intimacy, love? For once, finally? I had to know, as the unseen timer ticked down to zero. I had to believe I'd lived before I died.

"Please, Luke. Don't shut me out, not now."

"What do you want me to do?" he asked with a challenge in his voice. "Tell me what you want me to say."

I want it to be real between us. It was my plea this time, my unspoken words butting up against an uncaring lover. No, not uncaring. He was hurt and fighting back. I understood that, though I'd rarely done it myself. But that was Luke, who had clawed his way up until the world had given him respect. And this was me, who accepted what I was given and wondered, wondered, wondered if it would ever be enough.

"I'm sorry I pushed you. Forget I asked." I stroked his chest, hoping his heart would calm.

He sat up, pulling away. "You know what it's like. Right, Shelly? You know we don't like to be touched. So why are you all over me? Why can't I seem to shake you?"

Tears ran down my cheeks. I hated to see him like this, raging and hurting.

"I don't know," I said, shivering. I just wanted him to feel better. "I'll pretend he never told me."

"What for? You know the truth. You know that I was too much of a coward to tell you myself, even when I knew you did the same. You know that I took it up the ass since I was sixteen, but you know what else? I'm guessing you did too."

I recoiled. "Stop it."

"Am I right? If I guessed right, I think I should win a prize."

My breath exhaled in shaky jolts. "You're being cruel on purpose. To push me away."

"Way to state the obvious, Shelly. Next you'll tell me I know how to suck a cock. Probably better than you, and between the two of us, that's saying something."

I stared at him, burning the image of him into my mind. He was rabid, a cornered animal, a tortured one. And I couldn't help him. I turned and crawled to the other side of the cell. It didn't have quite the same effect without a slamming door and screech of tires, but we were beyond theatrics. There was only desolation here, only tears streaming down my face as I curled up, facing the wall. The problem with crying is that once you start, you can't stop. Soon my silent tears had turned into sobs that racked my body. I put my hand to my mouth to try to keep them in, but somehow that only made them worse.

Luke picked me up and cradled me in his lap. I fought him at first, striking out, landing blows only God knows where. It didn't deter him. If anything, he probably welcomed them, so rife was he with self-disgust.

"Oh God, Shelly. I'm sorry. Yes, hate me. I'm so sorry."

I curled into his warmth and his hate and cried into his shirt. He rocked me, murmuring endearments and apologies and self-directed epithets until my tears had dried.

My head felt hollow but strangely heavy. "Did you think I would judge you?" I whispered.

His laugh was hoarse. "I don't need you to judge me. I do that plenty for myself."

"You did what you had to do to keep your sister safe."

"I could have walked her into any police station. I should have. If I had, she would still be alive."

"You were a teenager. You couldn't know what would happen to her, especially after they had left you in that man's care."

"And I thought I could do better. I was so damn cocky. Isn't that funny? The gay-for-pay guy was cocky."

It was like watching myself from the outside. So full of anger and hurt, covering it all up with sexually insulting humor.

"How did she—" I bit my lip, stoppering the words.

"I wasn't her pimp, if that's what you thought. There are some lines even I wouldn't cross."

"I didn't think that," I said quickly and felt some of the tension leak from his body.

He swallowed. "I was gone every night. She was bored, like I told you. She started hanging out with a bad crowd who got her hooked on heroin. That was the point I really got scared. I knew we were both in over our heads, but I was so wrapped up in my own shit. I thought I could handle it all. I started being more careful with money, so she wouldn't spend it all on the drugs. That's when she started hooking, to make up the money. Most of the girls she hung out with were already doing it, so I guess it didn't seem like a big deal. I only found out later, after she had gone."

His grip on me tightened, and I couldn't quite breathe, but at that moment, I would rather have suffocated than deny him comfort.

"I failed her," he said, his voice cracking. "I failed her so bad, and I could never stop trying to make it right, even though I know it's too late."

I wrapped my arms around his neck, holding him to me. We shifted slightly so that his head lay on my chest. I wondered if he could hear my heart race, and I struggled to calm myself as if that could calm him too. At length, his breathing evened out, though small shifts in his body told me he was still awake.

Pulling himself up, he faced me, solemn and determined. His eyes were streaked red, though they didn't look nearly as bad as mine probably did—puffy and swollen from tears unshed.

He brushed a tear that had remained on my cheek. "I owe you an apology. The things I said were unforgivable."

"You were upset."

A ghost of a smile touched his swollen face. "I think you would excuse me from murder if I tell you I had a bad day."

"I forgive you."

His voice grew husky as he said, "I don't deserve that."

"Forgiveness isn't about whether you deserve it or not. It comes freely or not at all. Like love."

He swallowed. "You do love me, don't you, Shelly? And I don't deserve that either."

He was more deserving of love than anybody I had ever known, but it wasn't even relevant to how I felt about him. Love wasn't a choice; it was an accident. Not a climb but a fall. I had slipped somewhere along my prickly path and down, down to the murky depths, hurtling ever farther, ever faster, and the only question left was whether he would meet me at the bottom.

Chapter Fourteen

I CROUCHED BEHIND the flat of the table, which had been turned on its side, wondering how Luke had talked me into this.

It was a suicide mission. His.

The plan was chillingly simple. Luke waited, prone on the floor and armed with our crude and blunt weaponry. He would lure the men to his side and fight them, distracting them long enough for me to escape through the door. I had argued vehemently at the beginning, flat-out refused. How could I leave him to his death? I could go for help, but we both knew it would be too late for him. But then he had pulled me tight and said that if we did nothing, we would both die. Let him do this much, he'd said.

Live, he'd told me.

I understood about guilt, however undeserved, and how it would eat at him in these final minutes if he believed I would die. So I agreed, still unsure whether I could run away. There were moments that defined a person, choices that separated me from my mother. Could I leave him to suffer in my place? Could I live with myself after? It was the same as when Henri had given me that gun. Could I become a murderer? I would save myself, but there were things worth more than my life.

My ankles ached, cold from the chill of the floor. I missed his body warmth, the way he breathed.

It felt like days passed before footsteps sounded from outside the room. I strained to make them out, to separate them into parts and count how many men were there. Two, maybe three.

They paused outside the door. I heard the faint sounds of two men conversing—arguing. That gave me hope. Maybe it wasn't Henri. No one would argue with him.

I heard a creak, and yellow light flooded the room from the hall, stinging my eyes. A single man walked inside, to Luke. Clop, clop. I recognized his gait. Henri's gravelly voice muttered something from the center of the room. He always sent his men in first. What was different this time? Who still stood outside the room? This wasn't how it was supposed to go.

There was a thud, as if he'd kicked Luke, and an exhalation of breath.

"What's wrong with him?" came a voice from outside. My pulse beat a rapid tattoo in my temple, though I struggled to place his voice. Low, male. Unsurprising in our current situation. There were women who held power in this industry—Jade, for example—but they were rare. Confident, impatient. Those also were hallmarks of a man in power.

"How should I know?" Henri snapped.

The strange part was the power dynamic. I had never seen Henri before with a man more powerful than himself, at least without a full-fledged power struggle. But in Henri's voice, there was a tremor of uncertainty. A bit of subservience, which was why it took me so long to place. The Henri I knew would never submit, but now I wondered if that undaunted power was as much a mask as my own limitless capacity for subjugation, as if we had both played our parts to the fullest. As if we were each consumed by our roles. A social experiment, indeed.

The other man came into the room. It felt like déjà vu, like I should know him just by the way the air shifted at his presence. One of Henri's men? An old client? But this felt older than that—ancient, like I had heard this story in an old fairy tale.

Before I could figure it out, Luke made his move. A sharp cry of pain was followed by the fast exhalation of breath, the hair-raising sounds of two bodies in combat. There were only two men, neither of them paid henchmen; it was better odds than we had counted on. I scooted around the side of the table. A quick glance revealed a blur of limbs and boots.

I dashed out of the room, thinking of going for help, of getting the car, of doing something. *Let me do this much,* he had said, and I was, but he would let me do something for him in return. Well, he didn't really have a choice.

A shot rang out. I thought I heard footsteps. Bursting through the door, I sucked in lungfuls of outdoor air. The woods looked so peaceful. I headed for the line of trees, knowing that if either of them had followed me, I would be safer out of sight.

A flashlight chased my feet, and I stumbled into the woods, hiding behind a tree. I glanced around wildly. I would run to the car. I wouldn't think about Luke, not yet.

"Michelle Ann Laurent, come out here this instant."

The words rang out with crushing familiarity. My breath came shorter. I saw black spots covering the wintry foliage before me. I suddenly wished I had known. I should have. If Luke had wanted to show me mercy, he should have conked me on the head with that wrench. Anything to save me from this.

I thought of running again. It was what I had done in that hotel suite. What I had done for so many years. Why not keep going? Leave Luke behind.

Stepping aside from the tree, I said with as much casualness as I could muster, "Hi, Daddy."

"You went too far this time."

"Have I been a bad girl?" I smirked, wrapping the cloak of whorishness more tightly around me. Let him see what I had become, what he had made me. "Am I going to get a spanking?"

He came closer. "Don't make me come get you. It will only make this worse."

My laugh had a maniacal tilt, breaking cover. "How exactly could it get worse? Please explain that to me."

"I let you have your fun. But you always knew you'd come home."

He walked closer. Even in the twilight, I could make out the lines of his face, the gray of his temples. It made him more dignified. Objectively, I could see that he was handsome, to someone who wasn't his flesh and blood. I hated it, the way beauty could be a privilege and a curse. The way it turned me into a commodity. No, he did that.

"Why are you here?" I asked. "Why now?"

"I've never left. How do you think Henri found you? I had trained you. You were mine, and I wasn't going to let you go, working for a C-note a night. I told him where to find you. I told him to hire you. I've been here since the beginning, getting a twenty-five percent cut."

I felt sick but strangely unsurprised. "Henri isn't family."

He frowned. "No, but he was useful. For a time. He always had a weakness for that Chinese bitch. He should have killed her." His laugh sent chills down my spine. "And then he found the girl. You should have seen him, the proud papa. I almost bought him some cigars."

A gasp escaped me. Claire was his daughter? "Then why did he pimp her out?"

"Henri is unoriginal," he said flatly. "He tried to do

the same thing I did, but he didn't understand. I had groomed you from the beginning. So very early. He wanted to take a shortcut, and now look at the mess he made."

"Groomed me for what?" I spat. "For being a prostitute? Are you telling me you were that hard up for money that you needed a few extra grand a week?"

"It's not about the money you earned. That was nothing. This is a family business. How else were you going to run it if you didn't understand it? I couldn't just put you at the helm. They would have eaten you alive. But now…now you're strong enough."

"You're delusional if you think I'm going to run your business. This business. It disgusts me. The whole thing disgusts, the men and the women and—"*Me, me, me*. I disgusted me, though I couldn't tell him that. "The only reason I did it was because—"

"Because you had to? Because you didn't know how to do anything else? Other people may buy your excuses but not me. You're smart and beautiful. You could have done anything, but that's what you chose to do."

"I needed the money."

"Your friend needed the money, and you needed to be the one to give it to her, didn't you? That's your Achilles' heel."

"Friends?"

"Pride. You live for the gratitude, for praise. We all have a weakness. The only question is whether you let it rule you."

"Do you?"

He paused before answering softly, "I'm afraid so. It's you, actually, but you know that."

Yes, I knew it. I remembered the way his footsteps would pause outside the door before he came in…much like they had earlier tonight in the cell. The hesitation wasn't his conscience—it was his pride. He didn't want to be dependent on a little girl. "And you've always hated me for it."

His gaze flicked over me. "You look more like her."

"Is that all? Would it have turned out differently if I had looked like you instead?"

"I hated her too." He looked faraway. "That kind of power is unnatural."

I remembered the story my mother had told me about the princess in disguise. This was the lesson my father would take from it, that a woman held unshakable power, over her father, over the men in her life. The tale looked different to each listener, the lessons it told a testament to our deepest desires.

The most important question came to me, one I had first thought when he came into my room with a bag of her melted-down jewelry. "Why did she leave you?"

"It's dangerous too, that kind of power. I had to stop her."

"You killed her." The statement left me with the cold realization I had always known, or at least suspected. It was better this way, because she hadn't left me on purpose. But worse, so much worse. My hate for him, previously shriveled and tucked away, pulsed with new life.

He smiled, a little vacant, a little sad. "I knew you were stronger than her. She couldn't handle what I did, the way I supported our family. I couldn't let you go the same way."

"The devoted father," I scoffed.

"You can't question my devotion to you. From the moment she left us, I made everything about you."

"It was wrong," I said, knowing he would mock me.

But he didn't. His forehead creased. He seemed uncertain, as if he had pondered this before. "I kept you from ending up like her. She was so sure of herself. She wanted to leave me, to take you with her. You wouldn't have had a chance."

I wanted to laugh, but it caught in my throat. What chance? "Is this how you've justified it? The excuses you tell yourself so you can sleep at night? If you were so concerned about my safety, why did you let me prostitute myself? It's not exactly OSHA certified."

"I got you off the streets. Off those goddamn online ads where any pervert could call you. Henri knew what would happen to him if you ever got hurt."

"He hurt me, Daddy. Worse than you."

"He paid for that," he said evenly. "He's probably cold by now."

I blinked, turning to look at the building we had left. The gunshot. "Did you really kill him?"

"Yes, so you can thank me for saving that cop of yours. He was more trouble than he was worth too, always poking his nose where it didn't belong. I think he figured it out, but I'm assuming he never told you that."

My silence answered him. He hadn't.

"He's not who I would have chosen for you, but I think he loves you. The way I loved your mother."

I swallowed—no, not like that. Luke had kept his suspicions from me to spare me pain. My father caused pain and called it love. "I despise you. You can't understand how much I hate you."

"I can," he whispered. "I haven't been able to live with myself since she died. And then you left. It's been so hard, but I kept myself from going to you. Doesn't that count for something? Doesn't it show I care?"

I squinted, searching, as if I were looking for someone else inside him, someone who understood the wrongness of his actions and how very crazy he had become. I found nothing.

He pulled out a gun. I watched with a kind of disinterest. Would he kill me now? It didn't quite make sense, didn't fit with his plans for me to take over, to become stronger, but then, he was crazy. That was the problem I'd always had, a little girl trying to find the care and affections in the actions of a madman.

The metal met the palm of my hand as he pressed it

there. He maneuvered it in my hand so that it pointed at his chest.

"It's time," he said. "You can do this."

I recoiled, but he held me to him. "I'm not going to kill you. That's…that's suicide."

"Murder," he corrected gently. "It needs to happen. Otherwise you'll never move on. You'll never find peace."

Himself. He was talking about himself.

I jerked my hand away, my finger nestled against the trigger. He closed his eyes, taking a deep breath. "Do it."

"I won't."

A flash of anger crossed his face, and I waited for him to turn on me. He did, but not the way I was expecting. "I watched sometimes."

My voice faltered. "What?"

"Half the hotels in Chicago have peepholes between the rooms if you know where to look. If you grease enough palms. Henri would offer them a hotel room free so we would get the right one. You were good at it, Shelly. I was so proud of you."

I felt sick, like I really might throw up all over the gun, all over him and me and everything. I knew what he was doing. He was trying to rile me up, make me so angry that I pulled the trigger, but I was better than that—oh God, wasn't I?

"I wanted to leave you alone."

He was pleading now, for me to forgive him, for

me to shoot him—it all swirled together in one sick melee.

"It wasn't right, the way I couldn't stop thinking about you. That wasn't fair to either of us. I tried other women, other girls. Pretty ones with blonde hair. They even slept in your bed, but it wasn't the same."

My eyes burned with unshed tears. My finger trembled on the trigger. Almost.

A glint entered his eye. "Your friend's little girl is cute. Not to my usual tastes, but I can see the appeal. It was my money that paid for her birth, wasn't it?"

The report of the gun was loud in my ears, but it rang instead with *she's mine, she's mine too*. Had he really said that part, or had my mind filled in the blanks? He lay on the ground, unseeing. He jerked. Was he dead?

I rifled through his pockets. His wallet fell open to a school picture of me. I smiled brightly in the picture, my teeth a little too large for my face. I found his cell phone and dialed 911. A gurgling sound came from his throat. I had become what he wanted me to be—a murderer. I hadn't wanted to, but now...now I couldn't find any regret. Couldn't find any feeling at all. Not even the chill of the wind could touch me. When the operator confirmed that ambulances were on their way, I returned to the building.

Luke met me in the hallway, half dragging himself against the wall. I ran to help him.

"You're okay," he slurred. He seemed delirious with

the pain and blood loss.

Gently, I laid him on the floor. "I'm okay. Rest now."

His head was pillowed on my arm, tucked against my breast. My cheek lay against the concrete as I took comfort from him. I needed it, after the confrontation with my father, needed to know I was still alive, and that Luke was too, but just this. Just holding him was enough.

CHAPTER FIFTEEN

THE PARAMEDICS SPLIT us up, bringing us to the hospital in separate ambulances. I let them poke and prod at me. They were determined to do a rape kit on me even though I told them it didn't matter, it had never been rape. But I could tell by the doctor's expression that she didn't believe me, and so I spread my legs obediently and let her touch and didn't make any jokes about charging her by the swab.

The police questioned me, and I explained that the sex between Luke and me was consensual, since they'd find it in the lab report anyway. The two men exchanged a quick glance but kept their professional cool. They told me he was recovering well—but I knew it couldn't be too well if he hadn't come to see me yet.

The minute they were out the door, I wanted to leave in search of him. But the nurse must have filled my IV with something that put me to sleep. And they thought *I* didn't understand consent, I thought drowsily.

I drifted in and out of a dreamless sleep. When I woke up, the room was still quiet, but I felt someone there. Allie. She was curled up on the hospital bed at my side.

"Hey," I said, though it came out more like a croak.

"Hey yourself."

I read how bad I looked in her eyes. Sad. But not too sad, which meant I'd be fine soon enough. Good, because I never could trust those damn nurses.

"How are you feeling? Hurting? Thirsty?"

"A little of both, but wait, don't go yet. I just want to lie like this."

She looked shocked. She knew I didn't like touching. "Are you sure?"

"I'm working on it."

She grinned. "I'll take it."

Colin came in, holding Bailey in his arms. She squealed at the sight of me, but he held her back.

"No," I protested. "I want to hold her."

He eyed the tubes coming off me with clear doubt.

"It'll be fine," I assured him.

Bailey nestled between us, showing her frustration at my prolonged absence by smashing her face into mine until neither of us could breathe. She grabbed fistfuls of my hair and made a nest for herself in the crook of my arm. My lungs burned, my bruises ached, all of it too much and just right. I looked over her auburn curls at Allie, who watched us, her eyes bright. It was in her eyes, the soul-deep relief.

Over.

It was really over. There was no one to find me and force me back into the life. No one to hang over me like a heavy cloud. Even if they put me in jail for my part, I would have felt nothing but gratitude.

That wouldn't happen, though. The cops and the doctors veiled their pity behind professionalism, but the letter V might as well have been stitched across my hospital gown.

Victim.

And well, maybe so. I needed to take responsibility for every trick I had turned. It was the only way to stay sane. But as much as I would have wished it, I couldn't deny the truth of my father's words. He had trained me, and I had performed like an obedient bitch—so was it a hapless struggle or a choice? The way of the world or a sin? I wasn't sure it mattered anymore. I would never again have that pause outside a hotel room door. I would never again hear those unwelcome footsteps pause outside mine. Over.

Well, shit. "What the hell am I going to do now?"

Allie laughed, a little watery. "You'll think of something, and I'm sure it will make me want to pull my hair out, but it will be awesome."

"So basically I'm three years old like Bailey."

She nudged my foot through the sheet. "You are like my kid. And other times you're like my mom. That's what best friends do."

I lowered my lashes, and she gave me the moment I needed. Looking away, I said, "Speaking of kids, how's the girl? Did you visit the kennel, take her out for a walk?"

I was referring to the email asking her to keep an eye on Claire. I trusted Philip, but a little oversight never hurt anybody.

Her face screwed up. "Not exactly."

"Not exactly, you didn't check on her?"

"We didn't just take her for a walk. We took her home." At my alarmed look, she reassured me. "Nothing happened. They were driving each other crazy, and Philip asked Colin to watch her. So she came back to our house. It was completely safe. No one even knew she was there. You know Colin wouldn't have done it otherwise."

"I'm surprised he wanted to help Philip. Or that you did."

"Hmm." She paused, thoughtful. "I would have said I was doing it for her. But the truth is, I felt bad for him. I think he is really desperate for someone to love him."

I glanced at Colin, who stood just outside the room, visible through the half-raised blinds. "Yeah, well, he can join the club."

She raised her eyebrows. "Is that a confession I just heard? Do not give me that professional-working-relationship crap. Something must have happened between you and Luke."

The corner of my lips tugged up.

"See? I knew it. Details. I need details. Let me just give Bailey to Colin, and then–"

"Wait a minute. If you have Claire, then where is

she?"

Allie rolled her eyes. "She won't come in. I think she's scared, but of course she won't tell me. Also, remind me to send Bailey to a convent when she hits puberty. Teenagers are exhausting."

"Send her in."

"I'm telling you, she won't come."

"Tell her if she doesn't get her butt in here, I'm going to come out there myself. I have stitches and a hangnail here, so basically I might die. Does she want that on her conscience?"

"Okay." Allie dropped a kiss on my forehead and dragged a disgruntled Bailey into her arms. "You know, I expected Colin to be annoyed, having a teenaged girl around, but he doesn't seem to mind. I think he even leaves little stashes of cash for her to find. When she pitches a fit, he just shrugs it off. And then I realized he does the same thing to me."

I snorted. "Trust me, he does not see the two of you the same way."

"Oh, I know. I'm just saying, men will surprise you if you give them the chance."

"Subtle."

"When someone's as thickheaded as you…"

"Yes, all right. I'm working on it. See, I'm not denying there's a possibility for me and Luke. We could be together. Stranger things have happened." I grinned. "Though I can't think of any at the moment."

"Not strange," Allie said. "You're not Shelly's past

and Luke's job. You're just a man and a woman in love. Love is the great equalizer."

I was quiet for a moment. "That was deep. Oprah?"

She shrugged. "Saw it stitched on a throw pillow."

Allie left the room, and a few minutes later, a waif dressed in black lurked outside the door. Finally, Claire slunk inside. She looked nice in jeans and a loose sweater. Her hair had been cut so it didn't fall into her eyes, though she tried to reproduce the effect by hanging her head. I admitted to myself that Allie had been a better caretaker for her even if I hadn't wanted to involve her. Claire wouldn't meet my eyes.

"Do I look that bad?"

"No," she said quickly. "You look great. Really good. I mean, I'm so glad that you look so good and—"

"You mad at me?"

"No, not at all."

"You're doing it again."

She fidgeted with the hem of her sweater sleeve. "I made a little mistake. But the thing is, I couldn't have known it would lead to all that."

"Spill."

She told me that she had kept the gemstones I had given her in a stash with her other things. Except she winced a little when she used the possessive term. Stolen things, she meant.

"I took a pen. I just wanted to, you know, write with it or something. I had no idea it was a special pen or that it cost so much. Who pays a thousand dollars for a pen? So then he comes into my room and is looking all around, and I'm pretending not to know what he's talking about. And then he finds the whole stash, and he starts going through it and saying everything is his. Which it kind of was. But I told him the rocks were mine and that I was keeping them. Then he says he remembers them being part of some little statue thing in the library, and we had a fight."

"Lord," I said.

"Right? Anyway, he takes them, and apparently there are serial numbers on the diamonds. Can you believe it? He says he'll prove that they were purchased by him through a broker or whatever, and I'm like fine, because I know they're yours and even if you stole them, you didn't steal them from *him*."

"Appreciate the vote of confidence."

"So it turns out the diamonds were sold twenty years ago to some guy who Philip knows and hates. So then he thinks I was sent there to spy on him, like the stones were a payoff. He was mad."

Mad was an understatement. "He didn't hurt you, did he?"

"No, but he called Colin to come get me. And he wouldn't give the stones back to me."

"Probably for the best. Everyone knows diamonds are blood money anyway."

Her mouth dropped open. "You mean you're not going to get them back?"

"We'll consider it payment for room and board and

security. I know you were very concerned about inconveniencing him."

She looked mutinous, but she'd get over it. Eventually. "The important thing now is to get back your old life. Get back to living."

Her forehead creased. "I know it was scary, what with the threat of death and all that. But in some ways, it was easier like that. Just in limbo, no one expecting things from me. I'm not sure how to go back."

"I know, sweetheart." But we'd both have to figure it out.

CHAPTER SIXTEEN

LUKE FOUND ME in my hospital room and didn't leave my side. When they discharged me, he took me straight to the cabin in the country. He seemed to know that I could breathe there, heal there. But I was restless too.

Allie had come to see me here. Even Jenny had been to the cabin for a short visit, which was awkward. Major had brought her. They had escaped from the men who'd held them, and not knowing where to look for me, had holed up in the woods until the cops arrived. Rico had slunk away that night, not wanting to be questioned by the cops—apparently he hadn't exactly left the gang.

But there was one unanswered question that refused to let me rest. I asked Luke to drive me back into town. It was time to understand what had happened, time to pick up all the pieces so I could finally let them go.

The car bounced along the potholes in the parking lot, and I winced. When the car rolled to a halt, I sighed in relief.

"I'll get you," Luke said, coming around the car.

He opened the door and held out his hand. Gingerly, I stepped from the cab, careful not to jostle my leg. In an annoying twist of fate, the cut caused more complications and more pain than my old gunshot wound had.

"You wait here." I could see from his face that he was about to refuse. "I have to do this alone. She won't talk to me otherwise. Claire deserves to know, and so do I."

"Damn it, Shelly. You can't trust her."

"She's the only one in there. And you're right out here. I'll be fine. She was never the type to use force anyway."

"This is not comforting."

"Trust me," I said and won the argument. Trust was a slow climb for us both, but we had our eye on the peak.

"Okay," he said. "I'll be right out here. If anything goes wrong…"

I kissed him. "Love you."

He still looked startled when I did that, which was probably the best incentive to keep doing it. It touched my heart that he understood what a big step this was for me. It broke my heart that some part of him believed himself unworthy. I wanted to see the surprise fade, turn to acceptance.

"Hurry back," he said. His voice had taken on that slightly hoarse edge that meant arousal and approval. It wouldn't be long before he took matters into his own hands, finding us a quiet moment, a private space, an intimate touch.

I climbed the steps, glancing at the darkened window. The THAI MASSAGE sign was off, the waiting room empty and eerily silent.

Jade wore her customary loose-fitting clothes that seemed to hang on her rail-thin frame more than ever. I sat down in the chair while she got me a small glass of flat soda. Rituals were important.

Sitting across from me, she stared sightlessly at the calendar on the wall. It had a picture of a laughing family and a logo of some home insurance agent on the corner.

"I must thank you for telling me about the raid. I don't know why you did."

I had warned her beforehand. Most of the brothels in the area had been raided, but her house had been empty. Luke told me about the raids in advance, with a look that said he knew that I'd pass the information along. It had been a compulsion, one I would probably always have to some degree.

"I don't know why either," I admitted. But now that I had done it, I wasn't above taking full advantage. "Maybe now you'll tell me. Tell me the truth about Claire. I know you can."

"Yes. You deserve to know, after all this."

It took her several minutes to begin. I wondered if she had ever told this to anyone before and guessed that she hadn't. She wasn't the type to unburden herself to others. How lonely it was in that place of secrets and smoke. No one could hurt her there; no one could help.

"We have more in common than you think, you and I," she said. "When I was a girl, my parents sold me to Henri. I had six brothers and sisters. I sacrificed for them, like you sacrifice for your friend."

It didn't surprise me that she had got her start as a prostitute, working her way up to madam. It didn't even surprise me that she had been with Henri. It explained why she had so much hatred for him…while at the same time she couldn't help but obey him. He had that effect on people, and years of that abuse would make anyone a little crazy.

There was one big difference between us, though. She had forced other girls to whore themselves. I had been faced with the same choice once, and I had chosen to protect Claire instead. The thought didn't fill me with triumph or superiority, because I remembered how hard it had been. I knew well the trouble it had caused me to protect Claire instead of use her.

I spoke quietly, respect still lingering despite everything. "Somewhere along the way, it changed. You stopped sacrificing and started forcing others to sacrifice for you."

"Yes. I did that. They need to sacrifice for me when I give so much. One day, you will do same thing."

No, I wouldn't, but she wouldn't believe me. "Tell me why you really called me."

"I lived with Henri for years. I was his girl." Her

lips pinched together. "You know what that is like."

I knew. The scars I bore from those experiences weren't on my skin. Much deeper, in the darkness of my soul. I wouldn't have wished that on anyone. "I'm sorry."

"Then I got pregnant."

A small gasp escaped me. Henri had always used protection with me. He was actually a stickler for it. Other pimps would push their girls to go bareback because it brought in so much more money, but not him.

"He actually wanted the child," Jade said. "I wanted to get an abortion, but he wouldn't let me. I ran away, but by then it was too late. I tried everything to get it out of me. I almost died trying, but someone found me and brought me to a hospital. They kept me there until the baby was born, and finally I could get rid of it."

My eyebrows rose. She killed it?

"Adoption," she said. "Then I started my own brothel. I knew how to run it from being with Henri. For years, we were like that. I knew better than to poach from him, and he left me alone. But I knew he always looked for the girl. He felt that I stole her from him."

"Claire," I breathed.

"She did it herself," Jade said accusingly. "I gave her good family. Normal family. If she had stayed there like she should, he would never have found her. How could he? But she came to his place of business, getting a fake ID. Then going to his club. How could he ignore that?"

"He couldn't," I said, just stating a fact. He wouldn't have.

"I didn't want her. She was Henri's child. I know you think I'm a monster now after helping him, for what I did, but at least I kept her from him."

And it was the only reason Ella was still alive and relatively sane today. A child under Henri's control? Jesus. No one knew better than I the cruelty that could pass from father to daughter. Pimping her out had been the kindest thing he could do.

"She's safe now," I said softly. I didn't believe that Jade didn't care at all. She had involved herself in this, had tried to help Ella in her own way, by helping me. "I'll keep her safe."

"I do not know this girl. I don't want to know her. She is tainted by Henri, always." Jade looked down at her hands as they lay limp and open in her lap. "You stay safe. That's what I want."

CHAPTER SEVENTEEN

S OME SECRETS WEREN'T meant to be spoken. Like fire, they would burn anyone who touched them, the speaker and the receiver. Those were my secrets, and I kept them locked away in the box I had built, the emanating heat a melancholy reminder of what had been. Jade's secrets were different, because they had scorched us all. Like wildfire they had torn her down, leaving only a hollow bark where a strong, tender woman could have been.

I would always harbor some resentment for the fact that she helped Henri, but it hadn't been entirely unexpected. In many ways, they were birds of a feather. Both feared and successful pimps, both past their prime, struggling to hold on to the old power. Both had failed. They were irrelevant now, history in the Chicago flesh trade. It would be for other men and women to carry on the industry, for surely it would not end with two people dead and a handful of brothels shut down. It was the darkest side of man, and the most natural. To trade, to fuck. It was the oldest profession and the most enduring.

I turned to leave, kneeling at the small table to give

tithe. It didn't matter whether I liked the information, whether I liked *her*. She had told me the truth, and for that I would pay. But as I reached for the folded bills in my pocket, she came and stayed my hand with hers.

She held out her hand in a fist, facing down.

Cautiously, I held out my hand underneath, catching the familiar jade necklace that no longer hung at her neck.

"For her," she said softly. "It's the only thing I have to give. This and the truth."

I closed my fingers around the thin gold and jade, still warm from her body.

In the car, I showed Luke the necklace and told him what Jade had said.

He whistled. "Are you going to tell Claire?"

"I don't think it will help her to know. But…I just don't know. Do you think I should?"

"I'm not really the person to ask. I guess I'd want to know, if it were me."

"Yeah, that makes sense." But still, I wasn't sure. How could I hurt her that way? For nothing. She would gain nothing.

Her adoptive parents' house was a large colonial in an old neighborhood. Old money. Jade hadn't been kidding about setting her up with a good family. We parked in the circular drive, and I didn't argue when Luke escorted me to the door. A middle-aged woman cried when she saw me on the front step and grappled me for a fierce hug, which showed no signs of abating until I sent Luke a look of distress. He smoothly intercepted their thanks, assuring them that helping Claire had been no trouble at all. I didn't laugh at that, which I considered a major coup. She showed us upstairs to Claire's room, where Luke opted to wait in the hall.

The decor was very modern, with light wood paneling and ochre fabrics. There weren't any posters on the wall, any knickknacks on the desk, and I wondered if the sterility was related to her penchant for stealing.

Claire herself looked good. Young, especially against the backdrop of a teenage bedroom. She stood awkwardly, hands in her jeans pockets. I looked at her critically, thinking maybe I could see Henri's eyes or Jade's sleek, straight hair, but that was just the suggestion talking. For all I knew, Henri had made a mistake. Maybe it wasn't her. I found it didn't really matter.

"Did you talk to Philip?" she blurted out. Then blushed.

I suppressed a smile. "Not really. I did speak to Allie earlier, so she told me how he's been. Busy with work, I think."

"Oh."

I waited for the *did he ask about me?* But it didn't come. Smart girl. I understood the compulsion, but they were light-years apart. She was a mostly good girl in the senior class. Philip was a kinky bastard. She'd found a lifetime's rebellion in one petty crime, and he was in for life.

"Here." She gestured to the bed. "You can sit down, if you want."

I eyed the bed. This whole high school bedroom setup hit a little close to home. "No, thanks." Then realizing it had been curt, I said, "How has school been? Are you caught up?"

"Yeah," she said. "Lots of homework to make up, but I'll still finish the year out."

"Ah. Good."

She rolled her eyes, and I saw hints of the spirited young girl I'd come to know. "I'm sure you used geometry theorems every day."

"Every night, baby. My work is all about angles."

"Was," she said tentatively. "That was your work, but not anymore. Right?"

"Right," I said. "Though don't ask me what I'm going to do. I don't know."

I had some ideas. Marguerite had asked me to join her at the shelter. *Who better than to teach Jenny and the other girls how to function in society?* she had said. I knew where they were coming from, that much was true. But I wasn't in a position to tell them where to go next, not when I was still searching for that myself.

Claire shared a few stories from school, things about boys and class clowns, before broaching the topic I dreaded.

"Did you ever find out why he took me? What started it all?"

I swallowed. I could tell her now, and it would

make sense, but it would break her. What started the whole chain reaction was her deciding to be naughty, stepping out to the club with a fake ID. What started it all happened nine months before she was born. No, it had started years ago, lifetimes ago, endless cycles of abuse and betrayal. I didn't want that for her. I wanted this. The pristine room. The goofy friends who thought they knew everything.

"It was random," I said, and as the words left my mouth, I realized there was truth to them. I would never know whether other decisions, other roads would have kept me safer. I could be somewhere without this pain, without these scars—without Luke. There was only now, tomorrow. There was only love in all its forms, even the ones that made me lie to her. "His business was struggling, and he thought a new girl would bring in extra cash."

"Well," she said after a moment. "That sucks."

And yeah, it did. But I had gotten to know her, which mattered more than I could say. "Will you come visit me sometime?"

She made a face. "Where are you staying?"

I laughed. "Not at Philip's. I'm going to live outside the city for a little while."

A long while, if I had my way. But Luke's job was here, and so I was playing it by ear.

"I'd love to," she said. "I have to thank you for what you did in that hotel room. And after. I know no one else would have."

It was my turn to make a face. I had wanted to shake this need to please, this compulsion to keep everyone around me grateful to me. But here I was, thanked twice in two hours. It seemed I would never escape it, and maybe it had been a mistake to even try. These were my friends. Of course I should help them. It hadn't been the gratitude I needed then, but the company. There had been a void in me, and I had frantically filled it with fawning men and a neat collection of owed favors. The void was gone, filled with things far more weighty. Filled with hope.

I left her room with the jade necklace in my pocket. It was rightfully her inheritance, like those jewels had been mine. But they had been like poison, infecting me with their very presence. If Jade had wanted to be sure Ella received it, she could have sent it herself. By giving it to me, she was leaving it to my judgment. I would throw it away like the trash that it was.

CHAPTER EIGHTEEN

FROM THE BED, I watched the leaves drift to the ground through the window, a mural of greens, browns, and reds as autumn arrived. It was hard to believe that a few weeks ago, I had stared out the window, seeing only the gray tones of the city.

Luke came into the bedroom, carrying a mug of steaming tea.

I took it with thanks, wrapping my fingers around the hot ceramic.

"How's your leg?" he asked softly, but he didn't wait for an answer.

He crouched in front of me and carefully pulled up the long sheet. He cradled my foot gently as he examined the wound. It had completely closed, so the bandage was off. The raised, jagged line ran from my knee down along my calf. It would probably scar, just like the round wound in my shoulder.

Some days I felt like I was nothing but a collection of scars—a cautionary tale. Other days I found a certain quiet glory in the pain of my past. I had survived them. Sometimes triumph wasn't a fanfare but a series of small events: the first breath of morning, a warm body sharing the sheets, the sight of green eyes watching me as I came awake.

"It looks like it's healing well," he said. "How does it feel?"

"I barely notice it." At his disbelieving look, I said, "Except when I walk. Or, you know, move. Sitting's good, though."

"We'll sit, then." He sat on the edge of the bed, careful not to disturb my leg.

He had already been up and dressed for an hour. The cottage needed a lot of work before it was livable, but I had refused his requests to stay in a hotel while he did the work. I wanted to be here, even if the kitchen needed new cabinets, even if the water heater kind of sucked. I never wanted to see another hotel again in my life. Besides, this place filled a part of me that had long been empty. The wound on my leg was healing. More than that, *I* was healing. Both outside and inside were a slow-ass process, I was finding, but at least it was progress.

"I got a call from the captain today," he said.

My gaze sharpened. We had carefully avoided the subject of what would happen after his leave of absence. I strove to match his casual tone. "What did he say?"

"He asked about you."

"Really?" I laughed in surprise. "Has he found something new to charge me with?"

I immediately regretted my outburst. The captain of the CPD had put me through hell, and I wasn't sure

I could get over that. Far worse, he'd made Luke an outcast for fighting for me. So the guy had reinstated Luke. I still didn't have to like him.

Except I sort of did, because he was Luke's boss. I would answer the phone when he called the house for Luke. I would see him at the department's Christmas party. And I would deal with it, for Luke. It would just be another way of faking it.

Luke watched me with a resigned look. "You hate him."

"He's not my favorite person. But it's not like I have to work for him. And when I see him, I'll be on my best behavior, I promise." I never wanted Luke to feel ashamed of me. It was bad enough that everyone he worked with knew what I had been. That would already hang over him. I wouldn't make it worse.

He looked amused. "You realize your best behavior is also your worst."

A smile curved my lips. "You love that about me." I pouted. "At least I thought you did."

"I do."

His voice had gone low, his eyes a dark emerald color. He teased me about how much I talked about sex, but really he loved it.

"I've been here a whole week," I said in a singsong voice. "I'll start to get a complex."

"You're hurt," he said quickly. "You need to rest."

"I have been resting. In fact, I'm exhausted from all this rest."

"Oh yeah?" The glint in his eye said I wouldn't be falling asleep anytime soon.

I raised my eyebrow in challenge. "Yeah."

He climbed up beside me. I barely had enough time to put the mug on the bedside table before he pulled me up against his body, my back to his front.

Snuggling back into the warmth of his body, I said, "Not to complain or anything, but cuddling counts as resting."

"Hush," he said. His hand snaked over my hip.

I sucked in a breath. It had been so long…really, never. Never exactly like this, with Luke. We had a hundred different ways to explore each other, a million times to make each other come. I looked forward to every single one.

I had taken to the habit of wearing his undershirt to bed. Now he lifted the hem from my thigh and walked his finger beneath the waistband of my panties. I jumped at the touch of his hand on my mound, realizing I hadn't shaved all week. It had been hard enough to shower with my damn leg hurting every time a drop of water touched it. Plus it had felt kind of nice to take a shower without doing that sort of primping. Just getting clean without preparing myself for a man.

"Sorry," I said quickly. "Maybe this isn't a good time."

His hand froze. "What's wrong?"

"I'm…bristly."

He laughed softly. "Bristly?"

"You know, like a beard. But less sexy."

"I don't know," he mused. His fingers resumed their stroking. "I think it would be pretty hard for me not to find this sexy. A little bristle isn't going to cut it. Besides"—he touched my clit lightly, then backed away—"this was the spot I was going for. Not bristly at all. Very smooth. Only a little wet, but we can fix that." He dipped his finger lower, into the dampness that had pooled between my folds. Drawing it up, he circled my clit again.

"Oh, Luke." My heart swelled along with my clit. He made me feel so wanted, inside and out. I knew he enjoyed my body—the hard ridge pressed against my ass from beneath his jeans paid testament to that—but the way he touched me, it was as if that didn't even matter. Whether my hair was the old blonde or the lingering brown, whether my cunt was shaved or not, he was just as hard for me, just as ready.

"It's okay, Shelly. You can let go." He knew the effect he had on me. "I'm here with you. I'll do anything to be with you."

CHAPTER NINETEEN

I FELT MYSELF clench at his words. He said it to me
every day, reminding me that he didn't just want me
for my body, for what pleasure I could bring him. I was
trying, but it was hard to believe. It was hard to remember. He understood that too.

"That's right," he murmured as my hips began to
rock into his hand. "More."

"Ahh." I let out a small cry as pain shot up my leg.

He stilled. "What's wrong?"

"My leg. Sorry. It's brushing against the sheet."

He pulled the sheet off, then gently placed my leg
over his. This way nothing could accidentally brush
against the wound. The position also left me completely exposed, cool air wafting against my sensitive clit. I
shuddered from the chill.

"Shh," he soothed, his hand reaching for me, fingers pushing inside. I shuddered again, this time from
pleasure.

Held open by him, probed by him, I felt vulnerable. It was bittersweet, the lingering sense of shame
tainting the overwhelming pleasure. I whimpered.

"I know," he said, and the most incredible thing

was, he did. He knew what it felt like to be afraid to let anyone close. He knew what it felt like to be used. "Just tell me if you want to stop, and I will. I won't be mad."

I relaxed into his hold, leaning my head back. His mouth found the skin behind my ear, nibbling down to my neck. I pushed my hips into his hand, practically riding him as I sought my release.

"Yes," he muttered. "Do it. Use me."

My whole body tightened, squeezing his fingers and bucking against his palm. I couldn't find the peak. I could just push and writhe and plead with tiny moans, reach until I felt wrung out and stretched taut.

"Shelly." He sounded lost when he said my name like that.

I realized that my body was pushing back into his, that my ass was rubbing his cock, and he was probably about to come inside his jeans. That's what pushed me over, the thought of him spurting that way, making a mess of himself because he couldn't hold it back. With a cry, I came, grinding down onto his hand, bucking in his arms. He groaned, sucking at my neck as my body released liquid onto his hand. His fingers stilled as the last of the orgasm ran through me.

With a small sigh of contentment, I settled back. He jerked against me.

I smiled without opening my eyes. "So you didn't come in your jeans."

He laughed, a short, rough sound of strain. "No. It was close."

I pressed the curve of my ass against his erection, and he groaned. "Almost there," I said.

"Is that what you want?" he murmured. "Does it turn you on?"

"Yes," I said, strangled, and he chuckled hoarsely.

He pushed against me, once, tentative.

"Again," I whispered.

He held my hip this time, and just like that, his hand keeping my body steady for him to rub his cock against me made my arousal burn hot.

"Again, again."

He wasn't just pushing into me but pulling me back onto his body. His hands scrabbled for a better grip, as if he could get closer, as if he could pull me inside him and merge with me through the denim.

His groan was low and tortured and selfish—a man desperate for his release. Like every other time, I was a sex object being used purely for my partner's gratification. But this was different, because I was hot instead of cold, slick with arousal instead of slippery with lube. I was with Luke.

"Shit, shit, shit," he panted.

I smiled.

His movements grew jerky. I knew he was close, but I didn't want it to end. I wanted to go with him.

"Wait," I said, turning slightly. "Can you… Can we…?"

If I had seen his face first, I wouldn't have stopped him. It was all hollows and tension, want and arousal.

It looked like pain and felt like it too in the brusque way he turned me onto my back, in the grip as he spread my thighs.

"Your leg," he ground out.

"Fine," I gasped. I had no fucking idea, though. I couldn't feel anything but the ache in my cunt and the abrasive rasp of his denim and then the hard, painful press of his length against my clit. His body sank down onto mine. Without break, without reprieve, he began a hard-and-fast rhythm of bringing himself off, dragging me along. I reveled in his roughness, such a stark contrast to the gentleness he usually showed me—it was need. And it was trust, for now I understood that it was as hard for him to believe in the intimacy between us as it had been for me. My body sparked with a heightened arousal, but my heart warmed with tenderness.

"God, Luke. God."

"I know," he said. "Oh shit."

I kissed his temple.

His body tensed over me, against me, and I knew he was coming. I wouldn't make it, there wasn't time, but it was okay. And then his mouth sought out my nipple, sucking and—oh God—biting. It was too much, too hard and fast, too hungry and desperate and too damn close, and my body launched into another orgasm, my hips strained against his, and he forced them down, riding his release in the cradle of my body.

We curled up together afterward, catching our breath.

I rested my chin on his shoulder. "Hey."

"I'm a mess," he said, amused.

Glancing at the dark spot on his crotch, I suppressed a smile. "Was that second or third base?"

"I have no idea. But I'm pretty sure this means you're officially my girlfriend."

"If you insist."

"I do." He grew quizzical. "You know I want more than that, right? In the future. That's where we're heading."

I looked down where my finger drew figure eights on his chest. "I know. I want that too. But I kind of like this high school stuff." I felt a blush heat my cheeks. "I didn't get to have that."

He lifted my chin and kissed my nose. "Me neither. And I like it too."

After a few minutes, he checked on my leg, but the wound hadn't opened. It was a little sore from rubbing against the sheet when I was in the throes of climax, but so was my entire body. A session like that was draining, and I would have been more than happy to take that rest Luke had badgered me about, but I was restless. I opened the window. Fresh air wafted in, rich with the scent of twilight. We wouldn't be able to do this back in the city.

Luke groaned from the bed. "Why are you vertical?"

I swallowed. "You want to go back."

He was silent a moment; then he came to stand behind me, wrapping his arms around me. He spoke in a low tone. "I do. But I'm happy here too."

I shifted in his arms, turned my face into the soft hair of his chest. "What would you do here?"

"I'd find something." His shoulder shrugged beneath me. "I'm sure they need cops out here too. It would probably be less stressful."

I snorted. "Less stressful because you'd be handing out traffic tickets."

"I wouldn't mind, Shelly. Whatever we have to do, wherever you need me to be."

"Why so accommodating?"

"Would you rather I drag you back to the city and demand you have supper ready on the table?"

It didn't sound so terrible. Maybe what I had really meant was that *I* wanted to go back. "I think the work you do would be more meaningful there. I think you'd prefer it."

"But…" He raised his eyebrows.

"You might be ashamed of me. Word will get out about me in the department. It's one thing to grab a quickie on patrol; it's another to date me."

"Marry," he corrected.

My breath stuttered. "Excuse me?"

"It doesn't have to be now, but it will happen."

I blinked, incredulous and giddy that he would propose to me. Though he hadn't, really. "Isn't it supposed to be a question?"

"Would you have preferred rose petals and champagne?"

"God, no." I'd had more than enough seduction in my lifetime, more than enough false charm. I wanted the real thing. I wanted forever. "So what now?"

"Now we go back. I'll do the work I've been doing, cleaning the streets—" His hold tightened as I tried to object. "And if anyone has a problem with my wife, we'll deal with it like adults."

"That's what I was afraid of. I don't want any more violence."

He chuckled softly. "At night, I'll come home to you."

"Naked, except for my apron and high heels."

"Wearing whatever you want, doing whatever you want."

Which was what, exactly? That wasn't a question for Luke but for myself. I had never been the domestic type, and hadn't I already figured out that a regular job wasn't for me? I had been raised to do one thing only. Even the love of a good man couldn't make me forget all my training.

The bookstore was ages ago, a million miles away, but I might as well have been walking out the door, the rejected application damp in my hand. The life was the only thing I knew, the only one I had.

CHAPTER TWENTY

I STARED AT the unmarked building, red brick and blackened bulletproof glass. Luke sat quietly in the driver's seat beside me, giving me the space I needed.

"It's a little depressing," I muttered.

He made a small sound that could have been assent. Or not.

"I mean, just because it's a new start doesn't mean it's a better one. How can I know this is the right thing for them?"

Was it the right choice for me? I'd wanted so badly to make this right, without fully understanding what was wrong. I knew better now. It wasn't the actions of a single man. This would happen again and again, unless we did something. One girl, then another. With relief, I realized I hadn't been wrong before, bringing them here, supporting this place. But it had been a halfhearted effort. I hadn't been able to make the next step of helping them build a new life, because I hadn't been able to build a new life for myself.

"Wait here?" I asked softly.

His eyes shone with acceptance, approval. He pressed a kiss to my lips before I got out and rang the little doorbell. The wait was longer than usual, but I stood still and patient. Finally the door opened, just a crack. Marguerite was draped in shadows.

She squinted through the glare on the windows. "I shouldn't even have opened the door."

"Thanks for trusting me on this."

"That's your cop, I'm guessing."

"Just talk to him. He has ideas for how the police department can help you, so you're not wasting resources working behind their backs."

She frowned. "We do okay by ourselves."

"We can do better," I said gently.

Her eyebrows rose. "We?"

"I want to help. To volunteer, to teach, all the things you've been asking me to do. I'm ready now."

She didn't trust cops, and probably with good reason. But she didn't know Luke, not yet. With his help, we would be able to do more at the shelter. Give these girls a legitimate future with proper paperwork instead of a life on the run.

"Okay," she said with clear reluctance. "I'll meet with him. No guarantees."

I waved Luke inside. He got out of the car and strode over, his gait slow and unthreatening. But Marguerite paled as he approached, the pink of her lips pressing to white.

Well, that had gone downhill quickly. "It's okay," I said. "He's okay."

As Luke reached us, he looked at Marguerite with a

raw, open curiosity. He stepped closer. His eyes widened.

"Daisy?" His voice was a soft expulsion of air, of shock.

She gave a terse nod. "Luke."

"Is it really you?"

"I go by Marguerite now." She hesitated, pulling away when it looked like he would step forward. "I'm not sure this is even a good idea. I'm a completely different person now. I'm guessing you are too."

"Daisy. Marguerite. I want to know you, who you are now. I'm trying to catch up here, but give me a chance."

"I want to know you too," she said in a small voice.

"Okay," he said. "Okay."

Nice and soothing, and I recognized the tone of voice he had used for me once, his instinctual soft touch with an animal who has been hurt.

"That's a start. That's all we need."

WE RETURNED TO Luke's apartment, where we planned to stay until we found a house, something small for just the two of us and modest enough that I could still fill it with nice things. Luke made a decent living on the force, but the shelter wouldn't be able to pay me anything, at least until we got grants in place.

I was already reading up on that, studying the procedures and writing some very tame, G-rated firsthand accounts of my experiences to help encourage the wealthy of Chicago to open their pockets. We all lived here, the streetwalkers and those in the penthouse, stacked on top of each other. I had walked among the wealthy and privileged with no hope at all. I would do it again, this time with a message: *look down*.

We lounged in bed, in the same coarse blue sheets I had thought were unreachable.

"How did you know?" he asked me.

"I didn't," I admitted. Though I hadn't been shocked to discover it. It had been like remembering a detail of my childhood, one I'd never really had.

I had always felt a certain affinity toward Marguerite that couldn't be explained from our exchanges at the shelter. Family. She had felt like family, and Luke had felt like mine, long before I'd believed either of them could be possible. "She told me a long time ago about life on the streets. When you told me the whole of it, I put it together."

"She didn't seem that happy to see me." Disappointment trickled into his voice.

I linked my hand in his. "Give her time. She's survived this long by being tough. It wouldn't make sense for her to tear all that down in a day."

He smiled slightly, pulling me against him. "Thank you. It's inadequate, I know—"

"I didn't do anything, but I'm glad now that you can move on, you know. Get to know the real Marguerite. She's an interesting lady, I'll tell you that."

"Forget the past, you mean."

"Put it where it belongs, but don't forget. It made us stronger, all of us. You couldn't be nearly as good a cop if you hadn't gone through that. I hope that I can be useful to the shelter, because I know what these girls are going through."

"If I didn't know you better, I'd say you sounded like an optimist." His tone teased me.

A smile tilted my lips. "I think it'll be a long time before I get there, but I'm hopeful, and that's something."

"Yeah," he said softly, bending down for a kiss. "It's really something."

In the bedroom, he proved his words, feasting on me and offering himself up in return. He was my craving and my nourishment, my weakness and my rapture. Like a genie rubbed from a lamp, my arousal had been awakened by his tongue and his touch and his kindness, while his resolve as an officer of the law had only been strengthened.

He'd been willing to give up a life of rigid honor, while I would trade in my stature, my past, my everything to be with him. But in the end, neither sacrifice had been necessary. Instead we fit the pieces together, his work and my heart, his body and my lust, every part of us intertwined and flowing together—seamless.

THE END

Thank You

Thank you for reading Wild Dirty Secret! I hope you enjoyed Luke and Shelly's story. The next book in the Chicago Underground series is the story of Rose, Philip's sister, and Drew. Sweet is available now!

Don't miss a new release! Sign up for my newsletter today.

You can discuss this book in my Facebook group for fans: Skye Warren's Dark Room

I appreciate your help in spreading the word, including telling a friend. Reviews help readers find books! Please leave a review on your favorite book site.

> "This story was lovely and so engaging, I could read it over and over. The flow of it and the prose had the elegance of a ballet performance."
>
> ~ Ms Romantic Reads

EXCERPT FROM SWEET

D REW STEPPED INTO the spotlight, casting a long shadow over the silver-white side of his car. He opened his door and tossed his briefcase on the passenger seat. But instead of getting in and driving away, he paused. He turned back, looking directly at my window—at me. I froze, my throat going dry.

He must have known it was my room, though he'd never been upstairs. I didn't think he could see me. At least not clearly. We were twenty feet away, separated by double-paned glass, and the glare from the floodlights would overwhelm the thin light from my lamp. Impulsively, I pressed my palm to the cool glass. Could he make that out, the shape of my hand, the color of my flesh?

I leaned forward, painting my own reflection in the window. Wide, dark eyes set in the pale moon of my face, all framed with thick curtains of black hair. I looked like a ghost, something ephemeral and weightless.

That was how I felt sometimes too—not really there. I wanted to feel something, to see what it was like to participate, even if it was only a glimpse. He was waiting for me, leaning against his car.

Maybe he'd always been waiting for me.

Since that first meeting and the sudden heat that had sparked between us, he had been waiting for me to initiate something so he could be sure I was ready. Waiting and wanting, because he had some idea of my background, if not the specifics. The consideration in that gesture, the sheer expanse of it, took my breath away.

He remained still until the floodlights flicked off, blanketing him in night. My eyes adjusted, and he came back into focus again, somehow clearer in the dark. His arms were crossed as he leaned back against the car. The driver's side door hung open, an ignored invitation in favor of this.

I could see the glint of his eyes, his intensity unmasked. My imagination could fill in the rest—the short, stubby growth on his jaw after a long day of work, the shadows beneath his eyes.

How could I show him; what did he want? Silly questions. Of course I knew. It was primal, the urge to bare myself, to offer myself, and only my fears kept me in check. It wasn't the glass of the window or the bricks stacked beneath it. Only my fears kept us apart.

I toyed with the hem of my soft tank top, teasing him with a strip of flesh, blowing cool air across my belly. It wouldn't be like this with him. His breath was hot, his body a furnace. That much I knew from the study earlier when he'd murmured in my ear. The window pane was emanating cold, holding out the chilly night air but failing just a little.

He must be freezing, but he didn't look it, not even as a breeze ruffled a lock of hair over his forehead. He looked like he could wait forever, but why should he have to? I wouldn't be a coward, not tonight.

I had dressed for sleep after my shower, so there was nothing underneath the thin fabric of my tank top. I tugged the shirt off and let it slip from my fingers. My skin pebbled with goose bumps at the chill. My nipples tightened almost painfully. He might have been a statue, he was so still. I felt the opposite, tingling and aware. It was too much—too embarrassing, too revealing—but exactly what I had been waiting for.

What next? If there was a script to forbidden exhibitionism, I had never read it. I moved with pent-up desire, acted on ideas unformed. I trailed my palms up my stomach and lifted my small breasts like an offering.

I wanted his hands on me, wanted him to touch and caress and pinch me, so I did it myself, grasping my nipples between my thumb and forefinger. I squeezed slightly, and as if he were connected to me, as if *he* had done it, his body jerked infinitesimally.

Was he excited? I knew enough to look for a bulge at his crotch, but it was too dark to see. I wished he could tell me what he wanted me to do, but maybe that would ruin the illusion of safety. From fifteen feet away, I watched him lick his lips and heard the tacit message.

I put a finger to my lips and licked, slightly exaggerated so that he could see. He leaned forward slightly—*yes, more*. I sucked the finger into my mouth and could have sworn his hips moved slightly where they rested against the car. Trailing my wetted finger over my chest, I circled my nipple and pinched again, savoring the bite of cold air and hard pressure.

I let down my hair from my tower in the form of secret glimpses, and like Rapunzel, I needed exposure like I needed air. He joined me with his arousal, in the commands conveyed with his body. We communed in a language of our own. *Climb to me. I don't want to be alone.*

An ache built in my sex under the weight of his stare and my own touch. My hips moved in answer to his, finding an instinctive rhythm.

I reached for the band of my sweatpants, then paused. Panties too? Too much. I pushed down the pants but left the matching pink bikini panties on.

There was no way I could have heard, but I could have sworn he groaned. I imagined tiny molecules of air vibrating at the sound, traveling all this way and whispering against my lips.

I tucked my fingertips beneath the soft, stretchy hem of my panties, but then he wouldn't be able to see. Instead I slid my palm over my covered sex and slipped beneath the strip of fabric between my legs. Wet heat met my questing fingers, more slippery than I had ever felt it when alone in my bed. I teased myself along the slick outer lips before sliding upward in search of a particular place—*there*.

My knees threatened to buckle from the pleasure that coursed through me, from the hard training of the day. I braced myself against the window, one hand on the glass and the other on my clit. It did more than sustain me, it connected me to him, an arc from the outside in, and the result was electric.

He leaned forward, gripping the top of the open door. I watched his other hand ball into a fist before letting my eyes fall shut, imagining that hand on me, holding me just as tightly, bruising me so I would never forget.

Finish it.

I didn't know whether the words came from him or me, but I let the currents pull me along, let the arousal swirl faster and deeper until I couldn't find the surface, couldn't breathe—could only buck and moan and spill all over my furiously rubbing fingers. My stuttered moan was loud in my ears, filling my room before it dropped off into a sigh.

I let my hand fall away and opened my eyes.

He stood exactly as I'd left him, bristling with an almost palpable tension. After a moment, he detached from the car, moving slowly, like a man in pain, as if he'd been injured.

He turned away and rested his palms on the top of the car. With an unreadable glance back at me, he gingerly got inside and drove away.

I watched him go, sated but far from satisfied. Always wanting, always needing something above my reach. Dreaming of ballerinas when I came from the slums. Lusting after the smart, successful man in a well-tailored suit. One of these days, I'd reach too far. I'd fly too close to the sun, but even knowing so, I couldn't stop myself from spreading my wings.

Want to read more? Sweet is available now at Amazon.com, iBooks, BarnesAndNoble.com and other retailers.

Other Books by Skye Warren

Standalone Dark Romance

Wanderlust

On the Way Home

His for Christmas

Hear Me

Take the Heat

Stripped series

Tough Love (prequel)

Love the Way You Lie

Better When It Hurts

Even Better

Pretty When You Cry

Chicago Underground series

Rough

Hard

Fierce

Wild

Dirty

Secret

Sweet

About the Author

Skye Warren is the New York Times and USA Today Bestselling author of dark romance. Her books are raw, sexual and perversely romantic.

Sign up for Skye's newsletter:
www.skyewarren.com/newsletter

Like Skye Warren on Facebook:
facebook.com/skyewarren

Join Skye Warren's Dark Room reader group:
skyewarren.com/darkroom

Follow Skye Warren on Twitter:
twitter.com/skye_warren

Visit Skye's website for her current booklist:
www.skyewarren.com

COPYRIGHT

Cover design by Book Beautiful
Formatting by BB Ebooks
Edited by Ann Curtis

Manufactured by Amazon.ca
Bolton, ON

28515588R00266